CLOSE PROXIMITY

PERILOUS ALLIANCE – BOOK 1

CHRIS J. PIKE
M. D. COOPER

Version 1.1.1

Cover Art by Laércio Messias
Editing by Amy DuBoff & Tee Ayer

FOREWORD

Since the very beginning of my journey with the Aeon 14 novels, Chris has been my earliest beta reader who sees the books before editors or anyone else.

Chris has been instrumental in shaping the world and characters of Aeon 14, and now has finally stepped in to write his own tale here in the 'verse.

We chatted for some time about which time period would be right for Chris, and we settled on the years after Destiny Lost and the Battle of Bollam's World.

Both of us really like the area of space around the Silstrand Alliance, and we wondered what would have happened to the nanotech that Tanis sold S&H Defensive Armaments, and how were things faring in the pirate-ridden, coreward edge of the Silstrand Alliance.

Well, now you're about to find out in this exciting new adventure that follows Kylie Rhoads and the crew of the *Dauntless* in this, part of the expanding scope of the Orion War.

Sincerely, M. D. Cooper

TABLE OF CONTENTS

THE WORLD OF AEON 14

For the seasoned science fiction reader, there will be little here which they have not seen in another story be it space elevators, nano technology, AI, or mind-to-mind communication.

However, for those who may not know what a HUD is, understand the properties of deuterium, or be able to name the stars within the Sirius system, I encourage you to visit www.aeon14.com to read the primer, glossary, and timelines.

To get the latest news and access to free novellas and short stories, sign up on the Aeon 14 mailing list: www.aeon14.com/signup.

DERELICT

STELLAR DATE: 08.21.8947 (Adjusted Years)
LOCATION: Salvage ship *Dauntless* – Beyond Gedri's Heliopause
REGION: Gedri System, Silstrand Alliance

"We found her, Captain, and she's a beauty," Jim Rogers called out over the *Dauntless*'s audible address system.

Kylie Rhoads wanted to see the ship for herself; with any luck, this salvage would bring their next big payday. "I'll be right there," Kylie replied as she jogged down the long corridor from the galley and up the sloping ramp onto the bridge of her ship.

The *Dauntless* was a PetSil Scrapper hull with an unconventional configuration—courtesy of past owners. The main upgrade was the large, spherical bridge at the fore of the ship, providing an unobstructed view of space and their salvage. Suspended in the center of the sphere, three meters off the ground, was Rogers in the pilot's seat.

He was working the ship's four grappling arms, and as he spun and manipulated them, his seat moved too. Currently, he hung upside down while they approached their target, readying the arms to grapple the ship they had found.

"Howdy, capt'n." He waved awkwardly.

"The distress call?" Kylie asked.

"Was coming from her all right," Nadine—her communications and weapons officer—replied from her console on the bridge's deck. "It's been on repeat, and it's led us straight to her. She's a good-looking haul, isn't she?"

"Yeah and with all its core functions offline. Something took her out; she's cold as they come, Captain," Rogers said.

"Send a hail to be sure. Let's see if anyone answers." Kylie crossed her arms and hoped to God no one did. Legally or otherwise, they couldn't salvage a vessel with people on board, and they could use a new good haul to appease their boss.

"Yes, Captain."

"Maneuver on grav-drive only. If there's anyone on that ship, we don't want to spook them." Kylie leaned forward and gripped the railing at the fore of the bridge, staring through the plas at the view. The ship really was magnificent. Kylie couldn't believe their luck. The kind of payday a ship like that would bring? Man, they couldn't have bought this kind of luck.

It was a bit strange to find it this far out—well beyond Gedri's heliopause—but pirates and smugglers often did deals on the fringe of the system. Those dealings often went bad, and Kylie got the leavings.

The derelict was a Hedland 17-7 freighter, bulky instead of sleek, and designed to carry cargo, not human beings. All things being equal, Kylie would rather deal with stuff than people.

Rogers was more than capable at his job, but still, Kylie bent over a console to review the scan. The readings on the abandoned freighter confirmed everything on board was as quiet as a mouse. Life support was shut down, or malfunctioning, and the engines were offline. The hull had some light damage from whatever scuffle it had found itself in, but nothing they couldn't patch up. If not for the cold engines, it was space worthy and ready to fly.

Something had disabled this ship, all right. Now, it was adrift in space and ripe for the taking.

"Name?" Kylie asked.

"The *Titan-1*," Nadine piped up from the communications station she ran. "Big name for a freighter. Even one of this size."

"It's probably making up for something," Rogers said as he scrolled through his holodisplay. "Serial number matches a ship that does runs for the Black Crow."

Kylie sighed. It figured—the Black Crow was a nasty group of pirates, and all things being equal, Kylie would rather not run up against them. Even for pirates, their reputation was barbaric; they didn't deserve the ships they flew.

Kylie bet the *Titan-1* got caught with their pants down and had been taken out by the GFF—the Gedri Freedom Federation wasn't happy unless they had their piece of the pie. And the Black Crow was all about hogging the pie for themselves, which meant they often found themselves at odds with the GFF when they jumped through the Gedri system.

The *Dauntless* didn't have a license for this type of work outside Gedri's heliopause. Which meant they weren't supposed to salvage whole hulls. But what the Silstrand Alliance—the ruling government—didn't know, couldn't hurt them. A haul like this meant more money in their pockets and more food in their bellies. Also meant they could be choosier about what jobs they took for the GFF.

"Tap into their system and download their manifest. I want to make sure we know what we're looking for when we board." The rest could end up scrap metal, but as long as Kylie was paid for the job, she didn't much care.

Adding a bit of illegal wares to their coffers was always a good thing. Freight was freight, and as far as Kylie was concerned, if it was adrift at the core-ward edge of Gedri, it was fair game.

Whatever had happened to *Titan*-1 was the risk every freighter captain took getting this far into the fringe—the empty expanse between Gedri and the Scipio Federation—where the government was too far away to help.

Behind Kylie, Nadine spoke, "Close enough to send a hail…if you find it necessary, Captain." With genetically enhanced curves, azure hair, and piercing blue eyes, Nadine was the type of woman Kylie didn't mind being stuck in space with.

"It's always necessary. We won't be caught with our hand in the cookie jar while I'm in charge."

Nadine sighed and pulled up the holo system. "Yes, ma'am."

"What the hell is a cookie jar?" Rogers asked, and Kylie silenced him with a look. Her 'quaint' upbringing by technophobe parents often got a rise out of the crew.

"Most cookies come in those nice sealed packages," Rogers muttered.

Nadine sent the message across the void in a narrow ship-to-ship transmission. <*Disabled freighter* Titan-1, *this is the* Dauntless *acting on the authority of the GFF. Prepare to be boarded. Stow your weapons and remain in your quarters. We will be coming in hot.*>

Nadine threw a glance at Kylie. Her super-slick hair glimmered and changed color as light raced across each individual strand. "Message will repeat three more times, Captain."

Kylie crossed her arms and leaned over Nadine's display. "No heat signatures or movement?"

"None yet," Nadine confirmed. "If there are people aboard that freighter, they have an advanced way of masking it."

It made Kylie feel better, but she wouldn't completely relax until she had swept the decks of the *Titan-1* herself. "Hold down the fort here. Rogers, standard ship-to-ship docking procedures, and send me that manifest as soon as you have it."

"Yes, ma'am." Rogers spun in his seat to access the docking display. "I love it when she talks to me that way."

Nadine smirked at him. "You love it when she talks to you at all."

Kylie shook her head at the constant ribbing between those two. Like brother and sister, they sure could get into it, but it was kind-spirited—most of the time.

Kylie left the spherical bridge for the long corridor that connected to the rest of the ship. She passed by the crew quarters—positioned beneath the grappling arms—then turned past them. The corridor stretched down to the cargo area and engine room, but she took a left before going that far, headed for the starboard airlock

<*Winter, meet me, would you?*>

His gruff voice laughed across the Link, <*I'm already there. You know me better than that.*>

That she did.

*****

Kylie met Winter at the weapon lock-up right outside the airlock. She grabbed a pulse rifle, a standard helmet, and a heavy environmental suit in case things got dicey.

As she shimmied into her snug EVA suit, she glanced at Winter, who was checking his suit's seals. He was a big guy with pure white hair that had earned him his nickname. His eyes were a pale pink, yet no one dared make fun of him because his bulging muscles weren't just for show. Nadine might have liked shimmering hair, but Winter loved muscles. It was almost an addiction.

"You get any bigger and that helmet isn't going to fit around your neck anymore."

Winter's grin stretched ear-to-ear, and his white teeth gleamed behind his helmet's visor. "That's why you keep me around."

Wasn't much point in arguing with that; Winter's muscles had gotten her out of a lot of scrapes. He outfitted himself with a pulse rifle and some sonic grenades while she strapped a pulse-pistol to her thigh. A metallic clang let Kylie know that the umbilical had finished connecting to the freighter, and she sent up a communication to the bridge.

<*Open the hatch. We're ready.*>

<*Good luck, Captain,*> Rogers said.

Kylie didn't think she'd need luck, but in her experience, a little bit never hurt.

GOING IN HOT

STELLAR DATE: 08.21.8947 (Adjusted Years)
LOCATION: Derelict ship *Titan-1* – Beyond Gedri's Heliopause
REGION: Gedri System, Silstrand Alliance

Kylie and Winter stepped aboard the freighter. The *Titan-1* was pitch-black inside—even the emergency lighting was off. Kylie switched on her helmet's IR/UV cameras and a holo-image of the corridor came into view. It was long, with passages branching off, leading to various storage compartments.

Ahead, the overhead lights suddenly began to blink on and off as the ship detected Kylie and Winter, and tried to offer a warmer welcome. After a valiant attempt, the lighting failed once more and they relied on their helmets' enhanced optics.

<*Malfunction?*> Winter sent her an encoded message over the *Dauntless*'s shipnet, which reached into the freighter.

<*Or damaged in whatever fight disabled the ship,*> Kylie replied.

<*At least gravity is online. I hate having to float through these pieces of shit. Always end up turning a corner and smack right into a floating corpse,*> Winter said with a mental grimace.

Kylie was grateful, as well. Especially with how people usually soiled themselves after they died. Nothing worse than cleaning all that off an EVA suit after scouting a ship.

As they moved into the corridor, she picked up a weak wireless signal and Linked with the ship to access the logs. There was no mention of a battle. As far as Kylie could tell, it hadn't been boarded. She Linked the ship's net to a buffered portion of the *Dauntless*'s and pinged Rogers to let him know he could tap in and find the manifest.

<Nothing seems out of the ordinary so far. But I can't find any trace of organic matter. All the escape pods are here except for one. Maybe the bridge's logs will give us a better clue as to what happened,> Winter said.

They reached an intersection with a passageway running fore and aft. Kylie signaled for Winter to go left while she went right—toward the bridge.

<If there **are** *people here, I have a feeling they would have made themselves known by now,>* Kylie said. Empty ships always felt like tombs, but at least there was no one around to lob grenades at them.

<That's what worries me. If they aren't here, where'd they go? If they died, where are their bodies?>

<You got the creeps, Winter? Worried about the space-boogeyman?>

<I just like to stay alive, Captain.>

<Keep your eyes open and keep scanning. I've got your back.>

With each step, Kylie's magnetic boots brought her further down into the dark, quiet hall. Her breathing sounded loud in the helmet's confines. She was peering around a corner, surveying an adjoining passageway, when her comm lit up with a transmission from Rogers.

Rogers flashed his good-looking, spiced-up avatar at her and he kissed his bulging biceps. If Kylie hadn't been on a wrecked ship floating through space with no life support and no interior lighting, she might have smiled. *<What you got?>*

<Found the manifest you asked for. Well, I assembled it from a dozen different files across their net. These guys did not organize their data at all. Sending it over. You owe me cookies from that jar of yours.>

Kylie quickly scanned the contents and noted the usual list of items her crew wouldn't mind—fresh food and medicine. Even a few crates of liquor. That always made for a great party in the dark, but it was the high-end gear Kylie was excited to get her hands on—some upgrades for her ship and weapons for the crew. Plus a few tech items she had no need for, but could sell at Laerdo Station, or maybe hold onto until the next time they got to the Coburn Station auction house in Trio—they'd fetch some good coin there.

It was about time they had a couple nights off on some exotic luxury planet doing nothing but lounging in the sun, and being fed grapes by handsome men—or some beautiful woman. Kylie wouldn't have minded either.

Kylie pulled her head out of the clouds and sent a message to Winter. *<See anything down there?>*

<Nothing. No damage at all, cargo looks secure. I can't get the internal systems to spark up from engineering. There's an override from the bridge stopping it.>

<Okay. Rogers got the manifest. Meet me at the bridge and let's see if we can convince this old girl to power up.> To Rogers, she sent a private message. *<See if you can modify the manifest. I'm sending it back to you with some revisions. Few things have to be scrubbed before we turn the salvage over to Maverick.>*

Rogers avatar winked. *<You sure do know how to play them, boss.>*

Winner take all. Life wasn't much fun unless she was burning the candle at both ends. What Maverick didn't know couldn't hurt the crew of the *Dauntless*.

Kylie hit a dead-end and had to backtrack to get to the bridge. Taking another passageway, she spotted Winter bent over a terminal. His brow was furrowed, and he was reading something only visible on his HUD.

<What you got there?>

<They sent some strange distress signals before abandoning ship. Made it sound like someone boarded them.>

Odd, Kylie hadn't found any evidence someone had boarded the *Titan-1*, invited or otherwise. Kylie accepted the data transfer and looked over the logs. As far as she could tell, it was a garbled transmission sent in distress. She slapped Winter on the shoulder and pointed down the corridor. *<Yeah, it's weird, but maybe they were rescued after all, and that's why we can't find them.>*

<Uh-huh, sure. Like you really believe that.>

Maybe not, but Kylie wouldn't put her crew in danger, and so far there didn't appear to be any significant danger here. *<Come on, let's get this done and grab our new cargo. Then we can tow this bad girl back to Jericho and see how it shakes down.>*

<Drinks are on me,> Rogers added.

Winter nodded, but he held his weapon ready as he followed Kylie down the hall.

The terminal had held a map of the ship, and they used it to finally find their way to the bridge. Kylie hung back and monitored the entrance while Winter did his best to bring the ship back to working order.

Keeping an eye out wasn't the most stimulating work Kylie had ever done, but she did her best to stay alert and vigilant. Her mind was starting to wander when a signal from the *Dauntless* brought her back to the present.

<Captain.> It was Nadine's soft voice, but she sounded on edge. *<I've picked up an encrypted transmission coming from somewhere inside that ship; one that's not coming from you or Winter.>*

<Shit, man,> Winter said, and Kylie nodded in agreement.

So, there were people aboard the ship? Kylie immediately tensed and unholstered her sidearm. She looked down the corridor leading from the bridge. *<I'm still not reading any heat signatures other than us.>*

<They must be cloaking it somehow. Roger says it's possible; it would be expensive tech. Freighter ship like that shouldn't have the sort of stuff Rogers is talking about.>

Kylie sighed and glanced back at Winter as he continued to work on getting past whatever lockdown was keeping the ship offline. She tossed her head toward the door. <*Work fast, I need to check the signal out. Nadine, you decode that transmission. I want to know what they said, and who they said it to.*>

Winter nodded without looking up, his fingers flying across a console. <*If you need me….*>

She hoped that wouldn't be necessary. She smirked. <*Don't count yourself so lucky.*> She couldn't help razzing the big man a little.

Kylie headed out into the hallway before sending a transmission back to the ship. <*If you can pinpoint that signal's location….*>

In her mind, Nadine's glamorous avatar blew her radiant blue hair out of her face with a huff. <*I'm working on it…Captain. It's aft somewhere—maybe in the main cargo hold.*> Kylie liked it when Nadine focused on a task—it made her sound extra sexy.

<*Keep at it,*> Winter interrupted. <*If there are people here, we lock them down and keep them quiet until we reach Jericho. Let Maverick deal with 'em.*>

Kylie sighed. <*Give her space to work, Winter. If there are people on board, you know we can't salvage this thing.*> She hated a lot of things, but her least favorite thing in the world was human cargo.

Winter gave a mental grunt. <*Only if someone finds out about them.*>

She silenced him with a look from her avatar. <*We take advantage of people's misfortune. We do not cause it.*>

Kylie came to an intersection of two passageways and turned left, following the map Winter had lifted from the terminal.

<*Almost there, Captain,*> Nadine's excited voice chattered in her mind.

<*Play it when you find the signal.*> Kylie sent a 3D meme across the Link to Nadine of a sexy pinup model smoking an

old-fashioned cigarette. One, because she liked to flirt, and two, to keep the mood light. She knew her girl—great at her job and what she did, but stress tended to lock Nadine up.

Kylie reached the main hold. The door was open, and she eased inside. The hold was large, easily forty meters wide and twice as deep. Crates stamped with the logos of consumables lined the outer wall and metal cargo bins were stacked haphazardly in the middle of the room.

Kylie swept her eyes and weapon across the hold as she approached the containers. Nothing stood out, or made any noise. If there were bad guys on board, they weren't here.

Due diligence done, she holstered her weapon and stepped up to the first crate. This was where the good stuff would be.

As she looked for the first crate's locking mechanism, the lights came to life around her and Kylie allowed herself a small smile of satisfaction. Nice work, Winter. *<Get your ass down here and help me with these things, muscles.>*

<On my way.> At least he had the good senses not to make a joke. A quick check-in on her HUD said he was, indeed, running. A scary image to see in one's head. The man was large, and boy could he move.

Kylie found the crate's latch and was gripping the lid when Nadine called out over the Link. *<I got it!>*

<Good girl,> she said and waited for Nadine to play the transmission.

Nadine nodded and played the message. A deeper, huskier voice came to her over the Link. *<They took the bait.>*

Slowly, Kylie removed her hand from the shipping container as if it were a nuclear weapon. She backed away, glancing up at the walls and the ceiling. If someone was there, if someone was watching, they could be anywhere—especially if they had the sort of stealth tech Rogers had gone on about.

Something shimmered along the wall, but when Kylie peered closer, she couldn't make out anything other than crates and bulkhead.

Someone *was* there, she knew it. They weren't alone.

<*Who'd they send it to?*> Kylie asked Nadine.

Nadine gave an involuntary gasp across the Link. <*To the SSF!*>

The Silstrand Alliance Space Force—that was the last thing Kylie wanted to hear, but it made sense, didn't it? A freighter like this, adrift in space, with only minor hull damage and no signs of trouble or struggle inside…not to mention an easy-to-hack net and juicy manifest?

The SSF may as well have hung a sign on it that said, *take me.* And she'd fallen for it. *Damnit.* Kylie wanted to kick herself for being so naïve.

Rogers interrupted her train of thought. <*Get out of there, Cap. Get back to the ship.*>

She appreciated the concern and had the same idea, already running for the exit. She was almost out of the cargo hold when the door slammed shut and the mag-locks engaged. Kylie made a split-second decision and dove behind the food crates along the wall. A flash of light blinded her, and she shielded her eyes, unable to make sense of it.

<*A ship just appeared! Off the starboard side, Rogers,*> Nadine's mental tone was clipped and urgent. <*Tags say it's a merchant ship, the* Imperial Dawn.>

<*FTL dump?*> Rogers asked.

<*How the hell should I know? It wasn't there; now it is.*>

"Shit," Kylie swore aloud. She knew that ship; it was large and well-armed. There was no way her *Dauntless* could stand against it. If Rogers fought back, he would lose, and her ship would be the next drifting hull at the edge of the Gedri System waiting for salvage.

<*Get out of here!*> Kylie ordered Rogers. <*Let Winter and me handle this.*>

<*You don't have to tell me twice,*> her pilot replied.

<*Rogers!*> Nadine chastised.

<*Just joking. I'm powering up our beams. If they want us, they'll have to take us in a fight.*>

Powering the lasers? Were they serious? <*What are you thinking, Rogers? The* Imperial Dawn *can eat the* Dauntless *for breakfast. There's no way out of this situation for us. Run and I'll…catch up with you later.*> Kylie's argument was weak. She knew it, and Rogers would, too. <*Rogers, you answer me. Rogers!*>

There was no response from the *Dauntless*. Rogers either chose to ignore her orders—or was unable to answer.

Kylie frantically cycled her helmet through multiple scan modes, and when she landed on backscatter radiation, multiple figures appeared on her HUD—two on either side of the containers she was hiding behind, and moving fast. They must've worn some sort of stealth suit to mask their heat signature and their locations.

Probably military-grade.

If they'd wanted her dead, she'd be dead already. So, something else was clearly going on—if only she could figure out what that was.

Kylie lobbed a sonic grenade over the crate she'd hidden behind before peering around her cover, spraying shots with her pulse pistol at the closest figures. Her HUD highlighted a hit on one of the attackers and she smiled as the force flung that figure backward.

<*Anytime you want to open that door…*> Kylie said to Winter.

<*I'm working on it. Hang tight.*>

Like there was another option?

Concussive shots struck the stack of food crates she was hiding behind and the top one fell, landing less than a meter to her right and cracking open—the sight of bacon and apples interrupting Kylie's train of thought. What she wouldn't give for a piece of fresh fruit. Last time they'd had a supply of fresh apples, Rogers had eaten them all.

Staying in one place was going to get her killed, so Kylie rolled behind another stack and fired off a few shots in the general vicinity of her attackers. The enemy was closing in and there was only so much she could do to hold them off. She tossed another sonic grenade into the mix, taking the meager distraction it offered to rush to new cover.

<If you don't get that door—> Kylie broke off as two more figures appeared behind her.

Where had they come from?

Why hadn't they attacked earlier?

Kylie fell to her knees and pivoted to take a shot at the closest attacker when one of them lobbed a grenade straight at her. She jumped back to get clear of the blast radius, but it was too late. It hit her center mass and a nano-net wrapped around her. The buggy little bastards infiltrated her suit and attacked her nervous system.

The neural attack gagged her. Her lungs responded as if smoke was suffocating her, and she fought the net in a blind panic. It was all a mental trick, and one Kylie had been taught once to fight against, but that was a long time ago.

She clawed at her helmet, trying to remove it, forgetting the air on the ship was not breathable. Luckily, strong hands pinned her down and kept her from removing her helmet as she sent a distress call across the Link to Winter.

<You better be running for the ship. I'm going to need a rescue.>

Winter didn't speak but he flashed her his avatar, showing his arms held in the air before their Link connection was severed.

BOARDED

STELLAR DATE: 08.21.8947 (Adjusted Years)
LOCATION: Salvage ship *Dauntless* – Beyond Gedri's Heliopause
REGION: Gedri System, Silstrand Alliance

Rogers knew he couldn't just leave Kylie and Winter on board that freighter, but when the *Imperial Dawn* dropped out of the dark layer, he knew there was no time to lose.

"Get those beams powered up, we don't have much time if this is going to work," Rogers said as he activated his holodisplay and disconnected the *Dauntless*'s umbilical from the lifeless freighter. It was hard leaving the captain on board, but if he didn't, it would nix any chances they had of holding out against the enemy. "I'm bringing our shields up."

"Weapons ready here," Nadine said. "What's your plan, exactly?"

"Well," Rogers said as he boosted the *Dauntless* away from the *Titan-1*. "We're pretty sure some of their guys are on that ship, so we'll just tuck behind and use it for a handy shield."

"Rogers!" Nadine exclaimed. "Kylie and Winter are on that ship!"

"Yeah, but so are their guys, and it has no shields. They're not going to risk punching it full of holes."

Rogers spun the *Dauntless* and slowed it down, keeping only their dorsal weapons peeking over the disabled freighter.

A warning shot from the *Imperial Dawn* lit up the space above the *Dauntless*, and Rogers whistled. "Yup, they mean business. Nadine, hit them on their sensor array—maybe they'll decide we're not worth it."

"This is nuts." Nadine sighed but followed his direction.

Return fire lanced out from the *Dauntless*, easily shed by the *Imperial Dawn*'s shields.

"Damn," Rogers said, his expression growing concerned. "Their shields didn't even flicker; I didn't think they'd be that strong."

The *Imperial Dawn* boosted hard, arcing over the freighter and the *Dauntless*. It spun, lit its torches to break, and fired four separate beams at the same location above the *Dauntless*'s center engine.

Nadine's voice rushed out, "They just punched right through our shields."

"The reactor is overheating; I'm trying to get it shut down." Rogers swore. "Damnit."

"One hit and we've lost an engine!" Nadine exclaimed from her station. "These guys are having us for appetizers and drinks, and they haven't even asked us out on a proper date yet. We have to do something."

The enemy ship fired two more shots, disabling the shields over the Dauntless's other engines, and Nadine fixed Rogers with a hard stare.

<Vessel designated Dauntless,> a message hit their shipnet and came to them over the Link. *<You are under suspicion of piracy. On the authority of the Silstrand Alliance Space Force, and our letter of marque, we demand your surrender.>*

"Shit! A privateer," Rogers exclaimed. "What the…"

Nadine swallowed hard as she met his gaze at him. "This was a bait ship, and we wanted the payday so bad we fell for it."

"Yeah, but it was just sitting out here, fair game for salvage. What's their play?" Rogers replied.

"I'm powering down our beams. There's no way we can hold our own, let alone take these guys out," Nadine said. "They're not making kill shots. They want us alive…or something."

Rogers didn't bother to argue with her. He slid out of his chair and dropped to the bridge's deck. He grabbed the handgun he kept strapped underneath in case of an emergency.

"It's the 'or something' that worries me. Find a place to hide, and stay quiet while I deal with this." He stormed off the bridge, but Nadine followed close behind.

"There's no exit plan on this one, Rogers. We've been caught with our hand in the cookie box."

A shudder shook the ship as the *Imperial Dawn* grappled the *Dauntless*.

<Dauntless *crew. Prepare to be boarded. Assemble at your port airlock. On your knees, hands in the air.*>

Rogers gave an exasperated sigh and said, "It's 'jar', Nadine. Cookie *jar*. Now go hide!"

"Whatever!" Nadine's hands flourished in the air. "We're trapped. The *Dauntless* is a sitting duck, and now they're going to come on board and fry us."

"Don't you say that. She can…pull it together."

Nadine rolled her eyes. "Rogers, I love you, but you're delusional. We've lost. We need to shift gears or we'll never be able to help Kylie!"

She continued to follow him as he raced past the crew quarters and down the long passageway that ran toward the port engine. The enemy would expect him to come from the bridge, but if he could get past the airlock and take them from behind, they just might have a chance.

"If you're holding that weapon when they break in here, they'll kill you, and they'll be within their rights, Rogers. We fired. We fought. They have a letter of marque. We don't."

Rogers sighed. "But the captain. What about her? I know you two have been more than friends…more than once."

Nadine nodded. "Yes, and I'm twisted up inside, but if we die, we can't help her, and if we fight, we die. Come on, Rogers. We're outgunned and outnumbered. Please, see reason and listen to me."

The *Dauntless* shook again, and a loud clang sounded behind them as the enemy breached the airlock. Rogers blew out a long sigh and took cover, watching where the privateers would break through.

"I hate giving in. I can't, Nadine." Rogers shook his head and gazed around at his girl.

"It's not giving up. It's regrouping. We'll get them back."

"When?" Rogers asked, a deep growl to his voice.

Nadine shrugged. "I don't know." She placed her hand on the weapon Rogers held. "I don't want to watch you die."

Finally, with a resigned sigh, he turned it over to her. She tossed it into the corner as figures in powered armor burst through the airlock and scanned the corridor. She gave the intruding guard a pathetic glance and edged into view, her hands overhead.

"I'm here. I surrender. Don't shoot." She nudged Rogers, and he sighed before raising his hands and stepping out from his cover.

"That a boy," Nadine whispered.

"If they kill us, I blame you," Rogers said.

The armored boarders approached them with weapons leveled, while one signaled back through the airlock.

A man stepped into the corridor, and Rogers groaned. He was with the SSF, and a colonel, if Rogers read the rank on the man's collar properly.

"On your knees!" one of the armored figures called out.

Rogers knelt and Nadine followed suit. "Don't hurt her, we surrender, alright?"

"We're not junkers like you. Silstrand doesn't hurt its prisoners," the colonel said.

As he spoke, two of the armored boarders jammed tranq-wands into Nadine's and Rogers's necks. It might not have knocked them out, but Rogers instantly relaxed and Nadine swayed on her knees. She grinned and stared up at the officers. "Aren't you guys cute?" She pouted at them and blew them a kiss.

<*Nadine!*> Rogers chastised her across the Link, but his message never made it. Instead, it terminated at the edges of his consciousness, and the cocktail the tranq-wand had delivered made the words bounce around in his head. He groaned out loud and made a move to grab his temples.

One of the boarders cuffed him. "No more Link for either of you guys. Now, up on your feet. You have a lot of explaining to do aboard our ship."

"Shouldn't we get council first? A representative?" Rogers asked.

"From who?" the colonel barked as they walked down the bay toward the merchant privateer ship. "The GFF? Please. Move it, the both of you!"

"Are we in trouble, Rogers?" Nadine threw him a glance; she looked loopy, like the stun wand was messing with her more than it should have. If anyone on that ship took advantage of her…

"Yeah," Rogers whispered. "Big trouble."

*****

Back aboard the *Imperial Dawn*, Grayson took a sip of his coffee. Leaning down to access the holodisplay, he brought up images from the four holding cells. It was a motley crew that Kylie had put together. Who knew albinos even existed anymore? That recessive gene had been scrubbed from everyone's DNA, which meant the big man's look had to be a conscious choice.

It took all kinds.

Three of the four prisoners were awake, but still appeared dazed and out of it as they lay on their beds. Grayson was more concerned with Kylie; still unconscious from the effects of the nanonet and its neural attack. It'd be a few hours before she woke. When she did, she'd be pissed and ready to fight.

<*She looks well enough, Sir. Minus the whole unconscious bit,*> Jerrod, his internal AI, said.

<*Looks just like I remember.*>

<*She looks a little older to me. It's weird the way humans do that, isn't it?*>

Grayson didn't particularly think so. <*She's peaceful when she's…sleeping.*> More or less. He was worried about what would happen when she woke up.

<*She's not exactly sleeping, is she? Our men did that to her. Nearly killed her.*> Jerrod's voice would've been judgmental if he could be judgmental.

<*We didn't have a choice. She wouldn't give up. I know that, and you know that, too. The mission…we need her.*>

<*Oh yes. The mission,*> Jerrod said.

Grayson scowled but didn't argue further. Arguing with an AI never amounted to much other than a headache. Grayson had no proof Jerrod had done it on purpose, but sometimes he wondered if the synthetic mind he shared his head with could be spiteful.

The truth was, Jerrod was right. Grayson loved sparring with Kylie, and it looked like they were about to go another round. Too bad it was under these circumstances; he certainly missed the soft lines of her stubborn face.

What a future Kylie could've had—if she hadn't thrown it away.

The *Imperial Dawn*'s captain entered the privateer's bridge. "Call came in from General Samuel. He wants you to report immediately to the Trio System with the prisoners and their ship."

Grayson nodded. "Then let's not waste another moment here." The sooner they got to Trio, the sooner he could get off this freighter.

The captain nodded in agreement, probably also counting the minutes until he could get rid of Grayson—and his unwanted oversight. Even freighters on the up and up didn't like having an Alliance liaison on board. Grayson could appreciate that, but he had a job to do. "I'll be in your ready room. Let me know the moment the captain of the *Dauntless* awakens."

"Yes, Colonel." The captain sighed. Grayson caught the roll of his eyes and couldn't help a slight smile.

<*You enjoy yourself too much sometimes, sir,*> Jerrod said.

If he didn't enjoy his work, then what was the point of it all? It wasn't as though he had much else.

CAPTIVE

STELLAR DATE: 08.24.8947 (Adjusted Years)
LOCATION: Privateer ship *Imperial Dawn*
REGION: Interstellar Dark Layer, Silstrand Alliance

Pain thundered behind Kylie's eyes as she regained consciousness. She groaned and rolled over before pushing up into a sitting position. The room spun, and she grabbed the metal bedframe to stabilize herself. When her vision snapped back into place, the first things that resolved into any amount of clarity were the soft, gray tiles on the floor.

The room was small, nothing more than a three-meter-square prison cell. Steel walls, a small silver toilet in the corner; it all pointed to Kylie being on board a vessel—in the brig.

How did she get here in the first place? She couldn't remember much from what had happened on the *Titan-1*. Then she recalled falling unconscious with a woman standing over her in a shimmersuit. The kind that masked your movements and heat signatures—military-grade.

It had to be the SSF. Kylie had always said the only way she'd come back was to be dragged kicking and screaming.

Kylie clearly recalled the woman's face from when the nano field had hit her. From the grin she'd worn, she must have wanted Kylie to know she was beaten. That message had come through loud and clear.

Anyone using a shimmersuit and a nanonet was a cheater. Plain and simple.

Kylie rubbed her temple. <*Rogers, Winter, Nadine?*>

Her thoughts never left her head. They bounced around like it was nobody's business. Kylie grunted, the pain behind her eyes intensifying under pressure.

"We had to block your Link for now, to make sure you didn't plan a coup."

That voice…it was one Kylie hadn't heard in a long time, and her heart skipped a beat with surprise. She looked up, past the shimmering grav field across her open cell door. On the other side stood Grayson—in his Silstrand Alliance uniform, clearly here on business. His hands were clasped behind his back, and he stared at her as if she was a test subject on display.

Grayson's trim physique was tight, his jawline sexy as ever, but his blue eyes held only judgment. Kylie shook her head. "Here I thought you were going to leave me alone."

"We have, haven't we? Near a decade."

One year greater than that, but still. "Yet," Kylie whispered, "here we are."

"I knew you wouldn't be able to resist that freighter, but part of me wishes you had."

"And miss out on you taking the higher ground? The noble stance? What fun would that be?"

Grayson didn't even flinch. "I didn't come here to fight, funny as that might sound."

Kylie leaned back against the wall and crossed her legs on the bed. "Then why bother coming at all?"

"To make sure the effects of the nanonet were wearing off."

He could've done that through a holodisplay or a security vid—the room probably had vitals monitoring, too. Clearly, he didn't need to do that himself, especially now that he had gold oak leaves on his collar. "Full-bird colonel now, isn't that impressive?"

"Funny, you don't actually sound impressed."

Kylie smirked. "Next time I'll bring balloon animals, okay?"

Grayson chuckled. "You haven't lost your spunk. Little wonder you were never a good fit for the SSF."

No, but Kylie had tried. She'd really wanted to fit in with them and be the best damn space pilot anyone had ever seen. Young girls and their dreams. She shrugged and gazed away. "My ship? My crew? Winter?"

"Everyone's all right. Came quietly, which surprised me. Your ship on the other hand…."

Her heartbeat rose sharply, and Kylie leaned forward. "What the hell did you do to my ship, Grayson?"

"The *Dauntless* came at us hard. We were forced to take out one of the engines. She's repairable. I know what she must mean to you."

The same thing any ship meant to its captain, not that Grayson would understand a lick about that. A ruined engine would cost more money to fix than Kylie had—probably would have for some time. Of course, being locked up made that point kind of moot.

"Where's my crew? You break them, too?"

"Don't worry. I have them stewing in their own juices, but no harm has come to them."

Kylie shook her head. "Go easy on them. They're gentle."

Grayson smirked. "I won't hurt your crew. They're not what I'm after."

"Then what are you after?"

"You," Grayson said, and Kylie got the distinct impression he was playing with her. After all this time, nothing had really changed between them. She hung her head and studied her knuckles as she considered her next move. "I want to see them. I'm not going to take the word of the Alliance that they're all right."

"What about *my* word?"

Kylie licked her lips. "Like I said, I don't trust the Alliance. And you're *all* Alliance."

Grayson usually played things close to the chest, and Kylie was surprised to see his eyes narrow for a moment. So, beneath his starchy uniform, he still had feelings. "You play nice, and you guys get a meal together. How about that?"

Kylie shrugged. "I guess it's a start."

Grayson nodded and moved away from the grav field. Kylie couldn't let him go that easily. "When are you going to tell me what it is you're after?"

"That's not for me to say. General Samuel will fill you in when we arrive at Trio."

Well, there was a name she'd hoped never to hear again. Kylie sunk deeper into the mattress and leaned her head against the wall. So much for not attracting the attention of the Silstrand Alliance—now she was being dragged back to where everything had begun.

* * * * *

When Grayson had said that Kylie would have to play nice, he'd meant it. She'd needed to earn that dinner with her crew through good behavior, and she'd spent the first day locked down in her prison cell. At regular intervals, someone had brought her food and drink. It hadn't been unpleasant, but the most interesting thing was that the people who'd brought her meals weren't military.

It was plain to see—SSF uniforms were gray, and these guys wore blue shipsuits with no discernable markings. Their movements were casual, unlike the stiffs that gravitated toward the military. These men didn't appear to bear her any ill will. Instead, most looked uncomfortable and occasionally cracked a joke or a handsome boyish smile.

The *Imperial Dawn* was a civilian ship, but Kylie had always suspected that it dealt in more than just honest trading. What was Grayson doing on board and why had the SSF sent him there? It was clear General Samuel was using her past relationship with Grayson to his advantage, but why go through all the trouble?

Kylie played with the rations on the metal plate balanced on her knees. She picked up a bit of protein and popped it into her mouth with a smile. She gazed at the man who had brought it to her, now watching from the passageway outside her cell. He was young and good-looking with an olive complexion and dark, wavy hair. "Thanks for the food. It's delicious. Did you cook it yourself?"

He smiled and gave a little laugh. "No chance of that. I can barely boil water."

"Been awhile since I've had cheese. It's a real treat. Thank you." Kylie laughed as she slid the tray onto the bed beside her. She sauntered over to the grav field and leaned against the wall, placing a hand on her hip. "What are you guys doing out past the heliopause anyway? Some sort of secret mission?"

He tensed, and his shoulders shrugged up against his ears. "I don't really know. If you're trying to pump me for information…"

"I wouldn't dream of it. I'm just trying to make conversation. I've been locked in here for over twenty-four hours now—it's getting a bit dull."

He nodded. "Sure, yeah. I can understand that."

"You been out in the black long?" she asked.

"Long time. We live out here, practically, but once we drop you off, we get a bit of R&R."

"And what is it you're doing out here? What's this ship's business?"

He laughed and shook his head, gazing away.

"Oh, come on. What's the harm in telling me? What exactly can I do from in here? I'm not going to write my mom about it. I don't even have a pen."

"We're a merchant privateer, okay? We trade, and occasionally salvage a damaged ship—that we may, or may not, have damaged ourselves—for the SA."

So, that must be how they knew Grayson. They were legal pirates, and she was an illegal one. Typical.

"Thanks, junior." Kylie winked at him. "If I ever get out of here, I'll thank you properly."

He grinned. "And how exactly—" He cut himself off and jumped as if someone was yelling at him over the Link. From the way his cheeks blushed, Kylie suspected someone had.

"Sorry if I got you in trouble with your captain."

"I better go, but it's all right." He threw a glance at her as he left, his feet stumbling like a kid who'd had his first schoolgirl crush.

Kylie turned her arm over. She pressed a finger against the cuff of her purple jacket. A second later, it lowered its pheromone output. There was more than one way to get what she wanted.

Right then, she could really use a weapon and a plan.

* * * * *

After a day in the tank, Kylie's captors escorted her to a small room. In that room, her crew sat around a small metal table. Some of her anxiety dissipated just to see their warm bodies in the chairs. Winter and Rogers hunched over the tabletop, but Nadine's posture was straight as an arrow—same as always. She looked out of place in the jumpsuit they had given her. Always regal, no matter where they were, Nadine couldn't hide from her heritage any more than Kylie could.

In front of each sat a modest dinner. Kylie took the empty chair, and a guard set a tray of food in front of her. A piece of chicken breast, most likely overcooked, and some bland-smelling potatoes. Not the best food, but certainly not the worst, and Kylie eagerly picked up her spork.

She waited for the guard to move on to the back of the room before she allowed herself to glance at the faces of her crew.

Their serious expressions spoke volumes about the trouble they were all in. Winter's concern was the most masked, except for an occasional twinge at the corner of his eye, which would've gone unnoticed by most.

Nadine looked the most anxious. As communication officer, she didn't see action most of the time—what happened on the ship must have been dramatic. Her eyes fluttered about as she curled a tendril of hair around her finger, the beauty of her face marred by worry crease-lines along her forehead.

And Rogers was his usual calm, collected self, hunched over the table, eating as if it would be his last meal. How he could wolf food down like that even under the worst of circumstances?

"Everybody okay?" Kylie used her spork to pick at the potato and chicken mixture. Her initial guess was right—overcooked, but it could have been worse.

Her crew gave her a bunch of nods, and Winter grunted.

Nadine shook her head. "It was intense. I know we've got into scuffles before but—"

Kylie wanted to comfort her but didn't want to draw attention to their relationship. With the Link down, there was no way they could have a private conversation that wasn't going to be observed and recorded. "I'm glad each of you is all right."

Winter crossed his bulky arms and leaned back in his chair, with a shake of his head. "Doesn't make sense how they're even letting us speak to one another. I'd be careful what we say." Winter gestured toward the corner of the rooms and

Kylie didn't need to look to know he was pointing out the surveillance system. She had already spotted it on the way in.

"What the hell happened out there?" Rogers's eyes were angry. Not with her, but at what had happened and how their ship had been lost.

"It was a setup. We were meant to find that disabled freighter." Kylie followed her words with a sip of water from the glass on the table. "They were waiting for us."

Nadine held her breath, but it was Rogers who shook his head. "And we took it hook, line, and sinker."

"Why us?" was the only question Winter asked. "What'd you get us into, Kylie?"

She bristled at the question. It wasn't like she had done this on purpose, but the past had a way of catching up to a person, even at FTL. "I don't know. We'll find out when we arrive at Trio. They're taking me to see a general."

Nadine groaned, and Rogers rested his chin on his fist, gazing down at his food. No one at the table was a fan of the Silstrand Alliance, even less of their military. Kylie wasn't sure if there was anything worse that she could've told them. However, she always did her best to tell her crew the truth, when the truth could be seen clearly.

"We'll be there in just over a day now."

"These guys ain't 'Strands'." Winter leaned forward. "Unless I miss my guess, they're private. Civilian, not government."

Kylie could read between the lines. Maybe they could take the guard in the room, but they had no clear view of the layout of the ship. They couldn't access the ship's Link and they had no weapons. Four sporks weren't going to cut much of anything.

"There's a colonel on board; I met him. If there are other officers, I haven't seen them yet." Kylie turned her attention to

Rogers. "But those were SSF soldiers who took me down on that freighter; they have to be here somewhere."

Winter had that look in his eye that Kylie had seen before. Usually, it led him to do something reckless. "These guys have weapons."

"We can't…" Nadine said, lowering her voice. She leaned forward and whispered, "…hurt these guys."

"We need to get off this ship before we're locked up in some SSF prison and can never get out," Winter said.

Kylie held up her hand to stop them from going any further. Already Winter sounded heated, not that she didn't understand. "The *Dauntless*…can she fly?"

Rogers shrugged. "She'll fly, but shields are down, and the AP engine was damaged. Would be nothing but a flying tin can."

It was too big a risk for the crew, that was for sure. "We sit tight for another couple of days. What's the worst that can happen?"

Nadine relaxed, but Winter tensed. "They throw us in a prison cell for the next hundred years, if we're lucky. If we see a chance, we have to take it."

"They set us up for a reason. I don't think they went through all that trouble just to arrest a few junkers," Kylie said.

"Then what?" Rogers asked. "What makes us so damn special?"

"*She* does." Nadine's saddened eyes studied Kylie's face. "They want you back. You always knew this day would come."

But Kylie wasn't expecting it to come so soon, or that it would be Grayson who came for her. Of all the people to send after her, why him? "Hold tight, Nadine. I'm going to get you out of this yet."

"How?" Winter asked.

Kylie was still working on that part. As the guard in the back approached, Kylie slipped her spork up her sleeve. She cupped her hand to keep it secure as he forced her up from the table.

"Playtime's over. Back to your holding cell," the man said with a grunt.

"Be good. I'll see you guys real soon." Kylie let her eyes linger on Winter even if he refused to look at her.

Another guard entered the room, cuffed her hands, and escorted her to her cell. As they walked, Kylie studied the structure of the ship and peered down the intersecting corridors. Most were unguarded and half the crew they passed weren't even armed.

It was suicide to do anything, but Kylie still itched to make a move. Stay the course, be patient. That was what was best, but self-restraint and Kylie weren't exactly the best of friends.

Grayson was waiting outside Kylie's cell, standing with his arms clasped behind his back. He didn't smile at her, but he didn't look away, either. Instead, he met her gaze head on. "I told you, you could be rewarded if you played nice."

Kylie walked into her cell and waited for her handcuffs to be removed. She wished Grayson wasn't there to watch and her cheeks flamed red with embarrassment. "Why'd you do it?"

"To observe you. So, you'll realize there are benefits to good behavior." Grayson stepped into her cell instead of raising the stasis field. "So, you'd take me at my word."

There was a time Kylie would've believed him without the need for proof. "You told the truth. Good for you. I'm just glad you didn't hurt them."

"They've given us no need to, so far. I do hope you realize there's no way to escape, or commandeer this ship."

"You think I would put my crew's life at risk like that? I can read the odds. I haven't seen any of your SSF assassins, but based on what happened on the freighter, I'm sure they're around here somewhere."

"We don't employ assassins," Grayson said. "Standing orders from the general are for you to appear before him at Trio. He made no mention of your crew. You might not be expendable, but they are."

He was couth as ever. "Should I thank you for your fair warning?"

Grayson smirked, but sadness lingered in his eyes. "I wouldn't expect such a thing, but it had to be said, Kylie. Play ball and things will go your way."

He still said her name with a softened undertone that Kylie had almost forgotten about. With nothing left to say that would benefit her, she bit her tongue.

When he exited the prison cell, Grayson hit the panel to bring the grav field back online. His head hung low, and, Kylie thought he might say something out of character. Instead, she stepped forward. "Grayson."

"We chose our sides a long time ago." Sadness and anger mingled in his eyes. "So, let's not have a conversation neither of us wants to have."

He pulled the hem of his jacket down taut and pivoted sharply before walking away.

Grayson never looked back, and Kylie drew her lips into her mouth. For a moment, she had almost been vulnerable with him.

It left her feeling cold.

GENERAL SAMUEL

STELLAR DATE: 08.27.8947 (Adjusted Years)
LOCATION: Privateer ship *Imperial Dawn*
REGION: Outer Trio System, Silstrand Alliance

Kylie had been in a deep sleep when the ship's klaxon sounded, announcing the dump from FTL to normal space. The Trio System was a frequent stop for the *Dauntless*—being only a five-and-a-half-day jump from Gedri—and she had a good idea where the *Imperial Dawn* would dock. It wouldn't be long before she met the general once more.

Where Gedri was a half-forgotten system—one that only the Silstrand Alliance had laid a nominal claim to—Trio was the opposite. Like Gedri, it too sat on the coreward edge of Silstrand Alliance space, staring across the Yosemite Gulf at the Scipio Federation. But where Gedri was a haven for illegal trade and smuggling, Trio was a bastion of the Silstrand Alliance's civilization.

Its interstellar commerce hubs bustled with trade, and the SSF made sure the system was secure and well-ordered. Excepting one incursion by Padre's pirate ships a few years ago, nothing bad ever happened there.

It was a peace enforced at the point of a gun—or the point of the space force's vast navy. It was at one of their bases, which ringed the system, where Kylie expected the *Imperial Dawn* to dock.

She rolled over, attempting to get back to sleep. It would be many hours, at best, before the ship reached any port, and she wanted to be well-rested for whatever was to come.

Still, old habits were hard to break, and Kylie thought of all the bad ones, and scarce few of the good ones, as the hours rolled by—wishing she could be on the bridge, confirming approach vectors and reviewing insystem ship traffic.

Eventually, as sleep began to overtake her, another klaxon sounded, and she felt docking thrusters fire. Either the ship had jumped further insystem than normally allowed, or they were approaching a station she didn't know about.

Either way, very soon, it would be time to face the music. Too bad Kylie didn't even know what melody it was that was playing.

It was someone else's dance.

When armed Alliance soldiers came to collect her, Kylie finally recognized a face from aboard the damaged *Titan-1* freighter. "Well, if it isn't you?"

The woman with the tight ponytail didn't flinch. Her narrow face could stand a rearranging and Kylie wanted to volunteer for the job.

"Stand back. Hands in front of you."

Kylie did as she was asked, but didn't like it much. The cuffs dug into her skin as they were locked on much tighter than they needed to be. She cringed as the female guard shoved her forward. "Move!"

"What did I do to piss you off?"

"One of my friends is laid up in the medbay because you dropped a crate on his head."

Kylie turned down the hall, but the female soldier didn't let her get too far ahead. She kept a firm hand on her shoulder. "They were trying to kill me first," Kylie said.

"They were trying to subdue you. Not kill you."

"No one told me that, did they? Like it's my fault your bosses keep everything hush hush? Far as I knew, I was fighting for my life."

"Don't push your luck." The woman gave Kylie another shove, and Kylie stumbled forward.

Kylie recovered and continued walking down the narrow corridor. A few twists and turns later and they arrived at the docking bay.

Inside the bay, her crew stood single file with Winter at the front.

Nadine tried to glance back at Kylie, almost as though she sensed her presence. A soldier pressed his rifle against the back of her neck. "Eyes front, Ms. Devonire."

"Keep your hands to yourself." Kylie fumed. "That's a princess you're mistreating."

The officer snorted. "Not anymore she isn't. Just another cheap junker like the rest of you."

Cheap? Junker? Kylie's face twitched, and she itched to wipe the floor with him.

The officer glanced back at Kylie and his finger slipped off the rifle's trigger guard, hovering a centimeter over the trigger. Grayson, from his position at the front of the docking bay, didn't miss a beat. He lifted a finger to silence the soldier, who pulled his rifle back, but said nothing in support of Kylie.

Figured.

Winter tensed. He threw a quick glance at the soldier and then down at the man's weapon, Kylie didn't miss his intent. All the guards were armed. There were enough weapons for all of them, but she didn't think her crew would make it out alive. Getting off this ship would just land them in a fight for their lives across what she suspected would be a military installation.

The four of them would be dead in minutes.

Kylie wished she could tell Winter they only wanted *her* alive. Why bother transferring them all to the station? Kylie held her breath as a transmission from the station piped over the room's audible systems.

"*Imperial Dawn,* your passengers are cleared to disembark. General Samuel sends his greetings and is waiting for you in Ready Room Three. Welcome back, Colonel."

"Thank you," Grayson replied as he palmed the control that opened the docking bay door. As it slid open, Kylie peered outside, but the view left much to be desired. All she could see was the security checkpoint and a few more soldiers.

All at once, everything around her erupted. Winter slammed his elbow into the side of a guard's head. The guard flew to the side and Winter grabbed his gun, training it on Grayson. "Nobody move or the boss-man loses all his tiny little brain cells!"

Kylie's heart leaped into her throat. She lunged forward to get between the guards and Winter, but her escort kept a firm grip on her arms.

Nadine screamed, and the soldier guarding her wrapped his arm tight around her throat. Rogers spun and grabbed the weapon from the woman behind him, and Kylie cried out. This wouldn't play out well, not at all, but Winter had forced their hand. Damn him.

"Winter!"

This wasn't what she wanted. This wasn't going to work; even if they got off the station, they'd never get out on another ship. There was probably half an SSF fleet docked here. If Winter thought they could handle that, then he really had lost his marbles.

Grayson spoke calmly and quietly to Winter, but his eyes fell on Kylie. "You don't want to do this."

Kylie could only see the back of Winter's head, but she could imagine how twitchy his face must be. He probably had that whites-around-the-eyes look that made him downright scary.

"Oh yeah? I think I'm doing exactly what it is I want to do."

"You may want to look behind you. We have Ms. Devonire by the throat. There's a gun to her head. If you don't drop yours, we're going to take her out. Even if you get off the ship, even if you kill these guards and me, you'll never make it off the station. You're going to end up back in prison, or the incinerator, where you belong."

Nadine was gasping for air and Kylie's blood pressure shot through the ceiling. She was sure the boys would lower their weapons. There was no way that Winter, and especially Rogers, would trade Nadine's life for freedom.

Kylie was half right. Rogers handed his gun over to the guard and raised his hands. In retaliation, one of the soldiers sucker punched him, and he fell to the floor where the boot of another solider mashed his face into the deckplate.

Rogers choked, and Kylie let out a long breath. "Let him go."

Grayson's eyes didn't even meet Kylie's. Instead, they remained firmly on Winter. "That's up to him. What's it going to be?"

Winter hesitated. He didn't lower his weapon.

"Winter!" Kylie warned.

He wasn't going to give up. Kylie's eyes darted to Winter, then back to Nadine who still struggled to get free. Nadine's back was arched as she reached back to claw at the man's head. If the soldier didn't let her go soon, things would be bad. Real bad.

If Winter wouldn't give up his gun, it was time to make him.

In a split second, Kylie twisted her arm free and grabbed her hidden spork, driving it deep into her handler's ear. The woman screamed as blood gushed out and ran down the side of her head. She doubled over in pain and Kylie grabbed her pulse rifle.

Without warning, she fired it into the back of the soldier who was holding Nadine. The man fell to his knees, and Nadine collapsed, coughing, and stroking her throat as if she couldn't breathe. Kylie stepped beside her and glanced down. The purple color was draining from her cheeks.

She'd be okay. Thank God.

Kylie aimed the rifle at the guard who had his boot on Rogers's face, so he couldn't take the shot at Winter. "This isn't the way. There is no way out of here for us, don't risk the lives of our friends and crew to get out of here. I know you're afraid…" she addressed Winter.

"If we don't get out now, we're never free. Damn you, Kylie." He spat out the words, his weapon never wavering from Grayson's head.

"We don't sacrifice the crew to free ourselves. We're better than that." They might be scoundrels, but Kylie would never abandon her crew, not a single one of them.

Winter's voice strained. "I need you with me on this, Kylie."

She shook her head. "Never going to happen. We don't leave without them. Let me find a way out of this for *all* of us. Trust me. I've never left you high and dry. No matter what happens, I would never stop fighting for you."

Kylie held her breath for the two seconds that followed. She wasn't sure what would happen, but Winter slowly lowered his gun. Grayson took it from him with a nod. A second later, four guards rushed in and grabbed Winter, pushing him to the deck and shackling him hand and foot. Kylie had no sympathy for him. He had brought it on himself and every member of her crew.

She wouldn't soon forget that.

One of the soldiers took the rifle from Kylie, and another forced her down to the deck and checked her over for more hidden weapons. So much for gratitude. Kylie craned her head to look back at the crying woman with the spork jammed into her ear.

The officer's bulging eyes would have burned a hole right through her if they could. "You crazy bitch!"

Kylie smirked. Sometimes gratitude came in all shapes and sizes. She grinned as two soldiers took her by the arms and lifted her back up.

Kylie was escorted out last and Grayson shook his head as he took her by the arm. "You never learn, do you?"

"You should be thanking me for saving your life."

"You should be thanking me for not taking out your crew."

They passed through a long corridor, through a security checkpoint, and out onto the station's busy dock. More soldiers appeared and surrounded Kylie and her crew. Kylie wrenched away from one who grabbed her shoulder.

Grayson shook his head. "Will you ever make things easy?"

"Probably not, but you wouldn't have it any other way." Kylie's voice betrayed her more than she thought it would. She gave Grayson a sweet smile as she was led away. Another prison cell was in her future, but Kylie welcomed this one.

She was in no rush to meet the general. No rush at all.

*****

General Samuel wasn't a man Kylie could forget. But he *was* a man she had hoped never to see again. When he stepped into Ready Room Three, Kylie could have recognized the man by his deep, overgrown eyebrows alone. Did he not know about grooming combs? Tall and slender, like every man in the SSF, he stopped at the end of the table and scowled down at her.

"Rhoads," General Samuels greeted her in a gruff voice, just the one she remembered.

Kylie wiggled her fingers at him. "I'd stand, but your hospitality service here handcuffed me to the table." She swiveled in her seat to throw a glower at the armed guards standing by her side.

"You blame them after what you and your team just pulled? You seriously injured one of my officers with a plastic utensil."

"It was a spork," Kylie interjected.

"And," he continued at a louder volume, "the other officer is in critical condition."

"There wasn't a low-power setting, sir. I had to act fast before my crew was dead. Maybe even Colonel Grayson, too. Sorry, my crew panicked, but we're not used to your rules and law. We live outside it. When you corner a wild animal—"

Samuels grunted. "Still would have us believe you can't be tamed, Kylie? Is that your game?"

Kylie blinked. "It's not a game. I just want my ship back. I want my crew. I want to know why you came for me after all these years when before—well, to be frank—you just didn't care what I did or where I went."

"I'm sorry you think that," Samuel muttered. "Samantha, dim the lights and pull up the images."

"You named the division AI after yourself?"

"A coincidence," Samuel said as the lights dimmed.

Yeah, right…

A young woman's face hovered in midair. Pretty, though with almost plain features and fine blonde hair. Her bangs rested right above her eyebrows, and there was something angelic about her appearance—even if her green eyes held a great deal of distress.

"My daughter. Two weeks ago, she went missing."

"I'm sorry to hear that, but I don't know what that has to do with me," Kylie said.

Samuel paced back and forth as he spoke. "We have every reason to believe that Maverick has her. We don't know where he's keeping her, but it's imperative that we get her back. That we find her. She's not well and needs a dangerous operation soon, or she won't survive. Her nano isn't able to keep up."

Maverick, the crime lord who was the real power behind the Gedri System. He was ruthless and kept the other crime lords and pirate cartels in line. Without him, Gedri would fall apart—well, fall apart more.

He was also Kylie's boss and was expecting her to bring a sweet haul in soon—what she had hoped the *Titan-1* would be. A lot of junkers worked for Maverick, but not everyone got in to see him—not like her. Somehow, that information had landed in the SSF's hands, and now she'd bet they wanted her to do their dirty work.

"I'm sorry for your daughter's condition, but how do you know Maverick is responsible?"

"Surveillance vids outside her home, and from where she was taken. We tracked his men to Gedri. There's no other explanation."

"And now you want me to betray him? You think I'm stupid enough to get an entire system's worth of angry crime lords and pirates chasing me across the galaxy?" Kylie shook her head. "Even if I was that stupid, I'm not suicidal."

It went beyond that—not that she was going to share the details with Samuel. Once, Maverick had owned her, and he'd set her free—she had a price to pay, a big one, and she didn't want to betray him. If she did, his punishment would be far worse than any prison Samuel could throw her into.

"Maybe you don't care about yourself, or your own freedom, but I guess you care about your crew: Rogers, Nadine, Winter. From what I see in their records, they all have fairly checkered pasts but none more so than Winter. He has too much on his record for another warning. His illegal boarding of the *Titan-1*…" Samuel said.

Kylie blew out a long breath, desperate not to play his game. "You mean the bait freighter that you put out there for us to find? It was derelict. We have a salvage license from the GFF; you had no right to arrest us for that!" Anger rolled over her tongue.

"Cut the shit, Kylie. That ship was outside Gedri's heliopause. Your license ends where that star's foul wind stops. You could have flown on by. You didn't."

"It's entrapment. Even for you, it's low."

"Maybe." Samuel's lip turned up in a snarl as he leaned forward and pressed his hands onto the table. "I know enough about Nadine Devonire's troubles to know she doesn't want to get sent home to her family. If you want to stop me from doing that, you'll play ball. Or, do you need reminding about what awaits her when she returns home?"

Kylie turned away. She had heard enough, and from the scowl on Samuel's face, it was clear he knew it.

"I have an offer to make you."

"Fine. I'm listening," Kylie said, even though she didn't want to listen at all.

"We fix your ship and release your crew. You go back to Maverick with the *Titan-1* as your salvage. It'll give you the opportunity to get close to Maverick." Samuel turned the lights back on. "You rescue my daughter, do whatever you have to do. I'll make sure the four of you are never bothered again. You'll get your own letter of marque and complete immunity for past crimes," he finished.

Work legally? With no problems and no hassles? If that was true, Kylie would never have to see Maverick again. Or share his bed. It was almost too good to be true, which meant she couldn't trust it. Kylie couldn't let her guard down. "We'll get a free pass for everything that happened?"

"Everything that happened and everything that will happen on this mission. I'll see to it the SA grants you immunity for everything that you have to do 'til my daughter is back in my arms, Commander Rhoads. You know I have the power to do it."

"I'm not a commander anymore, General, but I appreciate the sentiment."

Old habits were indeed hard to break.

Samuel leaned closer. "This is the best offer you're going to get. If you say no, you'll be transferred to an SSF holding facility to await trial. It'll be swift. And it'll be the *Dauntless* that will find itself salvaged."

Kylie's tongue ran along her teeth. "Well, when you put it that way..."

Grayson entered the room, and Kylie wondered how long he had been listening. Obviously, he'd known going into the mission to capture her what was going to happen—what the endgame was—and he'd still set her up.

So much for any past feelings they may have shared. Grayson was loyal to a fault, and Kylie had never had any misgivings about who he was loyal to. The Silstrand Alliance had his body, mind, and soul. Kylie had just borrowed him for a little while.

"A few more points to cover. To make sure you follow the plan and do your damnedest to rescue my daughter, Grayson will be on board your ship."

A representative from the SSF, on her ship? That much Kylie could've guessed—it was smart business—but the idea of spending a prolonged period of time with Grayson was unfathomable even after everything that had happened. Not counting the things that had transpired on the *Imperial Dawn*.

Kylie did her best to keep her eyes front and center but couldn't resist a quick glance at her former lover. Grayson wasn't looking at her either, but he *was* smirking. That smirk she could never wipe off his face for good. It always found its way back.

"Just one more thing. To succeed in this mission, you will need to be fitted with a military AI. The process is relatively painless and will take about three days for full integration—"

Military AI? In her brain? New anxiety surged. Kylie tried to stand up from the table, and the cuffs around her wrists caught on the locking bar, jerking her back down. The officers behind her stepped forward just in case she tried to do anything. What could she try to do? She was out of moves.

Still, Kylie couldn't stop her charging heart from trying to break through her ribs at the mere suggestion that her brain would suddenly become home to another being—even if it was artificial. "No way! An AI? Not on your life. I'd rather go to prison. People go wrong when they have an AI. I've seen it before and even those that don't, they're never the same. Sub-humans."

Grayson wiped his mouth as his oh-so-intelligent stare cut through Kylie. "I know this is something you've strongly believed for a long time and it's not your fault. Your technophobe parents indoctrinated you long before you ever came to the academy. But there's another way. I've been living with my AI for over ten years and it's nothing to be afraid of."

Kylie's nostrils flared. "You're not one to tell me what I cannot be afraid of. My parents aren't technophobes. They're devout in their beliefs. They just chose another way of life that might seem arcane to you, but it's calm and pleasant and gave me everything I need to survive."

Samuels muffled a laugh. "Life in space on a freighter? A pilot? You loved your techno-free existence so much that you joined the Alliance?"

"You're twisting my past. It's not like that."

It wasn't. She hadn't run away because she'd been trying to escape. She hadn't joined the SSF Academy because she'd wanted to run away and hide. She'd just wanted to travel and explore new places, and with her piloting skills, maybe she could have done some good. Boy, had she been wrong.

None of which had anything to do with her parents or the religion they followed.

Kylie held her ground. "You can't change my mind on this."

"Then the deal is off," Samuel said with a grunt, clearly disappointed in her decision.

"I can do it without an AI. I know Maverick in ways other people don't. I don't need an AI to get the job done." Kylie's breath stuttered. "With my crew, this mission has a high likelihood of success. I can get your daughter back, I know it. At least give me a shot. If it doesn't work, you can stick us all back into lockup, and you get one more salvage ship ready for duty."

Grayson and Samuel stared at one another. Kylie suspected they were communicating over the Link. What she wouldn't give to have access to that little chat.

She straightened up, her shoulders rigid as she waited for them to speak. It was Samuel who finally did. "Grayson convinced me to go along with your plan. But if you, or your team, try anything funny you're not the only one who will be punished for this mission going wrong." Samuel nodded to Grayson and the guards before taking his leave.

Grayson unlocked her handcuffs, and Kylie rubbed her hands together to sooth her itching skin. "You put yourself on the line for me?"

Grayson shrugged. "Least I could do. I suckered you into this mess. Besides, I know you can get the job done. The two of us together…once we were unstoppable."

Kylie remembered. It was a long time ago, before she'd been booted out of the SSF with a dishonorable discharge. "And the *Dauntless*?"

"It's being worked on now. I knew you'd say yes." Grayson smirked and showed off his dimples.

Kylie did her best not to return his smile, or notice his stinking dimples. "And how long will it take for the station to make the repairs?"

"Thirty-two hours. Just enough time for you to get your crew on board with this mission. And with me."

Kylie snorted. Barely enough time for just one of those tasks.

GET IN LINE

STELLAR DATE: 08.27.8947 (Adjusted Years)
LOCATION: Silstrand Space Force navy base
REGION: Trio System, Silstrand Alliance

Rogers, along with Winter and Nadine, had been moved from their holding cells into more comfortable quarters—a small room containing a simple table and chairs with a gray loveseat in the rear and a small window overlooking the station's docks. On the dock, uniformed and civilian workers went about their business. The room's only exit was guarded by two silent officers, not exactly giving Rogers a good vibe about the situation.

When Winter began pacing in the middle of the room, Rogers's vibe went from bad to worse. He strode over to Winter, his fists clenched so hard that his knuckles turned white.

"Don't," Nadine whispered from her seat at the table. In her hand was a purple glass filled with filtered water, courtesy of the guard who had poured it for her.

Winter held his hand up to stop Rogers's approach, but he wasn't going to back down. He didn't care if the entire station descended onto them. What Winter had done was immature and selfish, two things Rogers wouldn't put up with.

He grabbed Winter by his shirt. "What the hell was that, huh? You don't make a move unless we all make a move! You broke the damn code, and for what? Yourself?"

Winter pushed Rogers back with a casual thrust. "Get off me."

Rogers lost his grip on the big man's shirt and plopped down into an empty chair. He stood back up and went toe-to-toe with Winter even though there was no way he could beat the hulking man's raw strength. "You don't get to say that. You don't get to act high and mighty. I have a lot to say to you, and you're damn well going to listen."

He paused, and when Winter didn't say anything, he continued. "You put us all in jeopardy. Nadine, the cap— you did more than put her in harm's way. She took a huge risk saving your ass. More than *I* would have."

"You took a weapon too," Winter said

Rogers nodded. "Had no choice and it nearly got me killed. If I didn't make a move, you'd be dead. You forced my hand with no plan, no backup. You're a sonofabitch, Winter. Always knew it, but you were *our* sonofabitch. Good for the team and all that. Now you're airlock trash for all I care."

Both men glared at each other and their chests puffed out. Winter began to circle Rogers, as if they were standing in the middle of a wrestling ring, and Rogers moved to face his would-be friend and shipmate. If he wanted a fight, Rogers was damn well going to give him one. Even though he couldn't come out on top, he'd damn well try.

"Don't. Not on my account," Nadine said with a quiet strength.

They both glanced at her as if they had forgotten she was there—and Rogers, for his part, had. Her sad eyes peered up from beneath her feathered blue bangs, and their gaze defused his anger.

"Sorry, Nadine." Rogers took a deep breath. "But it had to be said."

"I know, but please stop now."

"Just when things were getting good," one of the SSF guards said with a chuckle from her post at the room's entrance, and Rogers threw her a dirty look.

Winter bent down to make eye contact with Nadine. "I didn't mean...."

Her sorrowful eyes didn't leave his face, and the heartbreak of it all made Rogers look away. "You were going to let them kill me."

Winter shook his head. "It was never going to happen."

"Bull. Shit." Rogers squinted. "You panicked. You snapped. Just admit it. Everyone knows your history, getting sent back to prison for you might be the last time. To get away from that, you threw us all to the wolves."

Rogers turned and took a breath as though he was done, but then decided he wasn't. He came back and pointed his finger straight beneath Winter's nose. "As far as I'm concerned, you're no longer part of this team. And if we ever see Kylie again, I'll tell her how I feel."

Winter huffed. "You think she'll take your side over mine?"

Rogers nodded. "After what you did? She'll take my side. You'll be lucky if she ever lets you step aboard the *Dauntless* again. If my girl hasn't been scrapped yet." Rogers walked to the other side of the room and stared out the window to study the ships as they were loaded and unloaded. His anger slowly defused and he exhaled, nice and slow, trying to forget everything he had just said.

But behind him, it wasn't done. Winter sat down at the table. "Nadine," he whispered. "I never meant for you…it just didn't go how I thought it would play out."

Nadine shook her head. "You didn't think. That's the problem, and that's what Rogers is getting at, albeit less eloquently. You reacted out of fear, Winter, and that's something that puts us all at risk."

Winter stared off at the wall. "I guess an apology won't work."

Nadine smiled slightly. "But it's a start."

Rogers turned and leaned against the window frame, while Nadine and Winter got buddy-buddy. He wasn't so easily swayed. At that very moment, the door slid open, and Kylie stepped in.

She looked no worse for wear—in fact, Rogers thought she looked more refreshed than when they'd last seen her after the confrontation in the *Imperial Dawn*'s docking bay. She was back in her gleaming black leggings and form-fitting blue jacket, not the prison jumpsuit he had been half expecting.

Rogers stepped forward to greet her as Nadine and Winter quickly rose from their seats. Rogers was the first to speak. "You okay? What happened?"

*****

Kylie reached for Nadine's hand and squeezed her fingers, and a small smile passed between them. "I'm fine."

Winter licked his lips and immediately try to speak, but Kylie cut him off with a stern glare. "You sit down."

Winter's eyes flashed open wide, and his cheeks puffed out, but he didn't argue. He flopped into the seat and crossed his arms like a man-child who had just been scolded by his governess—which wasn't that far from the truth.

Rogers suppressed a chuckle and Kylie was glad for that. She wasn't looking to have a pissing contest.

"There's a lot to say." Kylie shifted her weight from one leg to the next, nervous with all their eyes on her.

"The *Dauntless*?" Rogers asked, the worry visible in his eyes even though he did a fine job of keeping it out of his voice.

"She's being fixed. In little more than a day, she'll be in ship shape and we'll be on board."

Winter's scowled. "Why? We should be in prison cells for what we did."

"You mean what you did?" Kylie leaned over and studied his face. "I made a deal to get us out of a royal mess we'd stepped into, and then you made it worse. You tied my hands, Winter. I don't like it when my hands are tied."

Nadine cleared her throat, and Kylie glanced at her comm officer. Well, maybe sometimes she did like to be tied, but that was beside the point.

"We're going to take the *Dauntless* and go on a rescue mission to save the general's daughter. Once that's done and she's back in his loving arms, we'll have our freedom. And a letter of marque." Kylie couldn't help but feel a little pride as she said it.

Rogers's eyebrows rose. "Damn, we're going legit?"

The excitement in the room rose as the uncertainty on Winter's face increased.

Nadine clapped with a happy, but demure, squeal. "This is so amazing. I always knew you could go legit, Kylie."

Her words of belief and encouragement made Kylie's heart soar. It wasn't often anymore that she was proud of herself, but right then she felt it.

"And we're going to have immunity. We get the general's daughter back by any means necessary."

Nadine expelled a long-held breath. "This is the best news I've heard since, well…since I was nearly killed—but then wasn't."

Kylie smiled and touched her chin "There's just one thing, an SSF representative will be on board the *Dauntless* to make sure we do everything we're supposed to. And it's not negotiable."

"Did you even try saying 'no'?" Winter asked.

"Don't," Rogers ordered. "You've lost your say in anything we decide. Anything Kylie decides, keep your trap shut."

Winter stood from his chair and kicked it back. "I'm tired of your sanctimonious bullshit, Rogers. You were there, same as I was."

Kylie put a hand on his chest and stopped him, ready to put all her might into it if he pushed. "Knock it off. The both of you. This is where we are. There's no going back and, of course, I tried. You think I want back in with the SSF?"

Winter glowered at Rogers, but answered Kylie, "Maybe you do."

"Then maybe you don't know her at all," Nadine said. "Maybe if you came out of the cargo hold once in a while and socialized with the crew, you'd see that's not who she is."

Winter stepped back to pick up his chair, and Kylie lowered her hand. They had a conversation in their future, a long one, but here, in front of everyone, wasn't the time or place. Winter could be reasoned with when it was one-on-one. What he'd done was inexcusable, if he didn't see that…well, Kylie hoped he'd come around.

"We're still a team. We're still together in this. If this is going to work, we need to get past everything that happened. The rescue won't be easy; if it was, they wouldn't need us."

Rogers nodded, and the crew fell in line. "Who has her?"

Kylie licked her lips. What she was about to say wouldn't be easy for any of them to hear. "Maverick."

Winter gripped the back of his chair while Rogers and Nadine groaned in disappointment.

Rogers leaned forward. "You expect us to grab someone out from under Maverick? You have any idea the bounty that'll put on our heads? He won't let that go, and none of the other syndicates will, either. We might as well spend our life in prison. Because if we go against him, getting spaced will be the best thing we can hope for."

"That's the situation, and if we work together, I think we can pull this off. Maverick…he'll be angry for a while, but we can talk him down. He's always looking for new legitimate connections to make his little organization look more on the up and up." Kylie threw a glance at Nadine to see how she was absorbing the news.

Her complexion was sheet white as she swayed in her seat. Well, it could've gone worse.

"We've always talked about getting out from under him. This could be our chance, and if an innocent young woman is under his control—"

"None of our business," Winter said. "We keep to ourselves. We—"

"It's our business now." Nadine took a deep breath and rose from her chair. "I guess you have a plan?" She stood closer, and Kylie welcomed it.

Kylie felt warm just having her nearby. Her fingertips touched Nadine's as she nodded. Simple touch was all that was necessary for her to feel alive, feel vibrant. There was so much in touch, human contact—what about that was so hard for the Alliance military and their AIs to comprehend?

"There's a plan and here's how it's going to go."

*****

As the evening drew to a close, the boys retired to their separate rooms, but Kylie stayed up and pored over the holoprojected notes she had spread across the table. She studied everything there was to know about the girl and Maverick's headquarters. Of course, she knew it better than the back of her hand, but worry kept her at it.

She poured another cup of coffee from the thermos and almost moaned at the rich smell that wafted out of her cup. Why couldn't she make coffee like that?

This mission had her nerves frayed. Preparing made her feel better, but now with the crew so fractured, she worried that if things went bad, they might fall apart. What good was she without her crew?

For all the stupid things Winter had done, he was right about one thing—kidnapped daughters happened all the time. Kylie made it her business not to care. She just went about her work salvaging lost and damaged freighters, turning a blind eye to all the circumstance that surrounded how they'd gotten there. Now she was going on a rescue mission? It left a bad taste in her mouth. Rescues weren't her thing.

Never care too much. Keep your head down. Don't get involved.

Whatever Maverick wanted with this Lana girl was his business, not Kylie's. Except now she was pitting herself against him. He wasn't an even-tempered man; there was only so much he'd be willing to forgive.

"You're thinking too much." Nadine's sultry voice was smooth as chocolate as she came up behind Kylie and ran her fingers down Kylie's arms, kissing her cheek. Kylie sighed and bent her head to the side, allowing Nadine better access to her neck.

"A lot is going to happen, and soon. There's so much to do, to plan for. Winter and Rogers—"

Nadine straddled Kylie's lap, each of her bare thighs on opposite sides of the chair. Her shirt was still open from earlier, and her black lace cami was visible. "No more talking about those two. Not until tomorrow."

Kylie kissed the rising cleavage spilling out of her lover's bra. She tasted salty but smelled sweet as candy. "For my little dignitary, anything."

Nadine laughed and wrapped her arms around Kylie's neck. "That was a lifetime ago. Power, prestige, I lost it all. But at least I got you in the process."

"A fair trade. When I think of how things could've gone today…" Kylie didn't let herself finish the thought.

"You saved my life again," whispered Nadine. "Just like you're always doing."

Kylie studied the planes of her lover's face, recalling Nadine's rebellion. She'd ventured outside her family's estate, with little idea of what she was getting herself into out into the dark.

Nadine's chuckle drew her out of her memories. "You've saved me from one bad decision after another."

Kylie smirked. "Every ship captain needs a princess, and you're mine."

Nadine didn't often smile around the crew; mostly, she saved it for Kylie. Something that sat just fine with her. "Oh yes, I like the idea of being a kept princess."

Their banter failed to keep their conversation light-hearted. Nadine's past was troubled, but Kylies own history—especially where Maverick was concerned—was far worse. For years, Kylie had been forced to be his…companion, for lack of a better word.

Until he'd let her go. And given her the *Dauntless*.

Nadine touched Kylie's cheek, her eyes filled with sadness. "It's only natural. You feel loyal to him in a weird and twisted way. Just as any long-time captive would." Then her expression sobered. "How do you really feel about betraying him like this? It might go beyond what he can forgive you for."

"Maverick is capable of a lot of things. Love and forgiveness isn't one of them. If he doesn't want people to turn on him, then he shouldn't go around kidnapping people's children."

Kylie knew that first hand.

Nadine studied her closely. "Maverick is unable to love, at least like a regular human being, but you're not."

Kylie gawked at her and pulled back. "You think I love Maverick? There's only one person for me, and I'm with her." She stretched her arms around Nadine and kissed the skin above her breasts.

"I know that, darling, but you feel you owe him. He released you after he kidnapped you and kept you as his sex toy. Think about how twisted that is, please. Before we face him again and he gets you under his spell."

She would think about it, but not yet. Kylie gave Nadine a long kiss. "Maybe…instead of all this talking, we should just move to the bed."

"Oooh," Nadine laughed playfully, pulling on Kylie's lip with her teeth. "I'm pretty sure I'm up for that. If only we had our toys."

There would be time for that later, Kylie hoped. If they were successful.

Nadine took Kylie's hand and led her to an unoccupied room. Biting her lip with a sinful guise, she helped Kylie undress and they slipped beneath the covers. Kylie lay still on her back and she guided Nadine's head beneath the sheets, where it needed to go.

As Kylie's breath quickened and her heart skipped a beat, she thought of Grayson and how he could mess it all up for her. She should've warned Nadine; it would've been the right thing to do. But to end bliss like this with the news of his pending arrival?

Kylie wasn't ready for that. Not at all.

CREWMEMBER

STELLAR DATE: 08.29.8947 (Adjusted Years)
LOCATION: Silstrand Space Force navy base
REGION: Trio System, Silstrand Alliance

When Kylie saw the *Dauntless* again, it was an emotional moment. She hadn't seen the damage her girl had taken in the battle, and Rogers's stories had made it sound bad. Still, seeing the ship again made it feel like going home. Maybe the *Dauntless* couldn't make her Momma Kate's special brownies, but it had been Kylie's special place for ten years.

The SSF engineers had done good work; the repaired sections were indistinguishable from the rest of the whip, which is to say they were dirty and carbon-scored. She looked out at the ship's massive fusion burners, and single antimatter-pion drive capable of boosting a ship up to ten times the *Dauntless*'s mass to a considerable percentage of *c*. Forward of the engines were fuel tanks and crew areas, fronted by the clear sphere that contained the bridge. Though it did not have a smooth, uniform hull, the majority of the ship had an overall conical shape.

Four grappling arms changed that profile, giving the ship a much more organic look. The arms branched off not far aft of the bridge and could extend over four hundred meters to secure salvage, or even tear sections of damaged ships free.

The ship was power and grace, and it was all hers.

It had taken time to piece the crew together, and, for a while, it had just been Kylie and the ship. Sure, it was smaller than your standard starfreighter and was always in need of some small repair, but there was nothing they couldn't solve together. A ragtag ship for a ragtag crew.

The *Dauntless* was virtually unchanged on the inside, except maybe a bit cleaner since the repairs. It was Rogers who got choked up as he leaned over a panel and stroked its plas covering the way he would touch a lover.

"Good to see her again?"

Rogers nodded. "Oh, baby, so very good."

Kylie scowled. "Did you just call me 'baby'?"

Rogers stood to attention sharply and cleared his throat. "Sorry about that, Captain. I guess I just lost myself…. And started talking to the ship. Again. Out loud."

Kylie clapped a hand on his shoulder. "No problem, Rogers. We all get worked up over her sleek curves."

"Do we ever." Rogers took his leave of Kylie and headed toward the bridge. She suspected he wanted to make sure everything was as he'd left it, though there was no reason to think it would be any different.

Kylie followed the amidships passageway to the galley. It wasn't much, and the equipment was well-used, but it was enough to make a decent meal. A dark, wooden table commanded the center of the room, worn and scuffed from years of abuse and drinking games gone wrong.

Usually, it was just big enough for the members of her crew to gather around, but somehow with Grayson sitting there by himself, it looked even smaller. When he saw her, he immediately stood. "Is your crew on their way?"

"Be here soon."

Grayson let out a long breath. It sounded shaky, and Kylie suspected that he was nervous. "Don't worry, they don't bite. For the most part."

"I'm looking forward to getting this over with and getting the mission underway. I've never been very good at beginnings."

"Or endings."

Grayson's eyes narrowed to a fine line. "Point taken."

"Just follow my lead and everything will work out in the end. This isn't a military vessel. Things work differently here."

"I'm fully aware," Grayson said.

Kylie headed over to the kitchen counter. "Can I get you something? The instant coffee's pretty good."

Grayson's eyebrows rose, and his nose scrunched up as if he tasted something horrible. "If it's anything like your regular coffee, I'll pass."

Kylie pulled a mug from the cabinet. "Suit yourself."

<*We're on our way,*> Rogers said.

<*Hurry,*> Kylie replied. <*I'm running out of things to talk about.*>

Grayson huffed. "I can hear that you know."

Kylie blew on her cup of coffee and smiled. "I know you can. Like old times, wouldn't you say?"

Grayson shook his head and placed his hand on the table, fingers splayed. "I'm not your enemy here."

"No? They're going to think you are."

"I can't help that, but you can smooth things over. If you want your freedom, you will."

Kylie gritted her teeth and considered sticking her tongue out at him as Nadine entered the room. Nadine's footsteps faltered as her eyes fell on Grayson and she gasped, her posture gone rigid.

"You couldn't tell me this last night? This is how you wanted me to find out?"

Kylie held her breath. It might not have been the best decision she'd ever made, but what was done, was done. The truth of the matter was, she hadn't wanted to have that conversation last night and still didn't want to have it now.

"This doesn't change anything."

"No?" Nadine's chest rose as she sucked in a deep breath. "He's your husband. How can that not change anything?"

Grayson raised his finger in the air. "Ex-husband, for what it's worth. I seem to have run afoul of some sort of domestic spat."

Kylie ignored him and wished he'd step out of the conversation. "The general appointed him. I have nothing to do with it. We do this mission, and then he's gone." She took Nadine's hand. "Then *we're* gone and can do whatever we want. Legally."

Nadine sighed and glanced at Grayson and then back at Kylie. "I know you don't like to talk about things. I've long accepted you are who you are, just as I am. Just as Rogers and Winter are." Nadine gently freed her hand. "But you should've told me."

She was right about that. <*Can we talk about this in private later?*>

Nadine didn't answer, and as Rogers and Winter stepped into the galley, Kylie thought maybe she really had screwed the pooch this time.

"Oh hell, no!" Winter shook his head. "Him? You couldn't have mentioned this last night?"

Kylie bit her tongue when she met Nadine's disappointed eyes. "I thought it was best to rip the band-aid off all at once. I need you all on board."

"He set us up, Ky," Rogers whispered.

"On orders. He's military, that's what he does."

"And if his orders are to kill us? If his orders change?" Winter asked.

"I promise not to kill you if you promise not to try to kill me again," Grayson said with a tilt of his head. "If you do this mission, I will honor the agreement. A letter of marque for your ship. A chance to go legitimate. It'll open a lot of doors for you. All of you."

He gazed at each of their faces, but he was greeted with uncertainty—that much Kylie could see.

"For now, he's just another crew member," she told them. "We all fall in line, for this one mission. Then we go our way and he goes his way. But for this to work, we need to work together."

"But he's not a regular crew member; he has an AI," Nadine said. "He could be plotting behind our backs."

"I didn't take you for an AI-phobe like Kylie," Grayson said with a curious expression. "On your world, all the elite have an AI. I'm surprised you don't."

"Who says I didn't?" Nadine raised an eyebrow. "And it's all subterfuge and lies. The royal family is anything but transparent with its subjects."

Rogers gave Grayson a sharp double take. "Great, someone to go around second-guessing all my calculations."

"Jerrod, my AI, will be verifying your calculations while we're aboard this ship. If I need your help, Rogers, I will ask for it."

Rogers stepped up. "You want to pilot the *Dauntless* yourself? Over my dead body."

Grayson held firm. "I wouldn't dream of it, but you will do as I say."

Kylie sighed as the tension in the room rose. "Settle down, Grayson. We're working together. We are not working for you. This is still my ship, and you're not in charge of Rogers. Be a team player, would you?" she reminded him.

"I am being a team player."

And that was the problem. He didn't know how to de-military, no matter the situation.

Grayson went on, "As much as it doesn't feel like it, for now, we *are* on the same team. I'll work with you, you work with me, and we get the job done. Do remember, an innocent woman is being held by a very terrible individual. Maverick isn't someone who is going to play nice and serve his captives tea."

Rogers crossed his arms but remained silent. Winter refused to pull his gaze from the floor.

Kylie took a deep breath and studied everyone's cold expressions. "We'll get through this. I know it won't be easy, but when we get to Jericho, we can't show Maverick that anything is wrong. We do exactly what it is we always do."

"Which is pretty much nothing," Rogers said. "I still get to fly the *Dauntless*, right?"

Kylie nodded. "Of course. As far as regular ship operations are concerned, Grayson isn't even here. He's asserting himself in all the wrong ways, but I still have your back."

"If you say so. Didn't much feel like it," Rogers said and walked out of the room. Kylie longingly watched him go. This was his home as much as it was hers. She wished things could be different.

Nadine rose and silently followed Rogers out of the room. Kylie knew that it was time for her and Winter to have a talk. <*Leave us, please,*> she said privately to Grayson over the Link.

He nodded. "I have some…preparations to make." Pausing at the door, he offered a parting remark. "I won't hold past actions against you, if you don't hold mine against me, Winter."

For his part, Winter crossed his arms and glowered at Grayson's back as he strode down the corridor. "Top notch guy. Bet he loves taking the high road."

"Sure does, but this isn't about him, Winter. We need to—"

"I know, I know," Winter said in a rush. "You know I panicked. I felt the walls closing in. If we had gotten off right then—"

"A SA officer wouldn't have been injured, I'd still have my trusty spork, and I would've gone into the meeting with the general from a stronger negotiation place. You didn't just screw yourself. You screwed us all. It can't happen again."

Winter snorted and gazed away. Kylie hoped her words were reaching him, but she couldn't be sure. When his face went this rigid, he was impossible to read. "And now you let him on our ship. It won't take long for him to take over."

"I won't let that happen."

"No?" Winter glowered and stepped up to her. "Seems you are rolling over easy enough already. If he makes a power play for control of the *Dauntless*, what are you going to do?"

"What I always do. Whatever is in our best interests. You might not see it, but I have your back. I need you to have mine. And anyone else that's serving on this team. Even if that person is Grayson—for the time being."

"If I can't?"

Kylie shrugged and infinite sadness washed over her. "You know the answer to that question, but I'm really hoping it won't come to that. Do we have an understanding?"

Winter struggled with the question for a short while before he nodded. "Yeah, yeah we do."

"If you ever put Nadine in harm's way like that again—"

"I won't. I shouldn't have. Idiots are born every day, you know? Don't get much bigger than me."

Winter turned around and left. Kylie let him go because she needed him to process all of this on his own. She understood his fear of tight spaces and the panic it sometimes caused him, which was why he favored the cargo hold so much. Awful as it was, if Winter's self-hatred made him a better team player, Kylie wouldn't just accept it, she would encourage it. Later there would be a chance to be a good friend.

But not now. Not before the mission.

* * * * *

Kylie stepped onto the bridge and reviewed their status with the tug. The SSF had provided them with the *Titan-1,* as the general had promised, to prove to Maverick they had been working. It would help get them in the door at Jericho—plus, money always softened Maverick up.

In the center of the bridge's sphere, Rogers was in his seat operating the grappling arms to secure the ship, and then they'd be on their way to Gedri. Kylie crossed her arms and took a deep breath as Rogers swiveled in his chair. Her eyes darted to Nadine, but she didn't say anything. Her comm and weapons officer appeared stoic as she studied something on her console. Right time, right place—and this wasn't it.

Tensions were going to run high for a while. Kylie thought of saying something when Grayson stepped onto the bridge. "Jerrod says your calculations are off .002 degrees. Readjust your grappling arms."

Rogers didn't flinch or say a word, but Kylie thought from how his fingers moved he might have taken Grayson's unwelcome advice. She poked her ex-husband in the chest.

<Don't second-guess my crew.>

<It's what I'm here for, Kylie,> Grayson said.

<Rogers is good at what he does. He's the best.>

<Even the best can make mistakes. He's a big boy. I'm sure he can take my advice.>

<It wasn't advice. It was an order. .002 degrees doesn't make a difference. Use your head.>

Grayson studied her eyes. *<Use yours. If we're going to get this done…>*

<Then we all need to get along. Get off my bridge. Next time you have something to say to a member of my crew, send it to me first. You're not in charge, Grayson.>

His eyes flicked back to hers, but he didn't say anything. Nothing changed in his bearing, he just turned and left the bridge. Kylie had a bad feeling about this.

She gazed back at Rogers as the grappling arms locked in place. With that done, his chair righted itself, and he gave a whistle. "Locked and ready to go, Cap!"

If he had been upset by Grayson, he didn't say so. Still, Kylie was sorry on his behalf.

"What's our ETA to the jump point?" Kylie asked.

Rogers glanced at the holopanel that floated in front of his elevated pilot's seat. "Your SA friends have a clear point not far from here. One that's not on the public charts. They topped us off on antimatter, so once we clear their station, it will only take us nine hours to get there."

A full antimatter bottle? That was the best news Kylie had heard all day.

"What's our dark layer travel time?" she asked.

"We'll hit the DL at about 0.57*c*, if I do everything right," Rogers replied, then turned his head and gave her the requisite 'cocky pilot' grin. "And I assure you, I always do everything right."

Kylie did the math in her head. It was 6.3 light years from Trio to Gedri, and the average dark layer multiplier between the two systems was 692. That put their FTL transit time at just shy of six days. Six long days.

"Nadine." Kylie looked down at her comm officer. "We've been away for a long time. Cue up a message for the GFF to send out the moment we dump out of the DL in Gedri."

Nadine activated her holodisplay. Her posture, picture perfect and erect, she barely glanced at Kylie. "Of course, Captain."

Kylie nodded and stepped off the bridge. Barely a day in and she had alienated over half her crew. Wasn't this going to be fun?

*****

Kylie stood at the back of the bridge, looking out through the glass dome at the *Dauntless*'s prow and into the Gedri system.

Where Trio had received the full works from the Future Generation Terraformers—with two terraformed worlds and a space elevator to boot—the ancient terraformers had completely passed Gedri by. Its primary star, which carried the same name as the system, was old and had long ago moved off the main sequence, with only a hundred million years to go before it burned out completely.

The second star—named Townsend—whipped around Gedri, only a scant thirty AU away. Luckily, Townsend was a low-mass red dwarf, and, from a navigational standpoint, was not much harder to deal with than a large jovian planet.

Townsend had captured three planet-sized worlds at some point in its history—probably stolen from Gedri long before the old star puffed up and turned orange. The only remotely habitable of the three was named Jericho, and that was where the *Dauntless* was headed.

The Gedri Freedom Federation held the most sway over the worlds surrounding Townsend. It was far from the official capital world of Freemont, from which the Silstrand Alliance liked to pretend it controlled the Gedri system.

But everyone knew it was on Jericho where the real power lay—and where the real decisions were made.

Politics in Gedri were complex. Officially a member of the Silstrand Alliance, Gedri's parliament was controlled by members of the GFF. When it was founded, the GFF had just been a freedom organization, which consisted of little more than pirates and outlaws banded together for protection.

But, over time, the GFF had become more organized and gained legitimacy. Now, it controlled the Gedri system and even sent representatives to the Silstrand Alliance Senate.

Underneath it all, though, the GFF's power still came from the crime syndicates and old families who had been operating their empires out of the system for centuries. The GFF was just a veneer of civilization over the syndicates' corruption.

A veneer that was at its thinnest at their destination of Jericho.

Kylie took her eyes away from the blackness of space and the glow of both the red and orange stars, settling her gaze on Nadine. Kylie and the boys were about to have their mission briefing with Grayson, and she decided it was best that Nadine wasn't present. Things hadn't become much less tense over the past five days in the dark layer, and Kylie needed the meeting to go smoothly.

She opened her mouth to speak and Nadine's posture stiffened, almost as if she sensed Kylie's presence.

Kylie let out a silent breath, turned, and left the bridge without saying a word. When she reached the main cargo hold, Winter, Rogers, and Grayson were all waiting for her.

"Nice of you to join us, Captain," Rogers said in a mocking tone, though his smile was genuine.

"Good, let's get started," Grayson said without preamble. He sent a data burst over the Link, and Kylie leaned against an open crate as she went over the files and scanned the vids of Lana's abduction.

"Picture A-1. This is the most recent image of Lana that the SSF has." The holographic image of the young woman's head rotated in the open space amidst the crew. Her expression was carefree, her skin tight and smooth, with a light dusting of freckles on her cheeks. Her hair was pulled back in a long braid, while her blonde bangs curled right on her eyebrow line. Blue eyes. Simple and pure—just the way Maverick liked his girls.

"Young, but troubled about the recent elections in Silstrand. She was on her way to a pro-Scipcio rally when she ran into trouble," Grayson explained.

Winter snorted. "And you tell me daddy general was okay with that?"

"General Samuel prefers to stay out of his children's affairs, but he did advise caution. Events like this can be rife with violence and offliners. I'm sure I don't have to tell you that."

Kylie nodded to Grayson and privately waved a white flag across the Link at Winter. "Continue."

"Video A-1. Here she is arriving at the transport platform not far from her dorm on Silstrand."

The video began to play, and while it showed events from a distance, Lana was easily distinguished by her long braid. Dressed casually in tight black pants and matching jacket, she carried an orange backpack. She stepped onto the platform, almost completely lost in the crowd at times as she awaited a transport shuttle. Several minutes later, a small shuttle arrived, and two men stepped out.

They brandished weapons and pushed the crowd back. Lana edged backward, and when the men approached her, the girl raised her hands. Kylie zoomed in. The wide-eyed terror was real.

One of the men shot her with a dart. Within a moment, her body went limp and her knees buckled—a clear sign she had been sedated. The other man caught her and carried her onto the ship.

By the time the authorities arrived, the shuttle was gone. Kylie paused her video and spun the shuttle around to catch the serial number on the back. The glow from the thrusters hid most of it, but she thought it could be deciphered with a little digital forensics.

She sent a private message over the Link to Nadine. <*Can you clean this image up for me?*>

<Yes, Captain.>

<Nadine…>

Nadine sighed with exasperation across the Link. *<I said yes, Captain.>*

<Very good. Thank you.> Kylie closed the communication and paid attention to what Winter was saying.

"A snatch-and-grab like that? In the middle of the day on a busy platform? In Silstrand of all places? It's not Maverick's style."

"Perhaps Lana has something on him and his organization. We don't know, but we can ask her when we find her," Grayson said.

"If she's still alive," Rogers said. "I know you told me you tracked her to Maverick, but you don't know where she is. What if she isn't anywhere? What if he used her and then disposed of her? It wouldn't be the first time."

"Or the first hundred," Winter added.

"Doubtful. You don't do a high-risk extraction like that, use the girl, and then just dump her like trash." Grayson took a breath. "However, if that's what we find, at least the general can get some closure and select his next option."

"Would that be revenge?" Kylie stepped away from her cargo crate into the center of the room. "Here I thought the SSF was too evolved for such a thing."

Grayson cast her a dirty look. "Things change when it's your daughter. Plus, the SSF has been looking for the right reason to take down the GFF for good."

Winter snorted. "Good luck to them."

Kylie nodded. "No kidding. That's not something I want any part of."

"You won't be. Just do your bit here. With luck, we'll get Lana back home, and we can go about our business. Separately."

So, she wasn't the only one who didn't like their arrangement. Not surprising, but it didn't make Kylie feel any better.

"You really think it'll be that easy?" Winter asked.

"Nothing ever is." Rogers shook his head. "This could ruin us."

"We can always head over to the Scipio Federation. If the SSF is going to wage war on Gedri, I prefer somewhere that isn't here," Winter said with a shrug.

"Let's try to be positive, gentlemen. Okay?" Kylie eyed Rogers and Winter. "Grayson, you said you tracked this shuttle to Maverick?"

Grayson pushed another document across the Link. Pictures of two men, presumably the ones who grabbed Lana—one bald with a scar running down the side of his face, the other with a tattoo over two-thirds his face.

How charming.

Kylie read through their criminal records and picked out the breadcrumbs that led straight to the GFF. Hitmen for hire with a history of violence, drug abuse, and trafficking. These guys weren't low-level scum; they were heavy hitters. They wouldn't have taken a job to kidnap Lana if it hadn't come with a hefty cash bounty.

Could she be alive? Maybe. Unspoiled? Probably not. Kylie felt for the girl, which was one of the reasons she hated these sorts of missions. Her emotions got all mixed up. She started to care a little bit too much, which led to inevitable heartache if she failed.

"If we doubt why we're doing this, just bring out image A-1 and look into her eyes," Kylie said to her men. "Generally, I know, we don't take sides. We do our job and get out. But if we can save this girl…"

"You don't have to sell us," Winter said. "We're doing this. I get it but don't expect me to start crying and making origami animals while we lay around and do each other's hair. I care about our crew, not some hapless girl."

Grayson scowled and stepped in front of Winter. Winter sighed and folded his arms.

"Get out of my way," Winter growled.

But Grayson didn't move. Kylie sensed a low boil of anger coming from his direction, but it didn't play out on his face. "Don't you care about the girl? Even a little bit? She could be tortured, forced to perform sexual acts against her will, and you're telling me you don't care?"

"No," Winter grumbled and pushed past Grayson and disappeared through the doorway, never looking back.

With a level stare, Grayson brought his attention back to Kylie. "Well, nice to see the kind of people you're keeping company with. Good job choosing them over the SSF."

"I care." Rogers raised his hand. "I don't want to die in a blaze of glory over this girl, but I care. Let's try to stay alive. Can we do that?"

Grayson nodded. "Staying alive is something we can all agree is a top priority."

"Good," Kylie said. "I can keep Winter in line. I know his bedside manner sucks, but he's not as rough as he pretends. He'll do what we want…as long as it goes through me, Grayson."

"Understood. Loud and clear."

Now they were making progress.

"I'm going to go check in with the ship," Rogers said. "When we drop out of FTL in Gedri, I'll let you both know over the Link."

"Thanks, Rogers," Kylie said and watched him go.

"He's a good man," Grayson said.

Kylie did a double take. "I'm surprised you can admit that."

"Well, he didn't try to kill me."

Winter *had* really lowered the bar.

"Want to tell me what your plan is?" Grayson asked. "How are you going to find out from Maverick where he's keeping Lana?"

"Once we've dropped off the hull, and taken the elevator down to Montral, he'll know and send for us. If he doesn't, well…there's always a party going on at Shade, his favorite nightclub, and he's there as often as not. If he's keeping Lana around for fun, then I'll see her. If not, it'll get trickier, but I have an in with him that most don't."

Grayson raised his eyebrows. "Oh?"

"He loves brunettes with purple streaks in their hair."

"Kylie," Grayson shook his head. "You…I can't ask you to…"

She pushed her hand against his chest. "We do what we do to survive. When I left the SSF, this is what I did. If I can use it now to clear this mission and reward my crew with a letter of marque, I will. Besides, I kind of owe it to all the girls I've seen…and never helped."

"All right, but I'll be listening, and if you run into trouble, we won't be far behind."

"I can handle myself, but thanks. Maverick knows not to mess up a good thing. He likes me too much. And before I forget, tomorrow morning, you're on breakfast prep. Six hundred hours, ship time."

Grayson's eyes narrowed. "Breakfast? As in cook?"

Kylie smirked. "Winter will be on rotation, too, so don't be late. He hates a tardy cook, but don't worry; I hid all the sporks." She sauntered away for the engine room to check on the system status before she retired to her quarters.

She willed herself not to look back. The last thing she needed to do was start throwing second glances at Grayson, especially with Nadine so mad at her. Though she wondered if Grayson still stared—if he still liked to watch after her as she left a room. She considered checking the ship cameras to see but thought better of it.

That was a wound she didn't need to re-open.

There was an engine to check out, and Kylie loved to listen to it hum. When she was most troubled, the sound of the engines always lulled her to a happy, comfortable place. She might've been born planetside, but space was her home. The *Dauntless* made her feel complete, and Kylie intended to never lose it again.

*****

Grayson watched her go with a deep sense of longing—one he thought he had gotten over years ago. But being back with her in the thick of it brought old feelings he'd thought long suppressed, bubbling to the surface.

He sighed and leaned his arm against a support beam while gazing at photo A-1 of Lana. *She* was the mission. She had to be, but being with Kylie again filled him with such an energy, as though a part of him came alive just to spar with her again.

<*Once she discovers the truth, we're both in a lot of trouble.*>

<*I know, Jerrod, I know. You better craft an exit plan for us. Once we deliver Lana, we need to get the hell out of here.*>

<*And the letter of marque?*> Jerrod asked.

<*There is no letter of marque.*>

<*The general doesn't usually lie like this. His word is supposed to be his bond, Grayson. If Kylie can't trust him, how can we? This whole thing makes me more nervous than an AI should be.*>

It made Grayson nervous, too, but he'd never say it out loud. <*He's getting ready to fight a war with Scipio, and we're expanding our territory. We have hard choices to make,*> Grayson said.

<Have you already made yours? Your elevated blood pressure and accelerated heart rate says you haven't. Don't worry, nano is assisting in regulating your functions, but I am going to have to recommend a high fiber diet from here on out.>

Good old Jerry, always looking out for him. <*My choices always align with the best interests of the* SSF.>

<That's good, because where you go, I go. At least for now.>

They had been together for ten years. Soon the SSF would have no choice but to part them and give Grayson a new AI. It wasn't something he really looked forward to. He liked Jerrod and they had worked well together.

Grayson turned and left the cargo bay in search of his quarters. He had made his decision, but it had been easier on the space station and before he had stepped on board the ship. Winter, he could leave or take, but the rest of them…

He wasn't sure what he would do if push came to shove. <*Jerrod, download the schematics of the* Dauntless, *just in case. We need to examine every weakness.*>

<Just in case of what?>

In case everything went sideways. Everyone but himself and Lana were expendable.

Even the ship. And Kylie. Grayson didn't want to think about that.

A HOMEMADE DINNER

STELLAR DATE: 09.05.8947 (Adjusted Years)
LOCATION: Salvage ship *Dauntless*
REGION: Outer Gedri System, Silstrand Alliance

Kylie lingered between a dream-like state and being awake when her comm chirped. <*Captain?*>

If it hadn't been Nadine, Kylie would've just rolled over and ignored it. Instead, she gave a little stretch and arched her back. <*What is it?*>

<*It's 0600 and I'm going over logs. I found something I think is worthy of your attention.*>

Kylie swung her legs over the side of her bed and rubbed her face. She was really going to need to grab some coffee to make it through the day. <*Okay, I'm listening.*>

<*Grayson's AI interfaced with the* Dauntless *last night after your meeting. He downloaded her schematics. It triggered the warning system I put in place, just in case.*>

Just in case. That was her girl, always thinking and planning ahead for the future.

<*Thanks, Nadine. I'll handle it.*>

<*Any idea why would he want that? Are we in trouble here?*> Even across the Link, Kylie could make out Nadine's rising anxiety.

<*I promise, I'll handle it. If it's anything to be alarmed about, I'll let you know. We won't do this mission unless I'm comfortable. It's his job to make us comfortable.*>

Nadine sent a relieved sigh across the Link. <*Thank you, Captain, but don't let him sweet talk you.*>

<*Never happen.*>

<*Right.*> Nadine cut the communication, and it was clear that Kylie's own motives weren't clear to Nadine. Maybe they weren't clear to any of the crew. She really needed to fix that.

Turning on the lights, Kylie rose and headed to her wardrobe. Time to get to work.

*****

Dressed in shimmering purple pants paired with a black jacket, Kylie entered the galley. The counter was covered in more potato peels than she thought could come from the handful of potatoes they had in stock. She picked up one of the spiral pieces and let it uncoil in the air. It reminded her of the breakfast-in-bed Grayson would whip up for her when they were stationed on-world.

"These look familiar."

"They always were one of your favorites," Grayson said.

Over by the stove, Winter cast her a glance as he tilted the frying pan, coating it in oil. "And to think your man Gray here didn't want breakfast duty. He's a whizz with a veg peeler."

Grayson sighed. "Please don't call me that."

Kylie smirked and sized him up—without trying to look like she was sizing him up. "I have to say; I'm surprised you kept up with the cooking skills."

"The SSF doesn't leave much time for extracurricular activities, but everyone has to eat. What are you doing up so early?"

"I got a call. Care to step outside so we can talk? Winter, do you mind?"

Winter snorted and added the potatoes to his sizzling frying pan. "Only thing I mind is talking when I'm trying to work."

Kylie motioned for Grayson to follow and led him out into the hall and down into a private nook. She propped herself up on a piece of exposed conduit, but Grayson stood erect. He crossed his wrists. The man never could relax.

"What's this about?" he asked.

"Your AI. He downloaded the schematics for the *Dauntless* last night—and not just the ones pointing to the nearest fire escape. Why?" She studied him intently. Kylie didn't trust AI and considered it possible that Jerrod did it without Grayson's permission. If any surprise registered, she wanted to see it.

Grayson's face barely flickered. If it was news to him, he didn't let it show. He had always been a great poker player. "Protocol. If we need an exit plan or get boarded, or any of the other dozens of situations we could get ourselves into. We need to be prepared for any eventuality. You haven't forgotten all the old rules, have you?"

"Hardly." Kylie's tongue ran along the inside of her cheek. Was he lying or was he telling the truth? The carefree way in which he answered said he was on the up and up, but she knew better than to trust everything he said at face value. He would always be SSF first and Grayson second.

If she trusted Grayson, could she trust his AI? It was clear *he* did.

"You could've asked me this over the Link?" he asked.

"I wanted to see your face when you answered. Look into your eyes and see if the words and the truth had any…disagreements."

"And?"

"I wish I knew." She scowled. "I guess I'll have to take your word, for now. If this mission is to succeed, we have to trust each other."

Grayson nodded. "I'll earn that trust. I promise, Kylie."

"But your AI. Jerry."

"Jerrod," Grayson corrected. "I know you don't trust AI, but he's had my back for over ten years since our pairing."

Kylie resisted an eye roll. "Of course, he has. He's in your back. Your brain. However it works. It's in his best interest to see you're all right, but isn't it possible he could have orders you don't know about?"

Grayson's lips drew together in a thin line and his brow furrowed. "No." His cheeks flushed and it was clear Kylie had hit a nerve.

"Okay, okay. Forget it, then. Back to breakfast. I'm going to relieve Nadine on the bridge. She needs some rest and she's probably starving at this rate."

She waited for Grayson to say something else, but wasn't really sure what she was waiting for. Kylie walked toward the bridge and pinged Winter over the Link. *<Keep an eye on him, would you? If you see anything suspicious, bring it to me before you act on it.>*

<You don't trust lover boy?>

<I want to.> Hopefully, that was all she'd have to say on the situation. Hopefully, it would turn out her fears were just old paranoia, old suspicions.

<Having him here is your idea. I vote we blow him out the airlock.>

Winter was nothing if not consistent. *<It wasn't actually **my** idea, and we can't do that, but I'll keep it on the back burner.>*

<All right. I'll take a back burner any day of the week.>

<Let's just…> Kylie sighed, *<…not rush in and do anything stupid. We're family. Such as it is. Let's not let a stranger mess that up.>*

Kylie ended the conversation as she rounded the corner and entered the bridge. Just like last night, Nadine was in the pilot's seat—which currently sat only a meter off the deck—with her legs curled up underneath her. She stared out the window. Her breathing calm, coming in long deep breaths, almost as if she slept, but Nadine was wide awake. She was studying space, her mind probably racing along with the stars.

They could swallow all your troubles away if you allowed them to. Kylie craved that.

"Nadine?" Kylie reached up and placed her hand on the back of the pilot's chair, causing Nadine to jump.

She slipped down out of the elevated seat, landing gingerly, and walked to her comm console where she sat down and pulled up a report. "Captain, I didn't hear you come in."

"Stealthy like a cat."

Nadine did her best to hide a smile, but Kylie saw it crinkling along the edges of her lips. "Anything from Grayson?"

"Just protocol. So he says."

"Is it? Protocol?"

Kylie nodded and slipped into the chair beside her. "It is."

Nadine scowled. "Then why that face? You don't trust him, but still you couldn't bring yourself to tell me he'd be here, on your ship. To let me discover that way, that we were about to be thrown together with your ex?"

"We just got out of lock up. We were having a nice night; I didn't want to…risk it all."

"But you *did* risk it all. Worse than if you had told me. Kylie, I'm a big girl. I can take the truth. He's your ex. Not a dirty secret."

It was true. All of it. So why did Kylie make such stupid decisions? She didn't know, but she wished she did. "Go get some rest…a shower. Breakfast will be ready soon. I'll monitor things up here for a bit."

"Yes, Cap." Nadine rose and stretched her long legs. "If it turns out he is lying, what's our next move?"

"I'm hoping we don't need a next move. I'm hoping I'm just jittery."

Nadine nodded as Kylie approached the pilot's chair and allowed the grav system to pull her up into the seat. "We've lived our lives on the fringe before. We can do it again."

"We'd be fugitives this time. A little bit different than salvaging abandoned ships and staying under their radar." Kylie gazed out into the black. The vastness of it always made her feel better. Like she could slip away, get lost, and no one would be the wiser. She'd done it once before.

"I don't want to make this harder on you. I can't imagine what you're feeling to have him here. I'll stay away if that's what you want, but if you decide instead you'd like to talk…"

The shock of her lie and seeing Grayson again must've finally worn off. Kylie didn't deserve someone like Nadine. Someone that was kind, generous, giving. How'd she ever managed to land a girl like that, Kylie didn't even know. To think she had put it all on the line for Grayson, someone who was the exact opposite of Nadine.

By the book. Rules. Military before personal.

It turned her stomach.

"Talk is better than staying away. Thanks, Nadine." Kylie tried to smile.

Nadine returned it. "Excuse me, Cap. Whatever they're cooking in the galley smells pretty good. I think I'm going to grab a bite. Did you want some?"

"Nah. I've eaten enough spiral potatoes to last me a lifetime. I'm sticking with good old-fashioned coffee."

Nadine raised her eyebrows. "Well, suit yourself."

Kylie swiveled in her chair as Nadine left the bridge. In just under twenty hours, they'd arrive at the Jericho. And, if Kylie's nagging suspicion wasn't wrong, all hell was going to break loose.

*****

Kylie was nursing hot coffee in a blue mug when Rogers slid into the chair beside her. He slouched down, legs wide, and threw his arms behind his head before settling in. "You missed a good breakfast. And a hearty lunch."

"I'll be around for dinner."

Rogers nodded and puckered his lips as he thought. "Pretty hard out there for you. Ex-husband, angry girlfriend, you nearly shot Winter…."

"It's a gangbuster week for me, what can I say?"

He grinned. "You know how to throw a great party."

"I'm just trying to give them some space before we arrive at Jericho. Once we get there, there's a lot we need to do. We need to pull together as a team. Think we can manage that?"

He crossed his arms and gave her a penetrating stare. Then it softened, and he laughed with that friendly twinkle in his eyes. "We can manage anything, but we need you, Cap. We need you to bring us all together. Hiding out on the bridge isn't helping anything."

Maybe not. Maybe Rogers was right, but Kylie wasn't ready to mingle with the crew. "Has everyone been behaving themselves?"

"Yeah, for the most part. Just a few spork jokes."

Kylie laughed. "I guess I'm never going to live that one down."

"Oh, I don't know. It'd be pretty cool accessory to wear on your belt, don't you think? Fastest spork-slinger this side of Trio. Instead of draw, you could yell scoop. It would blend in against those sparkly pants, too."

She nearly bust a gut from giggling so hard. When she settled down, she smiled at the joy on Rogers's face. "Thanks. I don't always make it easy, but you always have my back. The *Dauntless*'s back. She's your girl as much as she is mine."

"Amen to that, Cap. I hope it's always true." Rogers stroked the console and gave the old girl a hearty slap.

"It will be. Soon we'll embark on a new future. A new legitimate path. We just have to get through these next few days." Just the idea of it made Kylie long for something different. She couldn't wait to come out of the shadows.

Rogers leaned over the console and brought up the holodisplay. With a few flicks of his wrist, he rotated the planets and trajectory. "Well, they got the message Nadine sent, and they have a slot for our salvage in the Valhalla shipyard. Nothing to show they're suspicious."

"There's no reason to suspect us of anything—unless they have us bugged, or there's a mole in the SSF. In either case, we had better rest up and be prepared for a battle just to be on the safe side." With that, Kylie rose from her seat. "I'll see you at dinner. Chin up, we're going to get through this."

"And Nadine?" Rogers asked. "What about her? Will she get through this?"

Kylie shook her head. She knew Rogers was protective of not just the ship and herself, but Nadine, too. "She won't be in danger."

"She *will* be in danger." Rogers leaned forward. "She's going to go with you to see Maverick and find this girl. If things go galactically south, she's in trouble, and she can't fire a weapon like you can."

"I'll be with her. I promise. I'll protect her, Rogers."

He took a deep breath and sunk back down into his seat. "It needed to be said. I worry about you, but you can handle yourself. Nadine, she's a stars-be-damned princess."

"Not just to you. To me, too."

"It still needed to be said."

Kylie smirked. "I get where you're coming from."

"Good." Rogers nodded as he climbed up into the pilot's seat. He always preferred it up there, and Kylie couldn't blame him. It was the best seat in the house.

*****

Rogers had piloted the ship in a gravity-brake maneuver around Einendart, navigating its dozens of moons and flotsam and jetsam, like the professional he was. Now they were in clear space between the outer gas giant and Townsend. When they got closer to the red dwarf and its three planets, things would require a manual touch, but for now, the ship coasted through space guided by its autopilot NSAI.

For the last big meal before the op, the crew had gathered together for dinner in the galley. Kylie prepared an old-fashioned corn bread that her mother taught her how to make using slow-churned butter—a delicacy that her crew had come to expect at the evening meal when supplies were available.

Served up with Rogers's mock-tuna casserole and green beans, it was a comfort meal fit for a king, and one that reminded Kylie of being home. While they ate, everyone's mugs sloshed with too much spiced wine, carrying the evening's revelries well into the night. Long after the plates were licked clean, everyone still sat around the table swapping stories, which were met with hearty laughter.

Good for the spirit, and good for the team.

"What, exactly, is in mock-tuna casserole?" Grayson asked. Maybe he was drunk, maybe he was tipsy, but he was too professional to show it. That or his AI kept his blood stream regulated and clear.

"You don't want to know," Nadine said and burst out laughing. She was such a cute drunk.

Kylie leaned over the table to grab the bottle of wine and topped off Grayson's cup. "Tofu. Spongy, fermented, tofu."

Grayson turned several shades of green and everyone laughed, even Winter.

"I don't like my cooking to be mocked, but that was worth it to see you change to that color," Rogers chuckled.

"When we ship out from Trio, or Silstrand, we usually get to have real meat," Nadine said. "Chicken, duck, fish. Even some beef. Except for me, I'm a vegetarian."

"Until I met Nadine, I thought they were mythical creatures," Winter said.

"Practically are." Nadine gave a loud laugh.

Kylie held her mug up in the air. "Tonight, things could've gone way worse. The bread didn't get burned, the butter didn't curdle, and no one tried to kill each other. To tomorrow morning, lady and gents."

Winter and Rogers thrust their mugs into the air. "To tomorrow!" They chugged their wine just as Grayson held his up and gave a small nod of appreciation toward Kylie.

"You have to chug it," Winter said.

"Oh, no, I don't think I really—"

"Chug it!" Rogers banged his fist on the table. "Chug, chug!"

Grayson sighed and complied, tilting his head way back to get the final drops down his gullet. He launched into an uncontrollable cough, and his face turned bright red.

Winter held out a small bottle. "I spiked it with jalapeño bacon whiskey when he wasn't looking."

Kylie laughed and slid a napkin over to Grayson. "Your first hazing. I think you're officially part of the crew now."

Grayson covered his mouth with the napkin but couldn't speak yet.

Kylie excused herself and collected the dirty dishes and carried them to the sink. Nadine met her there with two bright red serving platters. "Things are going better than expected."

That was what worried Kylie the most. Winter, except for the harmless prank, was shockingly well behaved. Maybe he was taking her threats seriously for a change. Kylie shrugged. "Let's see what tomorrow brings us."

"And tonight, if you want company..." Nadine ran her hand along the countertop as she swayed on her feet.

"You're drunk."

"Not *that* drunk."

"Even so, I can't...not until you're level headed again. Sleep it off, and we'll see each other in the morning." Kylie filled the sink with soap and plopped all the dirty dishes inside. "Winter, your turn."

He sighed as he pushed back his chair. "Yes, Cap. This is why I'm always saying we need some hired help around here."

"Winter." Kylie put her hand on his shoulder as he stepped up to the sink. "You *are* the hired help."

Everyone laughed, and with that, Kylie took her leave for a little shut eye. Halfway to her quarters, someone called her name. Stumbling, she paused and turned around to face Grayson who was rushing after her. Great, just what she needed. To be drunk, impressionable, and vulnerable.

"Can I help you with something?" Kylie swayed side-to-side as he came to a stop in front of her.

"We didn't discuss the mission. I'd thought after dinner, we might have had time for a briefing. A group one, I mean."

Kylie snickered. "We did that yesterday. Everyone knows what they need to do. Tomorrow we get started. Tonight, we partied, and now we relax." Kylie slapped him on the back. "I know that's hard for you to understand, being a military man and all."

Grayson's eyes narrowed. Angry. Kylie had seen that look before. "That's not all I am. Stop marginalizing me."

"I'm not marginalizing anything. It went good in there. They're starting to like you."

Grayson blustered. "You used to be a military woman, too."

"But not a very good one," Kylie said with a shrug.

"You know the commitment and the risks we're all taking."

"I'm still taking those risks. Still committed, but now to myself and my crew. Not some huge alliance who doesn't care whether I live or die—that wants to stick AIs in everyone's heads. It doesn't care for you either, Grayson. If you die, they'll just replace you with someone else. That's how it works. Rank and file."

Grayson scowled, but he remained silent.

"Maybe you're more comfortable in a big organization, but I'm happier on my own. See you tomorrow. It'll be here before you know it."

Morning *was* coming all too soon, and then it'd be time to dance. Maverick was friend to no one. If he caught on that Kylie was snooping for information, she'd be the one who would need rescuing.

JERICHO

STELLAR DATE: 09.06.8947 (Adjusted Years)
LOCATION: Salvage ship *Dauntless*
REGION: Near Jericho, Gedri System, Silstrand Alliance

"On final approach to Valhalla," Rogers announced. "We'll be at handoff in about twenty-five minutes."

"Good job, Rogers," Kylie replied. "Nadine, anyone raise a stink over how long we've been gone?"

Nadine nodded. "Yeah, Benny groused about it until he saw the hull we're bringing in. *Titan-1* is way bigger than our usual hauls. I told him it was way out past the heliosphere. He bought it and was all but salivating at the price he could get for it—even as scrap."

"Not really a lie, either." Kylie grinned. "We were way past Gedri's heliosphere."

"Yeah, in Trio." Nadine chuckled.

"What the…" Rogers muttered as the ship lurched suddenly.

"What was that?" Kylie asked.

"Damn pirate scum," Rogers replied. "Was a Mark ship. Dumb bastards can't fly for shit."

"Mark?" Kylie asked. "I heard they all buggered off after that Rebecca bitch took over and got half their ships blown up out at Bollam's World."

Nadine shivered. "Even where I grew up we heard stories about that woman."

Kylie had never met anyone from The Mark during her time as Maverick's…companion. But back in the SSF she had been on missions to hunt them down. No one ever did find their secret base, but word was it had been destroyed almost twenty years ago.

"Yeah, well not all of them flew off to their deaths. Some new guy named Drew is trying to get them rolling again," Rogers said. "Going to be a tough run, though. None of the guys they have left can even fly, let alone take out some ship in the dark."

As she settled back in her seat, gazing up through the glass above her at Jericho, Kylie laughed at the thought of a bunch of incompetent pirates bungling their way through space, failing to take even one merchant ship.

"You could always work for them when you tire of us," Nadine said with a grin. "I bet they'd pay top dollar for a decent pilot."

Rogers laughed. "Not on your life, sister. This face is too handsome for the likes of those pirates."

Her crew's banter made for pleasant background noise as Kylie stared out through the bridge's sphere at the world of Jericho.

Once, in the days before the Silstrand Alliance was little more than a twinkle in Peter Sil's eye, someone had tried to terraform Jericho. She could see why—the planet was smaller than Earth-normal, but it was dense, giving it a surface gravity of 0.92*g*. There was even free water down there. Not enough to form oceans, but several large seas had pooled here and there.

As the stories would have it, the terraforming held for a while, almost a thousand years from what she had heard. Then something happened, no one seemed to know for sure what—maybe it was a war, maybe the Big OJ had blasted more solar wind than normal, or maybe it was just mismanagement. Whatever the cause, the atmosphere had thinned, leaving only half the pressure an unaugmented human needed to survive.

She shifted her gaze to the Valhalla shipyard, which was only thirty-two thousand kilometers above the planet in geostationary orbit. From their approach, Kylie could make out the largest of the cities, Montral. Well, she saw the light reflecting off its dome more than anything else. Also visible was Laerdo Station, atop the world's claim to fame, a functional space elevator that terminated in Montral.

"Penny for your thoughts?" Nadine asked.

"Just thinking about what Jericho must have been like, once. Someone must have really liked this place to build a space elevator...and to dome over the cities after the air thinned out."

Nadine nodded. "Yeah, it's a lot of effort for a world like this—but who knows...when it's the only TP in the system, you try to keep it intact as long as possible."

"I hear you can still go out and breathe the air in some of the deeper valleys," Rogers said. "Though I don't think I'd trust whatever the ruling families have dumped outside the cities not to eat my lungs."

"Maverick always talks about cleaning the place up, getting terraforming processes going again to build up the atmosphere," Kylie said.

"As if scum like him could pull that off," Grayson said from the bridge's entrance.

"Who knows," Kylie shrugged. "People say a lot of the old CO_2 generators are still out there in the wilds. If you could fix them and then get enough air for the plants to grow back, they'd make the oxygen, and it would be good to go."

Grayson laughed. "Just like that?"

Kylie scowled. "No, I didn't say it would be easy. I don't know how long it would take, but it's how they did it the first time."

"And look how well that turned out," Grayson said. "Now the world's just a dumping ground for Silstrand's garbage."

"I think I resent that," Rogers muttered.

"What did I say about playing nice?" Kylie asked Grayson with a raised eyebrow.

Grayson didn't reply, just folded his arms and leaned against a console. He pouted like a child and Kylie wanted to needle him about it but let it pass.

No one spoke for the remaining twenty minutes to the handoff at Valhalla. When it occurred, Rogers released the hull into the tender care of a Valhalla Shipyard tug.

<Now, Benny,> Kylie advised over the channel to the station's salvage chief, *<I've inventoried every inch of that ship, and Maverick is going to get the full report.>*

<Kylie!> Benny replied with mock chagrin. *<Maverick fills my credit accounts just like you. I'm not going to bite the hand that feeds me.>*

Kylie's virtual presence smiled. *<Glad to hear it. Oh, now that I think of it, we didn't finish inspecting all the crates in the stern port hold, so if you could finish that up, it would be great.>*

<For you, Kylie, I will gladly take care of it,> Benny replied magnanimously.

<Thanks, Benny,> Kylie replied. *<Pleasure doing business with you.>*

<And you, as always. Say hi to Maverick for me.>

<Wouldn't you rather I didn't?> she asked.

Benny laughed. *<Yeah, best not to. Never know what sort of mood he's in.>*

Kylie gave a parting smile and cut the connection.

"Standard arrangement?" Rogers asked.

"Yup," Kylie replied. "Made sure there was a little something extra for him, just like always."

"That's how things go out here, is it?" Grayson asked.

Kylie cocked an eyebrow at her former lover. "Gray…that's how things go everywhere. I did way more swapping and trading in the military than I've done out here in civilian life. If you weren't such a straight arrow, you'd see how things really work."

"Kylie I—" Grayson began, then stopped abruptly as he saw the broad smile on Kylie's face and realized that she was goading him.

"She really got you going." Rogers laughed.

"Yeah, I guess she did," Grayson mumbled.

"How long to Laerdo?" Kylie asked Rogers. She could have looked it up on the nav systems, but she always liked to ask. The bridge was too quiet half the time as it was.

"Heavy traffic today," Rogers replied as he brought up the reports on the bridge's forward holoscreen. "Gonna take at least four hours to get down there."

"No rush," Nadine said. "I've been on the horn with Laerdo control. They won't have a berth for us 'til then anyway. They'll forward the bay number as soon as they have one ready."

"Gotcha," Rogers replied.

Grayson walked to the edge of the bridge and peered out at Valhalla Station and the rows of ships slated for salvage or up for sale.

"I never imagined Gedri had this much going on," he said. "I had always written it off as a backwater."

Kylie rose and walked to his side, peering out into space, as well. "Rough, dirty, cutthroat, yes. Backwater, not so much. Gedri does just as much trade with the rest of the Silstrand Alliance as Trio. It does even more with the Scipio Federation. The Gedri System, especially Jericho here, represent the alliance a lot more than anyone would like to admit."

Grayson shook his head. "What a first impression. A failed world run by old crime families."

"It's not so bad," Kylie said with a grin as she slapped him on the shoulder. "You may even like it down there. You'll find it's one hell of a party."

Grayson didn't reply as he gazed out the window at the slowly growing world and Kylie looked into his eyes, trying to imagine what he was thinking, before letting out a slight laugh.

"You're enjoying this," Grayson said with a slight growl to his voice.

Kylie shrugged. "Fine. I promise not to enjoy it *too* much."

*****

The *Dauntless* was on final approach to Laerdo Station, and Kylie had summoned the crew to the bridge so Rogers could join in the final mission briefing before they disembarked.

"Okay," Kylie began. "Everyone stays armed. And everyone stays on alert. Grayson, you better go put on the civvies I left for you."

Grayson raised his eyebrows and then his mouth opened to argue.

Kylie knew the argument he'd make, and she didn't want to hear it. She raised her hand to cut him off. "If you plan to survive, you need to blend in. Look as unmilitary as possible. Stay close to Rogers. He can show you around without looking like he's showing you around."

"I could just stay on the ship…"

Kylie shook her head. The last thing she wanted was for Grayson to be alone on the ship. She wasn't ready to trust him that much. Instead, she wanted Rogers and Winter to keep an eye on him. "Too suspicious. Maverick's boys will board and check over the ship after we dock. If they catch you on here, there will be too many questions. You're going to need to blend in. Take in the sights. Have a few drinks."

Rogers threw him a charming smile. "Don't worry, I have a pretty nice pad here. Girls are pretty good, too—parts of them that are still girls, anyway."

"Mods are big here," Kylie explained. "The kinkier, the better."

"Pretend it's a holiday," Nadine said with a giggle. "If you can."

"Not sure how I feel about any of this," Grayson muttered. Even if he liked it, he wouldn't say.

"Don't worry, kink and mods are Harken's deal. Maverick prefers his girls pure," Nadine added. "That's where Kylie and I come in."

Kylie didn't want to think about Harken—Maverick's second-in-command. The woman made Kylie's skin crawl. Harken was the one that ran all the drugs and modded-sex boys and girls. Maverick liked to pretend he was above all that—as though he was a legitimate businessman.

"Like Lana." Grayson's voice softened with grief, and it surprised Kylie. They had both known Lana when she was a little girl, but Grayson had arguably seen her more recently, since Kylie had been away for eleven years.

The vein that ran down Grayson's left temple pulsed. "I don't like either of you getting that close to him. I've heard about how his tastes run."

"Nice to see you still care, but we'll be fine. We just need to walk around. Go about our business. The rest of it will fall into place. You'll see. It'll be easy."

Nadine smiled. "Like riding a hover cycle."

Grayson cringed. "I hope that bike is regularly sanitized."

Kylie smirked. "And that's the job. Don't worry, neither of us will do anything we don't have to."

Outside the windows, Laerdo Station loomed large as Rogers brought the *Dauntless* over the outer ring and down toward their berth. Nadine had gotten them an external slot—better if they needed to make a fast getaway—and Rogers eased the ship's starboard hatch up to the station umbilical with smooth precision. The station's docking arms extended, made a solid grapple, and Rogers powered down the grav drive.

"Home sweet home," he announced.

"Nice flying," Kylie replied as she glanced out at the rows of ships around them. Many were independent freighters, salvagers, and mining rigs. Others belonged to one of Jericho's ruling families, though most belonged to Maverick. He had really built up his empire over the past decade. He was king of the hill, and no one dared challenge him.

The thought made her blood run cold for a moment. *She* was planning on challenging him.

"I guess I'd better change, then." Grayson grunted as he excused himself to get ready in his quarters. Like it or not, everyone would need to be on deck for this one. Kylie just hoped his stomach was strong enough for what was about to follow. Undercover wasn't exactly his strength. Kind of how the military wasn't hers.

"Make sure he doesn't walk too much like a tin soldier," Kylie said to Winter.

Winter snorted. "Does he walk any other way? Man was probably bred in a military tank."

Inwardly, Kylie laughed. Based on the military family Grayson came from, it wasn't too big a stretch. "Then you better get him drunk. Get him relaxed, but nothing too dangerous," Kylie said.

"Don't worry, I picked one of my best vacationing flower print shirts just for him," Rogers said.

Kylie groaned. "Rogers—"

"Don't worry. I have everything under control." Rogers gave her a pretend salute. "We'll take good care of him and we'll be monitoring your comm. We might not be too close, but you aren't alone, Captain."

Kylie knew, but it was good to hear. "I'm going to fill out the docking plaswork myself and make sure the right people see me. We'll check in soon." She walked off the bridge and took the side passage toward the starboard airlock. Nadine joined her as she cycled the lock, and they stepped out together into Sweep AC-121's receiving and loading area.

A podium stood near the airlock, and Kylie approached it. She slipped her finger into a receptacle and winced as it took DNA samples. An IR scanner examined her eyes, and she Linked to the station's net and passed her auth codes.

<*Welcome, Captain Rhoads,*> the docking bay's AI greeted her. <*Everything seems to be in order with your check-in. Do you and your ship need anything? Supplies or services? There's currently a ten percent special for junkers.*>

Kylie thought it over and stuck with the plan. <*Just dinner reservations for me and my missus tonight. I hope the Caviar Club is still open and serving their steak dinner special?*>

<*Of course. A reservation for two then?*>

<*With a bottle of white bubbly. We're celebrating.*>

Nadine laughed nervously as Kylie pulled her finger from the podium's DNA scanner. Everything was scheduled, and the AI confirmed the time for dinner.

Kylie took Nadine's hand, and they walked through the sweep's long, curving deck until they came to a maglev train station. Once aboard a train, Nadine relaxed against Kylie. Neither spoke; instead, they simply enjoyed the quiet time together with no demands. And especially no Grayson.

The maglev stopped at the central hub, and the pair disembarked, queuing up for a ride down the strand to the planet's surface and the domed city of Montral. A lift-car arrived, and they boarded and found a seat. It would be a forty-minute ride down to the surface, and light music played around them while ads for just about everything imaginable danced on the walls.

"When we get down there, what do you think about some quick shopping before we head to my quarters?" Kylie asked as part of the script they had agreed upon.

Nadine nodded, but her distracted eyes flitted about. "I could use a new scarf."

"New shoes always hit the spot for me."

Privately, Nadine sent a message across the Link, <*You think it'll work? You think Maverick is keeping such a close eye on things, he'll pick up we're docked?*>

<*I'd bet my life he's already watching,*> Kylie replied.

Outwardly, Nadine shivered.

*****

The elevator passed through the glass dome of Montral, and Kylie stared out over the city where she had spent many of her recent years. The reddish-orange light from the suns always gave the city a sinister look to her eyes. Though the dome shifted the light closer to pure white, it was not enough that they resembled G-spectrum stars.

Still, it was enough that green plants could grow inside the dome—unlike the scrub and lichen that survived outside, where photosynthesis required planet life to be more brown than green.

Light glinted off the lazy river that wound through the city. Once it had been lovely and sparkling blue—or so Kylie liked to imagine—now it was sluggish and brown, only enough impellers still ran to keep the waters from completely stagnating.

As the lift-car dropped closer to the ground, tall buildings—some nearly scraping the dome—obscured the view, and Kylie turned her attention to Nadine.

"Wake up, we're down."

Nadine's beautiful blue eyes cracked open, and she looked up at Kylie with a sleepy love, and Kylie's heart melted. This woman was such a dream, and for some reason she was with Kylie, on Kylie's junker ship, snatching hulls out of the dark.

What had she done to deserve such a thing?

Just don't screw it up.

The two women took another maglev to one of the more upscale shopping districts, and Nadine's eyes lit up as she took in all the latest styles—many from Scipio—often available on Jericho before anywhere else in Silstrand space.

Nadine dragged Kylie up to the third level of the broad promenade, which was filled with high-end shops and boutiques. It was the perfect place to pick up a matching ensemble to wear for an elegant dinner.

Everyone, from the shoppers to those manning the doors, wore elaborate outfits consisting of complex polymers, elaborate lighting, and dazzling holoeffects. All the women's—and many of the men's—hair were done up in creative twists and gravity-defying shapes, their eyes dotted with all the colors of the rainbow. Even their multi-colored shoes and boots were extraordinary—many didn't even touch the ground as their wearers drifted by.

It wasn't somewhere that Kylie felt at all comfortable.

A short while later, inside a boutique, she leaned against a white column as Nadine tried on her fifth scarf. This one's material was velvet-soft and changed colors as she turned side to side. Nadine cupped her hands beneath her face and held her head high. "What do you think?"

"It's perfect."

"You've said that about the last three scarfs."

"Four, but who's counting?"

"*You* are, obviously." Nadine smirked but tried to hide it as she went for a blue scarf with pom-pom tassels. *God, not another scarf with tassels.*

"You've looked perfect in every one you've tried on. Is it my fault blue is your color?"

Nadine tossed the scarf around her hair like an elegant cowl. "Head outside. I'll be right there."

Kylie raised an eyebrow. It wasn't like Nadine to just dismiss her like that, but if she got the chance to get out of there, Kylie had to take it. "Sure, but you be careful."

Nadine laughed out her nose. "Yes, I'll make sure all the violent ho's don't get me."

Women. Kylie greeted the lady monitoring the front door. "I'm just going to step outside and catch some fresh air."

The highbrow woman with crisply-defined eyebrows that arched disdainfully, not to mention an hourglass body that was far from natural, barely looked at her. Instead, she pushed up her bangles and sniffed with disinterest. "Junkers like you belong on sub-level six. I think you'd find what you're looking for there."

Guns, ammo. The mercs hung out on sub-six and ran it with an iron fist. Once, it had been a level of the city, as the name implied. Now it was an entire section of Montral. Those who didn't belong, or showed a sign of weakness, were quickly dealt with. Even Kylie only went there when she absolutely had to.

Kylie smiled unkindly at the woman and stepped outside. The filtered air smelled fresh and clean. Leaning on her elbows on the white banister, Kylie watched the stream flowing through the center of the promenade. Others did the same as they collected on benches or hung around the trees. It was a tranquil place, and far up above, a holoprojection portrayed a beautiful blue sky and yellow suns.

It was all just a show. Salvagers. Gangsters. Junkers. Those who worked for Maverick, the other families, or did the bidding of the GFF. This city brimmed with them. Couldn't trust any of them and Kylie was one of them. So, what was it about her crew that made them different?

Maybe they weren't different. Maybe that was the problem.

Kylie straightened up as someone approached. She could hear his heavy boots as he sidled up behind her. She turned, and he caught her hand, slipping a card key into it. He was one of those seriously-modded guys with the requisite spyglass looking-lens fused into his eye. In a thick vest and heavy pants, he appeared bulkier than he was.

"Maverick says hello. He's looking forward to seeing you tonight." The man glanced at the store as Nadine exited. She held a small blue bag in her hand. "He wants you to bring your girlfriend, but leave your boy toys at home or on the ship. Maverick don't much care where they go, as long as he has you girls to himself."

Bingo.

Kylie tilted her head to the side as she slid the card key into her pocket. "We look forward to it."

"Change your clothes. New dresses are being sent to your apartment," the man ordered as he turned tail and hurried away. Probably the clean smell of the place gave him a headache.

"See," Kylie said as Nadine reached her side. "I told you it'd go according to plan."

Eyebrows raised, Nadine let out a deep breath. "This time I kinda hoped you'd be wrong. Plus…now I won't get to wear this scarf to Caviar Club tonight."

Kylie snapped her fingers. Couldn't Maverick have waited a day? "C'mon. We have to suit up, and I have a few little surprises of my own."

"Be careful, Kylie. If Maverick catches us…if he figures out we're up to something…"

Kylie didn't need to be reminded of any of that. She slipped her arm around Nadine's and led her toward the closest maglev station.

*****

Kylie's quarters were on level fifty-seven of a high-rise apartment complex on the eastern side of Montral. The view from the windows looked out over the bustling city center. Sounds of traffic filtered in from the open window in the bedroom and a gust of wind brought the smell of industry. The dark bedroom twinkled with lights from the billboards flitting by outside.

Except for a round bed—covered in burgundy satin sheets—in the center of the bedroom, Kylie didn't have many belongings. There was a large, abstract watercolor painting her parents had sprung for once. It was one of the only things Kylie really cared for about her quarters. Truth be told, she only kept the apartment in case of emergencies. It was a good place to hide a few extra illegal weapons when they took the *Dauntless* to more legitimate ports.

The building also had the added benefit of being protected by the GFF. She'd only have trouble here if Maverick turned on her. It was like an early warning system. It didn't make the idea of double-crossing him feel any better, that was for sure.

Both ladies put on the slinky blue dresses Maverick had sent. They shimmered with waves of light, and the shade of blue shifted subtly as they walked. Kylie's had a high collar but was sleeveless. She paired it with black gloves and jewels around her wrists. The dress barely covered her ass, and her luminescent tights gave her a soft glow with each step. When she talked, the fabric of the dress hummed.

Nadine's dress was short in the front but had a long, flowing train made of bundles of fabric. Her blue bangs waffled in the breeze, sparkling with light and color as she swung a pendant necklace on and Kylie helped her clasp it. She couldn't help a slow kiss against the nape of her neck. Nadine smelled good, always did, but tonight she seemed more delicious than usual.

"You like it?" Nadine's voice purred like a cat. "Just picked it up. Maverick's men are going to go wild for it."

Kylie's vision swam with stars as her lips lingered against the soft skin. "It's affecting my thinking. I'm not sure how I feel about Maverick getting this close to you while he smells it."

"It'll keep him distracted. That's what we want, isn't it? Put some on before we leave."

Kylie laughed. "I have my own secrets, darling. You keep yours for yourself."

"We will walk out of this alive, won't we?" Nadine's eyes opened wide and her expression grew serious.

Kylie sat on the bed as she put on her bronze watch, and drew a black fur shrug around her shoulders. It accentuated her hourglass figure even further. "If we keep to our parts, we can do this. When I'm in with Maverick, I'm going to pass the codes onto you. You need to check the place out. See if you can find little miss Lana."

Nadine's eyes widened. "Me? I'm not as good with the snooping and bullshit stories as you are, Kylie. If I get caught, I might throw up. And these are expensive shoes."

"It'll be easier than spending time alone with Maverick. I can't do that to you."

"I don't want to do it to you, either."

"But I can take it. You're the dignitary. I'm just..." Kylie said with a shrug before continuing, "…nobody."

Nadine sat down beside her on the bed. "That's not true. You know that. If there was anyone who defies their birth order, it's you."

Kylie was the middle of seven children which meant, to Nadine's family, that Kylie was a nothing. Something just lost in the shuffle of scholars and the affluent. Most people didn't care about that sort of thing anymore, but to Nadine's highbrow caste, birth order meant everything. She didn't know if it was important to Nadine; Kylie had never asked.

"I'll be fine, you'll see. But thanks for caring. As for you, young lady, all we need are the system scans. The rosters. Maverick is too organized. If Lana is in the club, or anywhere else in Montral, for that matter, he'll have it listed somewhere. Or you'll find her…" said Kylie, swallowing hard before continuing, "…in the cage."

Nadine shivered, and the color seeped out of her skin. "I've always tried to pretend that place doesn't exist."

"I know," Kylie cooed, feeling like maybe she might be sick.

"If I see it, if I know it's real, for sure…I don't know how much longer I can work for him," Nadine admitted.

Kylie took her by the shoulders. With luck, soon none of them would need Maverick, and they'd be out from under his thumb. "We focus on tonight, and that's that. We find Lana and get her out of here. We get her back, and we're done with Maverick and the GFF forever."

"And if she's in the cage. How the hell do you propose we get her out?"

"I'll come up with a plan. I always do."

Nadine kissed Kylie's cheek. "You'd better."

A NIGHT ON THE TOWN

STELLAR DATE: 09.06.8947 (Adjusted Years)
LOCATION: City of Montral, Jericho
REGION: Gedri System, Silstrand Alliance

Grayson had been nervous about missions before, but for this one he was nervous *and* out of his element.

Rogers had waited until Laerdo Station's elevator was congested with rush-hour passengers before leading Winter and Grayson to a rental agency near their berth. There, they selected a small but fast station-to-surface shuttle and took it down to Montral's external docks.

Though the city had a space elevator, the lift didn't have the capacity to handle the volume of cargo that seemed to move on and off-planet—far more than the official data on the world indicated. Much of the traffic to and from the city passed through these docks, directly from the warehouses sprawling outside the city's dome to the waiting ships in orbit.

Grayson wondered what sort of filth festered just beneath the surface.

Rogers deftly piloted the shuttle through congested traffic of autonomous cargo pods, shuttles like theirs, small transports, and even some ships in the three-hundred-meter range. Most came down on grav drives, but a few burned their torches at far lower altitudes than any civilized world would have allowed.

The docks and warehouses were extensive, stretching for kilometers east of Montral's dome. Some had grav or electrostatic shielding around them to hold in a thicker atmosphere, but others didn't, and workers in rebreathers could be seen hauling cargo in and out.

Rogers eased the shuttle into a tall hangar with a grav shield over the entrance, holding the denser air in. He set the craft down in a cradle, and a minute later they had disembarked. Some hard credit chits swapped hands with a dock worker who Rogers was friendly with, and the trio of men were off.

Winter took the lead as they entered a narrow tunnel, which eventually met with a wider thoroughfare leading toward the domed city. Thousands of people of all possible configurations surrounded them, and the sounds of cargo haulers a level below them in the tunnel, echoed up through vents on the walls—along with a host of industrial smells.

Grayson sighed as he pushed past some people who turned their heads to laugh at him. "Of all the things, I can't believe this is the only shirt you had for me. I look like a walking postcard."

"Sorry." Rogers cast Winter a glance and they both held in a chuckle Grayson didn't miss. They were both so juvenile. "It's laundry day."

"I'm sure of it." Grayson threw him a glare and was sure Rogers had done it on purpose "People are staring at me."

"You're imagining it," Rogers said.

Winter shook his head. "Nah, they really are staring at him."

Rogers let out a burst of laughter. "Relax, you're going to have a stroke if you keep that up." Rogers punched Grayson light on the arm.

Grayson wasn't amused and his eyebrows knitted together. He didn't say anything and wasn't certain if this hazing was supposed to endear him to the group, but he didn't like it. And it wasn't working.

After about twenty minutes of walking, they emerged in the Ventrella Commercial Distract—where all the best bars, clubs, and whatever else a vile junker's heart may desire—were to be found.

Unexpected sights were all around. The denizens of the Ventrella District wandered about dressed in tight leather, gleaming steel, or sheathed in polymers that Grayson was unable to identify on sight.

It was warm as they worked their way through the crowded streets, the smells of grime and chemicals from the docks now mixed with that of the unwashed masses of humanity.

Through it all, Grayson stayed close to Rogers and kept a watchful eye on Winter.

<You told Kylie you were going to trust Winter,> Jerrod said.

<Under the circumstances, I'm doing the best I can.>

<At least no one has tried to kill us yet today.> Jerrod sounded pleased with this statistic, but Grayson's stomach shifted uneasily—though it may have been from the odor wafting out of a drug-den they were approaching. He held his breath and kept moving.

A woman stumbled out, dressed in as little cloth as possible while still passing for attire. He hadn't realized that clothing came in such small squares. Maybe Kylie was right—maybe he spent too much time in military stations even when not on assignment. He didn't belong out here; he was a fish out of water. It wouldn't take long for people to notice.

"You're looking a little green around the gills. Lighten up." Winter slapped him on the back. From the smirk the man wore, he was clearly enjoying himself a little too much.

Grayson shrugged. "Me? I do this sort of thing all the time."

The look Rogers and Winter gave each other suggested they weren't going to fall for the little lie. Nervously, Grayson cleared his throat. "Oh, come on, you got me. I'm not used to this, alright?"

<*Is the understatement of the year,*> Jerrod said.

Rogers elbowed Grayson. "Don't worry, once we get past this stretch, we can relax a bit. What's important is that we do our best to blend in. To not draw attention to ourselves."

"So, if you could relax and not look like a military guy in civvy clothes, that'd be awesome."

"Then maybe you shouldn't have given me a pink flower-print shirt anyone could see from a kilometer away."

"Everyone loves a tourist, Grayson," Rogers said. A glance passed between him and Winter again, and the unspoken words made Grayson fume. "If you have something to say, just say it."

"You're so rigid, your damn arms don't move. You're like a…doll, man. A molded, plastic toy."

Rogers snorted. "Try swinging your arms more."

Grayson tried, but it felt unnatural.

Winter sighed. "Now you look like a damn puppet. Well, we tried. Far as anyone knows, we're here to show our buddy a good time, so let's see if we can fake it till we make it."

Grayson felt better even if nothing had really changed. He set his mind to focusing on the plan, and unconsciously relaxed as he followed Rogers and Winter through the crowd. They took a left around the corner of what had to be a whorehouse, judging by the men and women standing outside, and then crossed a bridge over a slow-moving river—something that was rather surreal to see here, even if it was a disturbing shade of brown—to what Rogers described as the 'mostly better' side of Ventrella District.

Once across the bridge, the crowds were smaller, and the sound of soft music wafted over the breeze—not a recording, or even synthesized—it sounded as though someone was actually strumming a guitar.

Rogers picked up on Grayson's shocked facial expression and gave a nod. "It's real, all right, and it's a beauty. Every once in a while, you find a real treasure, something that can bring you back to the good old days, even if you hadn't been alive to see them in the first place."

The music grew louder as they approached a smaller building. Outside, a row of patio tables with orange umbrellas were filled with patrons holding strong drinks and eating from large plates of food. The aroma was intoxicating—food aboard the ships and stations Grayson usually frequented wasn't bad, but it never smelled like this. The scent of rich gravies drenching flame-seared meat, of melted cheese, and spices that would set a tongue on fire.

<Your saliva glands seem to be working overtime, should I help you regulate them?> Jerrod asked.

<Funny,> Grayson replied.

A neon sign flashed above the metal door. It said *Nancy's Place*. A simple name for food that smelled so good, Grayson thought. They passed through the doorway, and his enhanced vision noticed a bit of carbon scoring on the wall that someone hadn't scrubbed all the way off—the place certainly saw more than just culinary action.

<Jerrod, run facial scans and see what it is we're getting ourselves into.>

<Of course, sir.>

Grayson followed his companions into the darkened establishment. They walked around the side of the bar to a table not far from the guitarist—a woman, and a lovely one at that, despite the fact that she had an extra set of arms. Grayson couldn't tell due to the placement of her guitar, but he suspected she might also be naked.

"It takes all kinds," Grayson mumbled to himself.

"Ain't that the truth?" Winter banged his fist on the table.

<Sir, I scanned several dozen of the faces, as requested. Many of these men and women have active warrants out on them, several of them for crimes which were of a rather violent nature.>

It was as Grayson had suspected. <*Thank you. For now, let's keep our mouths shut. Make a record of who they are and what they're wanted for. When we're done here, we can send the transmission back to the SSF.*>

<*Sure,*> Jerrod said. <*When we leave here, make sure you sanitize well.*>

A waitress with her blonde hair done up in a beehive—complete with small robotic bees buzzing around it—stopped by the table. She wore too makeup on her near-plastic face, and a beige-colored latex shirt embraced her voluptuous curves. It was matched with a black pair of dangerously short shorts made of the same material. Grayson glanced at the other wait staff—this appeared to be the uniform at Nancy's.

"Wow," her sultry voice oozed out.

Her expertly-manicured, and rather sharp-looking, fingernails shone with all the colors of the rainbow. She dragged them down Rogers's bicep. "I haven't seen you boys around here in a while. Oh, you pick up a new friend?" She threw Grayson a kiss and eyed his shirt. "He on holiday, or something? Rad and retro, honey."

He sat up straighter in his chair.

<*You don't want to know what she's wanted for, sir,*> Jerrod said.

"Don't you worry about him, Betty." Winter threw her a kiss. "He's all yours later if you want him. Just make sure nobody bothers us, and keep the drinks coming."

The waitress clung to Rogers's arm, but her eyes narrowed seductively, taking in the sight of Winter. "Whatever you say, hot stuff. But save me some for later." She sauntered away, moving like her hips were double-jointed. Grayson stared longingly after her.

Rogers laughed and picked a handful of peanuts off the table. "You'd better learn how to keep your eyes inside your head, Grayson. This place is going to eat you up alive."

Grayson glanced around the room. The place's wait staff were all fawning over patrons as if they were on something. "The staff here…?"

Rogers laughed, and Winter gave a slow nod. "You think we just come here for the food? We have to show our new crew member a good time, right?"

As he spoke, the drinks were delivered at a table by another waitress. Grayson cleared his throat, certain that he couldn't legally enjoy the 'good time' they wanted him to have. Not with women like this, and not when on duty.

"Ohh my…" she pouted and blew Grayson a kiss. "Later…you and me…you're getting a special, private showing." She snapped her jaw shut but bared her teeth for a moment.

<*Oh dear,*> Jerrod said, <*I think I'm frightened.*>

<***You're*** *frightened?*> Grayson felt green, and not with envy.

Rogers and Winter laughed as the three men lifted their steins of beer and slammed them together in midair. They each took a long draught and Grayson was impressed with the thick, malty flavor. He was going to need it to get through this night.

<*To tonight!*> Winter said over their private Link.

<*To Kylie…and Nadine,*> Grayson said.

<*That's real sweet. We can hear you, you know,*> Kylie responded even though she was several kilometers away.

Grayson knew. Of course, he did.

<*Have a good time and make sure everyone knows you're there. Party, do whatever, but make sure it's public…and not too illegal.*> Kylie's words were followed by a signal that she was going silent and would only get emergency messages.

Grayson tracked her and Nadine's movements. They were entering the area of Montral known as the Red Zone. Maverick's territory—it made Ventrella District look like a child's playground. Grayson took a deep breath as he studied his overlay and watched her tracker move further away.

"Let's order some grub, huh?" Winter leaned back in his chair. With two fingers in his mouth, he let out a loud, piercing whistle.

Rogers was more subdued, his eyes moving back and forth. He wasn't as good as Grayson at hiding his Link tells.

"If anyone can pull this off, it's Kylie," Grayson said.

Rogers blinked. "It's not Kylie I'm worried about. Pulling Nadine into this was wrong. She's one of us, but she's not like us. You know what I mean?"

Grayson understood. He had studied Nadine's history and her police record. In over her head was putting it mildly. Yet, she had gone along with the plan without much fuss—not what he would have expected for a woman with her upbringing. Other than her raw beauty, Nadine was rather unassuming. Was there something about her he was missing? "If there was another way…"

"Your type always says stuff like that," Rogers muttered. "It's why I ended my military service before it even started, pal." His severe look shifted into a wink as a trio of waitresses approached the group. "Ladies, ladies…" Rogers stood with his arms spread wide as two of the radiant women came in close for a cuddle. "If only I had extra arms to handle all you fine, fine women."

One of them laughed. "That can be arranged."

Winter puckered is lips together. "Damn, I love a good tease. Come over here, sweetheart." He slapped his lap.

Grayson picked up his beer and tried to pretend none of this was really happening.

"What do you say, Grayson?" Rogers asked. "You ready to party?"

Like he had a choice.

THE SHADE

STELLAR DATE: 09.06.8947 (Adjusted Years)
LOCATION: City of Montral, Jericho
REGION: Gedri System, Silstrand Alliance

The Red Zone.

A notorious district that most citizens of Montral would never think of entering. Reserved for the mercs, bounty hunters, and other employees of Maverick's syndicate, it was the pit, the bottom of the heap in Montral. From here, he ruled the roost.

For a guy who was the power behind the power in the Gedri system, Maverick liked to circulate with the lowest common denominator. Maybe he just didn't give a damn. That was certainly his style.

Outside, 'police' patrolled the entrance to the district. Kylie used the term as loosely as possible, because they were directly on Maverick's payroll—no equivocation at all. If you were in Maverick's good books you got in; if you had messed up—whether you knew it or not—you were dealt with.

Maverick only dealt with people one way, and Kylie thanked her lucky stars she was still around. It was a good thing he liked her. Had a thing for sweet brunettes with knowledge of the inner workings of the SSF.

Kylie and Nadine passed through the auth portal, avoiding the hungry looks of the cops, and into the Red Zone. On the far side of the checkpoint, a heavily-modded guard with an eyepatch gave them the once over. "You have a good reason to be here?"

Kylie tossed a disinterested glance his way, but Nadine held her head high. She must've been generating a lot of heat because the train of her dress turned an ombre pink and then purple. "Maverick's expecting us. He invited us. I suggest you don't keep him waiting." She flipped the private card the muscle had given her on the promenade earlier.

For a big guy, he paled quickly. He stood to the side. "Well, I can't tell that by looking at you. You better not have any weapons on you."

Kylie snorted. "Do these outfits look like they can hide weapons?"

Nadine huffed a laugh as they made their way through. *<Well, that went well.>*

Certainly, it could've gone worse, but the hard part of the job lay ahead.

They strode confidently through the Red Zone. Mercs patrolled the streets, relaxed and laughing amongst themselves—the men and women both throwing lewd comments at the two women as they walked past. Kylie didn't respond to the cat-calls. In all of Montral—but even more so in the Red Zone—there were only predators and prey. She preferred to be the latter.

A group of hoverbikes screamed by, and Nadine winced at the high-pitched sound of their engines. "Stars, I hate those things."

"Especially how they echo through the buildings around here," Kylie replied with a nod. "Almost there, just another two blocks."

"Somehow, I think it's safer out here," Nadine replied as they hurried along the streets toward the tall building ahead.

The dome-scraper stretched at least a hundred stories into the air above them—headquarters for Maverick's operation, the ground floor of which housed his premiere club, The Shade.

They climbed the broad stairs and crossed the red marble expanse before reaching the towering doors that led into the club. Massive, heavily-modded guards stood on either side, and they pulled the steel slabs open allowing the loud music to spill out into the early evening air.

One of the guards nodded, and Kylie shrugged. They *were* welcome, after all. The two women shared a reassuring look as they passed under the elaborate holosign and sauntered into the club's main foyer.

Kylie waited for her eyes to adjust to the dim interior while the music and loud voices thrummed around her. Once they had, she saw the usual tables filled with patrons happily imbibing drinks, and on the dance floor, a sea of human flesh and fashion writhed to the beats pulsing through the air.

Kylie and Nadine glided around the dance floor, closer to the bar where rows of girls and lithe young men slithered up and down poles. They ranged from some who were entirely naked and natural humans, to those in complex fetish gear, to others who barely appeared human at all.

The one thing they all had in common were thick collars connected to the floor by glimmering chains.

All the pole dancers were in euphoric throes of ecstasy, their brain patterns altered through mods and conditioning to get off on their dancing, and on being groped by patrons. They moved slowly and sensually—Maverick favored mods that slowed time down for these dancers, so their languid movements were smooth and measured.

Kylie didn't know exactly what it was, but he called it Precision.

<Scan all their faces.>

<I'm working it, Ky,> Nadine said. *<So far, no matches.>*

<Damn it…alright.>

They ascended the grand staircase toward the VIP area. Once at the red-carpeted second level, Nadine waved the key card across the door, and it slid open. Stepping into the lion's den, Kylie steadied herself for what she was about to see.

An intoxicating mist wafted down from the ceiling. Some sort of party was going on in the main VIP room. Women in tight rubber catsuits were on their knees, submitting to whatever acts the patrons—both men and women—desired.

The gags the women wore kept them from making much noise, even the slightest cries further diminished by sound-dampening tech. The drug-laced mist kept them docile while it kept them aroused. They paid good money to be here, women and men alike.

<*Quick, before our heads begin to swim. Catch their faces,*> Kylie said.

Nadine worked fast. They circled through the rows of girls in the center of the room. When nothing checked out, they headed toward the rear wall where women were strapped to the wall, while others were vacuum sealed in frames like pieces of living art.

Kylie hated this place.

<*Their nano will heal them. Maverick doesn't want them permanently damaged.*>

That wasn't the point though, was it?

Kylie peered up at a blonde woman and thought it could be Lana. She grabbed her chin, and the stoned woman moaned, her eyes rolling back into her head. "Lana?" Kylie whispered. It wasn't her. Disheartened, Kylie let her head go and it was like letting go of a rag doll.

"Hey!" a man called and grabbed Kylie's wrist. "That one's mine! Get your own."

"We're Maverick's, so I suggest you keep your hands to yourself," Nadine said hotly and her powerful glower—honed from her years attending her family's high-brow events—cowed the man into submission. Salvager, dignitary, it didn't matter. Nadine had a power behind her looks and words.

The man lifted his hands up. "Well, then you better go find him." He gritted his teeth. "And leave my bitches alone."

Bitches? Kylie's eyes narrowed as he left and she thought to give him a piece of her mind. Show him what a real bitch could do.

Nadine placed a hand on her shoulder. "Not now, Kylie."

Right. The mission. Since Lana wasn't on the VIP floor, they had to continue on. There was never much hope they'd find Lana before seeing Maverick, but they had to try, didn't they?

"What are you two doing?" a soft, sinister voice came from behind the pair and the hairs on the back of Kylie's neck rose.

Harken. Maverick's second-in-command was not a woman they had wanted to run into. She had a dangerous, quiet calm about her that had always unnerved Kylie. She had once been Maverick's slave, like Kylie, but Harken had fallen in love with the torture and the control so much, she now got off on it.

She wore a red latex suit with a restricting posture collar laced around her neck, red gloves, and puffy sleeves. Harken's matching red corset kept her waist cinched tight. Extra small, from the ribs Maverick had removed years ago as a cruel joke. Now, with plumped up breasts, it was evident Harken embraced body modification more than before.

A long red train on the back completed the outfit, and her makeup was always tastefully overdone. Harken came across as more regal and elegant than her clothing would suggest.

Still, though he now preferred his girls more vanilla, it was no wonder the blonde beauty with silky hair had been one of Maverick's favorite pets.

Kylie did her best to keep her voice even, though her head swam from the mist around them. "We're on our way to see Mav." She cocked her hips and tried to look commanding, but instead accidently stumbled toward Harken.

Harken caught her arms, steadying her. "Then I suggest you hurry and get to it before I put you up on the wall like my girls. And if I catch you inspecting the merchandise again,

Kylie, it won't matter if you are Maverick's favorite. Your head—and ass—will be mine."

"Appreciate the warning," Nadine said. She took Kylie's hand and led her away. "You okay?"

"I can barely see straight." Kylie's vision blurred and everything around her shifted in and out of focus. A fleeting thought that Nadine didn't seem to be affected came to her before the drugs washed it away.

"You'll feel better once we get upstairs. Come." Nadine took Kylie's arm as they walked around the bar at the side of the room. The wall featured expensive wooden paneling, and as they approached, a section slid aside, triggered by the special key card. A conveyance slid out of the wall, and they stepped inside.

Time to go see Maverick.

MAVERICK

STELLAR DATE: 09.06.8947 (Adjusted Years)
LOCATION: City of Montral, Jericho
REGION: Gedri System, Silstrand Alliance

The lights in the room were soft—what Kylie would have deemed almost romantic if she hadn't been sickened just to be there. Music pumped through hidden speakers, and tables in the center of the room featured some of Maverick's favorite food: marinated octopus tentacles, haggis, and the rank cheese he served on crackers.

There were two guards standing watch by the door to Maverick's private bedroom, but other than that, they were alone. Except for a giant viewing screen, which allowed them to see down to the lower levels of the night club. The one-way holodisplay gave them privacy.

"Girls, girls!" Maverick said from where he lay on the soft cushions of his sofa. "It's been so long since I've seen my favorites. What a sight you two are!"

Maverick raised his arms to invite them to join him. Dressed in leather pants, a respectful black jacket, and a fitted white shirt unbuttoned down to his navel. He wore a few jewel-encrusted gold chains—worth more than most people made in a year—but their size was understated. Diamond-studded rings adorned his left-hand. His chiseled jaw, blue eyes, and a mane of long, wavy brown hair made him easy on the eyes, and it fooled young women into believing he was a true catch, but Kylie knew the truth.

Every time she saw him, every time he flashed that smirk and looked at her as though he owned her, Kylie remembered what it had been like to wear his collar—just like the girls downstairs on the poles. His word had been her command.

Whatever he had wanted, whether it was sex, playing hostess for him, or just dancing for him and his guests, fulfilling his wishes had been her sole purpose in life.

When she was in space, on the *Dauntless*, she felt free of him, but now—here in his den—she knew that was a lie. Maverick still owned her. It made the promise of true freedom, from the SA of all things, that much more promising.

<C'mon, we don't have a choice,> Nadine said.

<I know.>

<I know you know. I just needed to say it for me.>

"Stop your little girl-talk and get over here," Maverick smirked. "You know I hate private conversations."

"Sorry, Mav." Kylie slinked to the sofa and settled on one side of him while Nadine sank into the thick cushions on the other side, her long leg draped over his. Their fingers traced figures up his chest. "You know how we like to toy with you."

Maverick grunted as he swung his arms around them. "I was beginning to think you were never getting back. Almost like you tucked tail and left our stretch of the stars. Then I thought, no, my girls wouldn't abandon me. Not when I have given Kylie Rhoads so much. I got you that damn ship, and I can take it away if you ever—"

Kylie put her finger to his lips to quiet him. "You talk too much, did anyone ever tell you that?"

His eyes narrowed. "Then you do the talking. Explain why it took you three times longer than normal to grab that salvage? What were you off doing that took you away so long?"

"There's a lot of empty space out there; these things don't just hang out in the black with beacons on them. It takes time to find them. Plus, it's a big ship," Kylie purred.

"If it's so big, why did it take so long to find? It looks like it'll bring in a lot of money, but not enough to explain the extra three weeks. If you've short-changed me…."

"What? I would never hold out on you!" Kylie feigned surprise and batted her eyelashes.

He nodded. "Better not have. We're searching the *Dauntless* now, and if we find just a hint of wrongdoing, one crate unaccounted for, your ass will be mine."

Nadine laughed—she had been quiet for so long, her voice surprised Kylie. "Her ass is already yours, isn't it?"

"If you think your little coy banter can sway me…."

"We wouldn't try that. We wouldn't." The words rolled off Kylie's tongue, maybe a bit too forcefully. She sat up straighter and took a glass of champagne as it rotated past on the spinning table in front of them. "Search the *Dauntless* as much as you want. Scour the logs. Listen to private conversations. Do what you like, but you won't find a shred of any wrongdoing on the *Dauntless*."

"Because you and your crew are so on the up and up, aye?" Maverick's eyes glinted with suspicion and a bloodthirsty desire for revenge—he hadn't proved Kylie had done anything yet, but his rage was right under the surface.

"Oh, Mav!" Kylie ran her fingertips over his arm and leaned into him. "Well, if it were the SSF searching our ship they'd find plenty wrong. But there's nothing there your guys will have an issue with. Just make sure to leave my crew's private stashes alone. I have to spend a lot of time with them out there—they bitch if they don't have their little pleasures."

Nadine gave a coy laugh, shifted closer to Maverick, and ran her nose along his cheek. Kylie forced down a feeling of jealousy. This was why she had brought Nadine. The woman could seduce a stone. At least Grayson listened and hadn't stayed aboard the ship—there's no way he could have pulled off any light conversation with whoever Maverick sent. She hoped the SSF techs were as good at scrubbing the logs as they claimed.

She forced herself to remain calm; if she acted nervously, Maverick wouldn't let her out of his sight. He seemed antsy and might kill her just on suspicion alone.

"Here I thought you invited us here to party," Kylie said as casually as possible.

"Business first. Then we party." Maverick lifted his arms over Kylie and Nadine's heads and stood. He glanced down at Kylie before walking to the center of the room to grab a handful of octopus tentacles.

Kylie resisted grimacing at the sight of him popping them into his mouth.

He chewed them noisily as he paced across the room to the window. When his back was turned, Nadine gave Kylie a wide-eyed expression and a brief nod toward the back.

Kylie sent a message over their private Link. <*No.*> There wasn't time to say more as Maverick turned around and wiped his mouth.

"Don't get me wrong," he said with a wide grin. "You're two of my favorite girls. The word attractive doesn't do you justice. You're sharp. You've brought me a lot of business over the years, but if either of you have double-crossed me, I'll gut you like a pair of fish and wear your skins to my next party." Maverick reached up and pulled a plasma sword from the wall.

He touched a button on the hilt and the molten star-stuff flowed out into a magnetic field. It wasn't a terribly effective weapon in real combat, but here, with the pair of them unarmed, it was more than a little threatening.

"I'll melt your innards…burn you to ash. No one will ever see you again. Like anyone would even bother looking."

"Rogers and Winter—" Nadine said, but Maverick interrupted her with a laugh.

"Those two will be dealt with swiftly. We've already found them. Though, they might not know it yet." Maverick flicked a piece of dirt from under his fingernail. "But if word comes in that you've stolen from me, they'll be dead before your bodies hit the ground."

Kylie rose from the sofa. "Maverick, your paranoia is getting the better of you." She approached him with a smile, but his jaw was set in stone even as her hand slithered up his chest. "Let's just let this all go. You know I've always been loyal. I've always—"

"Sit down." His eyes bored through her like those of an angry father. "Sit down and don't move until my squad reports in. Don't move a muscle." Maverick slammed his fist into the wall.

Kylie backed slowly away and sat down next to Nadine. Nothing ever went easy for her, so why was she so surprised that Maverick was suspicious?

<I've never seen him this paranoid> Nadine commented. *<Someone or something has gotten to him.>*

<Me either, but let's stay silent. If he sees we're communicating, he'll just get worse,> Kylie said.

Maverick studied them as he leaned against the wall. "Why so nervous, Kylie? Your heart and respiration are off the charts."

"You did just threaten to gut me like a fish. Excuse me if I like to go around wearing my own skin."

Maverick crossed his arms. "I watched you as you entered The Shade. You walked around more than usual. Studied the girls. What are you looking for?"

"Nothing," Nadine answered too quickly. When Maverick's attention shifted over to her, she recoiled.

"You misplace something?" Maverick's eyes narrowed.

Kylie put her hand on Nadine's lap. "It's been awhile, Mav. We like to look at your girls the same way you do. You know how we swing." Kylie blew Nadine a kiss.

Maverick took a heavy step forward. "Bring a few of the girls in here, then. I want to watch while you two have some fun."

"You can't be serious," Kylie said. "You expect us to have sex for your pleasure while we wait for the final word on whether or not you're going to kill us?"

"Why not? I'm a little bored. Are you a little bored, Kylie? Nadine?" A challenge flashed in his eyes, daring them to claim otherwise. Their window of opportunity was quickly closing around them. Kylie considered her options, such as they were with the two guards in the room.

"Bored doesn't quite cover it," Nadine mumbled.

Maverick lunged at her and Nadine shrieked and sank back into the sofa. Her arms splayed and her legs spread wide. Kylie jumped up and caught Maverick under the throat. "Touch her, and it's the end for you," she said. "I don't care who you are."

Behind her, the sound of pistols sliding out of holsters echoed through the room. Maverick laughed, and the door behind them slid open. "Aren't you interested to know what my squad found out first?"

Kylie glanced around him and counted half a dozen more of Maverick's men—all armed to the teeth. She took a chance to send her team a coded message. *<I hope you guys are ready to move. Run. Get lost and disappear now.>*

<Who says we aren't running already?>

Crap.

ON THE RUN

STELLAR DATE: 09.06.8947 (Adjusted Years)
LOCATION: City of Montral, Jericho
REGION: Gedri System, Silstrand Alliance

Grayson took a left hook to the face. He stumbled backward and slammed into the bar as a full-on brawl broke out around him.

<*Rogers could use some assistance,*> Jerrod said.

Lifting his hands up, Grayson side-stepped the hulking, angry, jealous girlfriend. "I swear, I didn't know she had a girlfriend and I promise you, I didn't touch her."

<*Well, you touched her a little,*> Jerrod said.

<*Not helping.*>

<*I have confirmation she's wanted in four different systems for very violent crimes. If I were you, I'd duck.*>

<*This information would've been helpful when she first walked into the bar,*> Grayson replied with a mental frown as he avoided a swing from the brute.

<*I thought we were drinking mai tais and blending in?*>

Grayson ducked as the woman threw another punch. He grabbed a chair and smashed it across the girlfriend's head, but the huge woman just kept coming. He glanced around, looking for an assist.

Winter had some guy's head under his arm and was driving his fist into the man's face repeatedly. Rogers was just beyond the large albino, fending off a crowd of short, very angry dwarfs whose beards nearly reached the floor. Well, life certainly wasn't dull around those two.

"My girl," the girlfriend said, pointing at herself before continuing, "my rules. You touched her and now I get to touch you. That's my rule."

"I didn't know the rules when I walked in here."

"You cross the Black Crow, they'll catch up to you."

Grayson had heard of the pirate organization before and what they were known for. It was just his bad luck to get himself into a mess like this. He pivoted and caught the woman's fist as it flew toward his face. "I thought you were the Black *Crows*. Like more than just one crow? But seriously, can we call this off? I really, really don't want to hurt you."

The girlfriend sneered and pushed her fist forward, and Grayson's boots slid backward on the floor. He knew that if he pushed back too hard, he'd lose his footing, and just as he was considering his options, his back foot hit the base of the bar. The girlfriend grunted and strained, but her fist didn't get any closer to Grayson's face.

The angry woman's eyes widened as Grayson pushed her arm down and across her chest. "I told you I didn't want to hurt you unless it's necessary."

The woman grunted with exertion, her face reddening as she tried to win the contest of strength against what appeared to be a much smaller man. In an act of desperation, she launched forward and tried to bite his nose.

"Whoa! Hey! Now…" Grayson said with a grunt as he threw a punch straight across her jaw with his left hand. Then he kicked the woman backward into a group of tables and continued, "…it's necessary."

Rogers grabbed Grayson's shoulder and yanked him back. "Yo! Loverboy, let's move it!"

The beast of a girlfriend rose from the ruin of the tables, sneered, and charged at them. Grayson threw a table into her path, which she crashed into, falling to the ground in a heap. He turned and followed Rogers and Winter around the bar.

Betty stood behind a velvet curtain, a wry grin on her red lips. Her plastic features finally showed some color as she flushed from the excitement, and her chest heaved as she took a deep breath. She slid a secret panel open to reveal a hidden exit. "We use this to bring in the illegal drugs. Well…the more illegal ones. You better use it now before the patrols get here."

Winter and Rogers wasted no time in disappearing inside, but Grayson paused. A gentle stroke of his hand across her chin caused her eyes to flutter shut. "And you, will you be all right?" he asked.

"She'll calm down." The waitress gave a cocky smile. "I'll be fine. It's not every day I meet a gentlemen."

"If you're in trouble—" Grayson began.

"C'mon, Romeo!" Winter's hand reached out from the hidden passage and yanked Grayson inside. The thundering scream of the jealous girlfriend was enough to get Grayson's legs pumping after Rogers and Winter.

"What the hell is a Romeo?" Rogers asked as they ran like lightning and dove between two tall buildings.

"Crap, Rogers, you are the most uncultured person I've ever met!" Winter said.

The passageway led them out the back of Nancy's Place, and they raced down an alley across the street, then through a park. After a few minutes of running between buildings without signs of pursuit they ducked into an alley used for waste removal.

Grayson bent over and drew in several deep breaths, his nano working to regulate his oxygen levels and blood pressure. Rogers and Winter had no such modifications but still breathed easily.

It was clear Grayson wasn't in as good a shape as he'd thought. It was embarrassing to be bested by the vanilla crew of the *Dauntless*, but he had been on the general's staff for a long time. He wasn't often running for his life. Even when he was younger and in the rank and file, Grayson had always been on an officer's trajectory.

"You have super strength?" Winter asked with narrowed eyes.

Grayson shrugged. "Not really. I can use my mil-spec nano for bursts of speed and strength, but nothing long-lasting. It breaks protocol to use it on civilians, too. I shouldn't have, but keeping my face from being rearranged didn't really give me much of a choice."

"So, you're telling me," said Winter as he puffed up his chest before continuing, "that during the prisoner transfer, when I pulled your gun on you, you could've disarmed me at any time?"

"If I chose to, yes. I decided to see how it'd play out."

Rogers glanced between the two. It looked as though he didn't get what Winter was driving at, but Grayson knew. It had only been a matter of time before it came out.

Winter shook his head. "You manipulated the situation. You could've put me down and you didn't? Because of what? Because you wanted leverage on Kylie when talking to your general?"

Grayson let the words sink in while he thought of his best response.

Rogers face cleared like a light had gone off in his head. "Ohh…you did *that*, Grayson? You were willing to put our lives, Nadine's life, on the line like that? For a few extra bargaining chips?"

"No. Absolutely not." Grayson stood up straighter. "I never manipulated you. I didn't set up what happened. But yes, I took advantage of the situation when it presented itself. No one made you grab my gun to try to shoot your way out of there. But when you did, yes, I used it to my advantage. Besides, I wanted Kylie to trust me. If I took the gun and you went for me, who knows who would've ended up hurt—or killed."

Winter went toe-to-toe with him. Not a good turn of events. "Maybe you should try putting me down now. We'll see who will come out on top."

"I'm not looking for a fight with you, Winter." Grayson's calm voice resonated through the alley. "That was the last thing I ever wanted. Even if you can't see that, it's true."

Rogers took a deep breath. "Just wait a second. Winter's right, you *did* manipulate the situation. Your actions put Kylie in a position where she couldn't say no to you or the general. Not if she ever wanted her ship back. You knew if it went down like that, she'd have no choice but to go along with your mission."

Grayson could see how protective Rogers was of Kylie—it was admirable. Some time, a long time ago, *that* would've been him. But…

He licked his lips and kept his voice even and steady. "Like I said, I didn't make it go down the way it did. No one made Winter pull a gun on me. Just like no one made you attempt to do the same. What happened, happened. Can't we just leave it at that?"

Rogers and Winter glanced at each other. Grayson held his breath as he waited for a response. <*You made sure that Winter had the smallest quarters. That ticking noise in his room kept him from a deep sleep,*> Jerrod said. <*And you made certain he saw your pistol, had clear access to it.*>

<*They don't need to know that. A stronger man would've made a more rational decision. No matter what I did, I still didn't make him grab my sidearm. No one is all powerful,*> Grayson replied.

<*Sometimes I forget how calculating you can be. And if Kylie hadn't done what she did to save your life?*>

<*She always would. I know her better than she knows herself.*>

<*Perhaps,*> Jerrod responded. <*We're not dead, so I guess that is saying something.*>

"You know what? Bygones," Rogers said. "We've all done things we're not proud of. Am I right?"

"You're wrong," Winter said with his hands balled into fists. "When we get back to the ship, Kylie's hearing about this. I don't want you anywhere near me, Grayson. You hear me?"

Grayson avoided his gaze. "All right."

"But I also need to keep an eye on you," Winter glowered. "So, I guess I'm not going to get everything I want. And when I don't get everything I want..." Winter slammed his fist into his open palm. "You better be on your best behavior. Am I clear, brother?"

Grayson nodded. "Crystal."

<*Run,*> Kylie said over the Link. The nervous tremor in her voice said everything Grayson needed to know. It also stopped him in his tracks.

<*Kylie, what's the matter?*>

<*Who says we aren't running already?*> Rogers replied, then glanced at Grayson and Winter, cocking his chin at the far end of the alley. Without question the men began to jog toward it.

<*You're being watched. The ship might be clear. If you can get to it, take off, and I'll signal when we're ready for emergency evac.*>

Rogers and Winter groaned across the Link. Rogers then said, <*It's not good when she defaults to military speak.*>

<*Lana?*> Grayson asked Kylie.

<*Not here and I don't...*> Kylie's transmission faded. No interference. No nothing. It was just gone.

<*Kylie?*> Grayson tried to keep the swell of panic under control. <*Jerrod, can you get anything on her?*>

<*I can't. It's as if she just...disappeared. I'll keep trying, but the comm management AI here are unhelpful and rude.*>

<*Pinpoint her location if you can.*>

"Captain's orders," Rogers said he peered out of the alley into the street beyond. "We get to the shuttle and take it up to the ship."

"She might be the captain, but I'm in charge of this mission. We don't leave Jericho without Kylie," Grayson said. "Or Nadine."

Winter snorted. "If you think this is going to get you in my good graces, you're wrong."

Grayson opened his mouth to respond but thought better of it, and silently followed Rogers and Winter onto the street. They blended in with the foot traffic, working their way toward the thoroughfare that led outside the dome to the docks, when a voice called out from across the street.

"There, I see them!"

"Aw shit," Rogers cursed, and broke into a run.

Grayson focused his augmented eyes at the crowd across the street. He saw a man, holding a rather lethal-looking rifle, waving to another group of well-armed men. Grayson didn't pause for a longer look and took off after Rogers and Winter.

A shot rang out from the other side of the street, and a window to his left shattered.

<These guys are shooting with civilians around!> Grayson exclaimed.

<We're in Ventrella District,> Rogers replied from fifty meters ahead as he ducked through a restaurant's front door. *<There are no civilians, just people who want to rob or kill you, and people who are waiting to be paid enough to make it worth their while to rob and kill you.>*

Winter followed Rogers through the door, and Grayson wasn't far behind.

<I'm beginning to understand that,> he replied.

Inside the restaurant, Rogers and Winter were nowhere in sight, but the trail of overturned tables and angry wait-staff was easy to follow. He burst into the kitchen, ran past a pair of yelling chefs, and out the back door into another alley.

Rogers and Winter were waiting for him.

"Faster, soldier boy!" Rogers yelled and took off again.

<*An alert has gone out city-wide for your arrest, or deaths, whichever is more convenient,*> Jerrod said. <*It wasn't just sent to the police—such as they are in a place like this.*>

<*Why am I not surprised?*> Grayson replied.

<*A million credits bounty—I wonder if* **I** *could turn you in.*>

<*Not funny, Jerrod.*>

The trio of men dashed down the alley as the sounds of pursuit spilled out from the restaurant they had passed through.

"We've got company," Grayson called ahead as pulse blast hit a garbage bin next to him and bowled it over. "They're shooting at us!"

"Well, shoot back!" Winter hollered.

Grayson pulled the pistol from the holster inside his jacket and twisted, firing several rounds at their pursuers, aiming high—no need to kill anyone, just slow them down.

A volley of weapons fire came back in response, and Grayson ducked behind a large steel bin. Ahead, Rogers leaned around the corner at the end of the alley, firing wildly down the street. Winter was wrestling with a man almost as large as he was and Grayson dashed from his cover, and punched Winter's attacker in the head, pulling the albino away and to safety.

Beamfire lanced down the alley and sliced the man Winter had been wrestling with to ribbons.

Winter let out a long string of curses, before giving Grayson a smile that was almost warm. "Still not in my good graces, but you're getting there."

DOUBLE DOUBLE-CROSS

STELLAR DATE: 09.06.8947 (Adjusted Years)
LOCATION: City of Montral, Jericho
REGION: Gedri System, Silstrand Alliance

"We didn't find anything out of order," the captain of the squad said. "She's on the up-and-up, just like she said."

Slowly, careful to make no sudden movement, Kylie released her hold on Maverick's throat. His eyes, still wide, followed her movements as she stepped back. "I told you we could be trusted." She adjusted the hem of her dress. "I'm hoping now we can put this little disagreement behind us."

Maverick didn't say anything, but the rage behind his eyes was easy to see.

"C'mon, Mav. You're getting way too paranoid. Maybe if you went off world a little more often you'd realize—"

"Nothing was out of order, you say?" Maverick's voice was too calm as he turned to address his men.

The captain nodded. "Paperwork, vids, cargo. Everything was as it should be."

"Nothing?" Maverick's eyebrows furrowed. "Nothing? Since when has a junker been so squeaky clean?" He turned his gaze to Nadine and then Kylie. "My girls might be gorgeous, a pleasure to look at and more to touch, but they've never been clean. You're thieves—you and your crew of misfits. So, the question that begs asking is…why'd you doctor the records?"

He approached Kylie, and she backed up. Holding out her hand, until Maverick walked into it. "You think I have the time necessary to go around doctoring logs, vids? If I had stolen freight, why didn't your men find it?"

"I don't know, so why don't you answer the question? What are you hiding!"

"All very good questions." A new voice came from the room's entrance. Kylie looked over Maverick's shoulder at the newcomer. Tall and wearing heavy combat armor—enough to take anything Maverick's guards could throw at him—his face showed splotchy skin, and his lips were pulled back in a menacing snarl. "My guess is they've come for the girl."

"Girl?" Maverick asked with a twist of confusion. "What girl?"

Kylie reeled at the thought. He didn't know? He didn't have Lana? He must've be faking, he was a liar. If he didn't have Lana, who did?

Without a moment's hesitation, the man fired his railgun in short bursts, mowing down the room's guards before they could fire a shot. He turned the gun on the squad captain.

"Sorry, but I don't answer questions. I'm the one looking for answers."

The squad captain reached for his pistol, but he was dead before his hand managed to pull it free.

Who the hell was this intruder? He had the look of a bounty hunter, but it wasn't anyone Kylie knew, and that surprised her. Anyone brazen enough to walk into The Shade—not to mention able to successfully pull it off—should be well known. But this man wasn't; he was a mystery.

"Who the hell do you think you are? You think you can just walk in here and kill my men? You'll be dead for this? Dead!" Maverick screamed and reached for the plasma sword that had fallen when Kylie grabbed him.

"I wouldn't worry about me; it's you who won't be leaving this room alive. I guess from your reaction and stress indicators, you really don't know what girl I'm talking about." The man scowled, and his eyes showed some small amount of compassion. "It's too bad. The GFF needs you to hold things together, but I really don't."

He was going to kill Maverick.

"Get down!" Kylie screamed and kicked Maverick out of the way and he spun away as the man fired his railgun. The blast grazed past Kylie's hip, the heat of its passage blistering her skin. Maverick wasn't so lucky—the round hit him in the back. He screamed as he fell onto his stomach, half on the sofa and half off.

"You're next," the man said as he trained his gun on the two women. Defenseless, Kylie searched the room for something she could use against this man. Maverick's plasma sword was useless against the bounty hunter's railgun. He'd fill her full of holes before she got in range. Then, her eyes lit upon a pulse rifle one of the guards had dropped. It was just a few meters away…

Nadine screamed and charged at the bounty hunter just as Kylie lunged and snatched up the rifle. <*Get down! Stop! Nadine, no!*>

But it was too late. Nadine took a shot right in her gut and collapsed on the ground just as Kylie fired off her own shot at the man. His armor took the brunt of the blast and he trained his railgun on her. Kylie knew she was a dead woman.

"Seems we're at an impasse, Captain Rhoads," the bounty hunter said in a low voice.

She glanced down at Nadine, moaning and clasping her stomach as blood seeped out between her fingers. Sweat beaded on her brow, and her lips were flecked with red. <*Why, Nadine? Why?*>

<*He was going to kill you.*>

Like Kylie cared about that? Had she spent the last five years making sure Nadine was okay only for it to end like this? She bit her lip and looked back up at the man who now held both their lives in his hands. "Tell me what you want."

"I can help your friend if you help me. My ship isn't far. I can get her on board, get her treated, but it's going to take a sacrifice from you. Are you willing to make a trade?"

A trade? Kylie wasn't going to barter for Nadine like she was an object. "She's a person you piece of shit. You help her—"

"I need more information on the girl. Where she is. Where to find her. From here on out, you work for me. Soon as you find out where Lana is, you can have your friend back."

"What's Lana to you?"

The bounty hunter smiled. "You don't know what she is! Oh, this is priceless. Since you're in the thick of it, and clueless, let me take this mess off your hands. It's more trouble than you want, trust me. If you agree, I'll take the missus to my ship, heal her, and contact you when all is well…but if you think of shooting me on my way out, I'll pull her head off nice and slow. Deal?"

Kylie stared at Nadine's pain-filled face. There was no real choice to be made. She nodded and lowered her weapon as a show of good faith. "Deal."

"Good. I'll be in touch." The bounty hunter swung his railgun over his shoulder and scooped Nadine up, draping her over his other shoulder. She cried out in pain and Kylie took an involuntary step forward.

"If she dies…"

The man laughed. "You're not really in a position to threaten anyone, but I understand you have pretenses to keep up—you're a big, tough girl after all. Oh, and don't try contacting her over your private Link. The connection has been terminated."

Then, like someone flipped a switch, the man disappeared. Kylie had never seen stealth tech like that before. Even Nadine was gone. There were no footfalls or anything; they were just gone.

Kylie pushed the impossibility from her mind—there was no time to waste. She turned Maverick over and saw that blood was pooling on his plush leather sofa. "Maverick!" She slapped his cheeks. "That bastard has Nadine. It's up to you now, do you understand?"

He groaned. "The round…it went clear through…" He grunted and held his hand to the hole in his chest to stem the flow of blood.

"Your nano will heal you if I let them. Answer me, Mav, do you know about the girl? Did you kidnap a girl from Silstrand?"

"Silstrand?" Maverick shook his head with a cringe. "If I knew, I'd tell you."

"Then who? If someone in the GFF kidnapped her, who would it be? Where would they be keeping her? Maverick, wake up!" Kylie slapped his cheeks.

"Harken," he groaned. "She's had a side project the last few months…I just thought…bored." Maverick started to slip away into unconsciousness.

"Where? Where's she running this project? Where!"

"Sending the information….to your Link…" Maverick's head rolled to the side. Kylie sat back on her heels and read the data as it came in. It all pointed to a dwarf planet out in the Gedri's scattered disc. Nothing but a cold ball of ice. Not terraformed. No significant population—the perfect place to hide something big, but a simple girl?

Lana couldn't be just a girl. No one went to that much trouble for something so plain. So, the real question was, what had Grayson gotten them into?

"What the hell?" an angry voice called out from behind her.

The voice was unmistakable, and Kylie raised her hands before slowly rising. She turned and saw Harken standing at the room's entrance. Her mouth hung open as she took in the sight of Maverick's body and the blood-stained carpet where Nadine had lain only moments ago. She glanced at the fallen guards and a sinister grin crept across her face.

"You stay *right* there. Don't move a muscle," she barked as her eyes ticked to the side, her tell for holding a Link conversation.

She was summoning reinforcements. Kylie grabbed the pulse rifle she had dropped. "Don't, Harken. I didn't do this!"

"Like hell you didn't. Stay where you are, Rhoads. You're not going anywhere!"

Kylie frowned, Harken didn't seem to care that she held a weapon—though the woman probably believed there was no way out for Kylie. She was almost right.

Without warning, Kylie fired a shot at Harken and then another at the room's window. She didn't even look back to see if her first shot had hit before she leaped over the shattered plas and down to the floor below. There was no time to question Harken—not if she valued her freedom, and her life. The only thought on her mind was to get out of The Shade.

And fast.

<*Guys I'm going to need extraction sooner than expected!*> Kylie called to her team as she pushed her way through the men and women in the VIP fetish party, eliciting cries of both anger and excitement. She crashed through a door, into a back stairwell and dashed down the steps as the lights around changed from a soft orange-amber glow to red and a klaxon wailed.

<*Get to the north docks, we'll pick you up there,*> Rogers mental tone sounded out of breath as he replied in her mind. <*Uh…the cab stand near that shitty shipping company we used one time.*>

"Grab her! There she is!" a voice called from further up the stairs, and a shot rang out, ricocheting off the steps at her feet.

"Lethal force? Really?" Kylie muttered as she returned fire with her pulse rifle. A curse came from above, and she hoped one of her shots had at least left a bruise. She kept to the outside wall as more shots rang out and the sounds of heavy bootsteps echoed down the stairwell.

She couldn't believe how quickly things had gone from bad to worse. Kylie stuffed her fears and doubt down deep—she needed to focus on Nadine. Do what was necessary to get Nadine back.

Kylie glanced up the stairs and saw a guard leaning over the railing one level up to get a clear shot at her. She didn't give him the chance and fired at his legs with her pulse rifle. The blast made his limbs go numb, and he lost his balance and tumbled over the railing with a scream.

One down, hundreds to go. She just had to get through the Red Zone without being incapacitated, killed, or captured.

Three things that were going to be near impossible.

She raced down the final flight stairs, past the unconscious body of the fallen man, and burst out into the main floor of the club. The music was still blasting, and the sea of bodies still writhed on the dance floor, but as she stood, looking for the best path through the never-ending party, shots rang out, and the patrons near her screamed as the glass lining the wall shattered.

"Shit!" Kylie swore and dove behind the bar to her right. She hunkered down and saw she wasn't alone. A woman wearing The Shade's uniform of thigh-high boots and a skimpy dress that didn't even cover her ass cheeks, crouched nearby with hands clasped over her ears.

"Great party." Kylie cringed as the weapons fire renewed and bottles above them shattered.

"They're looking for you, aren't they?" the woman asked.

Kylie nodded. "You won't tell, will you?"

"Your dress kind of makes you hard to hide, no offense."

Kylie glanced down at her blue glowing dress, now lit up like a neon sign. "None taken."

The woman grabbed a fallen bottle and pulled the stopper out with her teeth. "To a good party! Who needs a job anyway?"

Nice girl. Kylie crawled away, using the bar for cover. At the end, she ducked behind the chairs and tables lining the wall and ran for the door.

"Hey! Stop!" One of the guards at the entrance called out and Kylie clocked him as she ran past. He went down, but she didn't look back to see if he stayed that way.

The other man grabbed for her, but she ducked to the side and dashed out into the settling gloom of Montral's night. She didn't pause to admire the glow of the city's lights reflecting on the dome, just raced down the stairs as projectile and beam rounds filled the night around her.

By some miracle, she wasn't hit by the wild shots from Maverick's guards. Ahead, a pair of men on hoverbikes were pulled up at the corner, talking to a couple of women. Kylie took a deep breath and charged straight at them.

Her shoulder slammed into the first man and knocked him off his bike. She leaped onto its seat, cranked the throttle, and raced down the street, heading for the Red Zone's exit.

Over her eyes, Kylie's HUD flashed a dozen warnings. She was speeding, she was wanted for attempted murder, her crew was wanted for a variety of crimes...and the *Dauntless* was impounded.

Things had just gotten even more complicated.

<Change of plan...again...> Kylie messaged Rogers. *<Get to the ship and break the station lock on it. I'll get up there myself.>*

<Captain...> Rogers began, but Kylie didn't give him a chance to finish.

<Rogers, not now. I don't have time to explain. When I get up there, I'll be coming in hot! You have to trust me on this. Do what I say and secure our ship. Get her ready to tear out of there.>

They had to, because if they didn't, Kylie might never get Nadine back. Already her anxiety was mounting. Already Kylie wanted nothing more than to hear Nadine was okay, to listen to her lover's voice one more time. Even to listen to Nadine yell about how stupid Kylie was for making this shitty deal with Grayson would be better than not knowing if she was okay.

Kylie wondered if she really had been stupid to agree to any of this.

Most likely.

Ahead, the security arch and checkpoint for entry into the Red Zone loomed. A large truck blocked the road—undergoing an inspection, from the looks of it. Kylie didn't hesitate. She ramped her bike over the curb and crashed into a crowd of people, shooting wildly at the guards and police ahead.

No one cared about casualties. Not her, and certainly not Maverick's men as they fired back. Kylie poured on all the speed the hoverbike could muster and smashed it right into the large, heavily-modded guard who had given her and Nadine a hard time when they had entered the Red Zone.

"Shiiiiiit!" she screamed as she flew through the air and slammed into the window of a groundcar waiting behind the truck. The window shattered, but broke Kylie's fall well enough that her limbs all still seemed to work. She didn't bother looking to see if she was being pursued as she pulled herself off the car and onto her feet.

Getting back to the ship was all that mattered.

*****

Bullets flew all around Kylie as she dove behind an overturned table. Her pulse rifle was long gone, its batteries depleted two gunfights ago. The slug thrower she had found somewhere along the way was out of ammo and she tossed it aside. She looked around and saw a fallen plasma rifle at her feet.

One thing was for sure about Montral: a loaded weapon was never far away.

Plasma rifles had terrible aim, but shooting star-stuff at people also had a way of getting them to fall back. How many people had to die because of General Samuel's daughter? And why was everyone going through so much trouble to get their hands on some snot-nosed brat?

Grayson, the general, they had to be leaving out part of the story. Maybe that had been a given, and maybe Kylie should've pushed harder. Sure, they hadn't given her much choice, so maybe Kylie hadn't stopped to consider it. Hadn't stopped to think that maybe Grayson—with all their history—might not be telling the whole truth.

If they survived, if she saw him again, Kylie would make him explain himself.

She fired several shots. One took out a woman near the bar's door. The second tore through the guy standing at the window. The third, directed at the guy by the vending machine, missed. She ducked back down behind her cover as the patron returned fire. It was as if the whole city was after her.

OK, maybe *this* plasma rifle wasn't so bad.

"Why don't you just come out and make it easy?" the man called out.

Kylie fired blindly around the edge of the table. "I don't believe in doing things the easy way, if you couldn't tell."

He didn't reply, and she peered around the edge of the table to see him lying on his side, a hole burned through his chest.

"Well, lucky me," she muttered and dashed around the table, leaping over the man to jump through the shattered window.

Her legs ached as she landed on the street and the pain reminded Kylie that her arms were scratched and bloody. Her chest heaved as she bent over and caught her breath. She looked down at what little remained of her dress and thanked what gods were in the stars that she had worn underwear. No need to be flashing her nethers at people as she ran from them.

Nadine's going to kill me for ruining this dress; she really liked it on me, she thought and then stopped herself. That was if she ever saw Nadine again.

Kylie forced the thoughts from her mind and looked down the empty street. It was late, and she had gotten past most of the groups hunting her, but that didn't mean she couldn't run into more.

Going left would link up to a broad boulevard that would take her straight to the north docks—a smaller port than the one near Ventrella District, but closer to her current location. However, that road would put her out in the open. To her right was a warren of streets and smaller commercial buildings, but she didn't know the best path through them. The last thing she needed was to end up in a dead-end alley with a band of mercs after her.

She could query the city's nav NSAI, but that would be like sending up a flare announcing where she was. It sure would be handy to have an AI right about then.

Of course, she knew someone with an AI, didn't she? *<Grayson? Can you tell where the hell I'm going?>* She had to swallow all sorts of pride just to talk to him right then.

<Kind of busy at the moment.>

Kylie's eyebrow arched, and she let out an angry breath. *<Multitask, for star's sakes. If you can track my movements, you can tell I'm still in the thick of it. I need an out.>*

<You…all right…go straight through the building across the street. Then you'll need to take a left, right, damn…look, Jerrod will send you a map. Are you okay? How's Nadine?>

Kylie held a shaky breath. *<One thing at a time. How's that ship-taking-back going?>*

<It's going.>

Well, at least he wasn't dead yet. *<Rogers? Winter?>*

<Alive and kicking.>

Good news. Kylie let them get back to it, and dashed across the street to the building on the map. It was a low-rent apartment building, and she jimmied the door open before slipping through the long hall to the back.

She followed Jerrod's map until she rounded a corner and saw a group of mercs who had set up a roadblock. The street had a long line of groundcars backed up, and the mercs were checking them over before letting them through. A group of pedestrians were also milling about on the sidewalk, waiting for the heavily-armed men and women to let them past.

Kylie pulled up the map and looked for an alternate route. There wasn't a good one. Any way around this stop would put her on busier streets, and if this one was guarded, those would be, as well.

She leaned against a building, and considered going to the rooftops, when she noticed a partially hidden symbol on the building across the street. It was cleverly blended into the sign, but a keen eye could spot it.

It belonged to The Mark—the almost-defunct pirate outfit. It wasn't one of their more commonly used identifiers, but she had seen it on some cargo in one of their ships she had salvaged. Had been a good haul. A lot of fresh fruit and vegetables on it—even though someone had made a mess of the produce in one of the holds before the ship had slowly frozen in the dark.

She walked calmly across the street and checked the building's entrance for automated weapons. Nothing seemed to be visible—which made sense in what appeared to be a low-key stash house. She passed one of the Mark tokens she had picked up from that ship, hoping it would still work.

It didn't. She tried a few others she had gotten over the years, and just when she thought she might have to break in the old-fashioned way, one of the older tokens worked, and the mag-seal on the door unlocked.

"Score," she whispered to herself. About time something went her way.

The building was a maze of halls and small rooms. Most were filled with junk, but in one she saw the symbol again, hidden above the door frame. Bingo. The room was filled with stacks of chairs and tables, and Kylie moved them aside as carefully as possible.

Behind them was another door. This one was also sealed, and she Linked to its control pad and passed the same token as the front door, praying whoever set up this safe house wasn't too clever.

For the second time that night, her luck held, and the door swung open, revealing a treasure trove of weapons and armor.

"Finally!" Kylie exclaimed as she stripped out of the remains of her dress, and flipped through the racks of armor, looking for something light-weight, but still able to deal with beams and ballistics.

Most of the armor was heavy and bulky—and made for people a lot larger than her. Then she spotted a Sherman 843A full-body armor set and picked it out. Though better than the others, Kylie wasn't a big fan of the Sherman 800 series. The ballistic mesh went over the ablative plates and always bound at the joints.

She decided to take a look through the rest of the crates in case there was anything else. On the fourth crate, Kylie struck gold. Inside was a Trylodyne IA99 stealth suit and ballistic layer. She bit her lip, hoping it was sized right. The armor was worth half the value of the *Dauntless.* With it, she could slip right past the mercs guarding the adjacent street.

She shook out the ballistic under-layer and held it up. It was near perfect. Maybe a bit large, but it should snug up once she got it on. Kylie pulled it on and it made a physical connection with the hard Link at the base of her skull, courtesy of the SFF years ago. For the first time, she was glad for it as the armor wouldn't have worked without a hard Link.

She pulled the hood over her face—grimacing as the rebreather filled her mouth—and the armor snugged up and seal the hood to the full-body suit. Checks scrolled across her HUD and she saw that the suit's battery only had a half charge. It read good for ten hours, which should be enough to get back to the *Dauntless*. If it wasn't, she'd be dead.

It ran through a full diagnostic on itself, and her body, testing her reflexes and providing suggestions for the best augmentations. Kylie accepted the defaults, recognizing that this suit expected the wearer to have an internal AI to manage its complexities.

Still a lot better than her tattered dress.

Once the base layer finished its diagnostics, it indicated it was ready for the stealth layer. Kylie pulled the slick, oily-feeling layer overtop, and shrugged it into place. It self-sealed and adhered to the under-layer. Kylie held her hands up, now seeing through small optics on the outer-layer's hood. Her hands glistened in the room's dim light, and she allowed a small smile as they turned a matte gray, and then disappeared.

This was going to be fun.

The suit wasn't as good as the ones SSF black-ops units were allocated, but it could fool optical and IR detection, and provided the scan wasn't good, it would blend on UV bands as well.

Kylie practiced breathing through the rebreather, drawing on her training in the SSF. She hated the device, but it was necessary to contain all the heat her body produced—it wouldn't do to hide her body's heat just to have her breath pointing her out to any IR scans. However, it meant that the largest inhalation she could take was just a mouthful of air. It made for a lot of short, quick breaths, and she had to keep her breathing to a gentle rhythm and resist the feeling that she was hyperventilating.

The armor had two pouches on her thighs that could conceal a pair of pistols, and she selected a set of high-caliber slug-throwers for close combat. Inside the armor's case lay three combat knives, and she slipped them into hidden sheaths below her breasts. One of the features of the armor was that it moved her 'outer sensing' layer from her skin to the stealth layer's surface. The armor now felt like her skin, and secreting the blades away gave the uncomfortable sensation of sliding them into her body.

The last item in the case was a Spectre U5RA multi-function rifle. It had light kinetic, laser beam, electron beam, and pulse modes—all capable of firing in stealth. The rifle was also coated with the same material as her outer stealth layer, and when she picked it up, it faded from optical view.

Her HUD updated to show the weapon's loadout and heat levels. A red line showed where the weapon would be too warm for the stealth systems to mask. She didn't have the tech specs handy, but hoped it would allow for more than just a few shots.

Kylie slid the weapon onto a pair of latches on her back and filled every ammo pouch on the armor.

If she hadn't been running for her life, sick with worry about Nadine and her crew, she would have been giddy with how powerful the armor made her feel.

The reminder redirected her thoughts to what lay ahead. Get past the mercs, get a shuttle up to Laerdo Station, get the *Dauntless* free, then find Lana and trade her for Nadine.... It was a lot to accomplish.

The realization tightened her chest, and she forced herself to ease her breathing once more—shove down all the questions circling in her mind. They were in this mess, and she had to get them out.

She slipped out of the safe house and headed back onto the street, glad no one was around to see the outer door open and close on its own. She set a new token to the door's lock. On the off-chance, she was ever in Montral again, having her own personal arsenal on hand could come in handy.

She crept down the street, careful not to make any noise. The suit had sound-suppressions systems, but they required the wearer to have internal AI to control the remote sound-canceling drones. That was something Kylie would just have to do without.

She looked down the street where the mercs had set up their checkpoint. A Montral police cruiser was parked nearby and a cop was arguing with a lithe woman who seemed to be in charge of the merc group.

The sounds of their heated discussion reached her suit's augmented hearing, and she smirked behind the mask.

"Look," the cop said, his voice rising in anger as he spoke. "I don't care if Harken put out the mother of all bounties on Captain Rhoads, you can't just set up your own barricades and checkpoints. That's our job!"

"Like hell it is," the woman retorted. "You just want to get the bounty yourself. Any idiot can see that. You want to take us on? Go for it. There'll just be one more corpse in the gutter come morning."

"You think I'm here alone?" the cop replied. "Look above you. We have gunships everywhere. I say the word and your barricade turns into a pile of debris decorated with your guts. Now, take it down and get out of here."

The merc leader responded with her own threats of surface-to-air launchers and Kylie ignored the cop's response. In five minutes, they'd be claiming to have the might of entire armies at their disposal. The augmented vision Kylie's suit provided did confirm that the Montral police had a healthy number of gunships in the air, but none were in their immediate vicinity.

Their argument, however, provided a great distraction, and she disappeared into the milling crowd, only getting bumped twice. Luckily, half the pedestrians were drunk, and no one took much notice of being jostled or brushed past.

Kylie had just made it past the merc's barricade when a message flashed on her HUD and fed into her mind over the suit's hard Link.

<Power reserves at 5%. Disabling active camouflage.>

Shit! What happened to the ten-hour charge? No surprise, though, when a suit sits in storage for years.

"Hey! You there. Stop!" yelled a heavily-armored merc who stood just five meters away.

With the now-pointless rebreather in her mouth, Kylie couldn't give a snarky quip in response. Instead, she pulled one of the handguns from her thigh and fired three shots at the man, hitting him once center mass, then in the upper chest, and a final time in the neck.

She hadn't meant to let the weapon pull up so much as she'd fired. It had more kick than she'd expected, but the result was hard to argue with. The first two shots hadn't even dented his armor, but the third—by some miracle—found a weak spot in his armor and a spray of blood erupted from of his neck.

The man fell like a rock, but a dozen of his compatriots were already firing on Kylie as she raced across the street behind the dubious cover of a parked groundcar. She slid the pistol back into its holster, pulled the UR5A rifle off her back and fired several electron-beam shots over the car in the merc's general vicinity.

She heard cursing as the relativistic electrons hit the barricade with explosive force. She hoped she hadn't hit any of the pedestrians, but then again, they took their lives in their own hands being on the streets of Montral this late.

Return fire peppered the car, and Kylie flinched as three jagged holes appeared in the metal of the door two inches from her left arm. In another minute, it wouldn't offer much cover at all.

<Power at 20%. Reengaging active camouflage.>

The suit powered the active stealth back up, and Kylie wondered if it was in The Mark's hands because it was faulty surplus. She didn't give it any further thought and made a break for it as soon as there was a lull in the merc's weapon fire.

The armor's stealth held until she got a hundred meters down the street and around a corner, then failed again. Kylie didn't look back to see if the enemy was fanning out in search of her. She took off at a brisk run, the armor's muscle augments still operating at full power.

At her current pace—provided she didn't run into any more snags—it was still twenty minutes to the north docks. She had wasted almost thirty minutes obtaining the armor and maneuvering past that barricade. She wanted to ask Rogers how things were going with the *Dauntless,* but he hadn't sent her any distress signals and hadn't confirmed that he had secured it, either—which meant he was busy and didn't need a distraction.

She began to jog along the streets, the armor's exo-muscles giving her extra bounce and speed. Her HUD showed twenty minutes to the north docks. When she got there, she just had to figure out how to slip past the security and steal a ship.

And not get shot out of the sky on her way to the *Dauntless*.

VENTRELLA

STELLAR DATE: 09.06.8947 (Adjusted Years)
LOCATION: City of Montral, Jericho
REGION: Gedri System, Silstrand Alliance

Grayson looked back down the alley, checking if their latest pursuers were still closing in. With the bounty on their heads, the entire district would be out for them. He wasn't sure how Rogers and Winter had thought they'd make it to the docks on foot.

As if on cue, a groundcar pulled up at the head of the alley, and Betty—the waitress from the restaurant—peered out the window. "You guys want a lift, or what?" she asked with a plastic-looking smile.

"Right on time, Betty," Rogers said with a grin as he ran around the car and jumped into the passenger seat. "Not only do you make the meanest bacon, but you also make the meanest getaway-driver."

Grayson and Winter piled into the back, and Betty took off before the doors even closed.

"What are you doing here?" Grayson exclaimed as he fastened his safety belt.

"Saving you boys from certain death," Betty said with a laugh.

"Yeah, I get that," Grayson grunted as Betty whipped around a corner and he slammed into the inside of the car. "But why?"

"'Cause I don't want to see you get curb-stomped into Ventrella's landscape, sweetcheeks," Betty said in her trilling voice. "Plus, Rogers told me where to meet you back at the restaurant."

Grayson cast Rogers a searching look. "You did? I didn't see it."

"I have Link, too, soldier boy," Rogers said and grimaced as Betty careened around another corner. "I knew we couldn't get out on foot. It would take all day."

"You offer this sort of service for all your customers?" Grayson asked.

Betty laughed, perhaps the first real laugh he had heard from her lips. "Hardly, dear. I owe Rogers here for a thing awhile back." Grayson saw her expression grow hard, and she glanced back at him. "He and Winter get a free ride, but now you owe me one, Alliance-man."

"That obvious?" Grayson asked with a sigh.

"As the nose on your face," Betty replied. "Mind you, I used to be a sergeant in the SSF, so I know the stick-up-the-ass look of an SA officer any day."

"What?" Grayson asked. "A sergeant? What outfit?"

"The 43rd None-Ya-Business, sweetie," Betty laughed.

"Betty runs a merc outfit that operates out of Jericho," Rogers explained.

Grayson sat back in his seat. A former SA sergeant, and running a merc outfit? Betty's sexy outfit and curves had done a number on his powers of observation. Probably the whole point of her get-up.

"So that's your restaurant, then?" Grayson asked.

"Well, not on the official record," Betty replied with a laugh. "Oh, checkpoint ahead. Someone shoot at the cops, okay?"

Betty aimed for a space between the two parked police cruisers—which was almost wide enough for her car. Grayson leaned out the window and fired over the heads of the police, and at their cars. Even though the cops were all on the take, there was no way he wanted a police killing in a Silstrand system on his record. At the last minute, one of the cruisers lifted into the air, and Betty ducked her car into the new opening. A pair of turrets slid out from the cruiser's underside and opened fire on them.

"Shit!" Rogers exclaimed. "What did Kylie do? These guys aren't messing around."

"Knowing Kylie, something that we're all going to live to regret," Winter muttered.

"Die to regret is more like it," Rogers said in agreement.

Betty swerved down an alley too narrow for the flying cruiser to follow and glanced at her passengers. "Oh, she killed Maverick. Harken's in charge of his little outfit now. Real shit show. Harken is one hell of a bitch. Mav knew how to run things nice and easy."

"Killed him?" Grayson exclaimed. "Killed him!"

"That's the official word, though there are some conflicting reports that he escaped death by a hair. Either way, Harken's pulling the strings for now. Girl's always wanted his power and now she's seized it."

"To more pressing matters—the cops are gonna have a gunship here in no time," Rogers said. "When we hit the end of this alley, we're going to be a smoking crater."

"You'd think this is my first high-speed chase through Jericho?" Betty laughed. "Hold on!"

As she spoke, Betty cranked the wheel, and the car fishtailed through a narrow passage and into a sizable garage filled with cars.

"Out, fast!" she hollered, and everyone piled out of the car as if it was on fire. Once they were clear, the getaway car tore back out into the alley and continued on its way.

"Nice…a diversion," Winter said with a nod.

"Yeah, let's hope it lasts long enough to actually be diverting," Betty said as she sashayed to a limousine and held open one of the back doors. "Get in. We'll take this out the front, and be on our way."

Inside was a bar, with bottles lined on top, and weapons lined below. In the front, a man peered over the divider.

"Where to, Miss Betty?" he asked.

"We're going to head to that place down near the boulevard out of the dome, but take the scenic route," Betty replied.

"Yes, ma'am."

"Do you mind?" Winter asked, gesturing to the bar.

"Hands off, Meathead," Betty admonished. "That's for paying clients. And you need to stay sharp. We're not out of this yet."

The driver eased the limousine around the dozens of cars before exiting the garage onto the street in front of the building. They didn't spend long on the ground, as the car's grav lifts soon powered on and pulled them into the air.

"Let's just hope we don't get shot down," Rogers said as he looked at the police gunships hovering over the city.

"Not going to happen," Betty said. "They know not to hit a car like this. Besides, they don't know you have my kind of help."

"They must be suspicious, though," Grayson commented.

Before anyone could reply, a gunship only a few hundred meters away fired a missile at a ground target, and a fireball erupted in Montral's night, reflecting on the dome overhead.

"Not for a bit," Betty said with a smile. "Gonna take them awhile to sift through that wreckage to see if you're in what's left."

"Damn," Rogers whispered. "That's some serious shit."

"You should spend some more time in Jericho," Betty said with a frown. "Stuff like that is getting a bit more common here. Gonna get a lot worse if Harken really is in charge now."

"Sounds like a good reason to spend less time here, not more," Winter said with a frown.

Betty laughed. "You? I thought you liked this sort of shit."

"Not this much," Winter replied.

They rode in silence for the rest of the journey, setting down outside a nondescript apartment complex near the edge of Montral's dome.

"I've passed you the token to get in, Rogers," Betty said. "Head into the basement, and then to the southeast corner. There's a hidden passage that will get you into the maintenance tunnels. From there, follow my crew's marks to the exit on the far side of the dome. You should be pretty close to the dock your shuttle's at."

"Thanks," Rogers said and placed a light kiss on Betty's cheek. "Now I owe *you* one."

"Rogers, dear, this was on the house—for you at least," Betty replied. "But you, soldier boy—Colonel Grayson—I'll call on you sometime for you to return the favor."

Grayson wondered how she had learned both his rank and name so quickly. Not knowing what to say, he simply nodded before following Rogers and Winter out of the car. They stood on the curb and watched it lift away into the sky before Winter laughed.

"C'mon, boys. That was the easy part. We still have to get our ship out of lockdown."

LIFTOFF

STELLAR DATE: 09.07.8947 (Adjusted Years)
LOCATION: City of Montral, Jericho
REGION: Gedri System, Silstrand Alliance

Kylie cursed silently as the armor's stealth system shut off again. Having unreliable stealth tech was worse than none at all, and she set the system to stay off. It took on a matte black sheen that was still better than nothing, and she prayed it would be enough.

Ahead lay her final obstacle before she got out of Montral's dome: a fully-staffed police checkpoint guarded the road leading to the north docks.

She tried to reach Grayson again, but failed to make a connection. Rogers and Winter were offline as well. There were only two possible reasons for it. Either they were dead, or they had made it to their shuttle and had severed their connections so they could approach Laerdo Station as stealthily as possible.

She prayed it was the latter. This mission had gone badly enough without her entire team getting captured by…well, by Harken.

Kylie pushed the worry from her mind and surveyed the police checkpoint. There were at least twenty cops in full armor patrolling the point, plus another six with sensor suites, checking over every vehicle. Autocannons tracked each vehicle on approach, and two gunships hovered in the air above.

There's just no freaking way! Kylie thought to herself. She couldn't engage them directly; the gunships would blast her into paste within seconds. Her armor's stealth was too risky—

it had already let her down multiple times in the last few hours.

There had to be another way through the checkpoint.

As she observed the point from her rooftop vantage, a half-kilometer away, one of the gunships settled to the ground, and the pilot got out. He stretched and walked into one of the buildings near the checkpoint.

It could have been his dinner break, or he had to piss…or maybe both. Either way, that ship was her way out. The police gunships weren't rated for vacuum—they didn't have the power to break atmosphere, anyway—but there was a grav-shielded opening a dozen meters above the ground exit that air traffic normally flowed through. At least, when the city wasn't on lockdown.

Kylie didn't waste any more time. She dashed across the roof and leaped to the next building, glad the armor's muscle enhancers hadn't shown any indications of running low on charge. In fact, they now showed a twelve-hour reserve, up from the initial ten hours.

The battery meter moving in reverse wasn't especially comforting, but Kylie didn't have many options.

She ran through the streets, praying she wouldn't be seen, and two minutes later was at the entrance to the building the gunship pilot had entered. She peered inside and saw that it was a break room with a small lounge for the police who worked the checkpoint. The pilot stood at a counter, pouring himself a cup of coffee.

Kylie started to creep through the door when the man set his coffee down, and half turned. At first, she thought he'd spotted her, but he walked to a small hall and entered a restroom. She took a moment to regain her composure, entered the building, and crept to the restroom door.

She took a deep breath and raised her foot to kick it down—just as the man pulled it open. Kylie stumbled forward and crashed into him.

They both fell to the floor in a tangled mess of limbs and he got in a few good hits before she managed to slither behind him and wrap an arm around his throat. She prayed that her armor's Link dampening field had worked, or his friends were about to show up really fast.

He went limp in her arms, and she waited for a ten-count before pushing him off. The man flopped onto his face, and she looked him over. He wore a loose flight suit and an open-faced helmet.

Worth a shot, she thought to herself and stripped the man before carrying him into a toilet stall. Thanks to the tight fit of her armor, the flightsuit was no problem to get on, but the helmet was a bit snug. Even a passing inspection would reveal her armor's faceless visage beneath, and she hoped she could get to his gunship unnoticed.

"Chuck," a voice sounded in her ears. "Get back in your ship; we don't have time for breaks tonight."

Kylie swore in her mind and jogged out of the building and back to the waiting gunship, tossing a casual wave at the police at the barricade.

"Good, now get back up there," the voice said, and she nodded, hoping her silence wouldn't raise concerns. Her luck held; the pilot had left the gunship on standby—it didn't require any tokens or auth commands to get it airborne once more. She pulled the ship back up to the altitude the pilot had previously maintained, and followed a lazy circle above the checkpoint.

The external portal was open, though two physical doors could slam shut at a moment's notice. Kylie timed her ship's path, and at the point where she was closest to the dome, gunned the engines and raced toward the exit. The voice called out in her helmet, angry and demanding that she get back to her assigned patrol space, then became more furious and insistent that she land the gunship.

Kylie tore the helmet off and lined the gunships' cannons up on the mechanisms that operated the doors. Because the dome was pressurized, they would slam closed in case of any issues that could compromise the dome—like a loss of power shutting off the exit's grav field.

Her armor's targeting systems assisted her, adding a countdown to her HUD and, as she passed through the grav field, Kylie fired the cannons and prayed the ship would make it through before the doors hit it.

An audible *FOOM* sounded over the gunship's engines and nothing on her board lit up, so she assumed she was free and clear. A moment later, an explosion shook the gunship, and the console before her showed a dozen angry red warnings.

She'd forgotten about the defensive turrets outside the dome. Apparently, the police were taking a 'shoot first, ask questions later' approach. She dove the ship down as low as she dared, ducking behind a row of warehouses outside the dome as projectiles and beamfire arced over the rooftops.

The ship's console started flashing more lights, and a warning blared, 'weapon's lock!'. The system indicated that two missiles were on her tail, with only four seconds until impact. She didn't think twice as she tore the ship's door open and jumped.

RENDEZVOUS

STELLAR DATE: 09.07.8947 (Adjusted Years)
LOCATION: City of Montral, Jericho
REGION: Gedri System, Silstrand Alliance

Grayson peered across the dock's concourse and examined the squad of mercenaries who guarded the airlock leading to the *Dauntless*. Of the dozen men and women, three were massively-modded monsters. More mech than human.

The rest appeared more or less stock human—though it could often be difficult to tell. One thing was certain, they were all armed to the teeth. He caught Winter's eye and could tell the big albino was thinking the same thing. This was going to be a blow-through. Maximum force, into the lock, cycle it, and tear free of the station.

So long as Rogers could get the lock-down clamps free.

"You sure you can get the ship out of there?" Grayson asked.

"Gray, for the third time, yes. I docked us in a way that I can get the ship's grappling arms at the station locks. My girl out there has the best plasma cutters money can buy—or steal off wrecked hulls—but either way, those locks will be butter in no time. The tricky thing is that once we get aboard, we're gonna have five minutes tops before the station's autocannons cut us to ribbons."

"We need to wait for Kylie," Grayson replied.

"Except we haven't had contact with her since you fed her that map to get to Montral's north docks," Winter said.

"I wouldn't steer her wrong. We had no Link on the way up to Laerdo, and she probably didn't either," Grayson said with raised hands. "Given flight time, she should be back on our channel in just a few minutes."

"Well, she better," Rogers said. "Because I tapped the duty rosters for Laerdo's tugs, and there's a hauler slated to take the *Dauntless* to Valhalla in thirty minutes. We're going to have to take that ship in twenty at the latest."

No one spoke for several minutes, but the looks Rogers and Winter shared spoke volumes. If Kylie didn't show, Grayson wasn't certain he wanted to get on the *Dauntless* with these two.

As Rogers's informal countdown neared its final minute, a breathless voice came over their private Link.

<*Guys! You still here? Oh, man…still be here!*>

<*Kylie!*> all three of the men shouted in unison.

<*Stars, yeah, no need to yell. I just got onstation. I'm about a half a klick from the* Dauntless, *where are you?*>

<*Staring at her airlock,*> Rogers replied. <*Taking her is a one-shot-only deal, so we were waiting for you.*>

<*What's the opposition look like?*> Kylie asked.

<*Twelve mercs,*> Grayson said. <*Three heavies, all serious. Rogers thinks he can remote start the airlock cycling, so if we go in guns blazing, and time it just right, we can blast past them and get on and shut the door.*>

He felt Kylie sigh over the Link. <*Okay, well, it's no worse than any other plan we've had today. I can be there in five. Set a countdown, I'll hit it in sync with you.*>

<*How you going to get here that fast?*> Grayson asked.

<*Don't worry about me, set the countdown. I'll make it. I might have all the heat on the station up my ass, but I'll be there.*>

<*What do you mean 'I'?*> Rogers asked. <*Where's Nadine?*>

<*Down…well…I really don't know. She got taken by some guy, a bounty hunter, or assassin,*> Kylie stammered her response.

<*What!*> Rogers yelled. <*What do you mean? We can't leave without her.*>

<We have to. I don't know where she is, but the guy who has her wants Lana. He'll trade Lana's location for Nadine, promised to keep her safe.>

<And you trusted him?> Grayson asked.

<Stars…no, of course not, but what choice did I have? He took her and vanished…like just vanished. Look, we need to get onto the Dauntless. *Without a ship, Nadine is as good as dead.>*

The three men shared a look, and Rogers replied, *<Okay. Countdown set. See you in the airlock, Captain.>*

<You got it,> Kylie replied.

The five minutes crawled by, and the three men checked and rechecked their weapons and ammunition. They had to take the mercs by surprise. Hit them fast and hard.

Grayson sent a swarm of microscopic probes across the concourse and situated them on the bulkhead near the mercs. When Rogers triggered the airlock, he would have the probes hit the mercs and disable their targeting overlays. Hopefully, it would be enough to keep them in one piece on this suicide run.

When the count hit zero, Rogers triggered the airlock, and Grayson sent in his probes. Then, the three men rose from their cover and charged across the concourse.

Even though he had told them not to, both Winter and Rogers began screaming and firing immediately. By some miracle, they didn't hit any bystanders. Most of their shots were wild, and all they achieved was granting the mercs as much notice as possible that an attack was incoming.

Since there was no point in holding back, Grayson joined in the screaming and fired his two pistols as he ran. With his military-spec targeting overlay and nano-enhanced reflexes, he found his mark each time he fired.

Even though he wasn't missing, it took more than one hit to take these guys down. As they closed the distance, and several of the enemies brought their weapons up to return fire, he knew there weren't going to make it. They were going to die somewhere between seven and ten seconds.

Then something happened.

It took Grayson a moment to realize what it was and he almost stopped running until it dawned on him that someone was unleashing beamfire on the mercs. The relativistic streams of electrons smashed into the enemy, cutting them in half, before slicing deep gashes into the bulkhead.

"Shit!" Rogers screamed and skidded to a halt. A merc directly in front of him had a hole burned through her chest, and was trying to scream as her arms flailed wildly.

"Keep moving!" Grayson yelled and grabbed Rogers's collar, dragging him forward. The mercs were scattering, even the heavies, and five seconds later, the three men spilled through the airlock door as it cycled open.

They turned to see a gray figure dash in behind them and palm the panel to close the outer door.

<*Hi guys,*> the figure said and gave a wave.

"Kylie?" Rogers asked and the figure nodded.

<*Yeah, it's me. Really glad you were still here.*>

"So, we're really leaving without Nadine?" Rogers asked with a scowl.

<*I bet that guy that took her is already long gone. He didn't strike me as the type to hang out any one place for long,*> Kylie replied.

"Can't you talk?" Winter asked.

"No, she's wearing Trylodyne IA90 armor—full stealth with a rebreather to keep hot gas from escaping. Also, means you can't talk verbally," Grayson said.

"Must be working overtime," Winter snorted. "Captain has a lot of hot air in her."

<*Har, har, Winter,*> Kylie said as the inner airlock cycled open, and the sounds of weapons fire hitting the bulkhead behind them echoed through the air.

The team dashed through the inner lock, racing for the bridge.

<*Oh, and it's the Trylodyne IA99, not the IA90,*> Kylie added. <*Though the stealth is pretty flakey. Kind of a miracle that it held long enough for me to get down the dock to you guys.*>

"That's some serious armor. Where did you find it?" Grayson asked as they ran up the long ramp to the bridge.

<*I'll tell you if we make it away from Laerdo.*>

Rogers was first on the bridge and swung up into his chair in a single, smooth motion. Seconds later, he was swinging the grappling arms around and turning on the plasma torches.

"Gonna take three, maybe four minutes to cut these locking clamps off," Rogers said through gritted teeth.

<*I'm on engines,*> Kylie said as she sat at the auxiliary nav console and brought up the engine status. <*Ah shit, we're in trouble—they powered down the reactor. It's fucking cold!*>

"How long does it take to warm them up?" Grayson asked and saw Kylie's head whip around. He assumed she was staring at him—though it was hard to tell with the featureless face of her armor's helmet.

<*Grayson, really? Did you flunk out of OCS the first time? It takes at least thirty minutes to warm up a cold reactor. You can't just dump a pile of deuterium in there and say, 'max speed!'*>

Grayson grimaced. "Sorry, the SSF doesn't really let reactors go cold."

<*Yeah, well they don't get their ships locked down when they double-cross crime lords, either. I'm going to have to blast out of here on chemical boosters and grav drives.*>

"Will that be fast enough?" Winter asked from the weapons console.

"No, it really won't," Rogers said with a shake of his head.

<*If we can stay close to the station…too close to other ships for them to shoot at us till the reactor is warmed up,*> Kylie muttered.

"Can you take that helmet off?" Winter asked. "It's kinda freaking me out."

<*Would you like me to strip while I'm at it? Seriously, kinda busy here,*> Kylie said as her hands raced over her console, igniting the chemical thrusters, ready to punch them to max power the moment Rogers gave the word. <*It takes more than a few seconds to get this shit off. I might also puke when I pull this damn rebreather out—thing has been sitting on my gag reflex's last nerve for an hour now.*>

"What can I do?" Grayson asked, trying to change the subject.

<*You can sit down and shut up,*> Kylie said. <*You and I are going to have a talk when we're out of here. There's a lot more going on here than some girl's kidnapping—even a general's daughter. When we're safe, you're going to give me the full story.*>

Grayson swallowed. Kylie was pissed, and in that armor, there wasn't a lot he could do if she decided to take her anger out on him. He thought about a response, but Jerrod sent him a not so subtle mental feeling to do as he was told and keep his mouth shut.

"Aft clamp is cut, ten seconds on the fore," Rogers said.

"Okay, hitting the chem boosters in…five, four, three, two, one!"

The ship's inertial dampeners were not yet online, and the bridge rattled and shook as the chemical boosters flared against Laerdo station. Grayson hoped the mercs hadn't breached the station's airlock yet. If they had, they'd be really sorry.

Rogers brought up the ship's aft optical cameras, and they got a good view of the curved docking ring glowing red hot and venting atmosphere as they pulled away.

"Shit, they're never going to let us dock here again," Rogers said with a shake of his head.

<That's the least of our worries,> Kylie said as she dove the ship over a freighter, and around a row of pleasure yachts. *<Grayson, help on scan. See if anyone is chasing us.>*

Grayson nodded and sat at Nadine's station, flipping the system to run a full active scan. They needed to know the instant the station powered up weapons—or sent patrol craft to shoot them down.

"We could do a crash initialization of the engines," Rogers said from his seat. "Could have them warmed up in fifteen minutes."

<Do it,> Kylie said as she wove the ship through the rows of docked ships.

"Turrets are online, they're tracking us," Grayson said. "Not firing yet, though."

<I'm not giving them clear shots for long enough,> Kylie said.

"You're running out of ships to weave through," Grayson pointed at a gap in the docked ships ahead. "We're going to be wide open."

<Not if I can help it,> Kylie said with an audible grunt.

Grayson watched, impressed as she tucked the bulky junker in close to Laerdo and arced around the station's superstructure, clipping a few protrusions as she hugged it.

"You wouldn't believe what traffic control is saying on the comm channels," Winter said with a grin. "Should I pipe it through?"

A chorus of *No's* sounded both audibly and over the Link.

"Okay, okay, your loss," Winter shrugged.

"We have company!" Grayson called out as two cutters approached from opposite directions. The patrol craft was small and sleek, just large enough for a pair of pilots and a lot of firepower.

"Tracking them," Winter said. "Can I fire on them, Captain?"

<*Be my guest,*> Kylie replied. <*Not like shooting down one or two of their ships will affect how much Harken wants me dead.*>

"Did you do it?" Rogers asked. "Kill Maverick?"

<*No,*> Kylie said as she swayed in her seat along with the ship—though the internal grav dampeners had come back on, they were sipping from backup power and there were serious forces pushing on them as she wove around the surface of the station, more than the dampeners were rated for. <*Some assassin…or maybe bounty hunter…came in and shot Maverick. Then he took Nadine.*>

"Why did he do that?" Rogers's voice raised an octave. "What purpose…what…?"

<*He wants us to find where Lana is for him, and Nadine's his leverage,*> Kylie replied. <*Can we save the twenty questions for when we get out of here?*>

"If we get out of here," Winter said as he fired the ship's forward beam at the first patrol craft. The charged electrons were shrugged aside by the ship's shields, but Winter fired a pair of lasers at the ship and weakened its shields before firing another beam. That one penetrated, and an explosion flared on the patrol craft's port side. It listed to starboard and fell back.

Winter tried the same tactic with the other cutter, but it avoided his shots rather than take them on its shields.

"More company!" Grayson called out. "Four larger ships, look like they have some serious armament."

"Black Crow marauders," Winter said as he leaned over Nadine's console to look at Grayson's display.

<*We can't take them on, plus the station's cutters,*> Kylie said. <*We have to dump to the DL.*>

"What the hell?" Rogers craned his head around to peer at Kylie. "You can't be serious! We're too close to mass; we'll be smooshed in there!"

<*There has to be a clear spot nearby,*> Kylie said. <*We don't need an outsystem vector, Rogers. Just ten minutes in the DL and*

then we'll have reactors online. We can pop back out and light our torch so bright we'll fry anyone chasing us.>

Rogers swore and bent over his console, running through local dark layer maps, looking for a clear pocket and a safe vector.

"That's one hell of a bounty Harken's put on our heads," Winter grunted. "She's gonna have the whole system after us."

A beam from one of the Black Crow ships hit their shields, followed by a trio of missiles. The bridge shuddered as gravity systems tried to compensate while running on backup power. She glanced at Grayson, sitting in Nadine's seat and her stomach turned at the sight of the SSF colonel in her girl's chair. *Damnit,* Nadine. Just damnit.

"Got it! Got it! Got it!" Rogers cried out in rapid succession. "Give me helm; I'll get us in there!"

*****

Kylie relinquished control of the ship to her pilot and felt her stomach twist as the ship dumped into the dark layer with minimal shielding and grav systems on low power. They were safe, they were away, but a piece of Kylie wasn't. A piece of her was lost with Nadine and whoever her captor was.

"No one came in after us—that I can see with this ship's scan," Grayson said.

"We'll get company real fast once the Black Crow figures out what we did," Winter said. "Not a lot of places we could have gone, or where we can come out."

Kylie swallowed hard. <*The truth is, gentlemen, every pirate and smuggler who works for the GFF, every freelancer out there, they're all going to be looking for us.*>

"When this is over, the SSF can help clear your name," Grayson said.

Kylie laughed bitterly. *<Like that's ever going to happen. GFF would never believe someone like you. They only believe what Maverick and Harken tell them. Even if Maverick is alive…or lives…he may not clear our name.>* Kylie didn't think he would go to bat for her. It was probable that he'd throw her under the bus, just to get his jollies off. Just to punish her for her betrayal.

"What happened with Maverick?" Winter asked.

Kylie shook her head. *<I've never seen Maverick paranoid like that. I don't know if it was a mod gone wrong, or he simply just sensed the truth. But he knew we weren't on the up and up the moment he laid eyes on us.>*

Rogers turned to Kylie, though he kept one eye on the forward view, black as ever in the dark layer. It was on all their minds—one stray blob of dark matter and they were done for.

"You need to explain this a lot better than you have. Where's Nadine? You said a bounty hunter has her?"

Kylie held up a hand. *<Let me get this helmet off. I need to take a breath of fresh air.>*

The crew nodded silently and waited as she released the seal on the outer stealth layer and peeled it off, throwing it over the back of her chair. She sent the signal for the under-layer to separate from the helmet and felt it unseal.

Here goes, she thought to herself and took as deep a breath as she could with the rebreather in her mouth.

She slid her thumbs under the edge of the helmet and peeled it off her head, gagging, but not puking—thank the stars—as the rebreather came out of her mouth.

The inside of the helmet was soaked with her sweat, and her hair was plastered to her head. She knew she looked like shit, but it felt good to take a deep breath, which she did, followed by several more.

She looked at each of the three men and leaned against her console. "Everything went bad from the start. Maverick was suspicious and had the *Dauntless* boarded. Just when we got him on our side, this guy entered. Cloaked and armed like a damn mech. He took Maverick out—"

"So, Maverick *is* dead?" Grayson asked with wide eyes. "He's the real power behind the GFF—"

"Down, but probably not dead. He has tech that will heal him. Though I kinda wonder if Harken will let that happen."

"What else happened? What about Nadine?" Rogers asked.

Kylie glanced at him with forlorn eyes. "She took a bullet meant for me. Close range."

"And you just left her there?" Rogers's voice was almost a yell.

"Shit," Winter ran his hands through his hair. "She's—"

"No. Of course, I didn't! This bounty-hunter guy—I don't know his name, he didn't leave a calling card—he took her. He promised to heal her aboard his ship if I get him one thing." Kylie glanced at Grayson and studied his expression. She needed to see it. Needed to see what he did when she announced what was going on. "He wants Lana."

Grayson blinked but did little else. Still, given his poker face, she took it as surprise. "Lana?"

Kylie nodded. "Funny thing is, Maverick had no idea who she is, but he figured Harken did. Said she'd been running a project out in the disk. And the bounty hunter, he said a lot of people want to get their hands on Lana." She stepped up closer to Grayson. "Want to tell me why this is?"

"She's the daughter of a high-ranking general in the Silstrand Alliance. Why do you think? A bargaining chip, most likely, but you're looking at me like somehow I'm a bad guy in all this."

"Are you?" Kylie asked quietly with an even keel. "Is there something you want to tell us, Grayson? Or do I need to find a way to rip into your head and pull the information out? Is that the only way I'll ever know if you're telling the truth."

"I know you're angry—"

"Angry?" Kylie's nostrils flared. "You don't know what I am. Nadine is gone, this guy is holding her life over us, and if we don't deliver, we might never get her back. And now the GFF thinks I killed Maverick."

"You? Why *do* they think that?" Rogers asked.

"Because I was the one they found over his body—and like I said, that's exactly what Harken wants everyone to think. What I did get from Maverick points to Harken as the one who took Lana, and she sure as hell doesn't want it to get out where the girl is."

"Harken…" Winter muttered and shook his head. "Shit, she's more brutal than Maverick any day of the week."

"I guess you're lucky to have gotten out of there at all," Grayson said.

Kylie ground her heel into the floor. "You're not telling me anything I don't know."

"What are you going to do?" Grayson asked.

"Whatever I need to do to get Nadine back," Kylie said.

Grayson's eyebrows rose. "If you go against the SSF and General Samuel's orders—"

"Where were you these last few hours? Everything's gone nuts! One of our own is missing, and we're going to do what we need to get her back." Kylie glanced at Winter. "Sequester Grayson to his quarters."

"Happily," Winter grabbed Grayson's arm in a vise-like grip as Kylie reached into the colonel's jacket and pulled out his pistols.

"You can't do this, Kylie." Grayson attempted to shrug Winter off. "If you do this—"

"You know how good this armor is. I could beat you into paste—and a part of me really wants to. Go quietly or…" she let the threat hang.

"He helped us," Rogers said. "He went to bat for us. Put himself in harm's way to get us back to the *Dauntless*."

So, Rogers was his buddy now? "I said lock him in his quarters!" Kylie ordered. "I'm not going to say it again. When it's done, get back here. We're not out of this mess yet."

Winter tapped Grayson on the back. "You heard her. Move."

Grayson took a deep breath and took a step toward Kylie—nose to nose. "You're making a big mistake."

"I excel at those," Kylie said and pushed Grayson back into Winter. "Get him out of my sight."

*****

Winter held the door open, and Grayson stepped inside his quarters. He didn't say anything, just sat down on the bed and crossed his arms.

"She'll calm down," Winter said. "The captain always does. Sometimes she just needs a cooling off period. Untwist your panties and just let it happen."

Grayson remembered that about Kylie all too well. That wasn't what surprised him—what surprised him was Winter himself. "And then what?"

"Then maybe we can find a way to rescue Nadine and return Lana."

"If you don't, Winter…" Grayson let his voice trail off and met Winter's gaze. "You must impress the importance of that to Kylie. Since I can't, you'll have to."

"Winter, get back up here!" Kylie's voice came over the ship's address system.

"Duty calls. I'll do my best with Kylie and rescuing the girls—but not for you." Winter shut the door and locked it from the outside.

Grayson leaned back and rested against the wall before crossing his arms.

Jerrod finally broke his silence and said privately, *<If you want, I can talk to the ship's NSAI. It's archaic, a relic, but I'm sure I can appeal to its higher sense of decency.>*

<And where would we go? I'm not giving up yet. We have to get that girl.>

<You think Kylie can be made to see reason?>

<Reason? Maybe not, but will she play ball? I think we can convince her that it's for the best.>

<So, for now, what do we do?> Jerrod said.

<We sit here. We wait, and we exercise some patience.>

Jerrod sighed. *<Yes, sir.>*

<Stay sharp, when she comes, we need to be on our game.> Grayson needed to be rested. He tilted his head back and closed his eyes.

<Perhaps a game of poker then? Winner take all?>

* * * * *

"We're exiting the DL in two minutes," Kylie said as Winter entered the bridge. "Get on weapons; I have a feeling we're gonna come out hot."

"I can't believe we're still alive, in the DL this close to a star," Rogers muttered. "Let's never have to do this again."

"I've got something on scan," Kylie said as she re-ran the ship's sensors over the area where something pinged.

"Mass?" Rogers asked.

"Maybe…crap. It's a ship, matches one of the Black Crow profiles. It's only a kilometer behind us."

"Dumping out now," Rogers said and deactivated the graviton emitters that held the ship in the dark layer.

As the ship began to transition, Kylie saw something else move on scan. It wasn't moving in the fixed trajectory of a ship in the dark layer—the reactionless, frictionless sublayer of space that made FTL possible. The thing she saw looked fluid, sinuous, and it *turned* in the DL. Nothing could turn in the DL; it was impossible.

Then the stars of normal space snapped into view around them, and the image was gone.

Kylie sat stunned for several seconds. What had she seen? What was that thing?

"Readying weapons," Winter announced. "When those bastards come out of the DL, they won't know what hit them."

But the Black Crow's ship didn't appear. Kylie switched from passive scan and did an active sweep. Still nothing. Rogers caught her eye, and she saw that his were wide as saucers. He must have been watching scan, too.

"We never, ever do that again," he whispered.

Kylie could only nod silently, certain they had somehow avoided a very messy death in the dark layer.

After taking another moment to regain her composure, she triangulated their precise location, a position four AU outsystem from Jericho.

"Rogers," Kylie's voice cracked as she spoke and she cleared her throat. "Rogers, set a course for the nav point I marked. Best speed we can manage while keeping our engine wash pointed away from anywhere inhabited."

A NEW PLAN

STELLAR DATE: 09.07.8947 (Adjusted Years)
LOCATION: Salvage ship *Dauntless*
REGION: Near Townsend, Gedri System, Silstrand Alliance

Kylie made a pot of coffee, but it didn't taste right. Even after putting in the right about of sugar and powdered creamer, it was worse than her usual brew. About to dump it, Kylie glanced up when she heard footsteps come into the galley. "You sure you need coffee right now?" Rogers asked. "I think you should be reaching for tea. Or a sedative."

"You talking about our escape, or was I too hard on Grayson? What happened between you guys tonight, anyway?" Kylie shook her head. "You know what, never mind. It doesn't matter, but I don't think we can trust him."

"You said we'd never get through this if we didn't trust him. Now, look where we are," Winter said as he sauntered into the galley. He flipped a chair around and sat in it backward, leaning his arms across the back.

Kylie supposed she deserved that. "You think I haven't gotten my licks tonight? Go right ahead and have your piece of me, Winter."

Roger sighed and sat down. "Haven't we been through enough today?"

Winter tapped the table with his index finger. "He's been manipulating us and this entire situation ever since we stepped aboard the *Titan-1*. He let me take his gun when he could've stopped me. I saw what he could do tonight firsthand."

"I'm in no mood to defend Grayson, but no one made you reach for his gun. No one made you try to shoot your way off that ship. It was a no-win situation."

"You served with him. You knew he had military-grade nano."

"He's military, a colonel for starssakes," Kylie said. "It goes without saying. Once you reach the level he is, it's understood."

"Maybe for a space force dropout like you."

"Whoa!" Rogers lifted his arms up. "Time out, guys. Time out!"

But Kylie couldn't hear him. "If I'm so despicable, why are you on this ship anyway, Winter? Lately, you never agree to anything we do. You sulk in the cargo hold by yourself. You're only a member of this crew when it suits you."

"If that's how you feel, why don't you throw me off?"

"Maybe I will the first chance I get."

Rogers stood up and made the universal time-out signal with his hand. "Would you both please retreat to your corners and let us do something constructive, like work on saving Nadine? Who cares who knew what when? At this point, it doesn't matter. We can't take any of it back. All we can do is work the problem we have."

Kylie took a deep breath and crossed her arms. She paced backward. "Okay, okay. You're right."

"Damn right I am," Rogers said. "We all have to work together. We have the same goal. So, let's pull it together and remember we're part of the same crew."

"You're right. I'm sorry." Kylie rubbed her face, still feeling a little hot under the collar. "Winter…"

"Yeah." Winter's voice was clipped and he didn't look up at her. "Me too. Let's just not, okay?"

For an apology, it kind of sucked, but Kylie wasn't going to belabor the point. She took a moment to compose herself.

"Let's go over your meeting with Maverick," Rogers said, always able to get out of her what was important. "What happened?"

"The bounty hunter said other groups are searching for Lana. He was sent by someone with a lot of money to retrieve her. There was a gun fight. He shot Maverick when Maverick said he had no idea who Lana was. And I was going to be next. Except…"

"Nadine leaped in to save you," Rogers whispered. "Her heart is always in the right place. Her mind, however…."

"Why would anyone want a general's daughter if there wasn't something the SA is keeping from us?" Winter asked.

"Maybe she got in trouble. Maybe she stole," Rogers said. "Maybe she saw something she shouldn't have."

"Maybe they want to use her for leverage," Winter said. "Can't we ask her that when we find her?"

"We gotta get Nadine back," Rogers said. "We owe her that much."

Yes, yes, they did. Which meant they still had to go after Lana, even if Kylie didn't want to do the SA's dirty work for them.

"But all you know is that Harken is doing something out in the disk. Disk's a big place. Could hunt for years out there," Winter said.

"Actually." Kylie took a deep breath. "The information Maverick sent me had some specifics," she said as she shared the information.

It had the floor plan, how many people were employed there, and a few security system specs, but not everything.

Winter swore under his breath. "Looks like a high-tech research facility…fronted by a brothel of all things. This place isn't going to be easy to get into. And getting someone out?"

"First things first." Kylie took a sip of her bitter, lukewarm coffee. "The bounty hunter who has Nadine wants this intel. To get Nadine back, we need to give it to him."

Rogers rubbed his eyes. "You think that's a good idea? What happens to that girl if we pass this information on?"

"What happens to Nadine if we don't?" Winter asked.

Both their points were valid, and Kylie's thoughts swirled in both directions. She had to focus and couldn't argue with herself about what needed to happen. As far as she was concerned, only one thing mattered.

"I'll contact him, arrange a meeting. We make a copy of the schematics, and maybe we can…rescue Lana when our new friend goes there to get her. I don't know yet, but I do know we have to ensure Nadine's release. That comes before we do anything else."

Rogers and Winter exchanged a glance before Rogers spoke. "Grayson won't go for this. He has an AI. We'll be lucky if the SSF stays off our backs long enough to even get Nadine back."

Kylie nodded. "You're going to have to leave that to me, but first things first…I arrange a meeting at a neutral location with this bounty hunter. If you two are on board, Winter I need you to go over the engines and make sure they're okay after our rapid warmup. I mean everything. And Rogers…get your ass to the bridge and stay on standby."

"Can I have some of that bad coffee first?" Winter asked with a smile playing at the edges of his mouth.

"Are you serious?" Rogers asked. "I can smell it from here. It's probably toxic."

Kylie just smirked. "Go."

The men hurried from the galley and Kylie sank into a seat and stared at her gloved hand, suddenly realizing she was still wearing the Trylodyne armor. She flexed her fingers and stared off into the distance. What if she was making the wrong choice? What if the SSF and Grayson were both trustworthy? Kylie didn't know if she was making the right call, but it was the only call. If Nadine was on the *Dauntless*, then it would be different, but such as it was, all the decisions were already made for Kylie.

She hated not having a choice.

A message hit the ship and somehow routed past the main comm system straight to her. She had a sinking suspicion that it was her new friend. Abilities like that would go along with his general mystique. She accepted the message, and the bounty hunter's smooth baritone entered her mind. *<You don't call, you don't write….>*

<Is she all right? Before we do anything, I need to know that my crewmember is okay.>

<Touch and go, but she came through.>

Thank goodness, Kylie sighed with relief. *<Before we arrange anything, I want proof of life.>*

The man sighed, and a second later, Kylie's HUD showed a visual and she felt herself transported into a virtual space. She saw a small room, maybe a medbay of some sort. In a bed, Nadine rested, her eyes closed.

"Nadine?" Kylie's chest tightened just to say her name out loud. When Nadine's eyes fluttered open, Kylie felt an emotional high.

Nadine was close to tears. "Kylie? Don't…whatever Jason wants, don't do it."

Jason. So…the bounty hunter had a name, and Nadine had managed to get it from him. She was always working the mission; Kylie respected that about her.

"But you're alright? He upheld his end of the bargain?"

"I'm fine, Kylie. I'm fine." Nadine's voice was rich with grief. "I'm sorry. I didn't want this to happen."

"You're going to be fine, Nadine. Just let me worry about it, okay?"

Jason cut the virtual feed. *<That's enough. She's going to live. Do you have the intel?>*

Kylie let out a long breath but the anxiety held firm. *<Maverick had what I needed on his computer—Lana's probably at that facility of his that Harken has been using for a side project.*

Maverick didn't know anything about it. He apparently allowed Harken a bit too much discretion.>

<Good work. Show it to me. If it's everything I need, you'll get your little girlfriend back.>

<What's to stop you from keeping Nadine **and** *the intel?>*

<Nothing. But there's nothing to stop me from putting the rail pellet I removed from her chest into her brain, either.>

Kylie sucked in a sharp breath. *<Hey! No! I'm playing along here.>*

<Good! Keep it that way.>

The situation kept getting worse instead of better. Still, Kylie didn't think that handing over the data carte blanche was a good idea. So, she blanked out a few details, such as the installation's coordinates, environmental conditions, and the like, but left in the details about security and the structure itself.

She passed it over and forced herself to take calm breaths while she waited.

Jason gave a sigh over the connection. *<Unfortunately, this isn't enough.>*

<Isn't enough?> Kylie struggled to remain calm. *<Listen, you—>*

<It isn't enough,> he repeated with razor edge calm. *<I know nothing significant about their security, how many are on rotations, when do they switch. How do I get in? Where are the sensors and alarms situated? I'm going to need more than this to get Lana out in one piece. Until I get that information—>*

<Wait a second,> Kylie let her temper flare. *<I got you what you wanted. I did what—>*

<No, you didn't. I need intel I can use. So, if I were you, sweet stuff, I would make sure that you do some recon, and get everything I just mentioned. Actual intel on their security, when they switch off, best insertion points, egress, the location of the facility—which I can tell you scrubbed—then we can do business.>

<Listen to reason.> Kylie let her mental tone fill with desperation—something that wasn't hard to do.

<Don't leave me waiting too long, Kylie, or Nadine and I may have no choice but to get acquainted.>

He wouldn't dare. Maybe if she gave him the information that she removed. *<Wait a second…if you would just—>*

She stopped talking because the conversation had been terminated. There was nothing else she could say. Nothing Kylie could do. She was stuck between a rock and a hard place. Actually, a rock would've been more comfortable than where she was. Still, she had bought more time. Time she could maybe use to get Lana, and figure out how to save both women. *If* she could save them both…

Lana. Nadine. Whose life would she trade for another?

She considered the lack of lag in the communication. His ship was nearby, within a light-second—less than three hundred thousand kilometers, maybe even within weapon's range. And he could breach her ship's security.

They were nothing but pawns to this man.

Kylie picked herself up from the chair. She poured another mug of coffee and then made another for Grayson. Not much of a peace offering, but it was a start. She walked slowly out of the galley and turned down the hall toward Grayson's quarters.

When she slid the door open, Grayson's lack of surprise caught her off guard. Bent forward, he rested his chin in his hand and barely glanced over at her.

"I wondered when you'd come."

She hated when he said stuff like that. He knew her so well, did he? Kylie handed him the fresh mug of coffee. "Two cream. One sugar. Extra hot, just the way you like it." She slid onto the cot beside him as he slurped his coffee, still just as annoying as it had been through the course of their marriage.

"You had to know." Grayson licked his lips. "If I wanted out, I would've just opened the door."

"But you wouldn't have had anywhere to go."

"Any comradery I had developed with your crew is most likely gone." Grayson blinked. "I would just like to thank you for that."

"Rogers defended you. That might please you."

"Well…that's unexpected."

"But we get Nadine back. Nothing else happens until that happens," Kylie said. "Rogers seems to think we can trust you. Is he right?"

Grayson's eyes met hers and never wavered. A fierce passion raged in them. "Yes."

Kylie struggled with his answer because she didn't know if he'd ever been that good a liar. If he was telling the truth, that meant Samuel wasn't just keeping her in the dark—he had kept Grayson in the dark, too, and that was dangerous.

"Then we work together. Get Nadine back. Find Lana."

"I guess you really do love her, don't you?" Grayson's voice hushed, and for the first time, Kylie thought his feelings might be hurt. Even when she'd announced she was leaving him, had he ever shown anything other than stoic pride?

"I'm not sure I realized how much until all this started. If that's hard for you…well, I'm sorry, Gray," Kylie murmured.

He laughed. "This is all hard for me. Being here. Being down on that planet. Being with you when you can't look at me or trust me. Nothing about this is fun or easy, but…"

"You have a mission." Kylie nodded. "And I promise we'll get back to that. I don't want to let the general down any more than you do."

"Jerrod says our course has changed. Want to tell me where we're headed?"

Not particularly. "Can you promise me you won't report in to the SSF until after we get Nadine back? Tell them whatever you want after that, but I won't have you do anything until my crew is whole again. If you can't promise..."

"You'll what? Space me?" Grayson smirked. "I'll play along. I think it's in my best interests to do so, but if you betray the mission, Kylie...It'll be your crew who won't live to regret it. Not me."

Kylie could appreciate that. She stood and headed for the door. "I won't force you to stay in here. You can move around the ship."

"For now, I think I'll stay." Grayson took another sip of his coffee. "If it's all the same to you."

It was. Kylie left him there, feeling more cold and hollow than she could ever remember feeling before. But she got him to play along, and for now, that was all that mattered. It didn't matter that a part of her heart still trusted him—even as the rest of her screamed to stop.

Grayson was military. It ended there—plain and simple.

Unfortunately for her, nothing was easy. Nothing was simple. Not even her feelings for Grayson and where his loyalties lay.

*****

"What are you going to do?" Rogers asked Kylie.

Kylie sat with him and Winter in the galley. The pot of coffee had long gone cold. She told them about the conversation with Jason and the impasse she was at. To save Nadine, they had to sacrifice Lana to the bounty hunter. That would put them at the top of the SSF's most wanted list. It would match their position on the GFF's. Another option was to forget Nadine and hit Harken's facility, get Lana, and turn her over to the SA—which wasn't going to happen. Not while Kylie was still breathing.

The only real option was to get Lana, and somehow take out Jason when he traded for Nadine.

They had talked about it for hours, distilled the information, considered it from every angle. "We have no choice but to go in and scout out the facility like Jason wants us to."

"A facility that Maverick considers top secret? That Harken has a run of? You know how well she'll have that place locked down?" Winter asked.

"We do have the blueprints; we know it's fronted by a brothel. Given Harken's proclivities, it's a fitting cover for a top-secret lab. That means there's a way in, something we can leverage," Kylie replied.

"If it was easy," Rogers said with an even, level stare before continuing, "Mister Bigshot Bounty Hunter would do it himself."

"It's for Nadine; we don't have a choice."

Winter folded his hands and cast a steady glare out at Kylie. "I owe it to her just as much as the next person, but she wouldn't want us to commit suicide."

No, she wouldn't, but was that what Kylie was doing? She was wrapped up in so much drama over Nadine's kidnapping, she couldn't see straight.

"One person going in will have better luck than the four of us."

Kylie cocked her head back with surprise at the sound of Grayson's voice. She didn't think he'd ever leave his room. Despite their sickening worry about Nadine, the crew was just starting to gel again, and now he was going to mess up their dynamic.

"One person?" Winter was incredulous. "There will be tech, surveillance, armed guards."

"All hard, but not impossible for the right person with an AI. Someone with training." Grayson sat next to Kylie and stared deep into her eyes. She knew what he was saying, but an AI? It went against everything she held dear. Everything she believed.

"I don't trust AI," Kylie said bluntly.

"You either get an AI, Kylie, or you send me in. If you go in without AI support, you won't be coming back from that mission. You barely came back from Jericho as it was. If you hadn't lucked out and found that Mark safehouse, you'd be dead."

"You think if I had AI that would've gone differently? That Nadine…she might be with us?" Kylie asked.

Rogers and Winter sat up straight, pulling hands and elbows off the table as though it were electrified. Kylie saw them share a look, one that should have made her quell her roiling emotions—one that presaged Grayson's answer.

He didn't pull any punches. "Yes. One hundred percent. Absolutely."

How dare he. "You've wanted to get an AI in my head for years! It ruined us, and now you'll say anything to get it done. Is that it?"

Grayson shook his head, his tongue clicking against the roof of his mouth. He gazed away with disgust. Kylie could see it in his eyes. "What's ruined everything is your distrust for technology, and of AI. Your parents might have raised you as part of that cult—"

"A simpler way of life isn't a cult, Grayson."

"So, you really believe in it? You think there will really be a 'reckoning'? You think one day the AI will overtake us and reveal there is some master plan? And the ascended AI are controlling us?"

"I don't know," Kylie spat the words out. "I won't share headspace with something that might be under strict orders that I'm not privy to."

"Then we get another AI—a non-military one. An AI that's not under any special orders from the SSF," Rogers said, his tone calm and his hands raised.

His voice startled Kylie. She had forgotten that she and Grayson weren't alone. "What?"

"There's a guy not far from here. He works on a station in the scattered disk—not too far from our destination. Mining operation, but that isn't the only thing he trades in. It's a safe port too, GFF and Maverick won't hear about us while we're there." Rogers stood and touched Kylie's arm. "If it'll help Nadine, why can't we do it?"

Kylie's eyes widened in shock, and she glanced at Winter, who only nodded. "You both think this is a good idea?"

"If you won't, I can," Winter said. "No disrespect to your parents and what they set out to prove, but I don't give jack about that. What I care about is Nadine, and I know you do, too. So, either hook yourself up or get out of the way so I can do it."

Were her parents' beliefs really that arcane? Were they setting her back and putting Nadine's life in jeopardy? Kylie felt like everything, even her own belief system, was falling apart.

Rogers folded his hands. "And we know with Winter's bedside manner, Lana will go screaming and running in the opposite direction."

Kylie felt like she was being backed into a corner. Getting an AI in her head was the last thing she wanted. However, she also knew that if Grayson went in, there was a chance he'd rescue Lana and take her right to the SSF. Then Nadine would be lost—it was the epitome of a non-choice.

She tried to come up with another alternative, some way to go in alone. Nothing came to mind, but it did occur to her that getting the AI was short term. As soon as she got Lana, she could get the thing yanked. Kylie grasped onto that straw and spoke up.

"All right, I'll do it."

"Wait for a second." Grayson held his hands out. "How can we even be talking about this? You'll trust a black-market AI more than you'll trust the alliance? More than me? Kylie—"

"Set a course, Rogers," Kylie said and started out of the galley. The conversation, as far as she was concerned, had already ended.

"How does he even get these AI? Do you know? Do you even care?" Grayson pleaded from behind her.

Kylie really didn't.

HEAVEN

STELLAR DATE: 09.10.8947 (Adjusted Years)
LOCATION: Salvage ship *Dauntless*
REGION: Scattered Disk, Gedri System, Silstrand Alliance

Kylie stepped onto the bridge and gave the empty seat in front of the navigation console a long, cold stare. It had been empty before, but never for this reason. Never because Nadine was captured and in mortal danger. That was on Kylie, and, as she sank into the chair, what she had done weighed her down like a ton of stones.

"You didn't approve of the mission," she said to Rogers, who hadn't spoken since she entered the bridge. "I know you didn't. You told me as much and I promised to keep Nadine safe."

"We promise a lot of things," Rogers said without looking over at her. "No one can see into the future. If we did, things would be different, wouldn't they?"

It was true. Things would be so much different.

"You did the best you could. When you made your promise, you meant it."

His words lacked conviction. Instead, he just sat with a sad look on his face and Kylie was sad right along with him. "I think I'd rather have you yell at me."

Rogers leaned back in his chair and stared out at space. "Right now, I don't think I have the energy or the will to yell. All I can think about is Nadine and what she might be going through. Maybe that's for the best now, to keep us focused." He glanced back at her and Kylie was struck with how lost he looked. "But I don't hate you, Cap. Sorry, if that's what you need from me."

Kylie didn't think that's what she was after, but maybe he was right. Maybe that was exactly what she was after. She swallowed and bit her lip. "Thanks, Rogers. Maybe what I really need is…acceptance."

"Don't we all?" He chuckled.

"And Grayson? You don't think he threw us under the bus?" Kylie asked because Rogers's opinion was important. He could always see what was really going on and what wasn't. He didn't lie, didn't throw punches. If he believed in someone, it usually meant Kylie should too.

"I think when the gunfire broke out, he was surprised. Did you see the look on his face? When you said Maverick had no idea who Lana was?"

Kylie had to admit that she hadn't. She had been so angry, she hadn't seen anything.

"He was as shocked as the rest of us. I don't know if that means the SSF was just plain wrong or what, but he's in the same boat we are. For better or worse, we're all in this together."

She wasn't sure about that. "How much longer until we arrive at your friend's station?"

"Another ten hours or so."

Ten hours until she permanently changed her brain. Well, wasn't that nice? "I think I'm going to grab some rest and then focus on dinner prep. I apologize best on a full stomach."

Rogers turned his attention back to his console. "If it's all the same to you, I think I'll skip dinner."

"It's not all the same to me. We all need to be together. Now more than ever. If we're going to get Nadine back, secure Lana, and keep the SA off our backs, we need to be on the same page."

"We're going to need a lot more than that, Captain. We're going to need a stars-be-damned miracle."

*****

"Heaven? Your friend operates out of *Heaven?*" Kylie exclaimed.

"Yeah, it's the perfect place. Everyone is welcome in Heaven. No one judges you here," Rogers replied with a sweeping gesture.

"Pretty sure they got that metaphor wrong," Winter grunted.

"So, Maverick, Harken, the GFF, none of them will try to take us out here?" Grayson asked. "I can't see how everyone on this station will just ignore the bounty on our heads."

"That's the appeal of Heaven," Rogers said. "It's a safe zone. Everyone respects that—the system wouldn't function if there weren't places that worked as neutral ground."

"So long as we grease the right palms," Winter said.

"Well, Heaven doesn't run on goodwill," Rogers replied with a grin.

Winter stared at Kylie a second longer than he needed to. So, she threw Grayson a bone and included him in things. She didn't want him to feel worthless, but rather part of her crew—for now.

"Still." Kylie turned and tossed her hair to get a clear look at Grayson. "Why don't you have your AI keep an eye on things just the same. Make sure if a communication goes out to Maverick, Harken, the GFF.... Hell, just see if he can tap all the off-station comms. Even if we don't get hit here, we still need to know what's waiting for us when we undock."

Grayson nodded. "Consider it done."

"You don't need to worry about it," Roger said. "Like I said, a place like this couldn't run in the trade it does if it ratted out ships that had bounties on them."

"I'm well aware of how it works," Grayson said with a heavy sigh. "But like *I* said, I'm worried the bounty on our heads might be large enough that someone on this station won't care."

It was a point worth considering.

Rogers's board lit up with a message, and he glanced down at it. "Got our berth…taking us in. We'll have seal in twenty minutes."

Kylie turned to Winter and Grayson. "Stay here just in case something goes wrong. We need the *Dauntless* ready to take off if there are any problems."

Grayson's eyes showed that he took exception to that, but he didn't say anything aloud. <*Kylie,*> was the only thing he said across the private net. Kylie didn't dismiss his fear but she couldn't let it cripple her.

"I won't have what happened on Jericho happen here. Stay with the ship. Defend it, if necessary, and if there's any sign of trouble, we'll get out."

"If there was a way to talk you out of this, I would. Just be careful. And have her back," Winter said to Rogers.

"I won't let her out of my sight." Rogers and Winter clasped their hands together in a brief, but firm, handshake before it was time to go.

Once the ship docked, and the credits exchanged with the right people, Rogers and Kylie cycled the airlock and stepped onto the small station. It wasn't a flashy joint, but a place that worked well and worked hard. The people they passed all kept to themselves and looked like they would rather be just about anywhere else but out here in the scattered disk. But work in Heaven paid well and sometimes that was all that mattered.

"Just let me do the talking. I sent a message that we were on the way and told him what we needed, but sometimes Finn can be a little…tricky to handle."

Kylie's brow furrowed. "You are friends with this guy, right?"

Rogers waved his hand in the air in a so-so motion. "Friend might be a slight overstatement."

"Why didn't you say something before?"

"Because you didn't want Grayson to have any more ammunition to argue with you. We didn't need it, either. You know that. If we had to go back to Trio to get you implanted with an AI you didn't want…"

It would've taken forever and day. Kylie got that. "What's so special about your friend?" It didn't go unnoticed that Rogers was carrying a non-descript package wrapped under his arm.

"He's a foodie."

Kylie raised an eyebrow. "A foodie?"

"Yup. It isn't just that he likes food. He *loves* food. It gets him off in ways you and I get off on…well, you get the picture."

"So…what you're carrying is…"

"The bribe. He'll love this stuff so much, he'll be begging for more." Rogers gave Kylie another wink.

Kylie raised her eyebrows. She'd had no idea they had anything on board that Finn would want.

They headed down a flight of stairs that led to what looked like an even seedier section of the station. The lights were dimmer, and those they passed wore cautious expressions—never making eye contact.

"They just don't want anyone up in their business. C'mon." Rogers paused at a door at the end of the hall and banged his fist against it. "It's Jim Rogers."

Funny, Kylie always forgot Rogers had a first name. She hadn't used it in so long.

The door opened wide enough for them to wedge themselves through, and then it automatically shut behind them. They found themselves in a long hallway with a dozen video cameras watching their every move. Kylie followed

Rogers down to the end, where he disappeared through a door on the right. Kylie had a bad feeling about what lay ahead but couldn't turn back. They had already lost too much time, and Nadine needed them.

Nadine needed *her*.

She turned the corner to see a big man with dreadlocks and a more varied array of mods than Kylie had ever seen on one person. He stood, and two of his arms stretched up while the other pair placed hands on his hips "Rogers."

"Finn, my man."

Finn crossed both sets of arms. The muscles on the limbs rippled and bulged, showing off his rich tapestry of tattoos. The colors seemed to all blend together, almost as if they were in flux, moving across his skin.

Never mind, they actually were.

"Good to see you," Rogers said, flashing his warmest smile. "This is my friend who needs your services."

"Kylie," she extended Finn her hand for a shake but she wasn't sure which of his four hands to offer it to.

Finn glanced at it before accepting the handshake with his top left hand. "You're in the market for an AI? I have several good ones. Ripe for a new home. They're in the farm, been kept isolated almost too long. They'll be eager to be paired off with someone new. We offer them," Finn paused as he stroked his long beard. Then he chuckled and continued, "incentive."

"Does it hurt? How long will it take?" Kylie asked, trying not to wonder what sort of incentive Finn was talking about.

"Whoa, you don't trust my establishment here?"

"She trusts you," Rogers held up his hand. "I vouched for you. I don't do that for just anyone."

"I suppose you don't." Finn gave him the once over, his eyes resting on the package under Rogers's arm. "Is that it?" He licked his lips and Kylie saw that his tongue was forked.

He must have gotten it done on purpose—there seemed to be little, fine hairs on the tip. Gross.

"Always." Rogers handed Finn the mysterious package.

Finn held it to his nose and inhaled long and deep. "Ahh…bacon. By the stars, this is the stuff right here."

Kylie gave Rogers a sidelong look. That was her bacon, damn it. No wonder he hadn't wanted to tell her what it was. <*What the hell is up with his tongue?*>

<*Modified to enhance the taste buds and improve the sensory experience. I told you he was a foody.*> Rogers didn't skip a beat as a wide smile spread across his face.

"We have more where that came from if you do a good job. Organic, raised planet-side. No nitrates or vat-grown stuff," Kylie added

Finn chortled with excitement, and Rogers slapped Kylie on the back. "Told you you'd like her."

"Follow me." Finn pulled back the curtain at the rear of the room, and they stepped into what looked like a lab that also appeared to double as a weapons locker. Kylie glanced at Finn. "Seems you keep your business diversified."

"That's one way of looking at it. A lot of people get weapons for mods, so the work blends together." He slapped her on the back and Kylie coughed without meaning to. Damn, he was strong. "This chair is for you. Hop on." Finn turned and walked to the rear of the room while Kylie stared at the reclining chair with a pounding heartbeat.

She didn't really know about this. Rogers took her hand. "I'll stay with you, if that's what you want."

"Please," Kylie said. "I don't want to appear weak, but—"

He smiled. "I won't tell anyone."

"You might be a better friend than you are a pilot." Kylie pulled herself onto the chair and tried to relax. She leaned her head back and clasped her hands together.

Rogers scowled. "Did you just insult my piloting skills?"

"I'm not really sure," Kylie snickered nervously and cast an eye at Finn as he entered the room with a woman whose otherworldly appearance took her breath away.

The newcomer appeared to glide across the floor, her movements measured and precise, more synthetic than human. Her skin was luminescent, and her limbs seemed almost too long, impossibly slender. Her head was an elongated oval with wide cat eyes with a mass of tentacles flowing off the top. She tilted it side to side as she walked, as if she was searching for something.

"Gert here will do the procedure. She hasn't fried a brain in over twenty years."

Oh, great.

Gert gave a silvery laugh, and the tentacles on her head lifted up and danced around her face. They glowed, and silver sparkles danced along their length and arced between them. Her tight, single piece of clothing—which Kylie now suspected was maybe just her skin—changed color from a sedate blue to a light green streaked with yellow. "More like nineteen, but who's counting? I do all my own work, do you like it?" She twirled, and her tentacles flowed out around her before settling down again.

Kylie nodded. "Love it. Your look is very unique."

"Isn't it, though?" Gert purred like a cat and Kylie watched her neck pulsate. "I tell you, honey, once you start, you just can't stop."

"Like potato chips," Rogers said.

Finn's eyes widened. "You have some? If you could get me some of those, I would throw in some weapons. Plasma clips."

"Done," Kylie said. "Now if you don't mind—"

Finn grunted. "I *really* like you guys. But first, we talk business. The credits?"

"Ready to move as soon as Kylie wakes up and we have proof you didn't kill her." Rogers winced. "Sorry, Cap."

None taken? Kylie couldn't find the breath to answer. "Let's just make this quick."

Gert leaned over. "Call me Gerti if it makes you feel better, honey. Now start counting backward for me from ten and soon you'll be asleep. When you wake up, there will be new neuron pathways in your brain and you'll have a headache. It'll take three days for your brain to figure out how to work properly again. You probably won't be able to move for a few days, but once the AI helps you adjust, everything will get better exponentially."

Three days? Three days. God, Kylie couldn't remember the last time she was still for an hour, let alone days. Could she even do it? She wasn't sure.

Kylie sighed and gazed up at the ceiling. If this is what it took to save Nadine…. If this is what it took. "Ten… nine… eight… seven…" She gasped as they injected her with an anesthetic and rush of cold assaulted her brain.

She was ready to quit. Kylie wished she hadn't agreed and wanted to shout out, but her mouth wouldn't open. Nothing would work. Her mind was beginning to drift away.

If she continued to count, Kylie lost all memory of it. Her eyelids became heavy, and they closed.

COMING AROUND

STELLAR DATE: 09.11.8947 (Adjusted Years)
LOCATION: Finn's Mod Shop, Heaven
REGION: Scattered Disk, Gedri System, Silstrand Alliance

Grayson stood in Finn's outer room, arms crossed, staring at a display showing a variety of rather terrifying mods. He rested his back against the wall and tore his gaze from the display to look at the motionless curtain at the back of the room. Kylie was behind that curtain and had been for twelve hours. The procedure was done and had been a success, so why wasn't she awake yet?

<Gert says her vitals are normal. She'll wake up when she's ready,> Jerrod said.

<And if she's never ready? If she was a fool to trust these people and that freak show did nothing but a butcher-job on her?>

<Then you'll know one way or another,> Jerrod replied. *<I know she meant something to you once. I only got to meet her a handful of times, and by then she was just angry all the time.>*

<You came into play toward the tail end of our marriage. She wasn't like that…not always.> Grayson remembered a time when she was always happy. *<We need her to get this job done. Without her, the crew of the* Dauntless *won't follow through. Without her, we can't do what we need to, to rescue Lana.>*

<Oh, is that all it is?>

Grayson didn't say anything because he didn't know what to say. Since being aboard the *Dauntless*, everything had gotten complicated. It shouldn't have mattered if Kylie lived or died, but it did. To him, it mattered. Rules and regs aside, Grayson didn't want her to die. Maybe that made him weak, but it was the absolute truth.

But General Samuel and his daughter had to come first. They were, of course, the mission, but it hadn't been part of the mission for a bounty hunter to show up. He'd nearly killed Maverick, and gotten his hands on Nadine, neither of which were supposed to happen—or be Grayson's problem—but he still cared.

The general hadn't told him something. Just what it was, or why it was so important, Grayson had to figure out before it came back to bite them in the ass. He had served under Samuel for years and never had he felt left in the dark the way he did now. Samuel had always proven himself trustworthy, or so Grayson had liked to think. So, what was his game now?

Rogers rounded the corner from the outside hall and Grayson tried not to glower at the man. It wasn't his fault Kylie had agreed to get a black-market AI. Kylie did what she wanted, just as she always had, but Rogers was the one who had happily facilitated this whole mess. He was the one who had hooked her up. If something went wrong, Grayson would hold him accountable.

"They don't have much in the way of anything remotely edible here, but they do have everything else you *need*." Rogers offered Grayson a food pouch filled with a gray, slimy, nutrition-rich goo.

Grayson held up his hand. "I don't think I could stomach anything, but thank you. It was kind of you to allow me to be here when she woke up."

"She'll kill us for letting you off the ship, but being that you used to be married, I'm easily swayed," Rogers said.

Grayson nodded. "And the facility where we believe Lana is…once we get out of here, any idea how long it'll take us to get there?"

"Four days tops. How we'll get close enough to get Kylie down there is something else entirely."

The door opened, and both Rogers and Grayson straightened and turned. "Excuse me," Gert said with her hands folded in front of her. The beautifully exotic, green-skinned woman looked utterly inhuman with her simple features, button nose, and flowing tentacles. The way her voice pulsed was almost erotic.

"Kylie is starting to awaken."

DOUBLE OCCUPANCY

STELLAR DATE: 09.11.8947 (Adjusted Years)
LOCATION: Finn's Mod Shop, Heaven
REGION: Scattered Disk, Gedri System, Silstrand Alliance

Kylie had what must have been the worst headache in the galaxy.

She groaned and touched her forehead, but even just the simple movement felt foreign, like she wasn't even in her own body. Plus, the pain in her head intensified from the minute motion, and she hadn't even tried to open her eyes yet.

On the plus side, she *could* move her arm—mostly. It was more than Gert told her would be possible right off the bat.

<*It helps to take a long, calm breath.*>

The voice came from inside her own head, but it felt different than a communication over the Link. It was as though it didn't come from any specific place. It came from all the places all at once. In her mind, Kylie saw a smiling face. She couldn't quite make out the features, but its mouth was definitely smiling.

Kylie struggled to take a breath. Her chest was tight and she had a sinking sensation she was on the cusp of a panic attack. Could she even still remember how to breath?

<*You should try relaxing. I know it's a new process for you, but I've been through this a few times before. It'll get easier if you breathe. Picture something nice, like a flock of birds or butterflies.*>

"I'm not sure I remember how," Kylie muttered aloud even though she meant to say it in her head.

<*Well, one thing at a time, I guess, Miss Rhoads.*> The AI's voice was feminine, respectful, and calm. Kylie wasn't sure what she had been expecting, but this wasn't it.

"What's your name?"

<*You can call me Marge.*>

Marge. A strong name for someone who sounded so simple. "Then you can call me Kylie."

<*Like we're friends? Well, I like that.*> Marge sounded playful, and Kylie got the image of a little girl playing on a swing.

"What is that?" Kylie asked.

<*Just an image. I find showing images is an easy way to get across how I'm feeling in the early stages of joining. Eventually, you'll just get in tune with me as I will with you.*>

"So, eventually you'll know everything about me? Every thought?"

<*No, I can't reach right into your mind, but I can pick up on your active thoughts if you let me. You'll learn how to keep certain thoughts private, and others broadcast across to me, but it'll take time.*>

<*It sounds exhausting.*> Would she ever be able to relax again, or would she always be on guard? Kylie didn't know how she felt about any of that.

Marge showed Kylie an image of someone clapping. <*There you go! You did it! You talked with your mind. Bravo!*>

Kylie hadn't meant to. She had meant to think that thought to herself. She suddenly had buyer's remorse—she wanted to go back to how things used to be. She was hungry, thirsty, and she didn't want to lay in that bed for three days waiting for things to either get better—or get worse.

Suddenly, the curtain brushed aside. It sounded louder than it should have—like her ears were able to pick up every rustling fiber in the fabric. Kylie lifted both arms to cover them but the movement sent a wave of vertigo over her.

"She's awake," Gert said to someone. Kylie wasn't sure who until she got a whiff of spicy aftershave.

It was Grayson.

"Well, look at you," Grayson said as he sat beside her and Kylie felt an intense wave of emotion wash over her—one that shouldn't have been there. "Awake, blinking, and everything."

"It's not a time to make jokes," Kylie said. "My head has gotten very crowded and the headache…."

Grayson took her hand. "I know, but it'll get better. Your brain is undergoing an intense process but in a day or so you'll feel like yourself again."

"I don't have that long. Nadine…."

"Isn't going to be hurt. Jason knows if he hurts her, he doesn't get the information that he wants."

Kylie nodded and immediately regretted that decision. She closed her eyes and moaned. "Has your AI spoken to you yet, Kylie?" Grayson asked, and Kylie got a distinct impression that he did so to distract her.

"Yeah, her name is Marge."

Grayson's eyebrows lifted. "Oh, a female AI? Is she nice?"

"So far, but this headache definitely isn't."

<I'm so sorry about that. I don't mean for this process to hurt, but it's no picnic for me, either.>

<It's hard for you, too?> Kylie was surprised. *<I'm sorry. I didn't know.>*

<Being placed inside someone's head isn't easy. I'm my own person, but now my neural net is sitting in the spaces of your brain, and in your mind. It changes who I am a bit—though in your case, it seems like a good change. We're in this together. Sorry if I snapped, Miss Kylie, I'll try not to let it happen again.>

<It's okay. Please don't apologize. And it's just 'Kylie', remember?>

<I remember, just making sure. I don't want to offend you.>

Grayson smiled at her. "Did you hear anything I just said?"

"What?" Kylie asked. "Oh…I'm sorry…"

"You were talking with your AI. That's good, real good. Soon, you'll be able to talk to her while remaining aware of what other things are going on around you. Don't worry, Kylie. You'll come through this. Jerrod had a chat with your AI too and looked at the interface. It looks like they did things well here—a lot better than I expected."

Kylie hoped so. She had been raised to never trust AI, and now she shared headspace with one that she didn't even know. Nothing about this situation sat right with her.

"Rest, and before you know it, we'll be out of here." Grayson gripped her shoulder and kissed the top of her forehead.

"You really think I can do this? What we're planning to do…"

"We'll get it done. For Nadine and for Lana," Grayson said.

For Nadine…

<*Well, he seems nice.*>

<*He does, doesn't he?*> Kylie asked and wondered if it was true, if Grayson cared as much as he seemed to, or if they were involved in some sort of long-game, the rules of which she wasn't even privy to.

*****

True to everyone's assurances, after a couple of days, Kylie felt a lot better. She had gotten to know Gert, or Gertrude as she had come to call her, quite well.

Gertrude's upbringing and life on the station had been hard, a lot of jobs had required a lot of mods, and not good ones, either. She'd learned how to keep them functioning, and slowly saved the money to turn her body into something she liked, not loathed. Her work had attracted Finn's notice, and she took special pride in doing mods that were as beautiful as they were functional.

Despite her alien appearance, Gertrude was a kind, sweet woman. Kylie liked her quite a bit and found herself warming to Marge, as well. The new AI in her head seemed like a simple being at first but as Kylie trained with her, she discovered that Marge knew a lot about weapons and combat…and espionage.

Maybe it was part of the training all AI were part of, but Kylie had a feeling Marge had picked up a lot of her knowledge firsthand.

<*How is it you ended up in the company of Finn?*> she asked Marge.

Marge took a few seconds to respond. <*That's a long story and one I'm not at liberty to talk about. I'm sorry.*>

That told a lot more than anything else Marge might have said. Kylie didn't like it. It occurred to Kylie she might have stolen goods in her head. It wasn't like she could do anything about it now, and they had to get on with working together—especially now that Kylie was feeling better. Stronger. It was time to move on.

It had been two days, and Kylie was supposed to stay one more night, but that wasn't going to happen. She had to get back to the ship so they could continue on with what needed to be done. Kylie was ready, and in fact, if she didn't get on her way, she might jump right out of her skin.

Rising from the bed, Kylie dressed and donned her leather jacket while investigating the weapons in front of her. It was getting easier to control what she saw and what she thought, keeping her ideas private, but it still took a heavy dose of concentration.

<*You seem nervous. Elevated blood pressure,*> Marge said. <*If you want, I can check to see if Finn has communicated about you.*>

<*No,*> Kylie snapped. <*I just mean…no, thank you. You don't need to do that.*>

<You bought me so we could work together. So we could be a team.>

Kylie sighed and rubbed her forehead. *<Let's get to the ship and then we'll figure it all out. Okay? We need to work together, but not yet.>*

<You don't trust me.> Marge stated the sentence like it was a simple fact instead of like someone with wounded pride.

<It's not that. It's just…I've never had an AI before.>

<I've never been with someone who once followed the ministry of the AI Reckoning either, but I'm willing to look past it.>

That information was private. Kylie's pulse raced as she realized what had been revealed.

<I didn't mean to stumble upon it, but you keep thinking about it. I couldn't help overhearing it. You're pretty loud.>

"Let's just," Kylie said, sighing out loud before continuing, "get going." Marge didn't answer, and Kylie knew that meant she was going to get her way. The nice thing about Marge was she didn't assert herself past a certain point. Kylie was in charge, and her AI appeared to respect that.

Outside, in the front room, Finn wasn't around, but Gertrude was there, standing at one of the tables. "Miss Rhoads? What are you doing up?"

Kylie walked by Gertrude, giving her a brief wave. "So long, Gertrude. Thanks for everything."

Gertrude didn't let her go that easily, though. "You're not ready to go. You should be laying down. Resting. Your body is—"

"Building new neuron pathways, I know. Plus, it's under a lot of stress. I know that, too, but I have a long space flight ahead of me. It'll take me a few days to get where we need to go. I'll get plenty of rest."

Gertrude's tentacles flicked back and forth as her eyes studied Kylie's. They went from sunflower yellow to an angry red. "I guess I'm not going to change your mind on this."

"Not really. Thanks for everything. Girls like me, we can't stay still very long."

"Don't go get yourself killed," Gertrude said, her voice soft with a hint of what Kylie took to be a genuine worry.

<Well, she seems to care.>

Kylie ignored Marge. All she wanted was to get back to her ship and crew.

<You seem agitated. Did I do something wrong?>

<Yes. No. I just…can I have some silence, please? I'm still not used to sharing my headspace, and I want to keep my eyes peeled on this station.> It was hard enough to think as it was.

Marge fell quiet again, and Kylie was grateful for the reprieve but hated the idea she might have hurt its feelings. Her feelings. AI were living entities, right? But they were also machines. Advanced computers and advanced tech. Now another being was living in her brain, whether she wanted it to be or not.

They shared things. Knowledge. Body functions.

How would Kylie ever come to grips with that? God, what would her parents think if she ever got around to seeing them again? She wasn't sure if they'd even talk to her. She'd walked away from their life a long time ago, but this was so very different. This was a slap in the face to everything they believed. To everything Kylie had been taught: AI were dangerous and eventually would turn on humans. She didn't know if it was true, but her parents sure believed it—droves of people living on the fringe did, too, thanks to her father's teachings.

She climbed a long stairway and came to Heaven's docking ring. The *Dauntless* was just a few hundred meters to her right, and when she caught sight of it, all her worries melted away. The airlock was open, awaiting her arrival, and Kylie sprinted toward it, feeling a wave of relief wash over her. She stopped in her tracks when she saw Finn there, moving several large crates on wheels toward the exit.

"Finn," Kylie said, forcing her voice to remain level. "What are you doing on my ship…taking my things…?"

He chuckled and pulled four bags of chips out of the top crate—one in each hand. "I never had seventeen varieties of chips before! Ketchup *and* octopus flavored!"

Kylie laughed and waited for him to leave before closing the airlock. She walked as fast as her sense of balance would allow in the narrow confines of the ship and stepped onto the bridge with a smile on her lips. "I'm on board and ready for takeoff."

"Aren't you a sight?" Winter gave her a big hug. "It's a relief to see your brain hasn't bled out your ears, or anything like that."

Kylie couldn't fault his sentiment, though his delivery left something to be desired. She signaled Rogers over the Link. *<Get permission to leave. Get us out of here. You know what course to set.>*

<You've got it, Captain,> Rogers said with a jovial tone. *<And welcome home. The place wasn't the same without you.>*

Kylie didn't know if she agreed with Rogers, but it was nice to be back. It was nice to be home. She turned back to Winter. "Where's Grayson? Any problems?"

Winter shook his head. "Everything's been quiet as can be. He's in his quarters. I think he's just anxious to get started. Like we all are."

Except his reasons *were* different, weren't they? As long as he was agreeable and he did what needed to be done, everything would be fine.

INTEL

STELLAR DATE: 09.11.8947 (Adjusted Years)
LOCATION: Finn's Mod Shop, Heaven
REGION: Scattered Disk, Gedri System, Silstrand Alliance

<*Incoming message,*> Jerrod said. <*It's routing through a relay on the station. There's going to be some delay on top of the light-lag.*>

Grayson nodded, and Jerrod connected him. <*Grayson, report,*> the general's voice reverberated in his mind.

Surprised to hear from the general himself, Grayson sat down on his cot and steepled his fingers. <*General Samuel. We're on our way now to Lana's location. It's a secure research lab owned by Maverick, though it's run by his second-in-command, Harken. It'll be heavily guarded, and the crew of the* Dauntless *plans on doing recon only.*>

<*Convince them otherwise.*> General Samuel's tone was terse as it came across the Link. <*The sooner we get her back, the better.*>

We? Why did the general talk about his daughter like she belonged to all of the SA and not just himself? It's possible he was referring to himself and his wife, but he rarely even mentioned her. <*Yes, general. Kylie's under a lot of stress, but I'm sure—*>

<*Good. Use that to your advantage. You know her. Now, exploit her. Don't forget where your loyalties lie, Grayson.*>

Just like that, General Samuel cut off the transmission and Grayson was left to wonder about him. He hadn't asked about Lana—if she was all right or what her condition was. Did the General have some intel he wasn't sharing, or were they all operating blindly?

<*What's his game?*> Grayson asked.

<He often doesn't tell us everything. It's on a need-to-know basis, Grayson. You know that. You've been at this long enough.>

Everything Jerrod said was true, but Grayson was beginning to believe maybe he needed to know more. Maybe being with Kylie and her team had taught Grayson a bit more about transparency and trust than he'd realized. Whatever it was, he didn't feel right about what was going on. Something was up with Samuel.

He should share it with Kylie, but if he did, she might not want to go along with what he needed her to do. And if Grayson had to come clean about the marque, she'd space him—or worse, skin him alive.

His stomach grumbled, and Grayson stood and left his cramped quarters. Perhaps things would look better after a hot meal. He walked down the corridor and turned into the galley, nearly colliding with Kylie, who was carrying a steaming mug of that black tar she called coffee.

"Everything alright?" She eyed him up and down. "You look like you've seen a ghost."

"Fine," Grayson smiled. "Everything's fine. Just feeling a little peckish."

"I was too."

He stepped inside but glanced back at her. She had just come aboard and he hadn't properly greeted her yet, or asked her how she was. Grayson didn't want to make Kylie suspicious. "How are you doing? With Marge?"

Kylie gave a brief eyeroll. "All right, I guess. It's weird to share my headspace with someone else. I feel like I'm never really alone. You know?"

Grayson did at that. "Don't worry; you'll adjust. And now you'll always have someone to keep you company."

"Greeeat." Kylie's lips pulled together in a sarcastic display. "Like it wasn't hard enough to think on this ship as it is." For a split second, her eyes narrowed. "Are you sure there's nothing you need to tell me?"

"Nothing." Grayson licked his upper lip. "I'm on food rotation tonight. Spiral potatoes?"

"Sure. Why not? Some more potatoes before we get where we're going. Maybe chocolate pudding surprise for dessert while we're at it."

"Please." Grayson groaned. "Don't tell me what the surprise is…"

"You don't ask. I won't tell." Kylie continued her walk down the hall, and Grayson thought there was a definite bounce in her step. It was nice to be able to talk to her again. A lot of things were nice since being on the *Dauntless,* but Grayson had to put that out of his mind.

A young woman's life was at stake, and he had a job to do. Soon, Lana would be in his hands, and they would deliver her to the SSF. Stars willing, the crew of the *Dauntless* would be amenable, and survive.

Stars, let the crew—Kylie especially—be willing. Grayson didn't want to do what was expected of him if they weren't.

LANA

STELLAR DATE: 09.05.8947 (Adjusted Years)
LOCATION: Harken's Research Facility, Perseverance
REGION: Scattered Disk, Gedri System, Silstrand Alliance

Lana closed her eyes, but the pain raging in her head wouldn't be quelled. With a groan, she mashed her face into the thin, white pillow they had given her, but who were they? Lana didn't know. She had been waiting for a transport and then…then what had happened?

She had been kidnapped. Someone had snatched her as she stood on Platform 42 awaiting a shuttle that would take her out of Silstrand space forever. That would've shown Daddy a thing or two about her independence. School, college, it was for the birds. Lana was going to make a quick buck by doing something easy and then be set for life.

Turned out, things didn't always go the way you wanted. What she wanted more than anything was for Daddy to show up with his soldiers and save the day. Wasn't that a joke? She hated his rules and now Lana wished she had followed them in the first place.

Now, she was locked in this space-rotted room, and no one would even talk to her. Her trendy clothes had been taken and all she had were plain white pajamas. They itched, the bed sheets were rough, everything scratched.

She peered at the sheets; they looked normal enough, so why did it feel like they were tearing at her skin every time she moved? Even her eyes felt like they were made of sandpaper. Thousands of needles might as well have been poking her at all times.

What was happening to her?

"Help!" Lana screamed, and in response, her muscles spasmed, forcing her back into a painful arch.

<*You really have to calm down if you expect them to help us,*> her AI, Abby, said. Another gift from Daddy so she could ace her tests and do well at the same university her mother had attended. Really handy when it came to papers and essays but less handy when it came to skipping out of class to go to parties.

<*Isn't there something you can do? We have to find a way out of here!*>

<*You know I'm not that kind of AI. I'm more of a life coach than anything. But I guess what happens to you, happens to me. I'll do my best to try.*>

Well, that was something.

Her body barely felt like hers anymore. Lana gritted her teeth and gripped the sheets of her mattress tight. Something in her was changing, she could feel it. Something was wrong. They had told her it wouldn't hurt her, that it wasn't dangerous. But they'd lied. They had really fucking lied.

Lana squeezed her eyes shut and screamed.

The door to her room opened, and two men rushed in. They wore lab coats, but she was sure they must've been hired guns because they were strong. So strong. They grabbed her arms and forced her onto her back.

"Relax, Lana. You have to relax," one of the men said, his voice kinder than she would have expected.

"I want my father!" she screamed and gnashed her teeth at one of them. "You bring me my father!"

"I'm afraid we can't do that. I'm afraid you're going to have to trust us. We can help him." The kind man smiled, but Lana didn't believe a word of it. His eyes weren't trustworthy. There was something about him that was smarmy, just like the men who worked for her father.

"He'll be looking for me," Lana whispered. "If he finds out what you've done…"

"But he won't find out, will he?" Someone else entered the room, the staccato snap of a woman's heels a change from the men's heavy footsteps. Lana peered around the men restraining her and caught sight of long, dark hair. She remembered the woman's name from earlier. When they'd first brought her in…she remembered the woman inspecting her like a side of beef.

What was her name?

Harken. That was it. Harken.

"Let me go. He'll make you suffer!" The pain surged behind Lana's eyes, and she felt a wave of nausea come along with it. She moaned and let her head fall back onto the rough pillowcase.

<*Something is changing in your body,*> Abby said. <*I've never seen anything like it…your molecular structure, your brain, everything is changing, Lana.*>

Oh, stars. They had said she'd be safe. They'd said she could smuggle it in her body without it hurting her. Money and lies, they went hand-in-hand, right?

Lana stifled a sob and realized those around her were still talking.

"Have you figured out how to get it out of her yet?" Harken asked the lab techs.

When had they arrived? It was like the room was suddenly full of people.

"Not yet. It's changing her faster than we thought."

"Sedate her, then. We can't have her causing any trouble or hurting herself. We need to slow it down, too. We can't have her changing completely on us." Harken turned and left the room, not even sparing Lana a final glance.

One of the lab techs drew a hypospray out of her pocket, and Lana bucked and fought the two orderlies who held her down

"Stay away from me!" She got an arm free and swung at one of the orderlies, but he grabbed her wrist and pinned it against her side. Two more orderlies appeared and grabbed her kicking legs. Lana was completely helpless.

Her back arched as the cold hypospray touched the base of her neck. Warmth spread through her body and then it flipped and ran cold. Her fingers splayed against the sheets as her body was wracked with convulsions.

<*Daddy!*>

<*I can't reach him. They have us locked up in here good. Whenever I try to connect to their network, I'm blocked. I can't even get a timestamp from it,*> Abby said, sounding worried for an AI.

The drugs they had injected into her were making Lana's body go numb. She couldn't fight it anymore and before long, the only thing she could feel was the pain in her skull, but even that seemed so far off. Lana moaned; that was about all she could do.

<*Abby…*>

<*I'll do what I can, Lana. I'll do what I can so you survive this process but you are going to change—whatever was in that nano is rewriting every part of you. I'm going to do what I can to slow it…to keep it from killing the both of us, if I can….*>

That damn nanotech. Transporting it was supposed to be easy. Most people had nano, at least the rich did, so why was this particular tech so different? What made it so special?

And why did everyone want to get their hands on it?

Now, it was in the very blood that flowed through her veins, boring into every cell in her body. Whatever happened next, Lana was helpless to fight it. She'd be changed, used, and if they could find a way to extract it from her, Lana would be dead.

<Your father will send someone. You have to hang on.>

If that was true, Lana hoped they would hurry. She didn't know how much longer she had.

* * * * *

Harken strode down the corridor toward the labs in the research facility's central hub. She needed to ensure the scientists there had worked out the logistics necessary to extract the nano in a fashion that would allow it to be reprogrammed. So far, when they pulled it out of her and attempted to reset its ownership, the nanobots had died.

And now it was a race against time.

Reba raced after her, carrying a hyfilm note in her hand. "Ma'am! The GFF has been trying to get ahold of you."

"I have more pressing matters to worry about than the GFF, Reba, as do you."

She nodded. "I know Lana is top priority, but the GFF is calling you back in. Since Maverick's indisposed at the moment—while he heals."

"Unfortunate, but the attempt on his life brought a warning that someone is onto us and that we have the girl. It's only a matter of time before they find us."

Harken wasn't worried about Kylie and her rag-tag group of junkers. She was worried about the man she'd seen shoot Maverick—before she'd removed all evidence of him and pinned the whole mess on Kylie. Whoever that bounty hunter was, he had some serious tech. Tech she would love to get her hands on.

"They want you back on Jericho…to take over for Maverick."

"That isn't happening, Reba. Stall them. I don't care what it is you have to do, but there's no way I can go back at present. They'll need to wait."

Her hurried footsteps chased after Harken. "What do I say? What do I do? Jericho needs someone at the helm. People are going to start asking questions. People—"

"Enough, Reba!" Harken's temper erupted. Reba was a worm, but even this was a new level of annoying for her. "Do or say whatever you have to. This moment is critical and I can't be interrupted by a trip to Montral, and certainly not by you every ten minutes."

Harken opened the door to the lab and slammed it shut in Reba's face. She paused and then locked it for good measure.

The faces of her scientists inside were worn and tired as they huddled around a table covered in plas and hyfilm with a jumble of holoprojections dancing above. "I guess from the long faces that you need increased motivation."

"Harken, we've been here for days. The tech we need to extract the nano from Lana's blood in a null state…we just don't have it."

"And she's changing," another answered. "She's changing faster than we can keep up with. Soon, she'll be the most advanced human being the galaxy has ever known."

"Correction," Harken said. "She'll be one of at least two. Everyone in this room knows what Tanis Richards is capable of. Or do we need to review the vid again and refresh your minds?"

"No, we know what she can do," The scientist swallowed hard and gazed down into his coffee cup.

Satisfied, Harken smiled. "Good. If we don't want Lana to end up as another Tanis Richards, then we find a way to succeed. Otherwise, she could single-handedly take every one of us down and blast her way out of here."

"Well, we're not on the *Intrepid*!" one of the scientists exclaimed. "We don't have the tech you're talking about. Maybe if we were Silstrand Alliance. Maybe…."

Silstrand. Harken nearly laughed. They'd never pay as much as the Scipio Federation or the other buyer who was interested in this tech. Harken had been fighting against Silstrand's rule all her life and she certainly wasn't going to let them get their hands on something this powerful. It could change the Alliance's position in their never-ending struggle against Scipio, and the last thing Harken wanted was for Silstrand to come out on top.

No, she was going to bet on a different horse—the sure winner—and it would make her very, very rich.

"…we don't think we can extract it cleanly without killing Lana."

Harken snarled. Finally, they were getting somewhere. "Then let's look at all the options, gentlemen. The girl's survival has never really been an issue for me."

"She's just a girl."

Harken disagreed. "No. She's a goldmine, and when I send her lifeless body back to her father, I want him to see that I stripped it completely."

* * * * *

Days had passed since Lana had first awoken in this facility. They kept sedating her to keep her quiet, or maybe it was to slow the changes coming over her. The last time she had fallen asleep in a bed, but then they had moved her. Now Lana woke in a sterile cell that didn't even have a mattress or windows. It was a steel room, reinforced with something powerful. Lana couldn't see it, but she could feel it.

It made her insides shiver as if she could feel some sort of vibration. Lana had never felt anything like it before.

<*Some sort of biotech that can resist nano attacks. Almost like it has antibodies against other tech. Silstrand Alliance has uses for it in its prisons, but that's all military-grade,*> Abby said.

Military-grade? What kind of facility was she in, anyway? Who had her? Lana had to figure it out, and soon. If her father didn't send someone to rescue her, what would she do? Escape? This was way more than she had bargained for. Way more.

She stroked the metal panel that should've been a door, except it had no handles or even a sensor pad. The panel was completely smooth and almost entirely seamless. It must've only opened from the other side. If only she could figure a way to jimmy it…

<*They'd kill you if you tried. Whatever it is you're carrying inside, letting you go wouldn't be worth the risk. Please, Lana, just sit and let's wait,*> Abby implored.

<*I thought you wanted to get out of here,*> Lana retorted as she threw her hands in the air and turned around, leaning against the wall and sliding down to a crouch.

<*I do.*> Abby sent her a pleading face. <*But I also want to live. If you die, I might be lost right along with you.*>

<*Comforting thought,*> Lana responded as she wrapped her arms around herself. <*Keep trying the homing beacon. Daddy will send someone if he hears our distress call.*>

<*I haven't stopped trying, but it's not getting through. The signal is blocked here. Wherever this place is, it's remote, and this new room is buckled down tighter than your father's wallet.*>

Lana chuckled to hear something she often said repeated back to her. Then, she noticed a tingle in her hand. With wide eyes, Lana watched as her right hand changed texture—it was beginning to match her shirtsleeve merely by touching it.

"Oh stars!" Lana screamed and quickly uncrossed her arms and slapped her hand against the wall desperate for it to change back. Contact with the steel wall triggered a change, but not the one she wanted. Now, her hand took on a steely sheen, and the effect began to travel up her arm.

She shrieked and waved it in the air. "Help me! Abby!"

<Calm down. Lana, don't scream. They're sending someone. He's coming down the hall. If you don't calm down, they're going to sedate us again.>

Being sedated was the least of her problems. Lana glanced around for anything to cover her arm, but there was nothing. In a blind panic, she threw herself into the corner of the room, squatting down and wrapping her still normal arm over her changing one. What would they do when they found her like this?

She gasped erratically, unable to regulate her labored breathing. What was she going to do? Lana hung her head and focused on the door.

It was opening. Moving. She could hear something going on from the outside, and a split second later, she could hear their conversation.

<Something's going on in there, looks like she's freaking out. You grab her, and I'll give her a little something to take the edge off.>

<It's not working the way it's supposed to.>

<Yeah, I know, but Harken is almost ready for her. Soon, she won't be a problem.>

Harken? Lana's eyes widened. Where had she heard that name before? The knowledge was so close, but she couldn't grasp it. She waited for Abby to fill in the gap, but her AI didn't speak up in her mind like she normally would have. Not that it mattered, it sounded like this Harken wanted her out of the way—dead. Lana didn't want to die. All she had wanted was to get away, stick it to her dad. This wasn't what she'd signed up for!

The two orderlies entered her room, but neither of them appeared to see her right away. They cast about as they walked into the center of the room. One scratched his head. "Where the hell…"

They couldn't see her.

<*If I miss my guess, your body is camouflaged with the wall. I don't know how you did that, but it might have given us the time we need.*>

With the door of her room left open, Lana had to make a move. This might be her only chance.

She charged from her cover and it wasn't until she was right on top of the security guards that they saw her. One screamed and lifted his hands to protect himself as Lana smashed her metal hand into his face. He flew backward and she kept sprinting for the door as the other guard fired his weapon at her.

Lana ducked into a forward roll, escaping into the hall. For the first time, she got a good view of the facility. Metal walls and no windows, with security cameras everywhere.

<*Where do we go?*> Frantic, Lana sprinted down the hall. Red lights started to flash, and a siren wailed. It wouldn't take them long to find her.

<*Abby!*>

<*Turn left.*> Abby's voice was calm. <*Down the elevator shaft. It'll buy you some time while I figure out where to send you next.*>

Anywhere sounded good to Lana. The doors to the elevator wouldn't open. So, she forced them wide and jumped down into the shaft and onto an elevator car. She landed with a thud and the shock of the impact reverberated through her.

Damn, that hurt more than she'd expected it to. Lana couldn't believe what she was doing. How she moved. She'd never felt so fast, so powerful, as if her lungs could take in more air than ever before. She was going to be unstoppable.

<*We need a ship. We have to get out of here, Abby.*>

<*You can't fly.*>

<*Together, we can. Together,*> Lana said.

<All right. All right. There's a small cargo ship. It's docked a few levels up, on a landing pad, I think. We might be able to fly it if we can get to it but…I'm not this kind of AI, Abby. I was groomed and raised as a social companion for children. A high-functioning nanny, if you will.>

<Then, take care of me and get me back home,> Lana said.

Abby sighed. *<I'm finding the best route. Give me a second.>*

Lana wasn't sure if they had a second. The elevator car they had landed on lurched as it started to descend and Lana splayed her fingers out on the surface. She had to get off it and get moving up. She gazed upward. That was the way she had to go, wasn't it? Abby had said 'a few levels up'.

She jumped over and grabbed onto a ladder centered on the back wall of the shaft. Lana took a deep breath and started to climb up toward the next level. *<My headache's coming back.>*

<You're pushing yourself too hard. Your vitals are all over the place.>

There wasn't time to rest, if that was what Abby was trying to imply. Escape seemed so close, almost something Lana could touch. She had to keep going.

<Two more floors and we'll be on the level that can get us to the landing pad.>

<Okay.> Her voice shook, even from within her own head. Her body was changing. One minute, Lana felt fine, and the next, it was as though she might fall apart. Her body was fighting against something stronger than itself and it would tear her limb from limb.

Lana pulled herself up and through the elevator doors. She crawled into a service hallway, and the landing pad was visible through a window at the far end. From what she could see, it appeared to be a small cargo ship. If she could just get there…. She rose to her feet, broke cover and ran for the end of the hall and the door beside the window.

Lana was going to make it. She really was. She was going to…

<*Stop!*> Abby screamed. <*You're not alone. You're….*>

Security forces stepped out in front of her, and her over-sensitive hearing picked up footfalls behind her, as well. She was surrounded. Someone stepped through the doorway from the landing pad, and Lana took a tentative step back. It was a rather angry-looking woman…a woman she had seen before. Where had Lana seen her before?

<*It's Harken,*> Abby supplied.

The woman's lips twisted into an unpleasant smirk. "Take her to the lab. We're just about ready for her. And from the looks of it," she said, glancing down at Lana's hand before continuing, "not a moment too soon."

Lana's jaw tensed as vice-like hands grabbed her arms. "You're going to regret this!"

Harken laughed. "I really doubt it."

"Wait," Lana said to the security guards all around her. "I really…. Please. Don't hurt me."

Their stone-cold faces didn't seem to care one way or another. A needle jabbed into her skin, and Lana felt the walls begin to spin. Would no one help her? Would no one truly come?

PERSEVERANCE

STELLAR DATE: 09.15.8947 (Adjusted Years)
LOCATION: Salvage ship *Dauntless*, In orbit of Perseverance
REGION: Scattered Disk, Gedri System, Silstrand Alliance

The planet's name was Perseverance.

Kylie had spent years in the Gedri system and had never heard of it, but that wasn't too surprising. The dual-star system contained over three hundred dwarf planets, most way out in the scattered disk—out beyond the jump points, and without anything to make a visit worthwhile.

It was a pale gray planet, on the large side for a dwarf world with a diameter of just over four thousand kilometers. It had a dense core, giving it 0.65*g* on the surface. The wiki for the planet suggested that it was most likely the core of a larger planet that had been ejected in some cataclysmic event early in Gedri's formation.

The data entries on the planet showed that several new mining rigs had taken up work on its surface, drilling down for the rare elements below the ancient crust, tucked in the deep reaches of its once-molten core.

Supporting those mining rigs were the refineries, service companies, and, naturally, the brothels, drug dens, mod shops, and whatever else showed up to take the miner's hard-earned cash.

They were, of course, all run by Harken now—perhaps they always had been.

It was time to get down there, scout it out, and hope it was enough to secure Nadine's release.

At the controls, Rogers's back was ramrod straight and his shoulders tense. "I don't know about you, but this whole thing feels pretty ominous."

Kylie felt the same way, but she didn't want to say it out loud and jinx the mission. "We tackle this like we always do. A heist. An op. We land, and we do what we have to. Get this job done."

Winter sat at a console scanning the surface of the planet, getting the lay of the land around their target. "We're good at that. Even if we're nothing else, we got that."

The facility was near one of the massive mining rigs that hunkered down on the planet. Over three kilometers tall, with a base over two across, struts, beams, and cables splayed out from the facility, anchoring it to the planet as it drilled a thousand kilometers into the world in search of precious elements.

"That is one big rig," Rogers muttered as they began their descent toward the world. "Cool name too; it's called the *Unyielding Lance.*"

"I like that," Winter said.

"That new ident box you picked up from Finn better be clean," Kylie said. "GFF has a lot of patrol craft around. I guess they want to keep their investment safe."

"It's clean. Finn has never done me wrong. I have the old box wrapped in a faraday cage, too; its signal isn't getting out. As far as anyone looking at scan knows, we're flying the *Splendid Hero* here."

"Now that's a stupid name." Winter grunted.

"I don't care what the name is," Kylie said. "So long as it doesn't get us shot down on approach."

"No sweat, Captain." Roger gave a brave smile. "I'll have an approach vector from the planet's Space Traffic Control in no time—and there it is. We're cleared for our descent."

The ship's documented destination was the planet's main spaceport, but they would instead touch down outside one of the service towns near the *Unyielding Lance.* ATC may send them a nastygram, but on a world like this, out in the fringes of the Gedri system, people rarely landed where they were supposed to.

The service town Kylie had selected was a run-down place named Treatise. It was just ten kilometers from the brothel where Harken had her secret lab. Kylie drew her lips into a thin line. "Come in low enough so I can jump off near the facility. You boys have some drinks or something at Treatise, but stay close to the ship. If things go bad, I'm going to need a distraction."

"We excel at that." Winter laughed and slid a piece of gum into his mouth.

"That we do, boys. Winter, any last-minute advice?"

"Yeah, don't get dead." He stood up and towered over her. "Want me to come with you?"

Kylie shook her head. "No, Grayson's right. Me going alone makes the most sense. If I don't come back, you can find a way to rescue Nadine. You can't do that if we're all dead."

Winter rose his eyebrow. "Pull a fast one on this Jason guy that has her? You really think we could run a job like that?"

Kylie laughed and clapped the big man on the shoulder. "I have no doubt."

Not one for long goodbyes, she hurried out of the bridge and down the corridor to the port airlock. She was already wearing the base layer of her Trylodyne IA99 armor, and she picked up the armor's snug helmet and the stealth layer.

<You sure you have the bugs worked out on the stealth systems?> she asked Marge. *<Maybe I should just go with the base layer.>*

<Don't worry,> Marge said brightly. *<The stealth systems on this armor were made for someone with an AI, or significant internal processing power, to manage the stealth component. The armor's systems can do it for a bit as a fallback, but that's for emergencies only. It's why it kept failing on you—that and the batteries all needed a full cycle.>*

<So it's going to work?> Kylie asked.

<Of course, Miss Kylie. It's going to work perfectly.>

<And this sort of op, you've done them before? It is the reason I got you—I need to know you're ready.>

<Absolutely!> Marge said with a gleeful chuckle. *<I've been dying to go on a mission like this for so long. I got pretty tired being paired with smugglers and mod traffickers, I'll tell you. A salvager like you is a real step up for me.>*

<It's nice to impress someone.>

"Kylie!"

She turned her head to see Grayson dashing toward her. "Rushing to wish me luck?"

"Of course, but I have faith in you. I always have," Grayson said and she got the feeling he was leading up to say something else.

She kept her eyes on him. "What else is there? Something, I'm guessing."

He nodded. "If you get in there and you can get close enough to see Lana, to see what condition she's in, and if you can read the situation right…why not rescue Lana here and now?"

"By myself?" Kylie's mouth fell open at the level of faith he must have in her. "I appreciate the blind faith you have in me—" It wasn't as though she hadn't considered it—stars, she had debated it with Rogers and Winter more than once. None of them thought she could do it, but it seemed Grayson did.

"That's always been the mission. Rescue Lana and bring her back to General Samuel, so why all the back-and-forth with this bounty hunter?"

"To rescue Nadine." Kylie's cheeks reddened. "I should've known you'd try to bypass that little step—because it means nothing to you. *She* means nothing to you, which is fine, you just met. But she means a lot to me and I can't…I won't forget about her, Grayson."

Grayson held his hands up. "Hear me out. If we bring Lana to General Samuel, you'll have SSF warships backing you up when you meet this bounty hunter. We'll get Nadine back *and* your letter of marque." For a moment, Grayson's eyes shifted. "Just think about it, that's all I'm asking you. If you think you can get Lana and yourself out alive, just consider it."

Kylie nodded. "And you can guarantee that the SSF would help me rescue Nadine?" He was right about one thing; if Kylie could get Lana out, she'd have a better bargaining chip to get Nadine back from Jason—except with Grayson on board, he would insist they immediately turn Lana over to the SA. He may believe that General Samuel would help rescue Nadine, but Kylie wasn't so ready to stake her lover's life on it.

<*Are people just bargaining chips?*> Marge asked, and Kylie silently sighed. She had to get better at keeping her private thoughts private. Grayson was replying to her question, and Kylie pulled her attention back to him.

"Of course, I can," he said. "If you do this for General Samuel, you can have pretty much anything you want."

Kylie thought about that long and hard. Samuel was hiding something, and she wasn't ready to trust him, but Grayson…maybe. "I'll keep it in the back of my mind but I won't put the *Dauntless* or the crew in more danger than is necessary. Understand?"

Grayson nodded. "Understood. Now you be safe out there. You do what you need to, but get back to the ship in one piece."

"I—"

Her words were cut off as Grayson took her face in is hands and kissed her. Kylie was taken off-guard. She nearly stumbled backward, surprised to feel his warm lips against hers again. When it was through, their eyes locked on each other and Kylie lived through a lifetime in his. The years of courtship, the wedding, the painful divorce, it all played out in an instant in her mind.

His hands dropped to his side. He turned and walked away. Just like that.

<*Well, that's complicated,*> Marge said.

Wasn't that the truth?

*****

The kiss distracted her. Kylie tried to scrub it from her mind. Why would Grayson pick now, of all times, to do that? Was he trying to throw her off balance? Was it a good luck kiss? Or maybe he thought he might never see her again so why the hell not? Sometimes a kiss was just a kiss, and sometimes love dimmed into nothing but a single spark.

Always there. Always waiting.

Kylie had to push it all away and forget. She was doing this, after all, for Nadine, her lover. She didn't need feelings for Grayson clouding the issue. Things were good between her and Nadine. They had a wonderful rhythm. Kylie was accepted for who she was. It was a wonderful thing, so she couldn't let one little kiss cloud her mind.

She shook her head one last time to knock the distracting thoughts free, then pulled the armor's helmet on, grimacing as the rebreather settled in her mouth. At least it would do double duty and give her enough air when in Perseverance's thin atmosphere.

<*You're sure about the stealth layer?*> she asked Marge. <*It's not going to konk out on me when I'm sneaking past a bunch of guards, is it?*>

<*Miss Kylie! I would never put you at risk like that. Also, I'm in here, too. I don't want your head shot off any more than you do.*>

How comforting, Kylie thought and was pleased when Marge didn't reply. Maybe she was finally getting the hang of keeping her thoughts to herself.

Kylie slithered into the stealth layer and put the pistols in their holsters, then snapped the rifle into the latches on her back. She added enough ammunition for the trouble certainly awaiting her, and stepped into the airlock.

<*Coming up on our jump point,*> Marge advised, and Kylie palmed the panel to close the inner airlock door and open the outer hatch. When it slid aside, she braced herself against the winds that whipped into the small room, threatening to knock her down and pull her out the open hatch.

Outside it was dark; a world like Perseverance was always dark. From here, the Big OJ was little brighter than any other star. Ahead, *Unyielding Lance*'s running lights cast long, eerie shadows across the landscape as it tore its way to the center of the planet.

Kylie looked down at the ground rushing by over twenty meters below.

<*Any chance you can get closer, or maybe slow down more?*> she asked Rogers.

<*Sorry, Captain, this is as low as I can get without hitting any rock outcroppings.*>

<*What about* **me** *hitting rock outcroppings?*> Kylie asked.

<*This was your plan,*> Rogers reminded her.

<*Yeah, yeah, okay.*>

<*Good luck,*> Rogers said.

<*Thanks. You too.*>

Kylie slipped her feet into a pair of thruster boots that would slow her descent and forward motion. Hopefully, before she smashed into the ground, or into one of those rock outcroppings Rogers had mentioned.

<*You'll want to jump on three, it'll be safe then,*> Marge said.

On the count of three, Kylie jumped. The boots fired their retro thrusters on cue, and she hit the ground with only a moderately jarring impact.

She unslung her rifle and scanned her surroundings with the armor's enhanced vision. Nothing stood out other than rocks, and more rocks. Many of them showed signs of recent exposure to extreme heat—likely from when the *Unyielding Lance* lowered itself onto the world.

On her right, she could see the distant lights of the brothel, and she activated her stealth armor, pleased to see her limbs disappear from view.

<*Nice work, Marge,*> she said.

<*Thanks, Miss Kylie. I'm monitoring the stealth systems to ensure they stay within optimal ranges. I'll alert you if there are any problems.*>

<*Thanks,*> Kylie replied as she began picking her way across the rock-strewn landscape. She had four kilometers to cover and wanted to do it as quickly as possible.

From this far out, no guards were visible, but she imagined they would be soon enough. <*Make a digital record of our approach vector,*> Kylie ordered Marge.

<*Will do. Also, I am taking a snapshot every thirty seconds. Photographic evidence will help to make a compelling dataset for your bounty hunter.*>

That a girl, Marge. Kylie hated to admit that so far, having an AI wasn't exactly the worst thing that had ever happened to her. Was everything her parents and their group believed a lie? How long had she been hiding from this tech because of faulty information? Could everything her parents believed just be simple paranoia?

She drew closer to the brothel and its hidden lab, picking her way across a landscape littered with heavy-grade crates—supply drops that hadn't been collected yet. Her armor's sensors picked up movement beyond the crates. Kylie zoomed the optical pickups and detected a pair of all-terrain vehicles on patrol.

Patrols protecting a brothel? She was in the right place.

<*See if you can get into the facility's network. Find out if those vehicles patrol at certain times.*>

<*Okay, their wireless signal does reach this far,*> Marge said. <*Is it okay if I use illegal means to do so?*>

<*Of course it is. Whatever gets the job done.*> What a silly question that was. <*Is there a special reason you're asking?*>

<*I just need to make sure we're on the same page. I wouldn't want you to force me to shut down and ask for me to be extracted from your mind.*>

All this talking was just going to slow them down. <*Marge, consider this your permission to do anything that you think you need to do.*>

<*All right then.*> Marge sent a smiley face. <*Let's go kick some booty.*>

Kick some booty, oh boy.

As they approached the facility, her armor's thermal and UV optics easily picked out the individual guards. There were two up front at the brothel's entrance and a few on the roof, eyes keenly surveying the building's approaches as they held their weapons ready.

The building was a wide, three-story structure set back into a low hillside. Halfway up the hill, protected by high rock walls, was a landing pad with a small cargo ship and a pair of shuttles. She suspected the research-lab section of the building was set in the hillside. *Why would Harken bother fronting this facility with a brothel?* she wondered.

As she studied the building, a third shuttle passed through the atmospheric shield over the landing pad and landed. She cycled her vision to a higher zoom level and watched men and women, clearly dressed for a night of hard partying and sex, exit the shuttle and walk to a well-lit doorway. Of course, the well-to-do executives who ran the mining rigs—and anyone else with good money—would want a nice place to spend the evening, away from the mining towns where the regular workers socialized.

It gave them cover for whatever else they were up to—like kidnapping girls.

Kylie crouched low behind a pair of crates and watched the guards, timing their movements; she wasn't about to blindly trust her armor's stealth tech and walk right up in the open. Every fifteen minutes one of the guards would walk along the roofline to the far side of the building and survey the perimeter, leaving a blind spot that would allow her to sneak up the hillside to the landing pad.

<*I've identified their off-world comm tower. It could easily be disabled,*> Marge said.

<*Great work,*> Kylie replied, feeling like she was talking to a puppy.

<*Shall I disable it?*>

Kylie bit her lip as she thought it over. <*Not yet. We're still only on recon. We don't want to spook them unnecessarily. Standby, just in case.*>

<*Affirmative.*>

Kylie piggybacked on the brothel's public Link access and reached out to the *Dauntless*. <*I've arrived at the facility. Scoping out security outside and the entrances. I'll be attempting to enter soon, hopefully unseen.*>

She held her breath as she waited for someone to respond. It was Rogers. <*We're getting acquainted with the locals. There are some hot girls, and it seems they're from the brothel you're visiting—making a few extra bucks on their day off.*>

That piqued Kylie's interest. <*I wonder if you can get any intel from them.*>

<*What do you think I'm doing?*> Rogers asked. <*So far nothing, but I can't just ask if there are any kidnapped general's daughters in*

the place. I gotta say, though, these girls are souped up. Gorgeous. Flawless. Perfect, and with that smell.... They're an upgrade from the girls Maverick has at The Shade.>

Modified and synthesized for the perfect experience. Kylie wondered if they worked for Harken of their own freewill, or if the research lab subverted kidnapped girls and turned them into willing sex toys. There was always a market for that sort of thing. <*Thanks, Rogers. I'll keep my eyes open. You make sure you do, too.*>

<*Oh, my eyes are open, Captain. Wide open.*>

When the guard moved away again, Kylie crept toward the side of the building. She used the crates for cover, and then a parked ATV sitting near a side entrance. Laying on the seat was a black supply bag with an ID tag. Curious, Kylie took both and hurried along toward the building.

<*Seventy-five more seconds until the guard returns,*> Marge said calmly.

Kylie didn't respond as she scampered up the hill and crouched behind the cargo ship's front landing strut. There was a locked door nearby and a wide window beside it. From her position on the pad, she could tell the door led deeper under the hill, probably where she wanted to go. Unfortunately, there was no handle.

<*Think you can pop that door open?*> Kylie asked Marge.

<*I don't think so,*> Marge sounded annoyed. <*It's not on the network I have access to; it looks like it's hard-wired only. I can get that other door open, though.*>

Kylie looked across the landing pad to the door the group from the shuttle had gone through. A sign over the entrance read Harken's House of Harlots.

Seriously?

<*Okay, let's go,*> she said and rose, moving to the shadows. She walked slowly toward the entrance, trying to get a look

through the glass doors, checking for guards inside. Suddenly, a warning appeared on her HUD.

<*Um, Miss Kylie?*> Marge asked.

<*Yeah, what is it, Marge?*>

<*Well, your armor's about to shut down the stealth systems. It's processor is overheating all of a sudden. It checked out fine before…I don't know what's wrong with it.*>

<*Shit!*> Kylie swore and dashed back to the shuttle's cover. It looked like strolling right in was out of the question now.

<*Options?*> she asked her AI.

<*Well, I did see a balcony sticking out of the hillside when we climbed up. I think it was off one of the…you know, human carnal pleasure suites.*>

Kylie laughed to herself. Had she somehow gotten a prim and proper AI?

<*Okay, let's go check it out.*>

Kylie backtracked partway down the hillside and came to the balcony. She jumped over the railing and through the grav shield. Her suit registered breathable atmosphere, and she set her rebreather to pull fresh oxygen.

<*It looks empty,*> Marge observed as Kylie peered through the glass doors into the room.

<*Yeah, can you get these doors unlocked?*> Kylie asked.

<*Of course! I've found them on their network. Unlocking now.*>

There was a soft *snick* sound, and Kylie tried the handle. The door slid right open.

<*How are you getting into their network so easily?*> she asked Marge.

<*Oh, I have been in a number of GFF personnel over the years. They don't change their codes very often. A lot of the old ones still work.*>

<*And they just leave you with all this information when you get removed?*> Kylie asked.

<*Well…*> Marge paused. <*Not everyone I've been in has lived a long and fulfilling life, if you follow me. My last human died, and Finn rescued me with all my data intact.*>

Kylie didn't want to think of what that sort of 'rescue' would have involved and instead focused on the room she had walked into. The décor was gaudy to say the least, with a vibrating bed and beaded curtains covering a closet and the bathroom.

All the latest gadgets and gizmos available to modern humans, and still the most engaging thing was a bed that could vibrate on twenty frequencies. Simple pleasures sometimes really were best.

A pleasant smell managed to get past her rebreather. Kylie's armor analyzed it, showing a rather potent batch of pheromones that would intoxicate just about anyone, keeping them off their game.

<*Marge, I can't go through this place in my armor if the stealth system is still acting up. But if I take it off, I'm going to get high as a kite. Any way you can filter this stuff out so it has less of an effect?*>

<*I'll work on it.*>

Kylie set her rifle and handguns on the bed, shutting off its vibrator first so they wouldn't end up on the floor She shimmied out of the stealth suit, which she lay on the bed beside the weapons.

<*Okay, I've added nano to your nasal cavity and lungs. They'll filter out most of the pheromones. You'll be a bit giddy, but that should be the worst that happens,*> Marge said.

Kylie nodded and pulled off her helmet before pushing aside the beaded curtain in front of the closet. The thing was bigger than her personal quarters on the *Dauntless* by a long shot. She found the perfect black, skimpy dress with color-changing sequins, a shimmering page-boy wig that changed color in tandem with the dress, and a pair of black, thigh-high boots

Seemed like Momma was going to get a new pair of shoes. What better way to blend in at a brothel?

Kylie hid her armor and weapons in drawer at the bottom of the closet and dressed quickly. The tall boots went up under the dress, so she slid one of pistols into the top of her right boot. It made the boots rub together and squeak as she walked, but that was the sort of thing people liked in a place like this.

She piled her short, brown hair onto her head and pulled the wig over the top. It was loose at first, but it sensed her skin's warmth and tightened, its edges adhering to her skin. Handy. She wasn't the best at makeup, Nadine usually took care of that for her, but Kylie sat at the mirror and managed to throw on some shiny red gloss and simple mascara.

She looked like a different person as she sauntered out of the bedroom into a small hall. The gun between her thighs made her throw her hips, altering her gait—hopefully in a sexy fashion. Kylie heard music, laughter, and a few squeals of delight from down the hall. She followed the sounds, taking a few corners until she entered a luxurious lounge. Overhead, twinkling chandeliers cast low light on the occupants who were scattered throughout the room, standing in small groups, or reclining in deep sofas.

Kylie had spent a lot of time in Maverick's less-than-savory establishments. Generally, they were shady clubs with dark corners for grungy sex and whatever else the patrons wanted to get up to. But even for catering to a better clientele, this place seemed over the top. They must've been playing a new angle that Kylie wasn't privy to.

<Keep scanning the facility. We have to find where Lana's being kept.>

<I'm searching. There's an area protected by some sort of block. It's jamming my probes, but I'll keep trying,> Marge said.

Interesting. *<That's probably where we need to go, but I don't want to go in blind. Keep at it.>*

On the far side of the room was a door for wait-staff. If there was a way deeper into the facility, it would be through there. Kylie worked her way through the sitting area as the men and women she passed—lounging on cushions and drinking at the bar—undressed her with their licentious eyes. She played with the exquisite crystal necklace she had picked up from the room's wardrobe and flashed them some sexy glowers.

She was almost at the rear door, when someone tapped her shoulder. Kylie slowly turned around and came face-to-face with a beautiful woman whose hair cascaded around her face in long, golden ringlets. She was completely sheathed in black latex, and her waist was cinched tight in a black corset, but it was her eyes that held Kylie's attention—the strangest, palest, twinkling blue Kylie had ever seen.

"Boss wants a good time," the woman purred. "A few girls are being sent up to her rooms and I know she'll love the look you have going on. She loves the classy type." Her eyes narrowed. "Wait, I haven't seen you here before. Who are you?"

"I'm new. Came in on the last shuttle." Kylie pulled her shoulders back and placed her hands on her hips. With a flick of her finger, she triggered her own batch of pheromone spray.

The woman took a deep breath. "Mmmm…the guild doesn't always send us such a lovely find—we usually have to do some work before they look as good as you." She touched Kylie's cheek gently with her well-manicured fingers, each with a jewel-encrusted tip. "Gorgeous doesn't begin to define what you are. A gem in the rough. Ohh…I'm going to enjoy giving you some extra enhancements." She pushed her breasts into Kylie's.

Kylie had no idea what the woman was referring to and didn't want to find out. She knew it would be easy to subdue this woman, but once she did, her cover would be blown. However, going up to some low-life's room wasn't exactly something she had time for.

"I'd rather stay here, I think." Kylie's hands slid around the woman's tightly-cinched waist, mouth hovering a hair away from her lips. "With you."

The woman pushed into her, and her tongue flicked out, running over Kylie's lips before she stepped back. "Later, darling. Harken doesn't like to be kept waiting. Since she keeps us fed and clothed…."

Harken. Kylie's heart skipped a beat. "Okay, then, let's go. I haven't been up there before, so I might need someone to show me the way."

The woman held up two key cards. "I wouldn't dream of letting you up there alone. She has a few of those scientists with her, celebrating some big tech breakthrough. I'll round up the others, and then we'll go up…" She walked away, barely able to saunter in the tight skirt that welded her legs together. "What's your name, anyway?"

"You can call me Ana," Kylie said with a pleasant smile. She leaned against the wall and waited, jutting her hips out to one side. She just had to be patient. Just had to wait her turn and soon, she'd be with Harken, and the woman would take her to Lana. Whether she wanted to or not.

Then maybe all of this would be close to being over.

HEAD OF THE SNAKE

STELLAR DATE: 09.15.8947 (Adjusted Years)
LOCATION: Harken's Brothel/Research Facility, Perseverance
REGION: Scattered Disk, Gedri System, Silstrand Alliance

In a total, ten girls were picked, each elegant and glamorous in their own right. However, a certain type of girl was definitely in evidence. Elegant, dressed in long gowns, looking like vid-stars at a showing—in fact, some looked uncannily like a few actresses Kylie had seen in recent vids. In stark contrast, Kylie and her new friend, the Madam of the establishment—Giselle was her name—stuck out from the rest. Giselle was obviously playing to some specific tastes.

They rode an elevator down two levels, and then took a short maglev further into the facility, which triggered Marge to check in. *<This is the area I couldn't read past. Now that we're beyond the barrier, I might be able to find what we need.>*

<Hurry. We might need to get out of here fast if Harken recognizes me.>

They got off the maglev car and followed a short corridor to what Kylie assumed were Harken's quarters. Well, suite would be more accurate. The outer room they were led into had a large, sunken seating area. In the center, a low table held drinks and a circular sofa wrapped around it. The scientists Giselle had mentioned—strangely, all men, and many still wearing their lab coats—were easy to identify, as they spoke nervously while the girls were ushered in.

It couldn't be the first time these men had been in the company of beautiful women. Kylie wondered what had them so on edge.

Giselle nodded and prodded girls to stand in a line. Hands on their hips, each girl moved seductively in an effort to entice the men and be chosen first. Some tossed their hair, and others puckered their lips, blowing kisses. Kylie didn't want to be chosen by the scientists, so she didn't do anything provocative. She was waiting to see Harken. If she was picking a girl tonight, Kylie wanted to be that girl.

The scientists had ended their conversations as the women lined up, and two rose first, then the other four joined them and approached the women with broad smiles—like kids in a candy store. "They really are some of the best we've made here. Just as beautiful and lovely can be," one commented.

Proudly, Giselle smiled. "Of course, the girls I keep here are some of our finest stock. It's important to impress the buyers when they come around. For example, Tyna here loves to please. I think she'd just die if she didn't have someone to please." Giselle laughed as she touched Tyna's chin and the girl nodded emphatically. "The ways she's been modified to increase your sexual pleasure can't even be described. You have to feel them to believe."

Kylie finally understood what the brothel was all about. These women were enhanced and modified before being sold as sex slaves to the highest bidder.

That's what Giselle had meant by giving her extra enhancements. Kylie worried that somewhere in the facility, Lana was undergoing these sorts of modifications…maybe she was even one of these girls, made to look like a famous star, ready to be sold off.

No, Kylie knew that couldn't be it. That didn't explain the bounty hunter's interest. He wasn't the sort that got sent in on a job like that.

Kylie watched as the scientists paired off with the girls. She was one left of three that hadn't been chosen. Giselle gave her the stink eye. "I feel like you're not giving it your all, dear. I thought you'd be number one—not that you were intended for these men, anyway. Still, I wanted to test your curb appeal."

"I'm glad. These guys weren't really my type," Kylie said, and then her ears picked up the sound of the suite's door sliding open. Harken stepped through. She was dressed in a black A-line dress and a leather bolero. Her heels snapped a staccato rhythm across the floor as she approached Giselle. "Now *she* looks more my speed."

"Well, you have high ambitions, don't you?" Giselle laughed and ran her hands down her torso as she sidled up beside Kylie and whispered in her ear. "If you knew a thing or two about Harken, you wouldn't want to be chosen. I'm her favorite pet, and what she does…."

Kylie sucked in her breath as Harken drew closer, her cold eyes inspecting them. She held out her hand, and Giselle bent over and kissed it. "Darling, Giselle, you've brought me a sampler pack."

Giselle blushed as Harken took her by the waist and gave her a drawn-out kiss. "I wanted you to be sure that you had the best."

"As I always do. It's been awhile since I've tasted our wares, but tonight, I have a reason to celebrate." Harken moved through the remaining girls and inspected each one like they were a piece of furniture. She caressed their breasts, held their waists, and kissed every woman. When Harken had sampled all the others, she approached Kylie, who drew a trembling breath.

Harken's eyes bore into hers. "Well, nervous jitters? Oh, Giselle, did you bring me a virgin? Unmodified? How adorable of you."

Kylie shook her head. "I'll teach you a thing or two in the bedroom, trust me. I'm just nervous to see you in person–so sexy and alluring for a woman of such power." Kylie ran her fingernails down Harken's neck onto her chest, lifting them away before they slipped between her breasts. Peering up at her, she pouted and gave Harken her best puppy-dog eyes.

Harken's tongue flicked and touched her ruby red lips, and her eyes crinkled ever so slightly. "There's something familiar about you…."

"Why not sample me, then? See if my flavor strikes you. I won't bite." Kylie smirked slyly. "Unless you ask me to."

Harken's hand flashed out and took Kylie by the throat. Squeezing, not hard, but enough to give her a little scare. Kylie went with it and passionately kissed the other woman. She triggered the device she wore on her wrist twice, which flooded her senses with desire. Harken's hands cupped her ass, and she moaned. "This one. This one's for me, and we won't be disturbed."

Giselle's expression fell, and she gave Kylie a hard stare. "Yes, ma'am…whatever you wish."

Harken took Kylie by the hand and led her away. Kylie glanced back at Giselle, who shook her head. "You'll be sorry," Giselle mouthed silently to her.

Kylie doubted it. Soon, it'd be Harken who was sorry, and if she tried whatever it was Giselle seemed to think would happen in the bedroom, it wasn't going to work out the way she wanted. Kylie would teach her something she couldn't forget. She owed the woman for past indignities.

Harken's private bedroom was on the far side of the seating area, and Kylie glanced down at the doll-girls as they walked past. It made her sick to think these girls weren't here of their own free will. But they weren't her mission, and she followed Harken to her room.

Inside, it wasn't cozy or warm, but Harken did keep the lights muted. Next to the bed, there was a bottle of champagne and mood-enhancing snacks. She noticed that cuffs and straps were attached to the bedframe. She'd seen worse.

"Champagne? I have a lovely synthetic blend," Harken said as she slipped off her bolero and tossed it on a dresser.

"Sure. Sounds nice." Kylie sauntered over to her. Harken slid the champagne from the ice bucket and Kylie wet her finger on the ice. She picked up a glass and traced her finger over its rim, producing a soft, resonant tone that filled the room. She danced her fingers across the glass, altering the tone and playing a little song, before handing the glass to Harken.

Harken raised an eyebrow as she filled two glasses. "That's a nice little trick. I bet it impresses all of your clients."

"Oh, you'd be surprised the tricks I have up my sleeves." Kylie accepted the champagne glass from her and crossed her ankles, pushing her ass out to create the perfect hourglass look. She wanted Harken's eyes on her body as much as possible. Harken could run a facial scan on her at any moment, and then the game would be up.

"To adventure," Harken said with a hungry smile, and they tapped the rims of their glasses together. Kylie downed her champagne and licked her lips, encouraging Harken to do the same.

Harken took the bait, taking a long draught from the glass. "You're going to have the night of your life. I'm going to make you squeal." She grabbed Kylie by the waist, pushed back Kylie's hair and nuzzled her neck. "You might even scream."

Kylie moaned and tilted her head back. "Just what every girl wants to hear."

<*I found it! I know where Lana is being kept. They're prepping her for some sort of procedure. It's brand new and according to their logs, barely tested. They're not expecting her to survive. I'm digging, but the security system keeps blocking me out,*> Marge said.

<*What?*> Kylie started. <*What sort of sex-doll procedure could kill the girls? Though at least she hasn't been turned into one of them yet. Keep at it. I'll do what I can from here.*>

<*Okay!*> Marge never failed when it came to enthusiasm.

"What you did to me out there, I'd almost say you're using some sort of pheromone system to cloud people's minds. You should know, it doesn't work on me—been around it too much—but I appreciated the gesture."

Kylie shrugged as she reached back and tugged Harken's hair. "I just wanted to play with the big boss, not a bunch of squints who don't know how to please a girl. I wanted to take the best for myself."

"I like that." Harken laughed. "I like that in you. I can already tell that you'll be a great addition to my stock. But what I don't like…" Harken began as she slid her hand along Kylie's thigh and pulled out her pistol. "What I don't like are Maverick's scraps." She shoved Kylie down onto the bed and aimed the gun at her. "You think I don't recognize you? You think I don't know Kylie Rhoads when I see her? Whatever you're planning, it isn't going to work—for you, at least."

Kylie considered pretending to be worried but decided against it. "I just happened to be at the wrong place, at the wrong time. And now I'm here to collect what our friend, the bounty hunter, wants."

"And what's that?" Harken asked.

"Lana."

Harken laughed. "Unbelievable. If you think I am just going to let you walk in here and…" with a scowl, she stumbled forward. Her hands shook, and she was unable to hold the pistol steady. "What the hell did you…"

"I put something on the rim of your glass." Kylie shrugged. "It's what I planned originally to do to Maverick when we were rudely interrupted. So, if you could please finish passing out…"

Harken dropped to her knees. "You stupid, bitch. You'll never…" She slumped forward and face-slammed into the floor.

Kylie retrieved her pistol from Harken's hand. "Let me finish that for you. I'll never get Lana out of here. I'll never get away. How am I doing so far?"

Except for a snore, Harken was quiet. Beautiful.

<*Wait,*> Marge said. <*Open her mouth. One of her teeth looked funny.*>

Kylie did as her AI asked and looked at Harken's teeth. They all looked normal to her.

<*There. Her left canine—it's fake.*>

Fake teeth? Who would have fake teeth when a quick visit to a med-tech could have you growing a new one in a day?

<*Touch it. I want to see what she's hiding in there.*>

<*Hiding?*> Kylie asked as she complied.

<*Aha! It's her personal tokens. I have full access to the facility now.*>

<*Hope you have a route to Lana for me,*> Kylie said to Marge

<*Yes, but she doesn't have long before they do whatever it is they're going to do.*>

Kylie holstered her weapon and peered outside the bedroom. The scientists and the other girls were all occupied, none sparing so much as a glance in her direction.

She grabbed a couple of small sandwiches from one of the tables as she dashed by. She was going to need an extra bit of energy to finish this job.

A LITTLE FUN ON THE SIDE

STELLAR DATE: 09.15.8947 (Adjusted Years)
LOCATION: Treatis, Perseverance
REGION: Scattered Disk, Gedri System, Silstrand Alliance

Grayson watched as Rogers landed the *Dauntless* on the dusty dunes at the outskirts of Treatise. The pilot had skill, he'd grant him that. The *Dauntless* was markedly less aerodynamic than a brick, but you'd never know with Rogers at the helm.

Once the ship settled, they donned their environmental suits, locked everything down, and headed into the settlement. Once again, Grayson felt like a fish out of water, only this time, the stakes were much higher.

Most of the buildings looked like dormitories and warehouses. The only business appeared to be a pub, and it was a dive, at that. They cycled through the building's airlock, and by the time they took off their helmets and grabbed some stools by the bar, the bartender had given them the once over.

"New workers, huh?"

"That easy to tell?" Winter said and leaned his elbows on the countertop. "Give me whatever's freshest."

The bartender spun a glass in his hand. "I know pretty much everyone that comes through here. The *Lance* is big, but not that big. Plus, your friend there is looking a little clean around the edges."

Everyone threw a glance at Grayson, who turned a bit red under the collar.

"Oh, he's not so bad," Winter said. "Just likes to shower a little too much."

Everyone laughed at that, except for Grayson, who let out a huff of air and reached into a bowl of peanuts.

"Everyone deserves a break now and then," Rogers said. "How's business? Doesn't seem like a lot is going on here. I mean, not that I could really see."

The bartender shrugged. "The GFF is happy with what the *Lance* pulls out, but you're observant. They could double their production if they sent in more men who liked to work hard. No offense, but none of you guys look like you've worked hard a day in your life. Well, except maybe for that one."

He pointed at Winter.

Rogers chuckled. "You got us, pal. Got us pegged."

The bartender smiled and held his hands up as if to say, 'it was no big deal, this is just what I do'.

Grayson watched Rogers turn and survey the room. There were a few other patrons present, and in the back, a trio of beautiful girls was coming down a flight of stairs.

"Be back in a bit, I need to go get acquainted with the locals," Rogers said as he stepped off his stool and approached the women with open arms.

The bartender laughed. "Well, that's what they're here for."

Grayson nursed his drink while Winter started up a game of darts with several men from a nearby table. The time passed slowly as they waited for Kylie's call requesting distraction, backup, or rescue.

<*Rogers, anything from Kylie yet?*> Grayson asked.

<*Oh, yeah, she made it in and is scoping it out,*> Rogers replied.

Grayson looked across the pub at their pilot half-buried in women. <*What the hell, Rogers! I've been sitting here worried sick about her and you're over there having the time of your life!*>

<*Hey, you're a big boy. If you want to talk to Kylie, you know how.*>

<*Well, not really. How did she contact you?*> Grayson asked.

<*She piggybacked on one of the networks out there at the brothel. I imagine your AI could figure out how to reach her,*> Rogers

replied mentally as Grayson watched him suck on one of the girls' ears.

Grayson sat fuming for a moment before he took a deep breath and asked, <*Well, Jerrod? Can you?*>

<*Of course, I'm connecting out to the brothel's public network now.*>

Grayson waited several excruciating seconds. <*And?*>

<*I can't find her. There's no response when I ping her there.*>

<*Rogers, Winter, get over here. Jerrod can't ping Kylie,*> Grayson addressed the other men.

<*Really?*> Rogers asked. <*Let's play it cool. Keep trying for a minute. Maybe she's busy.*>

<*That's not how it works,*> Grayson replied. <*Jerrod pinged her and there was no response. Even if she was busy it would still show a connection.*>

<*Maybe it's time for that distraction,*> Winter suggested as he threw another dart.

Grayson sighed and turned back to the bartender, waving to get the man's attention.

"You know how you noticed we're new? Well, we're here looking for…alternate opportunities, let's say."

"Oh, yeah?" the bartender replied, setting down the glass he had been cleaning. "And what makes you worthy of any special arrangements?"

"I have information I can sell for a little employment," Grayson said and slid a credit chit across the bar.

Cautiously, the bartender picked it up and flipped over in his hand, seeing the symbol on the back. "SA? This can be verified?"

"It can." Grayson drummed his fingers along the bar top. "I have information that would help the GFF get out of a jam. A serious one. I'm high-ranking enough, and fed up enough, to sing for a price. If there's enough in it for me and my friends…"

"One minute." The bartender took the chip with him and disappeared behind a closed door.

Rogers sat down beside him and let out a long breath. "Are you sure about this? Maybe this is more distraction than we need."

Grayson smirked. "Afraid of a fight?"

"An unnecessary one? Sure." Rogers dipped his hand into a bowl and pulled out a fistful of peanuts. "Far as final meals go, this one sucks."

Winter chuckled as he rejoined them at the bar.

"Any moment now, he'll come back out and say someone will come talk to me. Meanwhile, security personnel will leave the hidden outpost to apprehend me, giving Kylie the opening she needs."

"I hope you're right." Rogers straightened up. "Because he's coming back."

The bartender returned with Grayson's chit and handed it back to him. "My boss is sending someone to talk to you. Until then, drinks are on the house." He clapped his hands and spoke a bit too loudly. "Why don't you tell me what it is you'd like? Something I can call up special for you guys?"

"Fried chicken?" Winter asked, and Roger promptly elbowed him.

"On second thought," Grayson said, sliding the chit back into his jacket pocket before continuing, "I might have been too hasty. I've changed my mind. We'll be on our way out. We have some emergency business." Each of them stepped away from their stools, and the bartender's eyes widened with disbelief.

"Wait a second, you're not just leaving, are you? Stay for just a few minutes. I swear we'll make it worth your while."

"We really have to jet," Rogers said and picked up his environment suit's helmet, turning toward the airlock just as it cycled open.

Two figures in heavy armor walked through, weapons held ready. The other patrons moved to tables farther from the entrance as the newcomers blocked the only way out.

One removed his helmet—which was decorated in an elaborate pattern that looked skeletal in nature—and gave a menacing snarl, complete with fangs.

"Gentlemen," the bartender said with an abnormal amount of glee in his voice. "I'd like you to meet The Boss, as he likes to call himself."

Great.

"Do your thing, Gray," Rogers said and ducked out of the way as The Boss lunged forward, reaching for his neck.

"Gladly." Grayson stepped in front of the armored man and threw a punch, nailing The Boss right between the eyes, but the beast of a man barely moved backward. "I think we might have a problem." Grayson called out as he was picked up and hurled across the pub.

Winter drew his weapon and fired at The Boss, hitting him center mass. The armor the huge man wore absorbed the shot, but it was enough to drive him backward. Winter flipped his pulse rifle around and bashed the other guy—who had been kind enough to remove his helmet after the Boss had—in the head, forcing him into the wall. Winter followed up with another blow to the skull that drove the man down into a table, which shattered under the armor's weight.

Grayson picked himself up, grabbed his helmet, and ran for the airlock. The inside door was still open, and the three of them piled in. Winter hit the control to cycle it, and Rogers pulled a concussion grenade from inside his suit and lobbed it through the closing door. It wouldn't kill, but everyone would wake up with a headache in a few minutes.

"Do you think this is a big enough distraction?" Rogers asked.

"I think it'll work." Grayson led the team outside, and they sprinted into Perseverance's cold, unforgiving atmosphere. They'd have to hurry if they wanted to make it back to the *Dauntless* in time to lift off before The Boss and his goons got to them.

<*I've found her!*> Kylie's voice was relieved as it came across their private net, but more than that, there was an awestruck quality to it. She almost didn't sound like herself.

<*Be careful, Kylie,*> Grayson said. <*Are you all right? Is she?*>

<*I'm going to need more time to get out of here, but be ready.*>

Grayson turned and gave Rogers a steady look as they charged up the ramp of the *Dauntless.* <*We'll be on hand. I promise you.*>

<*I'm going to hold you to that, Gray.*>

"They're coming," Winter said as they raced onto the bridge. "What do we want to do?"

"Punch it!" Rogers leaped into his seat, and, without securing his restraints, leaned forward and took the controls. The *Dauntless* boosted off the surface leaving a molten patch of rock in its wake.

"Stay low. Don't go too high. We want them to believe they can catch and apprehend us," Grayson said.

"What makes them wrong?" Winter asked.

"Good question." Rogers sucked on his bottom lip. "Someone man the guns and issue a warning shot to those nice gents taking off behind us."

RESCUE

STELLAR DATE: 09.15.8947 (Adjusted Years)
LOCATION: Harken's Brothel/Research Facility, Perseverance
REGION: Scattered Disk, Gedri System, Silstrand Alliance

Kylie snuck through the halls, following the route Marge had laid out. Her AI used Harken's tokens to take her through security measures she had never seen Maverick, or the GFF, employ before. The route was like a maze, the passages continually turning inward through layers and layers of automated security.

She stopped just inside a doorway, spotting a set of cameras before they caught her. Leaning back against the archway, Kylie asked Marge. <*Can you loop the video for those cameras?*>

<*I'm attempting to hack in now. Although, there are other sensors—they might figure out what we're up to with your heat signature hanging out here.*>

<*Will it buy us time?*>

<*Yes. Even though I don't know that more time will help.*>

Kylie sighed inwardly. <*Do it.*>

Kylie waited for what seemed like an eternity while standing in the open before Marge replied. <*Okay. Go. The coast is clear.*>

She passed through the doorway and down a long hall before she came to a wide window overlooking a lab. She didn't have time to focus on what was inside as voices came from a corridor to her left.

<*Two coming from the west side. You'd better hide and I'll jam their comms. It'll send them looking for help.*>

Marge almost read her mind.

There was some equipment in the hall, and beyond that, a table. Kylie dashed down the hall and squeezed behind a table leaning against the wall. As the footsteps rounded the corner and traveled closer, she held her breath and squeezed her eyes tight. Then whoever was approaching stopped and started to backtrack the way they'd come. Kylie breathed a sigh of relief.

<Unlock the doors to the lab. I want a good look around before I decide what I'm doing next.>

*<**Doing** next? I thought this was a recon mission. You're not going to go with Grayson's crazy suggestion that you rescue Lana, are you?>*

Kylie didn't respond as she waited for Marge to finish her work. She had two options: either leave now, or break Lana out herself. But Harken had made her, and would put the facility on full alert, and they might not get another chance. If they were experimenting on Lana—doing something that was going to kill her—then Kylie had to get her out. Even if Grayson hadn't reinforced the belief that she could do it, it was really the only option.

Kylie couldn't let Lana die.

Plus, the faster she rescued Lana, the faster Kylie got Nadine back. Grayson wouldn't like it, but she'd have to deal with him somehow.

Exchange Lana for Nadine and cut the general out. A letter of marque wasn't that important to Kylie if it meant being without her lover. If they met with Jason, the bounty hunter, maybe they could figure out why Lana was so special. Why everyone seemed hell-bent on obtaining her. Lana wasn't much older than a college student, so why was she so important?

Could she really let Jason have Lana, just like that? Once Nadine was secure, nothing was stopping her from rescuing Lana and then returning her home.

<*Doors are unlocked, opening them for you. I'm digging through the resource files here. It's huge. There's a lot going on.*>

Kylie went into the lab through the open door. There was a lot of equipment along the walls, and in the center of the room was a single bed on which lay a young woman.

The woman's back was arching and twisting as if she was having some sort of seizure. Her long, blonde hair was slick with sweat and spread around her head like a wavy halo on her pillow. Her face strained with exertion, and a sob escaped her throat. The freckles Kylie had seen in the picture were gone, as though bleached off, and her blue eyes were wide with fear.

She was just a kid.

"They're going to kill me," she whispered. "Please! Help me."

Her words moved Kylie. She nodded wordlessly and worked to remove the straps holding Lana's legs and arms down. She didn't consider the risks. Lana's life was in danger. She needed help, and she was a person, wasn't she? Not just a bargaining chip. Damn, why couldn't she have just been a damn bargaining chip?

<*Clear the halls,*> Kylie ordered Marge. <*Can we call out to the* Dauntless*?*>

<*Not yet. We're still inside the jamming zone. We need to move past the lab if we're going to send a clear signal.*>

Damn, but Kylie could do that well enough. "Can you walk?" she asked Lana.

Lana shrugged and then nodded her head. "I guess so. Maybe. Did my dad send you?"

"Yes," Kylie said, mostly to motivate her. "Now, we need to get moving before they find us. We have a lot of ground to cover." She extended her hand to the girl, but Lana recoiled from her.

"Don't touch me! Don't touch me!"

"I'm just trying to help." Kylie tried to keep her temper under control. "If we don't get moving soon, we'll be a little bit dead. So, if you please—"

"You can't touch me!" Lana sobbed and put her hands over her ears like she was trying to block something painful out of her mind. "I'll hurt you if you touch me."

"Lana."

<*Wait! Stop. She's right. I found her records in the lab's logs. There's something in her they want. Something in her blood.*>

Kylie's hand froze in midair. <*Is it contagious? Is it safe to take her out of here?*>

<*It's not contagious…but it can be transmitted—maybe. It's highly advanced nano. It's rewriting her entire body on a molecular level. I've never seen anything like it. What she's carrying is worth more money than most planets will see in a lifetime. Stars, it may be worth more than the entire Gedri system.*>

Kylie's mind swirled with everything her AI had just said. She tried to get a grasp on it. Is that what everyone was fighting over? Was that what Grayson and the Silstrand Alliance wanted? This advanced tech…was Lana even General Samuel's daughter?

Lana sobbed into her pillow and her heart-struck grief sealed the deal for Kylie. She wrapped a sheet around her hands so she could safely grasp Lana's shoulder. "Whatever this is, I'm not going to leave you behind. Stay with me. Can you do that?"

Her tears tapered off and then Lana nodded. "Where will we go?"

"Leave that to me," Kylie said with gritted teeth. She helped Lana off the bed, and a minute later, they sprinted from the lab together. Kylie went first and Lana followed behind, trying to stifle her sobs. The simple truth was, if Kylie couldn't get out of this maze and reach the *Dauntless* in time, there might not be an escape for either of them.

BACKUP

STELLAR DATE: 09.15.8947 (Adjusted Years)
LOCATION: Near the *Unyielding Lance*, Perseverance
REGION: Scattered Disk, Gedri System, Silstrand Alliance

Rogers howled with delight as the *Dauntless* dove low and away from the GFF cutter that had been pursuing them. Grayson loved to see a man enjoying his work, but this was a bit more extreme than he could tolerate.

<*I have Lana. I'm going to need an extraction.*>

Grayson closed his eyes and took a deep breath. Thank the stars for small favors. The rest of the team wasn't as joyful as he was.

"Whoa!" Rogers said out loud while Winter broadcasted across the system-wide Link.

<*Wait a second,*> Winter said. <*We talked about that. This was just supposed to be recon. A scout mission only, Kylie. Let the bounty hunter do the heavy lifting and let's get Nadine back.*>

<*Sorry,*> Kylie said though her voice lacked any remorse, <*but they were going to kill her, and she's in a bad way. I didn't have a choice.*>

In a bad way? Grayson struggled to keep his emotions in check. He had watched Lana grow up. He'd seen how she'd gone from a naïve child to a young woman who had wanted nothing more than to break free of being 'the general's' daughter. Was Lana disillusioned and rebellious? Maybe, but that didn't mean he wanted to see her hurt. Far from it.

<*Is she all right? What happened?*>

<*I'll fill you in later, but something is happening to her, and I only have my armor and no environmental suit. So, my egress options are a bit limited. We were trying to get to the landing pad*

where there are some shuttles, but they've cut us off from those…so, if someone wouldn't mind offering us a little assistance….>

<*We'll be right there!*> Rogers said, and the *Dauntless* banked hard, making a quick one-hundred-eighty-degree turn as the atmosphere howled around its hull, and headed toward the facility.

Grayson rose from his seat and rushed off the bridge.

"Wait a second!" Winter chased after him. "Grayson, what do you think you're doing?"

Already in the weapons locker, Grayson grabbed an environmental suit and began putting it on. "Simple matter is, Winter, if the *Dauntless* attacks that facility head on, Kylie and Lana might die in the extraction, or they may have surface-to-air defenses that will take this ship out. Tell Rogers to slow down. I'll drop out, and I'll do what what's needed to get them both safely back. Jerrod will send you the coordinates for where to meet up with us."

As he spoke, Grayson grabbed a duffle and put two spare suits inside, just in case jumping out a window ended up being the best way out of there.

Winter wasn't having it. "Nothing about what you just said is 'simple'. What makes you the choice to go? She's *my* captain. *We're* part of her crew, not you."

"While that might all be true," Grayson said with a sigh. "I have a military AI and you don't. Neither does Rogers. If anyone is going to go in there and get her out with a high chance of success, it's me."

Winter stared him down for a long time. "So, help me…if you don't come through for her, Gray. I will hunt you down myself."

"And I wouldn't question it for a minute." Grayson offered him his hand and Winter looked at it before giving a single, firm shake.

"Get in the airlock. Rogers will come in low and drop you as close as we can, but no guarantees the enemy won't kill you as soon as you show up on their scan."

Grayson was willing to take that chance. He grabbed a sidearm and a few grenades, and hurried to the airlock, cycling it open while still pulling on his helmet. Once the pressure equalized, the outer door slid open to the sounds of the low-pressure klaxon.

He shielded his face from the blowing sand, trying to get a clear view of the dark ground that raced blow.

<*Sir,*> Jerrod said, <*SSF Command has an incoming message for you, top priority. They expect us to have Lana in hand and ready for the trade-off when we leave Perseverance. They will be ready in two hours.*>

<*Acknowledged. Send them back a communique regarding what's about to transpire.*>

<*Ready, sir. If Captain Rhoads puts up a fight during the trade off, you are aware of what you're expected to do? You might not be able to protect her any longer.*>

<*And you think I should take her out? Just like that, after everything we've been through and everything she's done to save Lana?*>

Jerrod paused. <*Well, I don't know. We've always done what the SSF orders, no questions asked. Should we be doing something else?*>

<*I'm not sure.*> It wouldn't come to that. Kylie would just have to be made to understand. He wasn't ready to say goodbye to her again, but if the SSF had its way, this time, it would be permanent.

KEEP MOVING

STELLAR DATE: 09.15.8947 (Adjusted Years)
LOCATION: Harken's Brothel/Research Facility, Perseverance
REGION: Scattered Disk, Gedri System, Silstrand Alliance

Kylie knew she couldn't outsmart them forever. Eventually, her streak of luck would break—which it did just as soon as they got out of the maze of labs and were nearing the area where Harken's suite was located.

Shots rang out as she peered around a corner, striking the wall near her head. Kylie ducked back, taking a deep, steadying breath as she considered how close she had just come to biting it.

She glanced back at Lana to be sure the girl was alright—well, alright insofar as gunfire was concerned. Lana hunched under a blanket they had found along the way, pale and shivering, but still standing and looking like there was a bit more fight left in her.

Kylie pulled her weapon out of her boot and leaned around the corner, fired, and pulled back.

<How'd I do?> Kylie asked.

<One coming up from your left. I'm working on jamming their comms so at least they won't be able to work together,> Marge responded calmly.

<Thanks.>

<Like I said before, we share the same body. I want to survive this just as much as you do.>

Kylie appreciated that.

The enemy returned fire and Kylie bit her lip while she waited for a break so she could return the favor. If she had something other than just a pistol, she could mop the floor with these guys, she was sure of it. But as it was now, with a young woman in her protective custody, good enough would have to do.

She glanced at Lana again to see her fingers on her lip, twisting it as she gazed at the wall like something was there. How Kylie was going to get her through this…

"Hang in there," Kylie said and went to place her hand on Lana's but then remembered what Lana said. She couldn't be touched. Kylie didn't know why, but she didn't want to risk hurting her. "We'll get you through this."

Lana just shook her head, with tears in her eyes. "I should've…I never should've volunteered. This wasn't supposed to happen." Her face scrunched up as she neared a full on sob. Kylie wanted to ask her a million questions but now was not the time.

She had to clear a path.

The enemy stopped shooting. Kylie crouched low and ducked out into the hall, shooting one guard in the chest and clipping another in the shoulder. She paused, and no return fire came, so she beckoned Lana to follow. It took some prodding, but the girl got moving again, though she was doubled over, grabbing her stomach as if she was going to throw up. Kylie pulled at the edge of her sleeve and led her down the hall.

<Reinforcements are coming. They're locked on your position.>

<Are they tracking her?> Kylie asked.

<I think so, I'm picking up a faint signal from her.>

Shit. Kylie looked left and right down the narrow corridor. *<Can you unlock one of these doors? We need to get inside.>*

<I'm working on it. Got it. Sure is handy having Harken's codes. I hope she doesn't wake up and change them.>

Silently, Kylie thanked her by using a mental image. She kicked the door open and was about to duck inside when the sound of boots thundering through the halls stole her attention. Kylie turned to see three heavily armored soldiers in

GFF military colors—not Harken's regular merc types—round the corner. This was a change; she hadn't seen any overt GFF presence here at all until now.

The soldiers held CFT shields with pulse-rifles resting in cutouts on the side. Their visors were down, and they closed ranks, overlapping their shields. They looked ready to go to war with someone. Kylie glanced down at her dress and boots—which offered her no protection at all—and felt a suspicion it wasn't with her.

"Send the girl over to us, and we won't open fire," one of the soldiers called out.

"I'm afraid that isn't going to happen," Kylie said.

She moved to grab Lana's elbow and pull her into the room, and Lana screamed, her mouth appearing amost unhinged from being open so wide. She yanked her arm free, and Kylie was thrown across the corridor where she slammed into the wall.

She hadn't expected that.

Lana rushed the guards, and they held their fire, glancing uncertainly at one another. As she neared them, Lana raised her hands and silver filaments flowed out from her fingers. They were barely visible, but Kylie could see the strands streak toward the soldiers and dart up under their helmets. The soldiers began to convulse and fell to the ground in seconds. Tendrils touched the soldier's weapons, and they exploded, shredding the soldiers' bodies.

The debris was everywhere. No one was putting that mess back together.

Kylie began to form a clearer picture of why everyone wanted to get their hands on Lana. What she had witnessed must have been some sort of nano attack, but to have so many nanobots that they were visible and could just fly through the air and attack targets…

<Have you ever…>

<*No,*> Marge answered. <*Not in all my travels and all my human masters have I ever seen anything like that. I sense she has an AI. I'll try talking to it.*>

Sounded like a good idea.

<*Too bad she detonated their rifle's power cores. They would have been a lot better than this pistol.*>

<*I'll ask her AI not to do that if I can reach it,*> Marge replied.

Lana collapsed to the floor and Kylie rushed toward her, but then stopped, now understanding the danger in touching the girl. Lana curled into a fetal position and rocked back and forth, her fingers tangled up in her hair. "It hurts…it hurts…" she muttered. "It's everywhere. It's everywhere."

"We have to move," Kylie said quietly as she crouched next to her, a hand reaching out tentatively. "We need to move you, Lana."

Lana shook her head. "I can't. I can't…."

"Try. If you stay out here, they're only going to send more men. You'll have to go through that again. Understand me?"

Lana's eyes met Kylie's, and she nodded. With a struggle, Lana sat up and opened her hand, revealing a silver circle on her palm. Metallic filaments rose up from the remains of the soldiers and flowed toward her, disappearing into the silver circle, which then faded back to the color of her skin.

Kylie took a deep breath, and she kept her distance as Lana struggled to her feet. There was no way Kylie was going to touch her now.

They ducked into the room they'd been about to enter before the firefight, which was dominated by a long table surrounded by chairs. There were no windows, but a door was present on the rear wall.

Once inside, Kylie closed the door and heard it lock.

"Marge, find out where we are," she said aloud for Lana's benefit. "And find a way to get us out of here when the *Dauntless* arrives."

<*This conference room has a dampening field. I suspect it's to keep communications in here private. I've used it to mask our location for now, but with that explosion, it won't take them long to come and sweep the area.* >

Good enough for now.

Lana slid down the wall, settling in a squat. Rocking on her heels, she chewed on her thumbnail. "I can't hear her anymore."

"Who?" Kylie asked and crouched beside her.

"My AI, Abby," Lana said her name like it caused her great pain and squeezed her eyelids shut tight. "She's not there anymore."

<*She's still there,*> Marge said to Kylie. <*She's working so hard to keep Lana's pain at bay, she's gone silent. I don't think there's much left to Abby. She's desperate to save Lana.*>

<*Will Abby survive?*> Kylie asked.

Marge took a moment to calculate. <*I don't know, but if she doesn't, Lana won't either.*>

A strong need to protect and console the young woman in her care washed over Kylie. <Dauntless*, where the hell are you?*>

<*I'm on site.*> It was Grayson.

Kylie had never felt so relieved to hear his voice. <*Where are you?*>

<*Hold on…shooting some guys,*> Grayson replied.

Geeze, what was he doing? She sent him her location over their private connection. He, in turn, sent his. It was inside the brothel. It felt like a league away.

<*You're pinned down,*> Kylie said.

<*I'll manage.*>

Sure, he would. Kylie glanced down at her living, breathing weapon. Lana's head was against the wall, and she moaned. Her teeth chattered, her legs stretched out one after the other. Kylie didn't know how much longer she would even remain aware of what was happening around them.

<*We'll work our way toward you,*> Kylie said.

<*Kylie, I don't think—*>

<*There isn't a choice, Gray,*> Kylie said angrily. <*Lana isn't going to make it if we have to wait.*>

The silence she met was unexpected and she felt a flash of grief coming from him. So, he did care about this girl. <*I'll work my way forward. Let's meet in the middle.*>

It sounded good to her. She turned her attention to Marge. <*Can you convince Abby to administer some sort of pain relief to Lana? We need her able to move.*>

<*I've tried, but Abby isn't answering.*>

Kylie tried not to think of what must be happening inside the girl. If she had nano this advanced, imagine what the GFF could do with it?

They'd probably launch into an outright war to separate from Silstrand—their populace be damned. If the SSF got it…well, maybe that was the best choice. They'd use the tech to solidify their position against the Scipio Federation and clean up Gedri, that much was a given.

None of which were her problem right now, all she had to do was get out of there.

"We need to move," Kylie said in her sternest voice—though her heart ached for what this girl was going through—and nudged Lana with her boot. "Lana, help is on the other side of these walls and we have to get to them. Do you hear me? Lana!"

Lana's eyes opened. Something about them wasn't exactly human anymore. Kylie couldn't put her finger on it, but it was the way they focused and contracted. Almost as if she had been modded right before Kylie's eyes.

There would be no helping this girl.

Kylie pushed her negative thoughts to the back of her mind. "C'mon, girl. Don't give up here."

Lana rose to her feet, holding onto the wall for support. "I don't know if I can make it. I don't know…" Her legs crossed each other as she stumbled forward like a drunkard.

"People are waiting for you. General Samuel sent us for you. Let's get you back home to him and your family. Everything else will come out the way it's meant to, but we are going to get you home, Lana." The words most likely sounded as lame to Lana as they did to Kylie, but it was the best she could muster at the moment.

Lana's nostrils flared as fresh tears sprung to her eyes. "He's going to be so mad at me. He's going to hate me." Her face scrunched up tight.

The girl's words caused fresh pain to well up in Kylie's chest. Maybe it was because it had been so long since she had seen her own family. "Why would he be mad?"

What did you do, Lana, Kylie thought to herself.

"I…" Lana closed her eyes, and it was clear she couldn't answer, but Kylie would find out. One way or another.

"Another time, then," Kylie said and opened the door.

Once out in the hall, Marge lit up the route out of the maze of hallways on Kylie's HUD. She was surprised by how little resistance they met, and she was able to deal with the few guards they encountered without Lana's new abilities coming into play.

She suspected that all the forces were being driven toward Grayson's location. He certainly knew how to throw a party, and he'd probably gone in with a full-frontal assault on the facility.

They finally reached the maglev tram only to see a pair of guards protecting the car. Marge remotely opened the tram's door, and the guards turned, each taking a shot in the back of the head from a kinetic rifle that Kylie had managed to salvage from a guard she'd taken out.

They boarded the car, and Kylie checked the rifle. Just two more shots. The charge and reservoir on her plasma pistol were almost dry, too. Grayson better be waiting when she got to the brothel, or this would be the end of the road for her and Lana.

She glanced at Lana, who gazed up at the ceiling, her mouth dangling open. The girl was going to be no help in rescuing herself from here on out, but at this point, Kylie would count it as a miracle if she didn't die before they reached the *Dauntless*.

Lana's head jerked downward, and her eyes rolled back. "I feel like I can see the individual molecules in my hand." Her fingers splayed wide, and she stared at them curiously before turning her attention to Kylie. "And I can see a stream of code running through your body. Why do you fight it?"

Her question made Kylie stiffen. "How'd you get hold of this tech, Lana?" Kylie asked softly. "Did you know…"

Lana shook her head. "I knew I was transporting something. A simple procedure. I swallowed a pill, and they put this device in me. Wasn't supposed to be traceable." She lifted her shirt and Kylie could barely make out the signs of an incision on her stomach.

"Then I was taken—kidnapped by these guys—and a fight broke out. Let's just say, the container didn't survive. Now it's in me. Now it's everywhere." Lana was on the verge of an ugly-cry meltdown, so Kylie held back on the stream of questions forming in her mind.

Why would you do this? Who asked you to do it? Where were you supposed to take it? Those were probably the most important questions of all. It didn't surprise Kylie that Harken would want to intercept Lana and steal the tech for herself. Probably going to replicate it and sell it to the highest bidder.

It's what they did. It's what Harken did. She was part of the machine that was trying to rob Lana of her life.

"Your father will forgive you, Lana. Father's do that."

Her words of comfort covered the young woman who still shivered under the blanket. She seemed to breathe easier and the sob that was about to break free disappated. "Thank you," Lana said and stretched out her hand toward Kylie.

In that moment, Kylie forgot what was happening to Lana and squeezed the young girl's hand. For a split second, she held it there, then snatched it back. Lana stared at her with wide eyes, and Kylie feared what might happen as she stared at her hand—but nothing did, and they were distracted from the near miss as Marge issued a warning.

<They're waiting for you at the end of the line. Six strong, plus a commander.>

The moment of truth was upon them. *<I hope you're charging from the rear, Grayson,>* Kylie said.

<I'll come for you. Believe it.>

She did, she was counting on it.

SHOWDOWN

STELLAR DATE: 09.15.8947 (Adjusted Years)
LOCATION: Harken's Brothel/Research Facility, Perseverance
REGION: Scattered Disk, Gedri System, Silstrand Alliance

Kylie stepped out of the tram, gripping the kinetic rifle and aimed it at the group of GFF soldiers standing on the platform awaiting her arrival. She hazarded a guess that they wouldn't kill her on sight. Maybe it was a fool's gamble, but those were her favorite odds.

In the midst of the soldiers stood Harken, arms crossed, and a smug expression on her face, though beneath it, Kylie could see a smoldering anger.

She wondered if the GFF soldiers were invited, or if they had come of their own accord.

"Nice little nap?" Kylie asked with a cocked eyebrow.

Harken took a breath. "Time for jokes is over, Rhoads. You have what's mine, and you're not getting out of here alive unless you return it."

"She's a person and not an 'it'. You can't own a person."

"That's where you're wrong. I own lots of people, and the tech inside of her—"

"Is stolen, too. She made a few mistakes, but we're going to fix that as soon as we can."

"We all deal in stolen property. Even you, don't you? Junker. Smuggler. Whatever it is you're calling yourself these days."

"At least it got me out of the club," Kylie said.

"This talking is getting us nowhere." Harken glanced at the soldiers.

"What? Have a hot date? Hope it goes better than your last one," Kylie said, trying to get a rise out of the woman.

Harken's lips compressed into a fine line before she opened her mouth to hurl what Kylie expected to be a venomous response when Lana stepped up beside Kylie. She placed her hands on the railing that ran along the edge of the platform and Kylie felt a hum, a vibration, coming right off the girl.

"Let her go to her ship, and I'll come over to you. I'll stay," Lana said with more energy than Kylie though she had left in her.

Kylie's mouth fell open. "Lana…so help me…"

Lana shook her head. "I know what I'm doing. I know what I can do, Kylie. Trust me."

She didn't want to stay; she would do whatever it took to get out. Kylie could see it in Lana's eyes and in the sour expression on her face. "Okay…" Kylie said sadly. "Be careful."

"No false moves," Harken said. "You walk over to us slowly with your hands up, and we'll take you back to the lab. Where it's safe. We can keep the pain from hurting you any further."

Kylie bristled as Lana stepped off the tram. She must've had a plan, but Kylie wasn't sure what it was, and she was more than a little nervous about what she was about witness. Holding her breath, Kylie watched and waited as Lana put one foot in front of the other.

Moving closer and closer to the enemy.

"Lower your weapon, Rhoads!" Harken ordered.

Kylie shook her head. "Not until I know she's safe!" Which meant never. While she was in the hands of the GFF, Lana would never be safe.

"I can't hear her anymore," Lana said. "I can feel her, but you did something to Abby. You hurt my AI."

"What?" Harken was taken back by her accusation. "You need Abby to help you through this process, Lana. We didn't do anything to her."

"You tried to take the nano from me, and when that happened, Abby got hurt. The nano attacked her because she was trying to help me!" Lana took a deep breath and lunged forward.

Harken stepped back, and a weapon fired. Kylie couldn't see who fired the shot, and that meant just one thing. She dove to the ground an instant before an explosion shook the platform. "Lana!" Kylie screamed trying to see through the smoke and fire.

<*Kylie, why the hell didn't you stay on the tram?*> Grayson said, his voice strained with worry. <*Where are you?*>

He was there. He had caused the explosion. What happened to Lana? Where was she?

<*On the ground, by the tram…thanks for the warning, by the way.*>

<*Sorry, I wasn't quite ready yet, but Lana forced my hand. Where is she?*> Grayson replied.

Kylie struggled to her feet and peered around the platform. Four of the GFF soldiers were down, and two more were struggling to their feet. Kylie shot one and Grayson appeared through the smoke on the far side of the platform and fired at the other.

Harken was nowhere to be seen.

Kylie cast about looking for Lana, finally spotting her behind a bench. She was on the ground, an arm wrapped around her stomach, and her teeth chattering in pain.

"You'll be all right," Grayson went down on one knee to help her, his hand extended out to clasp Lana's shoulder.

"Don't touch her," Kylie said. "The nano…they might jump to you."

"Nano?" Grayson asked.

Kylie nodded. "She was carrying some sort of advanced tech…crazy nano abilities. I don't know where she got it, or who offered her the deal, but she was smuggling it somewhere. Isn't that right?"

Lana confirmed Kylie's statement with a slight nod of her head.

"Smuggling it out of Silstrand space?" Grayson asked. "Oh, Lana..." He spoke the words as though Lana's actions hurt him. As if he cared about the girl. Kylie didn't know what Grayson knew, but it was clear her actions had surprised him.

"We have to get her back to the *Dauntless*. We can help her there."

"I have spare suits," Grayson took off his backpack began pulling them out. "Where's your armor?"

Kylie glanced down at her tattered dress. "I had to do a bit of infiltration; it's a few levels down, tucked away. There's a balcony we can get out of. Is the *Dauntless* close?"

"As close as they dare," Grayson said.

Between them, Lana struggled to her feet. "I'm ready. I want to go, please don't leave me here."

Kylie had to resist the urge to touch the poor girl. "No one's leaving you."

They moved past the fallen GFF soldiers, and Marge highlighted the route back to the room she had entered through, as they slipped down vacant corridors.

"Did you kill everyone here?" she asked Grayson.

"No. When I approached, the shuttles were taking off, full of clients I bet."

"You know...there was a cargo ship up there, too, did you see it?"

Grayson shook his head. "No, must have left before I got here."

They reached the room, and Kylie ducked behind the curtain and pulled off the dress and boots, leaving them on the floor in a heap. Certainly not her problem. She pulled on her armor, grabbed her guns, the armor's stealth layer, and stepped out into the room. Grayson was peering out the window, and Lana sat on the bed, panting heavily.

Kylie wanted to say something to make the girl feel better, but nothing came to mind. She had no idea what they could do for her, or what she should do with her.

"Put the helmet on," she advised, and Lana looked at the clear sphere like it was a snake.

"I can't…It's full of air, I can see it," Lana whispered.

"Grayson? Care to help?" Kylie asked as she stuffed her non-functional stealth layer into his duffle along with her pistols.

"C'mon, stand up, I'll help you with it. See? I have mine on and it's fine. I can breathe okay," Grayson said as he stood in front of Kylie.

"Yeah, why don't you all stand up?" a voice asked—a voice Kylie knew all too well.

Her head whipped around and she caught sight of Harken standing in the doorway, holding a rather impressive-looking railgun.

"Aw, shit," Kylie swore.

"You know what?" Harken asked. "I don't need you for anything. You're the very definition of expendable."

Kylie's eyes widened, and time seemed to slow down as she watched Harken's finger slowly squeeze the railgun's trigger. Maybe that was what happened right before death. She tried to tell her body to move, but it was too slow as the railgun fired.

Then, a figure moved in front of her with blinding speed, right into the path of the railgun's slug.

"Lana!" Kylie screamed as the girl was thrown back into her. She heard pulse shots and knew Grayson was returning fire, but that didn't matter anymore. Kylie was supposed to protect Lana, Kylie was the girl's rescuer, but she had failed.

She pulled herself up and leaned over Lana's prone form. There was no exit wound on her back. A railgun shot should have left an exit wound. She hoped her armor's gloves would protect her as she flipped Lana over and saw that the round had hit Lana in the stomach—which appeared to be made of a silver metal.

Then, before her eyes, it turned back to flesh and began to bleed profusely.

Kylie grabbed a corner of the bed's blanket and used her armor's augmented strength to tear it off. She wadded it against the wound and pressed hard.

"Grayson!" She looked up to see him firing a shot through the door as Harken dashed down the hall. "Help me!"

Grayson reached into the duffle and handed her a canister of biofoam. "Seal her up and make sure it bonds to the suit or she'll die outside."

Kylie nodded and applied the foam as Lana began to moan and loll her head.

"I can't believe she just ran off like that, what a loser," Kylie said as she peered down the hall.

"I got a lucky shot on her. Get your helmet on," Grayson replied. "We need to move."

Kylie complied. She pulled it on as she turned to look down the corridor one last time, only to see a dozen GFF soldiers round the corner and rush toward them. She didn't hesitate and fired her rifle on its electron beam setting. Blue-white lightening streaked down the corridor and tore a hole right through one of the soldiers. The rest dove into doorways and took cover.

Behind her, Grayson yanked the sliding glass door open and picked Lana up in his arms.

<*C'mon,*> he hollered over the Link.

<I can't, these guys will just shoot us in the back if we run. I have to take them out.>

Grayson's expression was pained. <*Kylie, don't be stupid. If we separate—*>

<*I have the armor, I have a better weapon. You go, I have this!*>

Shots rang out from the corridor, and Kylie flattened herself against the wall. She scowled at Grayson—though he couldn't see it through the helmet—and waved at him to go. <*I'm not hurt. She is. We need to get her to the* Dauntless, *or all of this is for nothing. Is that what you want?*>

<*Of course, it's not what I want but…*> Grayson sighed. <*Please be careful.*>

Kylie smiled, even though it was hidden by her helmet. <*It's my middle name.*> She leaned around the door and fired again, putting a hole in one of the GFF soldier's arms. She pulled back again and glanced at the balcony. Grayson was already gone.

GETTING OUT OF DODGE

STELLAR DATE: 09.15.8947 (Adjusted Years)
LOCATION: Harken's Brothel/Research Facility, Perseverance
REGION: Scattered Disk, Gedri System, Silstrand Alliance

The wind had picked up while he was inside, creating a full-scale dust storm.

Grayson was glad the environmental suit had a small scan suite as he carried Lana down the hillside and sprinted across the rocky landscape, or he would have been lost in the rock-strewn terrain. So many questions swirled in his mind about what Kylie had told him. If it was all true, if Lana had been transporting advance nanotech, had the Silstrand Alliance known about it?

Stupid question. Of course, they knew about it. That's why General Samuel was so desperate, even willing to make a deal with a group of illegal junkers to get access to the right people. Grayson had just been stupid enough not to ask any questions. Just to follow orders. So he'd said 'Yes, Sir' and went in to rescue Lana, thinking she was nothing more than a damsel in distress.

The Silstrand Space Force had sent him in blind. Samuel, someone he had worked under for years, had let it happen. Maybe he was even the one pulling the strings. That he cared for his daughter at all was now more than a little dubious. Maybe all Samuel and Silstrand cared for was this tech and what it could do for their soldiers and warships.

Through the swirling dust, Grayson finally spotted the *Dauntless,* hovering low, half-hidden behind a rock outcropping. "We're almost there, Lana."

She moaned in his arms, her voice coming through the suit's comms. For now, that was enough for him.

They ran into the airlock, and Grayson punched the control to cycle it. The moment the inner lock door began to open, he pulled his helmet off and Lana's, too. Her skin had gone pasty white, and his augmented vision could see that she had a high fever. "Hang in there, Lana." He carried her out into the passageway and almost ran into Winter.

"What the hell? Where the hell is Kylie?"

Grayson pushed past him. "Lana's hurt. Injured bad. We need to treat her wounds."

"Where's Kylie?" Winter grabbed Grayson's arm.

He nearly snapped. "She's on her way. Circle around, keep an eye out for her signal. Pick her up the moment you see her leave that damn facility. If you're not going to help me save Lana, get the hell out of my way."

Winter blew out a worried breath. "Easy, man. Easy. Yeah, I'll help you. Rogers, you catch all that?"

<I wouldn't be me if I didn't.>

Grayson might've smiled under different circumstances. He carried Lana into the ship's medbay. He looked around at the ancient equipment and half-stocked cabinets as he laid Lana down on the table. With what they had here—with what was inside Lana…was there even hope?

Winter helped him get Lana started on an IV drip. When he tried to unseal her suit, she swatted him away. "You can't…touch me."

"Lana," Grayson whispered. "If I don't get this off and find a way to close the wound, you're going to…. We can't lose you."

"I can't control it. I don't know how. It's too strong." Lana's chest heaved. "I can barely breathe and keep it in check at the same time. I don't know what will happen if you try to operate on me."

"We could sedate her. That might make whatever's happening a little easier," Winter said.

"Do it."

"That's what they kept doing. Sedating me. I thought they were trying to hurt me, but I think they were just protecting themselves from me." Lana laughed at the foolish notion. "I really wish I was home."

Winter added something to the IV drip, and Grayson bent over to whisper in her ear. "We're getting you there. I promise. Bet your puppy really misses you."

She laughed. "He's all grown up and old now, Gray." Her head tilted to the side as she drifted off to sleep. Grayson relaxed, wiping his face.

Winter raised himself up to his full height and stared Grayson down. "You want to tell me what the hell is going on?"

Grayson peeled off his gloves and slammed his fist into the wall as he bowed his head, taking deep breaths.

"Yo, Grayson. I'm not done talking to you!" Winter yelled.

"I have no idea what's going on," Grayson said, rage filling his voice. "Isn't that obvious to you? All I know is, she was shot. We have to stop the bleeding but to do so, might be dangerous for both of us."

"That wound's a mess…but I don't see any foreign objects, it's just bleeding from everywhere. What if we cauterize the wound? Seal it up? Will that buy us some time?"

Sure, but it could also make them very dead if Lana reacted badly and lashed out at them. "Let's do it, but hurry before I change my mind."

Winter opened up a cabinet to get the necessary equipment, and Grayson busied himself gathering gauze and ointments. He had no idea if this was going to work, but if he had to go to the General and tell him his daughter was dead…

Would he even care? What was important, Lana or the tech?

<Sir, I know this changes things…> Jerrod interrupted his thoughts.

<You have no idea,> Grayson said and could feel his cheeks beginning to redden. *<You have no idea at all.>*

<They're asking for a status update. They want to know if you're ready to make the exchange.>

Grayson glanced up at Winter as they prepared to save Lana's life. *<Tell them when we're ready to make the exchange, we'll contact them. Not a moment sooner.>*

<Yes, sir,> Jerrod said without missing a beat.

<And if you tell them, Jerry…If you tell them anything that's happened here or about what her skin did, how fast she moved, without my strictest authorization, you'll find yourself operating a tug.>

<Point taken, sir, but I am not the enemy. I was just as clueless about all this as you are.>

<I'm sorry, Jerrod. You're right. Emotions are just wound tight. When last I'd spent time with Lana, she was a much younger girl. This is all…going to take me some time to get used to.>

Winter's sleeves were rolled up, and he held a medical laser. "Ready?"

"As I'm ever going to be."

CAPTAIN ON DECK

STELLAR DATE: 09.15.8947 (Adjusted Years)
LOCATION: Near the *Unyielding Lance*, Perseverance
REGION: Scattered Disk, Gedri System, Silstrand Alliance

The ATV bounced across the uneven terrain, and Kylie twisted around, firing wildly with her rifle. She didn't know why she bothered. There was no way she'd hit her pursuers. It was nearly pitch black and a storm had kicked up, with the high winds blowing sand everywhere, the enemy wouldn't even hear the shots.

She was just wasting ammo.

Kylie pushed the ATV to its limits, straining to see through the storm, looking for any sign that she was going the right way.

<I can't raise the ship on comms,> Marge said. *<But I can't pick up the brothel's net anymore, either. This storm is highly ionized, it's blocking all the signals.>*

<God, I hate this planet,> Kylie said as she jerked the ATV's handlebars, narrowly avoiding driving into a gully. It was a close call, but she remembered the gully from her way in and turned left, praying the *Dauntless* was somewhere close to where it first dropped her off.

She approached the area she hoped the ship was in and stopped the ATV, peering through the blowing dust and sand for any sign of it. Nothing was visible, and nothing showed up on her suit's limited scan.

Her armor picked up a series of snaps, and it took her a moment to understand she was being shot at. She couldn't see who was doing the shooting, but dove behind the ATV on what she hoped was the safe side.

She caught a brief IR bloom and fired her rifle's kinetic round in its direction. The shot was punctuated by a blinding flash of light, and for a moment, she wondered if she had hit something explosive.

<*That wasn't you,*> Marge advised. <*It's lightning strikes on the* Unyielding Lance. *They're rather impressive.*>

<*I'll say,*> Kylie muttered.

Another lightning strike lit up the area around her, spotlighting the dozen figures closing in on her. She fired at one, and then another, but by then the light was gone and she doubted her shots had hit anything.

The enemy was still shooting, and the incoming weapons fire was tearing her ATV apart. In a minute, it wouldn't offer any more cover at all—or its batteries would explode. She was getting ready for her last stand when suddenly the sound of an autocannon tore through the darkness.

<*Was nice knowing you,*> she said to Marge.

<*What's that?*> another voice asked.

<*Rogers, you glorious bastard!*> Kylie cried out, never happier to hear his voice.

Floodlights lit up the terrain around her, and Kylie saw several motionless figures on the ground. She didn't look for the rest as she ran for the ship's waiting airlock and dove inside. The outer door hadn't even finished closing when she felt the ship pull up and boost hard.

She tore off her helmet as soon as the pressure equalized and tossed it and the duffle on the ground as she dashed down the passageway.

<*Get us out of here, Rogers!*>

<*Already on our way, Cap! It's good to have you back.*>

The feeling was mutual, and she wanted to take a moment to enjoy it, but Kylie had other things on her mind. <*Where's Lana? Is she…is she going to pull through?*>

<*Medbay. Winter and Grayson were patching her up.*>

Kylie turned down a side-passage and entered the medbay, where Grayson was standing by the bed. Lana lay unmoving on top of the sheets. Her rapid breathing hinted at continued distress. "We did what we could," Grayson said mournfully. "We sedated her so we could get through the procedure. She should be fine."

"I'm sensing a big but."

"She's not stabilizing. It's nothing we've done, and I don't think it's from being shot either. What's happening to her body…it's put a lot of stress on her. There might not be anything we can do other than to get her help. Help that the *Dauntless* just isn't equipped for."

Kylie knew what he was getting at. "But Silstrand can help her? You want us to take her there instead of trade her for Nadine?"

"That was always the plan, Kylie."

"Your plan," she said bitterly. "I don't have a plan because I was roped into this from the very start."

"Kylie…" Grayson sighed.

"If I'd known that Lana had been kidnapped for more than her good looks, if I'd known she was carrying dangerous tech, do you think I would've let Nadine walk into Maverick's den with me? You think I would've gone?"

"I didn't know. I swear it."

Kylie tore her eyes away from him because she didn't know if she could trust his words. She should've been able to. He'd just risked life and limb to save her and Lana. She'd seen the look on his face when Lana's steel-skin had turned back to flesh, but she still couldn't be sure that he wasn't pulling one over on her.

It wouldn't be the first time, would it?

"How can you expect me to believe Samuel didn't know? He went through a lot of trouble to get us to go on this mission for you."

"I don't know." Grayson's tone was morose. "All I know is, I wasn't informed. I can't speak to the knowledge he has, Kylie."

"If he didn't tell you, then we're really screwed, Grayson." Kylie shook her head. "If the Silstrand Alliance knew, and let's say for a moment they did, what would they do with it? What happens to Lana?"

Grayson thought it over, switching from one foot to another. "They use the nano to improve their weapons, ships, tech. All of it. They find a way to manufacture more and then…they wipe out the GFF and secure ourselves against Scipio."

Kylie fell silent. "So, it's been about war from the very beginning."

"It's also about not letting this nanotech fall into the wrong hands. Whoever has it will have a leg up. If the GFF were to use that tech, they'd take over. They wouldn't be happy any longer in just Gedri. They'd branch out. Who knows who could stop them."

Funny, Grayson sounded a lot like someone who knew about the nanotech to begin with. "You sure you know nothing of this?"

"I didn't know Lana had it. I didn't even know it was lost, but it's been rumored that S&H Defensive got their hands on advanced nano awhile back. They've been studying it and figuring out how to use it for years in a locked-down facility. No one even knows where it is."

"Clearly, someone does, because it got out, Gray. It got out and got stuck inside Lana. Now we're right in the middle of it, and we have a girl on my ship who might be dying."

"You think I don't know that?" Grayson's voice rose in volume and pitch. "I've known Lana since she was less than ten years old. You think I want to watch this happen to her?"

Kylie's mouth snapped shut. Grayson did really care for this girl. "S&H Defensive, will they be looking for it?"

Grayson nodded. "They will. Silstrand. The GFF, and any group that hears a rumor about what we might be carrying, will come looking for it."

Great, so they had a giant target painted on their backs. It was so much more than what Kylie had bargained for. "And Silstrand can remove it? From her blood?"

"I don't know, but we won't know until we get there," Grayson said quietly.

"I need to get Nadine back. You know that."

"Your desire to only rescue your girlfriend is childish and selfish. We're talking about tech that could change the balance of power across the entire alliance and beyond. Maybe every system there is."

Kylie narrowed her eyes. "You're the one who put me in the middle of all this!"

"And here I thought we were making progress with each other," Grayson shook his head. "Seems you still only care about yourself, Kylie."

"That's not fair." Kylie's nostril flared. "It isn't like that, so you stop looking at me like that, Grayson, or I swear to God…."

"Lock me in my quarters, then. Lock me in my quarters and arrange a swap. But Lana might be dead before you get there. And if she isn't, you're giving what's inside of her to the highest bidder. With luck, it's just the GFF and not someone who will do things a lot worse. A whole lot worse."

"You think this is easy for me? You think I want to make this choice?" Kylie wanted to scream. She wanted to throw things. She couldn't imagine being in a worse situation than the one she was stuck in now. Having to choose between the woman she loved and a stupid college kid who'd made the wrong choices in life—and now could change the balance of power forever.

"I've told you before that if we get Lana home, the SSF will have your back. We'll get Nadine."

"That was before I knew about the nano Lana was carrying. If the SSF kept that from us, who knows what else they're keeping. And you can't give assurances if they don't trust you either." Kylie pointed her finger at him.

Grayson sighed. "Kylie—"

"Don't. You can't explain so don't make excuses for them." Kylie left the room feeling utterly defeated and worse than when she had entered. Still, she hadn't made up her mind. She didn't know what was the right thing to do.

What would Nadine want? What would Nadine say to her if she could? Kylie wished she was there. Instead, Kylie was going to have to settle for second best.

*****

Kylie changed out of her armor and back into her regular clothes, then walked to the galley and sat down at the table with a long sigh.

<Looks like we got away clean,> Rogers messaged her. *<Storm masked our escape.>*

<That's some good news, at least.>

<Where to, Captain?>

Kylie had no idea. *<Power down, we'll drift for a bit, nice and quiet while we work out our next move.>*

She made a pot of coffee, and a few minutes later, Winter and Rogers joined her. They downed several cups of the strong brew as she filled them in with every detail she had. The longer she went on, the greener Rogers looked, but Winter seemed to take it all in stride.

"I don't see the problem. We need Nadine back," Winter said with a shrug.

"And if Lana dies before or after the trade?" Kylie asked.

"I'm more worried about the tech she has inside of her," Rogers said. "I know that makes me sound like a horrible person."

"That's because you *are* a horrible person," Winter said.

"But if someone real bad gets hold of that tech…" Rogers shook his head. "It's game over, man. Not just for Silstrand. Maybe for all of us. We can't just have that happen."

Kylie held her breath and sighed. "I was afraid you might say something like that."

Rogers winked at her. "If you asked me, then you must be prepared for what I had to say, you know? You must've wanted someone to tell you that."

Maybe she did. "We can't just leave Nadine."

"We send a communication to the bounty hunter. We tell him that we have the information he needs. Your AI collected information, right?"

Kylie nodded.

"Okay," said Rogers, before continuing, "we send the data. Arrange a meet up with him. He doesn't need to know we rescued her. Meanwhile, we drop her and Grayson off with Silstrand Space Force. They get their girl, we get our letter of marque, and everything goes back to business as usual."

Kylie considered it. The bounty hunter was probably close by, but with the storm raging on Perseverance, there was no way he could know what happened down there. It just might work.

"You're making a lot of assumptions," Winter said and took a sip of his coffee. "A lot of assumptions."

"That's what we do. It's worked out pretty well so far, don't you think?"

Winter shook his head. "I nearly got Nadine killed when I pulled my little stunt with Grayson, and you were all over me. I don't see how what you're suggesting is any different."

"Winter—" Kylie started, but Winter wasn't ready to be shut down just yet.

"You rode me for it. Hard. I felt guilty. You even got me to play nice with your ex. Now you've seen this girl, and you feel bad for her? What about Nadine? You just going to trade her in for this new model?"

"That's not what's going on here, and you know that!" Kylie rose from her chair at the same moment Winter did.

"Maybe you've just forgotten who we are. We're junkers. We work in the fringe, Kylie. We don't save people. We take what we want when we need it. Right now, we need that damn girl to save one of our own."

"Is that all we are? Is that how you really feel?" Kylie asked.

Winter nodded. "I'm just surprised it's not obvious to you. If you go along with this plan, if you bring Lana to the SA and screw Nadine in the process, then I'm done with you. Done with this ship. Just drop me off at the closest spaceport." He paused to look at Rogers. "And you should think about getting off, too. Won't be long before she trades us all in on some damn crusade to save the galaxy."

He stormed off, slamming his fist on the entryway as he did, and Kylie sank back into her seat. Rogers hadn't moved or spoken during the exchange, and Kylie couldn't help but wonder what he was thinking.

"Who peed in his organic craft cereal, huh?" the pilot finally said with a wan smile.

Kylie snorted out a laugh. "Do you agree with him? Do you think I'm going soft?"

"Me and Winter, we're not exactly cut from the same cloth, you know?" Rogers leaned back. "He cares only about what's right in front of him. Next big score. Sure, it's fun, but what we're talking about here…This bounty hunter, whoever he represents, they can't get their hands on this tech, Kylie."

"So, we're off to save the galaxy. Here I thought I was done with that."

"Maybe you were. Maybe it's the galaxy that wasn't done with you yet."

Well, that made Kylie feel out of control of her own destiny. Something she hated. "Jason left me a data dead-drop on a comm relay satellite. I'll send him a message and tell him we have everything he needs and we'll send a data sample. For now, let's set a course for the SSF base near Freemont. I'll have Grayson arrange a transfer."

Rogers stood from the table and left the galley. Kylie leaned back in her chair. Even though they had a plan, she didn't feel good about it. Rogers was right; Kylie had to protect the tech and Lana. Winter had been a good friend, most of the time, and a better shipmate, but if he couldn't see that…

Nothing was going the way Kylie expected.

Now, if she could just keep Lana alive long enough to get her help, Kylie would consider it a full-fledged victory.

As she stepped out of the galley, Grayson ran by. "What's going on?" Kylie asked.

"It's Lana," he said, his voice raised in panic as he continued, "she's crashing!"

*****

Kylie followed Grayson down to the medbay. Grayson's simple words were correct: Lana was in full cardiac arrest, and she was seizing. "You left her alone?" Kylie asked angrily.

"I had to grab something. I'm not medically-trained and the equipment you have here…"

"Okay, okay. Let's stop fighting and figure out what the hell we're going to do,"

<The defibrillator should shock her back to a normal sinus rhythm.>

Kylie grabbed it. She peeled back the sheet they had placed on Lana and stuck it over her heart. *<What do I do?>*

<I'll handle it.>

Kylie stepped back as the defibrillator shocked Lana's body with an electrical charge. She didn't know if it was working; Lana was still spasming.

Grayson was studying the vitals display and tapped it with his finger. "It didn't help. Her blood pressure too is high, and her heart can't establish a normal rhythm."

What could they do? By the stars, what if rescuing Lana killed her?

Winter entered and pushed her to the side. He glanced at the vitals and sighed. "What the hell are you guys doing?"

"Trying to save her," Grayson said defensively.

Winter opened one of the cabinets and pulled out a vial. He squirted two drops beneath Lana's tongue with a dropper. Immediately she started to squirm and he held her mouth closed. She fought against him, but a moment later, she was still again.

"That was risky," Kylie said. Winter had just given Lana one of Maverick's more exotic designer drugs.

"Had to do something, right? Save the lady everyone cares so damn much for. Can't use that stuff again, it'll take a day to clear out of her system." Winter left just as quickly as he arrived, muttering something under his breath.

Kylie stared after him, and Grayson did a double take. "Should I ask what that's about?" he asked.

"You don't want to know."

Grayson let her comment lie and inspected the monitor. "Her vitals are returning to normal. Her heart is still erratic but we've bought her some time."

"Do you think we'll reach the SSF base before…it gets bad?" Kylie asked.

"I don't know," Grayson said softly and glanced back at Lana. "I'm afraid I really can't say."

"Then I'll stay with her," Kylie said and stepped closer to the bed. "If anything goes wrong, she shouldn't be alone."

Grayson placed a hand on her shoulder. "It's possible the nano will finish restructuring her to handle its…whatever…and she'll simply wake up. Be unstoppable." There was more concern in his voice than was necessary. Than usual.

"You think she'll hurt me?"

"Maybe." Grayson rose his eyebrows. "To get away from General Samuel, anything is possible. You should know."

That she should.

ANOTHER DOUBLE-CROSS

STELLAR DATE: 09.15.8947 (Adjusted Years)
LOCATION: Salvage ship *Dauntless*, near Perseverance
REGION: Scattered Disk, Gedri System, Silstrand Alliance

<*And you really think you can meet that timetable?*> Jason asked. <*It seems rather aggressive.*>

<*We'll be there,*> Winter said. <*Be at the coordinates and I can guarantee that the* Dauntless *will be there, too.*>

The bounty hunter sent a smug expression across the Link. <*Pleasure doing business with you, Winter. Your reputation as a hothead seems unwarranted.*>

<*I don't know about that, but keep Nadine alive and well. You do that and I'll be easy to deal with.*>

The bounty hunter sent a short vid to Winter. Nadine sat in a private room on what looked like a comfortable bed. There was a window overlooking a planet—Chiras if his guess was right—and she wore a new blue and white dress. It was more fitting for a woman of her stature than the one she'd worn the day she'd gone into Maverick's club.

<*She'll be fine. And you'll be handsomely rewarded. Is the girl still alive?*>

Winter thought it over. How much information was too much information? <*She's breathing, and the tech she's carrying is safe. So, don't worry about that.*>

<*So, you discovered what she is carrying? Did she tell you?*>

Didn't Jason know the nano was in her blood? Well, that was interesting. <*Something like that. Listen, I have a lot to do so if you wouldn't mind…*> Winter peered around the corner onto the bridge. Rogers was by himself.

Good.

<As you were. I look forward to concluding our deal.> The bounty hunter cut the signal as Winter stepped onto the bridge. He took a deep breath as he came up upon Rogers. He had always been a friend—a buddy. Winter couldn't say that about a lot of people.

Rogers's chair floated in the center of the bridge, as he casually piloted the *Dauntless*. "Hey, bro, you have that cooling off period you needed?" he asked without turning his head as Winter's heavy footfalls approached.

"Yeah, I did." Winter gripped the top of Nadine's chair with one hand, while his other raised his sidearm. "Everything's a lot clearer now."

"Great," Rogers said, still looking ahead into the void. "I'd hate to lose you. I mean, except for Grayson, you're the meanest cook we have on board."

"I'd hate for you to lose that." Winter gripped his handgun with both hands, and it was only then Rogers turned around and let out a gasp.

"What the hell—"

Spinning the weapon in his hand, Winter slammed the butt of the pistol right between Rogers's eyes. The pilot slumped in his seat and Winter imagined he would get a nasty welt. Winter felt a moment of remorse but knew that this was the best way forward, even if no one could see that but him.

He hefted Rogers up over his shoulder. After a double-check that no one was around, he stepped into the passageway and stowed Rogers's body in a supply closet. Winter locked the door, and then smashed the mechanism to make certain Rogers wouldn't be able to break up his little party.

"Sorry, friend," Winter muttered to himself.

Rogers might hate him and have one hell of a headache, but at least he'd survive. In the end, who knew, maybe everyone would even thank Winter for what he was about to do. If Kylie couldn't make the right choice for the crew, then he'd have to do it for her.

He'd consider asking for forgiveness later.

OVERWATCH

STELLAR DATE: 09.16.8947 (Adjusted Years)
LOCATION: Salvage ship *Dauntless*, en route to Freemont
REGION: Scattered Disk, Gedri System, Silstrand Alliance

Kylie yawned as she stretched her arms overhead. Seated on a stool beside Lana's bed, she waited for a sign that the girl might wake up. Or be okay. Or not. Something.

So far, Lana was sleeping peacefully, and that was better than pain and convulsions. But the worry was still there. There was so much worry.

"I'm going to grab a cup of that horrible coffee you have. You want some?" Grayson asked from where he leaned against one of the counters.

She nodded. "Please. And thanks."

"Thank you—for being so reasonable about all this. I know it isn't an easy decision."

"It's always hard for me to do the right thing. You should know that," Kylie said with a wry smirk.

"Can we try not to fight for just a few hours?"

"Sorry. Really. I wasn't trying to fight. I was trying to be funny."

Grayson's sour expression just proved that Kylie's humor had been off the mark. Had she ever really been funny?

"Coffee sounds nice." Kylie tried to sound as demure as possible, but she wasn't sure it worked. She wasn't sure if Grayson cared much for her humor or when she was trying to be kind. Now the idea of her, the memory of her, that was a different story. But the reality of who they were? Funny thing about ideas, they often shifted and changed—sometimes until they morphed into dreams.

He left the room without a word, and Kylie's mind wandered, worrying about what the future would hold.

"You guys married or something?" Lana's soft voice asked.

Kylie's eyes widened as she realized that Lana was conscious. "Oh my, you're awake! How are you feeling?"

"Run through. Tired but…better. Hungry." Lana struggled to sit up, and Kylie helped her.

"We'll get you something," Kylie said. She reached out to Grayson. *<Lana's awake! And she's hungry. Grab her a protein pack and some water.>*

<This is good news. Great news!>

His happiness was infectious, and Kylie found herself smiling. "I wasn't sure if you were going to survive."

"Neither was I, to be honest. My AI, she's slowly coming back to me now. Thank you. I think she was always there, but I couldn't hear her." Lana shook her head and gazed around the room. "Is this your ship?"

Kylie nodded. "Not much, I know."

"It's okay. It's fine. Anywhere is better than where I was. Guess we're on our way back to the SA now, huh? To see my dad."

"You'll have some explaining to do, but he'll be happy to see you."

"Sure, he will." Lana's tongue clicked firmly into place. "He'll want to open me up. Get this stuff out of me just as much as the GFF did. I know my father."

"Lana…" Kylie said softly. "We all have issues with our fathers, trust me, but they do still love us. If there's a way for the SA to get the nano out of you safely, I'm sure they'll do it."

"You don't know. You're not me, so you just don't know." Lana lay down on the bed, rolled over to face the wall, and crossed her arms.

Kylie thought to say something but then decided maybe Lana needed space, and she stepped out into the hall. When

Grayson approached, he was almost bouncing with excitement.

"Afraid I forgot your coffee. Why are you out here in the hall? Is Lana…"

She held up her hand to stop his mad dash of questions and statements. "She's fine. I think she wants to be alone. College girl 'I need my space' sort of alone."

"Ohhh…" Grayson said, and Kylie had a feeling he had no idea what she meant by that. "I'll just drop off her food. Maybe you should get some rest."

Kylie shook her head. "I think rest is the last thing I can get right now." She paced the hallway and waited for Grayson to rejoin her. When he did, they fell into a natural walking rhythm together, and the comfortable silence they shared said everything, and nothing, all at the same time.

"Does her being awake and stable change anything for you?" Grayson asked tepidly. "If you've changed your mind about going to the SSF…"

"It occurred to me, I admit, but just because she's stable, doesn't mean she's okay. And now that I've talked to her…"

Grayson smirked. "You care. The great Kylie Rhoads actually cares about someone."

"I care about a lot, Grayson. That's not fair. Once upon a time…I still care." She cared about the *Dauntless*, her crew, and in a passive sort of way she cared about what happened to Silstrand and Gedri. She cared about Lana and Grayson, too…it just made choices harder.

Not easier.

Kylie opened the door to her quarters. "If you want to come in for a minute…we haven't really had a chance to talk."

Grayson's eyebrow rose. "To talk? I think we've talked about a lot of things."

"We've needled and argued but we haven't talked." Kylie took a deep breath and felt the reluctant truth she had been thinking about when not running for her life. "Not about that kiss, we haven't." Kylie stepped inside her quarters and Grayson followed behind. She sealed the door, and Grayson leaned up against the small table in her room.

His hands shoved deep into his pockets. "It was out of line. I know that, but I wasn't sure…wasn't sure if I'd ever see you again."

"Better than the last time we said goodbye, I guess. More fun anyhow." Kylie stepped up close to him and resisted putting her hands on his shoulders. "But I'm with Nadine. She's being held against her will and now isn't the time…."

"It's never been a good time, has it?"

Kylie shook her head. Maybe once it had been. When she had been a bright, naïve cadet just earning her bars from the SSF. "I have to focus on rescuing Nadine."

Grayson swallowed hard. "I wasn't trying to confuse your mission. I wasn't trying to do much of anything, to be honest. I just…reacted without thinking."

Well, wasn't that something? Who knew Grayson was capable of such snap decisions? "So, we'll deliver Lana to the SSF and then your mission is done. You can get off the *Dauntless*. I won't hold you to helping me rescue Nadine. Your part will be done and you'll have what you wanted…your duty is to the SA."

"I stay on until the mission is done. Far as I'm concerned, that extends to rescuing Nadine just as much as Lana. She was lost during our mission, after all. The one I was supposed to stay in charge of, and it went sideways. That means rescuing Nadine falls under my purview. And when we get to the SSF base at Freemont, that's exactly what I'll tell Samuel."

He was so different than he used to be. His words, his conviction, it almost knocked Kylie over. "Thank you," she said quietly, humbly. "When I first saw you standing outside my cell, I said you hadn't changed, but that's not true. You've changed a lot, Gray."

Grayson grunted. "Maybe I grew up. Or maybe time apart from you taught me a thing or two I had to learn."

"Like what?" Kylie asked, even though she knew she shouldn't. Even though she should've kicked him out of her room before the heat intensified between them. But she couldn't look away, and she couldn't ask him to leave.

"Sometimes people have to find their own way. Maybe they need to stumble and fall, and none of it can be helped. I couldn't force you to do the things I wanted to do just because it's what I wanted you to do. And the truth is…we don't work." Grayson said. "Everyone's told me that from the very beginning. I thought they were wrong, but they weren't."

His eyes didn't seem to agree with what he said. Neither did his hand, as it stroked her hair away from her face and Kylie's heart pounded in her chest. It was wrong. None of what they were doing was right.

"Still," Grayson said mournfully before continuing, "I never thought I'd see you again. And if I did, I never expected…to feel the way I do. That's why I kissed you."

Grayson leaned in to kiss her again, his hands already on her waist, ready to take it to the next step.

Kylie thought she'd let him, too. She thought she might even follow him into bed if he asked. Luckily for her, Marge barged in. *<We've changed course.>*

Only Kylie heard it. She put her finger to Grayson's lips to stop him and he scowled just a centimeter from her face. *<How far off course are we?>*

<Way off. We're on a heading for Chiras—looks like one if its moons…most likely Eris.>

That wasn't just a slight variation. That was huge.

"What's wrong?" Grayson asked.

"We're off course. We're headed in the complete opposite direction." Kylie went to the door, and when it didn't open, she swiped her hand against the console.

Nothing happened. Well, that wasn't right. Kylie tried it again with the same result.

"Doesn't anything work on this ship?" Grayson asked.

"Ha, ha," Kylie said. "Marge, find out what's going on."

<*Rogers? Why'd you change course? Rogers?*> He didn't answer, and Kylie didn't even sense his presence on the Link. Where the hell was he?

<*I'm afraid we're in lockdown,*> Marge said to both of them. <*I can't override it; the remote command codes have changed.*>

"Lockdown?" Grayson asked. "Who the hell could authorize such a thing?"

"Only one other person other than me has that code." A sinking feeling hit Kylie's stomach. "Winter. It has to be Winter." When Grayson scowled, she explained further. "He didn't think going back to the SSF was such a great idea."

"Perfect. So, we're headed to…"

"Trade her in for Nadine, if I had to guess."

Grayson sighed. "That man is more trouble than he's worth."

Kylie couldn't argue with him about that…at least not at present. <*Winter, get us out of lockdown. Open the doors and let's talk about this like adults.*>

<*Sorry, Kylie, but that's not going to happen until I get Nadine back. Until the exchange takes place, you'll just have to sit tight.*>

<*You can't just do this. I'm the captain of this ship!*>

<*You mean 'were'. Until you started making decisions that benefited Silstrand and not us. Grayson's got into your head.*>

Kylie's eyes fixed on Grayson and wondered if part of that was true. Was she so desperate to be accepted by him even after the years that passed, the divorce? <*She won't let you exchange her. What if she tries to kill you?*> Winter didn't respond.

Maybe he was willing to risk it. Even if Lana didn't kill him, Kylie just might.

"We better get these doors open," Grayson said and tried to pull them apart with his hands.

"Grayson, what are you doing? You know that won't work."

"We have to try. If we've gone off course—"

His words were cut off as they both felt the ship jink to the side. The *Dauntless*'s internal grav compensators weren't made for that sort of maneuver. Kylie grabbed onto her desk to keep from falling over. "That felt like…"

"Evasive maneuvers," Grayson nodded. "Jerrod, send a secure message to that ship and tell them what's going on in here."

He said it aloud for her benefit, that much was obvious. "What *is* going on? I feel like there's something you're not telling me. Again." Kylie's chest tightened under a rising pressure.

"It's a Silstrand Alliance cruiser. If we're not going to rendezvous with the SA, they're going to take us in. By force."

"By force?" Kylie repeated the phrase back to him, trying to wrap her head around what it was Grayson knew and when exactly he had known it. "Do you want to explain yourself?"

"I've been in contact with the SSF. Of course I have, that's my job."

Kylie nodded. She hadn't heard anything yet that she hated. "Go on."

"We went to rescue Lana, and the SSF wasn't far. Far enough that they wouldn't show up on anyone's sensors, but they wanted to be close in case anything went wrong."

She was still listening and getting less happy about what she was hearing. "So, they babysat us. Typical for the SSF."

Typical for Grayson, too, even though she didn't want to admit it.

"Right. Once we had Lana, I was to convince you to take her to the base at Freemont, and if you couldn't or wouldn't, they'd move in."

"And take her." Kylie's lips drew thin and determined. "So, that's what they're doing now. They're going to disable us and then board. Like good old times, huh?"

Grayson gave her a look. "I didn't tell you because…"

"Because then you wouldn't be able to convince me to do anything. I know my character flaws well enough, Grayson. I just wish you had trusted me enough to do the right thing."

"I'm sorry," he said quietly. "But now that we're headed off course, I can try to reason with them. I can tell them Winter took the ship…"

"And what happens to him?"

"You care?" Grayson asked coolly. "After all this…"

"Just answer the question."

"They throw him in the brig, and he never sees the light of day again."

Maybe he deserved it, but Kylie hated the idea. "And the rest of us are just allowed to go?" Kylie didn't think so. "They'll take us all in. We can kiss that letter of marque goodbye along with any chance of freedom."

"Yes," Grayson said and turned back to the door. "The cruiser out there isn't answering my communications. They might think I've been compromised."

If they lost faith in Grayson, then things didn't look good for the rest of them. Kylie grabbed a butter knife from the table and used it to unscrew a panel beside her door. <*Marge, see if you can update us on what's going on out there.*> Before Marge said anything, Kylie pulled on a bundle of cabling and began separating them, ready to strip them with her teeth.

"You're going to hotwire the door?" Grayson's voice was puzzled.

"You have a better idea?" Kylie asked.

<Kylie, stop,> Marge said.

<What, Marge? I have to get us out of here,> Kylie snapped. She didn't mean to, but her AI was breaking her focus.

<Just put your finger on the control circuit, I may not have the command codes, but it's not like your ship's interior doors use encryption or anything.>

Kylie did as instructed and felt a tingle as a batch of nano left her body.

<Okay, the way your ship's access codes work, they're all validated against a central store. I'll just alter this door to think that I'm the central authority. Give me a minute.>

"Bet you wish you had opted for an AI years ago," Grayson said with a smirk.

"Shut up."

ESCAPE

STELLAR DATE: 09.16.8947 (Adjusted Years)
LOCATION: Salvage ship *Dauntless*, en route to Freemont
REGION: Scattered Disk, Gedri System, Silstrand Alliance

Rogers's head was throbbing so much that he thought his eyes might pop from the pressure. Or maybe he'd just throw up. Maybe both.

Rogers couldn't remember where he was or how he'd gotten there. With a long groan, he opened his eyes in a narrow squint. His vision was blurry and whatever room he was in appeared to be split in two. A few blinks later and it snapped back together, revealing the small closet on the main level of the ship.

Close to the cockpit and away from the weapons locker. Rogers was cozying up with cleaning supplies and disinfectant. The smell was enough to increase the intensity of his headache.

Man…

He pushed himself up to his knees and touched the blood on his forehead. Dried now, it hinted that he'd been hit rather hard over the head. Who the hell? Did the ship have an angry stowaway?

The girl. Lana. No, it hadn't been her. Someone else had been in the cockpit with him right before Rogers was struck. That's right, it all came back into place, and now Rogers growled his name. "Winter."

The supply door only had a manual release, and as he grabbed it, his suspicions were confirmed. It was locked from the outside. <*Damn you, Winter.*>

<*You'll get over it. Once Nadine is back, you'll forgive me.*>

<We made a choice—a decision—and this sure as hell isn't it.> Rogers stood and rifled through the contents of the shelves, looking for something he could use to pry the door open—as if something like that was even possible, but he had to try, didn't he?

<You and Kylie made a decision, and I wasn't included. I'm doing what's right for this crew.>

<What's right for this crew means not giving the wrong group the tech Lana is carrying. Can you think of anything but yourself? Try it sometime.>

Rogers fell to his knees as the ship jinked sideways. Was something attacking his ship? *<Winter, what the hell is going on?>*

He waited for a reply, but Winter blocked him out. He wasn't going to say anything. Hot damn it all to hell. *<Captain? Kylie, are you there? Ky—>*

<Rogers, thank God you're all right. Where are you?>

<Supply Closet B. The one closest to the bridge. Winter didn't want to waste much time, it seems.>

<Okay…we're working on getting out of my quarters. Marge is almost there, but you're going to have to make it to the bridge. Do you think you can neutralize Winter?>

Him, taking out Winter? Had they lost their minds? Rogers thought he'd be more adept at taking out a primal snow beast—actually, Winter wasn't that far from *being* a primal snow beast. *<I'll try, but I'm going to need backup.>*

<Soon as we can. Marge says up above you is one of the service tubes that runs to the bridge. It's a tight fit up there—you'll have to remove panel two and three to access it.>

Rogers couldn't believe he'd forgotten about that service tube. He'd spent more than one shift in there fixing flight control systems. He blamed the headache. *<Right, of course. I see them. I can do it but…>* his words were cut off by another shudder in the ship.

<*We're under attack, Rogers. There isn't time for buts if we're going to get our girl through this.*>

That was enough for him. Rogers swept an armful of supplies off the shelves and climbed them, bracing his back against the wall.

<*So, your quarters, huh? You and Grayson? Anything you want to tell me?*>

<*Shut up. Just get moving.*>

Rogers smirked as he reached overhead and undid the twist-locks that held the panel in place. Nice thing about a ship is that anything that needed to be opened for maintenance was never screwed or bolted on. The never-ending vibrations would loosen anything over time. The spring-loaded twist locks, however, held things tight, and released like a charm—a minute later he had pulled himself up into the service tube.

He oriented himself toward the bridge and took a deep breath. That was odd…he heard something.

"Help!" a voice called out. "Help me!"

It was female and not the captain. Must be Lana, and boy, was she freaking out. The lockdown must've scared her. "Lana?" Rogers called, but he doubted she could hear him. <*Kylie, Lana's freaking out. I can hear her. You might want to get to her when you can.*>

<*Got it. We're almost out. We'll grab some weapons and check on Lana. Godspeed, Rogers.*>

Her words caused Rogers pause for a minute. He hadn't thought God or any of that was important to Kylie anymore. With a shake of his head, he began to shuffle forward in the tube. It was only ten meters to the bridge; he could do it in no time. What he would do when he got there was another question entirely.

A metallic clang echoed through the ship, the shock of it nearly knocked him out of the tube and back into the supply closet. This one wasn't a weapon blast or evasive maneuvers, but something else. It was metal grating against metal.

Something had grappled onto the *Dauntless*. They were going to be boarded. Rogers rushed forward on his elbows and knees, slithering toward the bridge as quickly as he could. His girl wouldn't be taken. He couldn't let that happen.

If anything bad happened to the *Dauntless,* to Kylie, Rogers didn't think he'd ever forgive Winter. Not in this lifetime and not in the next.

THE GENERAL'S DAUGHTER

STELLAR DATE: 09.16.8947 (Adjusted Years)
LOCATION: Salvage ship *Dauntless*, en route to Freemont
REGION: Scattered Disk, Gedri System, Silstrand Alliance

The ship's erratic movements terrified Lana. Someone, or some group of someones, was coming for her. She just knew it but what could she do about it?

"Hello!" she called out in terror and banged on the door. Why couldn't she get it open? Why didn't anyone answer? Why was she locked in like some criminal?

"Hello!" Someone had to be out there somewhere. It wasn't like they could just walk off the ship and disappear into space.

<*The ship seems to be in some sort of lockdown,*> Abby said.

<*Can you bypass it?*>

<*I'm afraid not. Even if I was skilled enough, a lockdown like this would need to be shut off by a member of the crew—or maybe by someone who knew the ship's schematics. Neither of which we are.*>

<*I kinda figured that part out myself.*> Lana ran her hands through her hair. If someone was coming for her, she needed to defend herself. <*Are we safe in here?*>

<*For now, but if we are boarded, it won't take them long to find us. The ship isn't very big.*>

So, in other words, they were sitting ducks. Great. "I really, really wish Kylie was here." Lana hadn't known her long, but the captain had gotten her away from that Harken woman. That meant something. Lana wasn't sure if she could trust Grayson—he was one of her father's cronies, after all—but she definitely could trust Kylie.

She banged on the door again. "Is anyone out there? Hello? Please, help! Someone answer!" Lana didn't want to be dissected—or whatever was going to happen to her.

She dropped her hand to the door's manual release, pulling on it with all her might. It wouldn't budge. She let out a long sigh and was about to let go when she felt her hand tingle the way it had before when she'd sent out a nanocloud—or at least she thought it had been a nanocloud—to kill the three soldiers back near the labs.

A moment later, the door latch made a snapping sound, and she pushed it open. Her nano—Lana hadn't thought to even try it. Had the tech opened the door itself, as if it had a mind of its own, or was she able to control it on a subconscious level?

<*See if you can find the rest of the crew. Kylie,*> Abby suggested.

That was good advice. Gingerly, Lana stepped out into the hall and peered around. Her heart pounded so fast, it couldn't be normal. Was it stress? <*We need to find a weapon. I'm not going with anyone!*>

<*I think you are the weapon, Lana.*>

She was the weapon. Lana didn't know how to process that and decided the best way forward was to just not think about it. She'd just get flustered, and when that happened, the nano was harder to control. So, she skirted along the edges of the hall, looking for someone that looked familiar. A friendly face.

Down the hall, Lana heard metal scrapping against metal. She crept forward and peered around the corner. There was nothing there. Maybe the sound had carried from further away than she'd thought. How was it she could even hear it?

The thumping continued, and it was growing closer. So loud it almost hurt. Lana grimaced and pressed her hands over her ears to ward off the pain.

<*You're picking up sounds at minus fifty decibels from at least forty meters away. Incredible, your hearing is so magnified. It's a marvel.*>

She could really do without it. Lana fell silent as she identified the sound of heavy boots hitting the deck—they were getting closer. If she didn't hurry, they might find her. Lana crawled as quietly as she could until she found herself at what appeared to be an open weapons locker.

Finally, at last something was going her way.

Lana went through the weapons and picked up a pulse rifle. It was heavier than she'd expected and Abby voiced concern. <*Don't you think that's a little much to be leading with? The last thing you ever shot was a water pistol.*>

She wished she had taken the shooting lessons like her dad had always wanted. <*Pretty sure I can use my nano to help me aim. I can see things differently than I used to. I can…focus more.*>

<*Perhaps, but you can't control it yet. It could be dangerous.*>

The *Dauntless* rocked to the side, and a metallic clang assaulted her ears. <*Not more dangerous than getting seized by whoever is coming on board.*>

A point that Abby couldn't counter.

She stepped out from the weapons locker at the precise moment a scary albino man forced his way inside. He wore a dangerous scowl and Lana nearly screamed, but he put his hand over her mouth.

"Quiet," he ordered. "Name's Winter. I'm first mate on this ship. You're Lana, right?"

Lana nodded, her eyes wide. Winter? Had she met him before? Something about him seemed familiar.

"Good. I'm going to remove my hand and then we're going to talk. Quietly. You got me?" Slowly he removed his hand and Lana took a shallow breath.

"I thought…"

"I know, but it isn't important. We're been boarded, and I'm going to need your help to get rid of them. Okay? But you're going to have to do everything I tell you."

Lana stood up straighter. “Just tell me what it is I need to do.”

Winter grinned. “That a girl. I knew I could count on you.”

GRAPPLED

STELLAR DATE: 09.16.8947 (Adjusted Years)
LOCATION: Salvage ship *Dauntless*
REGION: Scattered Disk, Gedri System, Silstrand Alliance

"The stars," Kylie whispered, then continued, "they're gone."

Through the viewports in the weapons lockup, no stars were visible. Kylie surmised they must be blotted out by the SSF cruiser that had grappled on to their ship. It was getting closer, which meant in a matter of moments, the cruiser would extend an umbilical and board the ship. They would take what they came for, which at this point might be all of them.

Winter had royally screwed them. It had been a mistake to trust him again—that much was clear. No more second chances.

"Jerrod says the cruiser was in a fight. Some of its key systems are offline, but it seems to be functioning well enough to take us on. He thinks perhaps they're not responding because they can't," Grayson said.

The thought left Kylie's stomach feeling sour. "Who would've engaged that thing in a firefight?" They were on the fringe, but taking on an SSF cruiser was no laughing matter.

"We can ask them later," Grayson said grimly. "We can still make this right. We can resist them when they board."

Resist them when they board? Was that really his plan? Kylie was in no rush to end up dead. "They'll just send more. It didn't work out so well for Rogers when he resisted you boarding, did it?"

Grayson handed Kylie her rifle. "Don't go soft on me now, Captain. If we resist, if I can have a few moments to talk with their commanding officer, I can fix this. I'm not Rogers. I know these people, and even if *I* don't them personally, *they'll* know of me."

His words made sense, but still Kylie wasn't sure. "Fix it for who? Me? Lana? The *Dauntless*?"

"Don't give up. I'm not going to hand Lana over if it means the end for you or your crew. Even this ship of yours."

Seems the *Dauntless* had worked its way into Grayson's crusty old heart after all. Kylie took the weapon he offered, shouldered the rifle and led Grayson out of there. They ran to the medbay as the lights aboard the *Dauntless* dimmed.

Once they got Lana out, they should split up. Kylie didn't want to make this easy for the SSF soldiers, especially if it was the last thing she ever did. As they approached the medbay, Kylie realized the door was open. She and Grayson exchanged a glance before bringing up their weapons and sweeping through the room.

Lana's blanket was on the floor in a pile, but there was no sign of a struggle. Nothing of the room or even the door panel was damaged. Kylie didn't get it, and then it dawned on her. "Her nano."

"She broke out," Grayson said with a nod. "I suppose now we have to worry about what happens if the SSF gets her before I get a chance to plead my case."

<Stand down, Silstrand Alliance representatives are now boarding. Move to a central location near the airlock. Stand with your fingers interlaced behind your heads and no one will be hurt. You have two minutes.>

<Can you slow them down?> Kylie asked Marge.

<I can try to jam the airlock and keep it from cycling, but it won't hold forever.>

But it might give them time to find Lana, and that was the most important thing. If Lana was hiding—or worse, if she was planning an assault—she might be hurt or killed.

"You don't think she would attack, do you?" Grayson asked.

"You saw the things she can do. If she thinks she's threatened, I think that's exactly what she'll do," Kylie said as they rushed from the medbay.

"Once they can see what she's capable of…" Grayson warned. "We must keep it from them as long as we can. If I can negotiate a peaceful surrender before they witness anything crazy, it'd be in everyone's best interests."

But to kill her and just take her nano? Would General Samuel really be okay with that? What was more important to him? The tech, or his daughter?

Kylie hoped to God she didn't have to find out the answer to that question.

LOYALTY

STELLAR DATE: 09.16.8947 (Adjusted Years)
LOCATION: Salvage ship *Dauntless*
REGION: Scattered Disk, Gedri System, Silstrand Alliance

Kylie looked worried as they rushed down the passageway, but it wasn't her that concerned Grayson so much as it was Jerrod, who was growing increasingly agitated for an AI.

<*What you're doing breaks protocol, Grayson. You know that. We have a mission and—*>

<*And I'm doing what needs to be done in this instance. The* Dauntless *didn't mean to go off course,*> Grayson replied.

<*Well, of course, I think you can explain that, but you can do that after the successful exchange.*>

<*Absolutely not. If I wait, I'll lose all my negotiation power,*> Grayson said. <*They'll lock Kylie up, revoke her immunity—*>

<*So that's what it's all about, then? Your ex-wife? Grayson, if you refuse to submit to the SSF officer in command, you'll be considered insubordinate. You'll be dishonorably discharged, at best, and what happens to me? I've been a military AI for my entire existence, and that isn't likely to change, no matter how much I like you,*> Jerrod said.

Grayson stifled a sigh.

Kylie gave him an eye. "Everything okay?"

"Fine," Grayson said in a short, agitated tone. <*We've been together for ten years. You know my motivations, my thoughts. I'm loyal to the SA. You just have to give me time to work this out. Jerrod, you know me. We've been through the thick and thin together.*>

<*And are again, but you make some good points, so I'll concede, for now, Grayson. If things change, if I suspect you've been*

compromised, you'll leave me no choice but to take you in. You can understand that, I hope.>

Grayson peered back at Kylie as she took up a position behind some conduit near the airlock. <*I understand, but I do hope before you do anything either of us will regret, you'll weigh your actions. Above all else, we can't harm innocent lives.*>

<*Who gets to say who is innocent and who isn't, Grayson?*>

That was a question he couldn't answer.

REPEL BOARDERS

STELLAR DATE: 09.16.8947 (Adjusted Years)
LOCATION: Salvage ship *Dauntless*, en route to Freemont
REGION: Scattered Disk, Gedri System, Silstrand Alliance

<Stand down, Silstrand Alliance representatives are now boarding. Move to a central location near the airlock. Stand with your fingers interlaced behind your heads and no one will be hurt. You have thirty seconds.>

The statement was broadcasting on a loop as Kylie took a defensive position behind a conduit stack near the airlock. She wasn't in the mood for a game of hide-and-seek. Her plan had been to turn Lana over to them and she was going to do just that. With an explanation.

Grayson took up a position across the corridor from her. They gave each other a worried glance as the airlock opened.

They just needed enough time to plead their case.

Kylie also hoped that Rogers would make it into the bridge and take out Winter just in case they needed to get out of there on a moment's notice.

As the airlock opened, Kylie tensed and Grayson gave her a level look that put her at ease. He was wearing his serious-commander expression, and at the last minute, he rose from his cover and stood in the center of the corridor, his arms crossed behind his back. She wondered if that was the right move, but these were his people, after all. He had probably worked with some of them shoulder-to-shoulder. If he couldn't get through to them, then no one could.

Kylie just wanted to give him a chance. She'd hope they'd listen to him.

She was about to find out as several soldiers rushed out of the airlock and took cover on the far side of the corridor. Their guns were drawn, but at the sight of Grayson, they faltered. "Colonel Grayson, sir!"

Grayson nodded solemly. "I really don't wish for my head to be blown off before I've had a chance to grab a good dinner. If you could please lower your weapons, we can arrange for a transfer."

Kylie kept her rifle trained on the soldiers and waited for their response.

"Not until she does, sir."

"Not going to happen," Kylie said. "You either listen to Colonel Grayson, or we stand here all day at a draw."

"I think you should listen to us, Commander Rhoads," General Samuel said as he stepped out of the airlock with another three soldiers covering him.

Man, it must have been a tight fit in there.

Grayson visibly relaxed. "Sir!"

Samuel nodded in response. "Colonel, from your reports, I suspected you would be en route with my daughter. When you changed course…."

"Not our doing," Kylie said, and the authority in her voice stole the general's attention.

"Oh?" Samuel raised his eyebrow.

"One of my crew went off-mission. It's unfortunate, but we are handling the situation."

"Let me guess which of your crew that could have been? I'm going to go with Winter. Am I close to the mark?"

"Dead on, sir," Kylie said. "If you'll have your soldiers lower their weapons, then I'll lower mine. We can discuss what happens next and you can see your daughter."

The general waved his hand to issue the order to his officers. "That's my show of good faith. Your show, allow Grayson to take your weapon, Rhoads."

She bristled as Grayson approached. He held out his hand, and there was something kind in his eyes. Kylie thought it over for a moment before she handed the rifle to him. He wouldn't let anything bad happen, and she had to show faith that the general would keep his word.

"Good." General Samuel smirked. "Now, let's get back to the business of my daughter. Where is she?"

"Safe. Where she'll stay until we hand her over. I need to make sure that our deal still holds. My crew will be free to go and the letter of marque…."

"I'm afraid not. No. The agreement was you bring her to me. Since you failed to hold up your end of the bargain, the deal is off."

Kylie took a deep breath. "Now, wait just a second! I explained!"

"And I don't believe a word you say. As for the letter of marque…well, maybe it's better that Grayson explains that one at another time. Bring me my daughter."

Kylie's eyes shifted from Samuel to Grayson. Why couldn't Grayson even look at her and why hadn't Samuel even asked how his daughter was faring? "If you think I'm going to just let you walk on board and take someone off my ship without my permission—"

"No one is asking for your permission." General Samuel pointed his finger past her. "The ship isn't that small. Find her. Colonel Grayson, do your job."

Was Grayson really going to side with Samuels on this? Kylie watched his jaw muscles tighten. He was considering it, wasn't he? Well, at least he was conflicted about it.

"You don't care for her at all, do you?" Kylie asked the general. "All you want is what she's carrying."

"So, you figured it out?" Samuel asked. "All right. My daughter's always had problems with authority, with me. I wouldn't want harm to come to her, but she signed herself up for this under my nose. She kept it from me. She broke the law, and now she expects me to save her. Is that right? So, I'll save her. I'll save her, and she'll solve all of Silstrand's problems. War is approaching us on all sides; she carries the advantage we need.

"Now, Grayson, follow out your orders, or we start firing. Kylie spends her life in Silstrand prison or floating through space, you decide."

Kylie peered up at Grayson's face as he took a deep breath. For a split second, she thought he would do what he was ordered, but then he pivoted and aimed his rifle at General Samuel while simultaneously tossing Kylie's back to her. "Sorry, sir. I can't do that."

The soldiers' weapons snapped back up, all aimed at Grayson. "Careful what you do next," General Samuel said with a smirk before continuing, "more than your career is on the line here."

Grayson's scowl deepened, and his voice was scornful. "Kylie put her life on the line. She saved your daughter, and you have no idea what Lana has been through, sir. If we're going to arrange for a transfer, let's do so, but the crew of the *Dauntless* deserves your respect and has earned the immunity and the letter of marque you promised them."

Samuel's eyebrow twitched. "She got to you again, didn't she? Puppy dog, doe-eyed, Rhoads. She's always had her hooks in you."

"If we could keep calm…" Kylie said, but her words broke off as Rogers broke in.

<I'm on the bridge, but there's a problem. Well, two problems. One, Silstrand is grappled on tight. We can't break free.>

<And the second problem?> Kylie couldn't resist raising her eyebrows.

<Winter isn't here. There's no sign of him.>

Crap. That meant he could be anywhere.

Kylie returned her attention to the conversation that continued to play out in front of her.

"The full pardon you promised for Kylie, Nadine, Rogers, and even Winter, if he'll take it. That's what I require from you, General."

"Shoot him," the general ordered. "For defying a direct order and siding with common criminals, thugs, and members of the Jericho crime syndicates."

What? No!

Kylie leaped in front of Grayson with her arms spread. "Don't! You can't!"

A scream echoed through the passageway behind them, and the SSF soldiers all looked behind Kylie and Grayson. The pair turned to see Lana being led over, held at arm's length by Winter. He had a weapon right against the back of her head, and his hand was wrapped around her neck.

"I believe we can end this all right now," Winter said.

Lana's lip quivered, and a stream of tears rolled down her cheeks. "He told me about your friend. He told me about Nadine."

Winter really was a pile of shit. "Lana...."

"I won't go with them. I won't go with my father or back to Silstrand. Not until you get your friend back. She can't die because of me. It isn't fair."

"In other words, advance on us and I blow her fucking head off," Winter said. "I'll do it. Don't tempt me."

"He's telling the truth," Kylie said dryly. "He's just that kind of guy."

"Lana, you can't possibly mean what you're saying. I'm here," General Samuels opened his arms. "I'm here, and I'm ready to take you home. Your dorm is just as you left it. Your friends are waiting for you."

"I can't go back, Daddy. I'm sorry. Everything's different now."

"Different?"

Lana nodded, and Kylie had a sinking suspicion the girl was about to tell him about the nano. "Lana…" Kylie warned.

"The nano, it broke out of the container I was carrying. It's in me now. It's…" Lana raised her hand as if to show them. A cloud of particles, too small to see other than as an indistinct haze, swirled around her hand. Almost like a dance.

General Samuel stepped forward. "You mean…it's in your blood? It's merged with you?"

Lana nodded. "It's in me now. I can…do things. That's why I can't go with you. I can't go with anyone. Once Nadine is free, I have to just…go away." She glanced back at Winter. "He made me see how dangerous I am."

"What can I say? I have a way with words." Winter gave a cruel smile.

Kylie had no idea how Winter had twisted the truth to manipulate Lana, but he'd succeeded.

Samuel lifted his hand toward Lana. "Fascinating. You've become the most advanced human Silstrand has ever known. Smarter, faster. A weapon…." His eyebrows arched. "A weapon we need, Lana. What's in you could save countless lives."

"Or spark a war across the whole Orion Arm. I may just be a dumb college-girl, but I watch the feeds. I know what's going on. Everyone wants me."

"We're your people! Your home. You'll come home with me now, Lana." Samuel pushed past Kylie and Grayson, reaching for Lana's outstretched hand.

"Winter!" Lana shrieked in panic.

Winter yanked Lana back, out of the General's reach and his finger slipped off the trigger guard, ready to pull it. He was going to do it. He was going to kill her just as he said he would. Kylie dodged around Samuel, lowering her shoulder to knock Winter back just as a filament of nano leaped from

Lana's hand toward the general, streaming into his eyes. He screamed and fell to the ground.

Lana turned to the group of soldiers and raised her hand. Kylie couldn't scream fast enough. "Lana, get down!" She altered her trajectory and crashed into Lana, forcing her down as focused pulse blasts rippled the air above their heads. Kylie was on top of Lana and found herself wrapped in a swarm of nano. The nanoscopic robots surrounded her in a glittering haze. She swatted at them as if they were bugs or smoke, but it was no use.

As the nano-fog cleared, Kylie held Lana close to her. The young woman's eyes were wide, staring up at the ceiling. Her forehead was crumpled where multiple pulse shots had hit it. Blood was seeping out, and more than a little gray matter was visible around the edges.

Kylie looked at her hands, covered in the young woman's blood, and screamed. Everything she had gone through to protect her. Everything they had done to win. None of it had mattered, and now she sat, cowering beneath a hailstorm of pulse, beam, and projectile rounds as Grayson and Winter lay down suppressive fire.

<Get us out of here, Rogers. Get us out of here!>

<They're still clamped onto us. I can use our plasma cutters to get us free, but it's going to put some holes in their ship and vent the airlock and umbilical…>

Grayson heard the conversation over the Link and pointed his rifle at the prone general's head.

"It's about to get real cold and airless in here," he yelled at the soldiers and nodded at a pair. "Everyone but you two fall back, or the general breathes his last. Then you can take him."

The soldiers ceased fire, as did Winter. They glanced at each other, and one, with a lieutenant's insignia on his armor, nodded. They fell back and the two men Grayson had called out came and grabbed the unconscious general by his arms and carried him to the airlock.

As soon as they were through, Grayson ran forward and palmed the control to seal the inner door.

Kylie didn't give a shit whether the general was safely through the umbilical and called up to Rogers. *<We're clear! Go!>*

With a rending sound that set Kylie's teeth on edge, the *Dauntless* broke away. She didn't know if the SSF soldiers had made it back to their cruiser or not. Or, if any of them had realized Lana was dead. To be killed for this tech, by her own father's soldiers…it was horrible…beyond thinking…such a waste of a life.

"Kylie," Winter said.

"Shut up! I'll deal with you later." Kylie trembled with rage, her voice filled with malice. "Go to your quarters and don't you dare show yourself. Don't you dare."

Winter turned and walked away without a word while Grayson fell to his knees beside Kylie. He stroked Lana's hair back and both of them sat in bitter silence. "Are you…"

"Okay?" Kylie shook her head. "I'm so far from okay. Gray…" She squeezed her eyes shut and fought off the urge to sob.

Grayson moved closer. He placed his hands on her knees and just sat with her. The body of a dead young woman between them. The one they were meant to save.

<I wish I could tell you that it's over,> Rogers said. *<But the cruiser is in pursuit, and a new ship is showing up on scan.>*

<How close?>

<Less than a light second, and closing in fast. I think…it's the Barbaric Queen.*>*

Pirates, one of the Black Crow ships. Kylie sighed and gazed down at Lana's face. "I don't know if I have the will to get up."

"The Silstrand cruiser will destroy us to keep this nano from falling into enemy hands," Grayson said. "If we can't shake them and the *Barbaric Queen*..."

In other words, Kylie didn't have any other choice. She stood, even though her legs felt like they were rubber. "Get her to the medbay. Put her on the bed. We can at least do something nice for her for...for the time being."

Grayson nodded, leaving so much unsaid. He picked Lana's body up and Kylie ran toward the bridge.

Her hands were still covered in Lana's blood, and she looked at them, feeling nauseated. They tingled slightly, and she wiped them on her pants as the ship rocked, jinking to avoid enemy beamfire. She stumbled onto the bridge as the ship shifted vector again.

"Nice to see someone. If you could man the guns," Rogers said from the pilot's seat. It pivoted back and forth as he did his best to avoid both ships.

Kylie slipped into Nadine's seat and brought up weapons. "Shields aren't going to hold much longer."

Rogers didn't respond, but tension on the bridge rose.

She powered up the weapons and reviewed scan. The Silstrand cruiser, listed as the *Hanover* on her screen, was close, just twenty thousand kilometers on their port side. The *Barbaric Queen* was further aft, just under fifty thousand kilometers—within effective beam range.

The *Hanover* was firing at both ships with lasers and particle beams, though the *Barbaric Queen* was only shooting at the Silstrand ship—for the moment.

"Coming up on Einendart," Rogers said as the *Dauntless* approached the massive gas giant in Gedri's outer reaches. Einendart was surrounded by dozens of major moons, a ring of dust and debris, and more flotsam and jetsam than scan could keep up with.

"I'll try to find some cover. We're close to Dredge—there are a few stations and shipyards there. Maybe they won't shoot if they think they'll hit civilians," Rogers said.

"We can hope," Kylie muttered as she adjusted the ship's shields to protect the engines from the *Hanover's* weapons fire. They weren't making kill shots, which was a small blessing, but Kylie was certain that if her ship were disabled, they would all wish they'd died in a fiery explosion.

"Communication coming in from the *Barbaric Queen*," Kylie said and pumped it through the speakers.

<*Well, well, Captain Rhoads. You seem to have a little problem…*>

Kylie was always one for witty exchanges but she wasn't feeling quite in the mood. She jammed his transmission. "Can we make an FTL jump or not?"

"Shit, Captain, really? This close to Einendart? No way! I'll need to slingshot around the planet and get on an outsystem vector first."

<*There's a clear pocket in the dark layer nearby,*> Marge spoke on the general shipnet. <*It's not on the official maps, but one of the smugglers I used to be with knew about it.*>

"Send me the coordinates." Rogers grunted as he boosted past a small space station at a thousand kilometers per second, drawing fire from its defensive turrets.

<*I've loaded them into the nav systems,*> Marge replied.

"Shit! That's tiny! I have to shed all this *v* or we'll get smushed in there."

<*Do a polar slingshot around Dredge and then do a max burn. It should put you right on target,*>

"You say that like it's going to be easy." Rogers grunted.

<*I can fly the ship if you want,*> Marge offered.

"No!" Kylie and Rogers yelled in unison.

"I got it," Rogers added.

Scan threw out an alert and a dozen missiles appeared on the holodisplay, closing on them. The weapons weren't moving at relativistic speeds, but they traveled erratically, jinking fast enough that the *Dauntless*'s targeting systems couldn't get a lock on them.

<*More Black Crow ships ahead,*> Marge advised.

Kylie shot down three missiles, then two more, then another four. She bit her lip, trying to get a targeting lock on the last three as a proton beam lanced out from the *Hanover* and hit the *Dauntless.*

"Oh fuck, they took out our shields," Kylie swore.

"They want those missiles to destroy, not disable. If they can't have Lana, they're not going to let anyone get her," Grayson said as he strode onto the bridge.

Kylie tasted blood as she got a lock on the three remaining missiles and fired. Two blew, but one shot missed.

"Max burn!" Rogers warned and a klaxon blared that the internal grav compensators wouldn't be able to fully protect them from the force. Kylie grasped the chair as the ship shuddered, and caught sight of Grayson as he flew across the bridge and hit a bulkhead.

"Dumping to the DL in five, four," Rogers began his count as Kylie watched the final missile fly past the ship and arc around. The ship had slowed, and the missile had picked up more *v.* It jinked wildly, and Kylie fired every shot that looked even remotely close. They all missed.

"...two, one," Rogers completed his count half a second before the missile hit.

Alarms wailed as the starscape and the looming orb of Einendart disappeared. They were in the dark layer, and the ship was still intact.

Kylie looked at the automated damage reports scrolling across the console.

Correction...mostly intact.

Rogers turned in his seat and cast Kylie an incredulous look. "We made it. I can't believe it. We actually did it."

"Good work, Rogers." Kylie's breath came in ragged gasps and realized her hands were shaking.

"How'd we do? How's Lana? Is she still…" Rogers asked as he rose up off the floor. He used the edge of a console to stand, but otherwise appeared okay.

Kylie sank in her seat and felt the nausea return. "I'm afraid…"

"The SSF took her?"

"It's worse than that, I'm afraid. A lot worse."

LAYING LOW

STELLAR DATE: 09.16.8947 (Adjusted Years)
LOCATION: Salvage ship *Dauntless*, dark layer, near Einendart
REGION: Gedri System, Silstrand Alliance

Several hours later, the ship was still tucked safely in the small, clear pocket in the dark layer. Repairs, such as their external bots could manage in the DL, were still underway, but no other ships had transitioned into the dark layer near them.

Kylie worried that they would need to wait a lot longer before they exited. The SSF probably had backup by now and had chased off the Black Crow ships, but either way, the word would be out. Everyone in the system would know they had Lana, and what she was capable of.

Kylie suspected that in a better facility, Lana's injuries would not have been fatal. But the *Dauntless* had no cryopods to hold her in stasis, and there was nothing they could do for such trauma. By the time they had returned to the medbay to view the young woman, her body was cold, the life long gone from it.

They placed Lana in one of the small holds, and lowered the temperature so the body would be preserved. Kylie couldn't bring herself to space Lana, though the dark layer may be the best place for the tech her lifeless flesh held.

She mattered. People mattered. Kylie wasn't ready to flush that all away.

Rogers stood next to her with his hands in his pockets. Whatever was going to happen next, neither of them knew, but it was far from over. Nadine was still gone and Kylie had so many broken promises that she had to keep.

So many.

"She deserved better," Rogers said. "I didn't know her but still…I know you worked hard to save her."

Everything he said was true, but Kylie didn't have the heart to respond. Lana was too important to dump, but they couldn't give her a proper funeral, either. So, what were they going to do? Keep her on ice forever? Or trade her body to Jason? Just the idea of something so distasteful…

She left Rogers without speaking and walked down the passageway to where Grayson stood outside the airlock, a large bruise evident on his forehead from when he'd hit the bulkhead. Within, Winter paced and raged.

"Let me out of here, Kylie." Winter slammed his palms on the glass. "You know I can't take these small spaces. Let me out!"

He should've thought about that before he'd betrayed us, Kylie thought as she stood beside Grayson, and they leaned against each other, listening to Winter's maniacal raving.

"I was just doing what I thought was best for the crew. C'mon, Kylie. You know me better than this!"

She did. Which was why she wondered how Winter's actions had caught her so off-guard.

"Should we space him now?" Grayson asked.

"I wouldn't even enjoy it," Kylie said. She didn't know what to do with Winter, but dumping him into the dark layer wasn't what she had on her mind. He deserved to be punished for what he'd done, but what would that punishment ultimately be?

Kylie had other plans.

"A pot of bad coffee, then?" Grayson asked.

"Sure," Kylie walked away with Grayson while rubbing her hand on her arm. It was weird, her skin was tingling again, almost like her arm was asleep, and the feeling was spreading from her arms, down to her legs. She wrote it off as a reaction to the stress of the battle. Still, she was uncomfortably aware of how taut her shirt's fabric was against her skin. Every sensation felt like a pinprick, Kylie was suddenly aware of everything.

She forced it from her mind, as they sat at the table in the galley and stared at each other over their cups.

"You know, everything you did…" Kylie said. "Your career with the SA…"

Grayson kept his head down when he answered. "I'm hoping Jerrod can help make them understand why I did why I did. How they left me with no choice."

Kylie hoped that was true. Funny…years ago, all she had wanted was for him to pick *her* over the SA, but now that he effectively had, it left a bitter taste in her mouth. Now what would they do? Was Grayson just going to become a member of her crew? If that happened, where did it leave them? Kylie didn't voice her questions because she needed more time to think.

"Will Jerrod talk with the SA soon?"

Grayson nodded. "He slipped a drone out of the DL. It will boost a ways away before it sends its message. Don't worry, he won't disclose our location. His neck is on the line, same as mine."

Kylie hoped that was true. "With Winter under lock and key, I'm going to need someone to help fix my girl and bring shields back online."

Grayson nodded. "Leave it to Jerrod and me. We'll have it handled."

"Great," Kylie said with audible calm, hiding the unease she felt. Could Jerrod—an AI in the service of the SSF—really be trusted if Grayson was no longer part of the military? How could she ask him about it when the AI was always there, always listening?

Grayson rose, placed his cup in the sink—the man never washed his own dishes—and left the galley. Kylie stared after him, wondering what their next move could possibly be.

<*Hate to break up this party, but we have a problem,*> Rogers said.

Kylie immediately headed toward the bridge. <*What now*?> Couldn't they get a break? At least for a few minutes to take a breather?

<*A GFF ship just transitioned into the DL. We're almost entirely powered down, so they haven't spotted us yet, but there's not a lot of places we can hide in this pocket.* >

Of course, and here they were without shields. Kylie needed a miracle to get out of this one. <*I'm on my way. If they send a communication, see if Harken is with them.*>

<*And if she is*?>

Kylie thought about that. <*Send flowers?*>

She sprinted down the passageway when an intense pain tore into her brain. She cringed and found herself unable to convince her leg to take another a step forward. Grabbing her head, she groaned. Her vision split and Kylie saw colors—purple, black, and gold charging toward her. She could see the metal in the ship unlike any way she had seen it before.

As though it was a breathing, organic thing. The molecules moved like an independent machine. What the hell?

Time seemed to slow. Kylie wasn't sure if she remained conscious, but eventually realized that she was on the deck, her face pressed against the cold steel.

<*Marge?*>

<*Lana's nano…I think you've been infected. When you tried to save her…I'm working hard to protect your brain and body functions from it, but it's taking all my processing power to keep up with it. I'm afraid I might not have the proper permission to do what is necessary.*>

<*Whatever permissions you need,*> Kylie said. She heard a noise coming and glanced up. Grayson was making his way up the ramp, his movements strangely wooden. He couldn't have brought the shields back online so quickly, could he?

"Grayson—"

There was an unusual look on his face, an expression of deep concentration that was abnormal, even for him. When she said his name, he wouldn't even look at her and his movements were stilted, almost mechanical—like he wasn't in full control of his limbs.

What was wrong with him?

"Gray? Can you hear me?"

He swung his arm wide and she felt her body move—lighting fast—barely avoiding the fist aimed at her head.

"Grayson! What's gotten into you?" Kylie's tried to move, but her legs wouldn't respond, then they gave out all together and she fell to the deck plate and crawled to the other side of the passageway.

She pulled herself to her feet just as he turned and charged at her, going for her neck. Kylie pushed him away, but it was like trying to move an elephant. He was strong and more than that, his eyes were vacant and detached, almost like he felt nothing for her at all.

Grayson? "Jerrod?" Kylie asked in horror.

His eyes flashed with recognition. Grayson wasn't in charge anymore. Jerrod was. Was there any wonder why she hadn't wanted a military AI? The control they could exert over Grayson or anyone dumb enough to have a government AI in their heads?

Kylie tried to duck again, but her body felt like it was stuck in mud—like the messages weren't getting to her nerves in time. Grayson grabbed her by the throat and slammed her up against the wall. Kylie gasped for breath as her body trembled and shook from the transformation it was undergoing.

Things were changing. Things were changing fast.

<*Grayson, if you're in there. If you're there somewhere, please answer me,*> she pleaded over the Link.

There was no answer. Instead, Grayson let her go. He let her go so he could kick her down the passageway like a football.

Kylie's body flew past the airlock. Things seemed to slow down and it occurred to her how comical it must look to Winter as he banged on the window. "Kylie!"

<*Kylie?*> Rogers asked. <*Captain, the GFF ship is hailing us. What do we do? Cap?*>

If she could get to the airlock in time, maybe Winter could stop Grayson. She was crawling toward the access panel when something tugged at her pant leg. Glancing over her shoulder, she saw Grayson and his unemotional eyes staring back at her.

Kylie screamed as he pulled her back toward the cargo bay, and everything went black.

EPILOGUE: THE HAND

STELLAR DATE: 09.16.8947 (Adjusted Years)
LOCATION: TSS *Armored Night*, departing Chiras
REGION: Outer Gedri System, Silstrand Alliance

In the ship's small galley, Jason poured two blue drinks and set them on a metal tray as a transmission came in from his handler at the agency. He triggered it to display as a full holoprojection.

"There was a problem with the SSF," Petra Cushing said. She leaned forward and folded her hands. Her beautiful green eyes sparkled and her sleek black hair seemed to shine extra bright. "They tried to take the girl but failed. Now it's going to be up to you."

"I have what they want," Jason sipped his drink. "They'll give me the girl."

"They better. This tech can't get in the hands of Silstrand, the GFF, or anyone else. It'll disrupt everything. It must be contained."

"I have it handled, that's why you brought me in on this. Are you sure the *Dauntless* still has the girl?"

"As far as we can tell, yes. Arrange that transfer soon. If you can't bring me the girl, she must be destroyed in a way that the nano will not survive."

Jason nodded. "Whatever you wish."

"Good," Petra replied. "Sera Tomlinson is following this operation personally. It won't go well for any of us if we screw it up."

Jason nodded. "Understood."

"Good." Petra ended the transmission and Jason topped off his drink to neutralize his nerves. Petra was a beautiful and cunning woman, one that was distracting in a lot of ways—on purpose, he suspected.

But Sera Tomlinson...*she* was another thing all together. To be under the eye of the President's daughter added its own stresses to the job. That girl must be in possession of something very important to have the Director of The Hand giving it her personal attention.

He picked up the tray and walked down the passageway to his ship's aft lounge. Within, sofas and love-seats were arranged to take in the view through the broad window. The planet of Chiras dominated the view outside the plas, its planets and stations glinting in the light of Gedri's two stars.

Nadine sat on a pearl white sofa. She wore a green dress and her hair was pinned at the nape of her neck. As usual, she was a sight to behold.

"Every bit as beautiful as the royalty you are," Jason said and set the tray on the glass table in front of her.

He watched her pick up her drink and take a dainty sip. Everything she did was executed with measured purpose. Even the way she licked those lovely, plump lips. Jason ached to taste them. Still, as far as babysitting jobs went, this was one of the more pleasant.

"Are they coming for me?" Nadine asked, a cloud of doubt passing over her aquiline features.

Jason nodded. "Soon. They ran into some trouble, but they're coming now. I'll be ready for them."

Nadine sighed and set her glass down before turning to peer out the window. "It wasn't supposed to be this hard. I wasn't supposed to..." She twisted the soft fabric of her dress into a knot.

Jason touched her face and pulled it over to face him. "You did what The Hand ordered, just as we all do. This time, it just led you places you didn't expect."

"No," Nadine said softly, quietly. With a reflective look, she turned her gaze back to the window.

"It's only natural that after five years you'd become accustomed to the crew. And to Kylie. The humanity of that, I can understand. However, Petra—and certainly Director Tomlinson—will not."

"Sera Tomlinson?" Nadine asked. "She's checking in on this op?"

Jason nodded. "That's what Petra tells me."

Nadine's brow furrowed. "And if I can't suppress my feelings? If I can't…turn on them?"

"Then you really will be my prisoner. Our organization doesn't brook disobedience. You know that."

Nadine sighed and Jason thought she might've finally understood what he was saying and where he was coming from. "Kylie was just supposed to lead us to her parents, eventually. This, I never imagined. How she, or I, ended up in the middle of all this mess…."

"None of us expected this. We'll do our job. We'll get the tech, just like we're supposed to."

"And then?" Nadine asked. "Then what do we do?"

"What we do best." Jason slid over closer to her and pressed his mouth hard against hers.

Nadine pulled herself away from him. "Perhaps, but my body isn't for sale."

"C'mon, Nadine, we've got some time to kill. You sell your body for the job already, what's a bit of fun on the side?"

Nadine stood from the sofa and walked over to the window, her arms wrapped tight around her torso as if she felt the chill of space. Jason watched the way her shoulders hunched.

Her behavior surprised him. "Once you were the best of the best. If you can't go through with what needs to be done…"

She turned her head so he had a view of her profile and her quivering chin. "What's necessary will be done, but for now, leave me. I wish to be alone."

"Whatever Her Royal Highness wants." Jason sketched a mocking bow, picked his drink off the table and downed it in a single gulp. He grimaced as the liquid burned its way down his throat.

Then, he left without so much as a word.

He turned back to cast an appraising eye on her. Nadine might've gone soft, but beneath, she was the same woman, and that meant she couldn't be trusted. Out here, in the Inner Stars, no one could.

THE END

*****

Continue the story of Kylie, Grayson, and the crew of the *Dauntless* in book 2 of the Perilous Alliance Series: **Strike Vector**

THANK YOU

If you've enjoyed reading Close Proximity, a review on amazon.com and/or goodreads.com is greatly appreciated.

To get the latest news and access to free novellas and short stories, sign up on the Aeon 14 mailing list: www.aeon14.com/signup.

Sincerely, Chris J. Pike & M. D. Cooper

AEON 14 BOOKS

Keep up to date with what is releasing in Aeon 14 with the free Aeon 14 Reading Guide.

Origins of Destiny (The Age of Terra)
- Prequel: Storming the Norse Wind
- Book 1: Shore Leave (in Galactic Genesis until Sept 2018)
- Book 2: Operative (Summer 2018)
- Book 3: Blackest Night (Summer 2018)

The Intrepid Saga (The Age of Terra)
- Book 1: Outsystem
- Book 2: A Path in the Darkness
- Book 3: Building Victoria

- The Intrepid Saga Omnibus – *Also contains Destiny Lost, book 1 of the Orion War series*

- Destiny Rising – *Special Author's Extended Edition comprised of both Outsystem and A Path in the Darkness with over 100 pages of new content.*

The Orion War
- Book 1: Destiny Lost
- Book 2: New Canaan
- Book 3: Orion Rising
- Book 4: The Scipio Alliance
- Book 5: Attack on Thebes
- Book 6: War on a Thousand Fronts
- Book 7: Fallen Empire (2018)
- Book 8: Airtha Ascendancy (2018)
- Book 9: The Orion Front (2018)
- Book 10: Starfire (2019)
- Book 11: Race Across Time (2019)
- Book 12: Return to Sol (2019)

Tales of the Orion War
- Book 1: Set the Galaxy on Fire
- Book 2: Ignite the Stars
- Book 3: Burn the Galaxy to Ash (2018)

Perilous Alliance (Age of the Orion War – w/Chris J. Pike)
- Book 1: Close Proximity
- Book 2: Strike Vector
- Book 3: Collision Course
- Book 4: Impact Imminent
- Book 5: Critical Inertia (Sept 2018)

Rika's Marauders (Age of the Orion War)
- Prequel: Rika Mechanized
- Book 1: Rika Outcast
- Book 2: Rika Redeemed
- Book 3: Rika Triumphant
- Book 4: Rika Commander
- Book 5: Rika Infiltrator
- Book 6: Rika Unleashed (2018)
- Book 7: Rika Conqueror (2019)

Perseus Gate (Age of the Orion War)
Season 1: Orion Space
- Episode 1: The Gate at the Grey Wolf Star
- Episode 2: The World at the Edge of Space
- Episode 3: The Dance on the Moons of Serenity
- Episode 4: The Last Bastion of Star City
- Episode 5: The Toll Road Between the Stars
- Episode 6: The Final Stroll on Perseus's Arm
- Eps 1-3 Omnibus: The Trail Through the Stars
- Eps 4-6 Omnibus: The Path Amongst the Clouds

Season 2: Inner Stars
- Episode 1: A Meeting of Bodies and Minds
- Episode 3: A Deception and a Promise Kept
- Episode 3: A Surreptitious Rescue of Friends and Foes (2018)

- Episode 4: A Trial and the Tribulations (2018)
- Episode 5: A Deal and a True Story Told (2018)
- Episode 6: A New Empire and An Old Ally (2018)

Season 3: AI Empire
- Episode 1: Restitution and Recompense (2019)
- Five more episodes following…

The Warlord (Before the Age of the Orion War)
- Book 1: The Woman Without a World
- Book 2: The Woman Who Seized an Empire
- Book 3: The Woman Who Lost Everything

The Sentience Wars: Origins (Age of the Sentience Wars – w/James S. Aaron)
- Book 1: Lyssa's Dream
- Book 2: Lyssa's Run
- Book 3: Lyssa's Flight
- Book 4: Lyssa's Call
- Book 5: Lyssa's Flame

Legends of the Sentience Wars (Age of the Sentience Wars – w/James S. Aaron)
- Volume 1: The Proteus Bridge (August 2018)

Enfield Genesis (Age of the Sentience Wars – w/Lisa Richman)
- Book 1: Alpha Centauri
- Book 2: Proxima Centauri (2018)

Hand's Assassin (Age of the Orion War – w/T.G. Ayer)
- Book 1: Death Dealer
- Book 2: Death Mark (August 2018)

Machete System Bounty Hunter (Age of the Orion War – w/Zen DiPietro)
- Book 1: Hired Gun
- Book 2: Gunning for Trouble
- Book 3: With Guns Blazing

Vexa Legacy (Age of the FTL Wars – w/Andrew Gates)
- Book 1: Seas of the Red Star

Building New Canaan (Age of the Orion War – w/J.J. Green)
- Book 1: Carthage (July 2018)
- Book 2: Tyre (2018)

Fennington Station Murder Mysteries (Age of the Orion War)
- Book 1: Whole Latte Death (w/Chris J. Pike)
- Book 2: Cocoa Crush (w/Chris J. Pike)

The Empire (Age of the Orion War)
- The Empress and the Ambassador (2018)
- Consort of the Scorpion Empress (2018)
- By the Empress's Command (2018)

The Sol Dissolution (The Age of Terra)
- Book 1: Venusian Uprising (2018)
- Book 2: Scattered Disk (2018)
- Book 3: Jovian Offensive (2019)
- Book 4: Fall of Terra (2019)

APPENDICES

Be sure to check www.aeon14.com for the latest information on the Aeon 14 universe.

TERMS & TECHNOLOGY

AI (SAI, NSAI) – Is a term for Artificial Intelligence. AI are often also referred to as non-organic intelligence. They are broken up into two sub-groups: Sentient AI and Non-Sentient AI.

c **–** Represented as a lower-case c in italics, this symbol stands for the speed of light and means constant. The speed of light in a vacuum is constant at 670,616,629 miles per hour. Ships rate their speed as a decimal value of c with c being 1. Thus, a ship traveling at half the speed of light will be said to be traveling at 0.50 c.

Cryostasis (cryogenics) – See also, 'stasis'.

Older methods of slowing down organic aging and decay involve cryogenically freezing the organism (usually a human) through a variety of methods. The person would then be thawed through a careful process when they were awakened.

Cryostasis failures are rare, but far more frequent than true stasis failures. When true stasis was discovered, it became the de-facto method of halting organic decay over long periods.

Dark Layer – The Dark Layer is a special sub-layer of space where dark matter possesses physical form. The dark layer is also frictionless and reactionless. It is not fully understood, but it also seems to possess many of the attributes of a universal frame of reference.

Deuterium – D2 (2H) is an isotope of hydrogen where the nucleus of the atom is made up of one proton and one neutron as opposed to a single proton in regular hydrogen (protium). Deuterium is naturally occurring and is found in the oceans of planets with water and is also created by fusion in stars and brown dwarf sub stars. D2 is a stable isotope that does not decay.

EMF – Electro Magnetic Fields are given off by any device using electricity that is not heavily shielded. Sensitive scanners are able to determine the nature of operating equipment by its EMF signature. In warfare it is one of the primary ways to locate an enemy's position.

EMP – Electro Magnetic Pulses are waves of electromagnetic energy that can disable or destroy electronic equipment. Because so many people have electronic components in their bodies, or share their minds with AI, they are susceptible to extreme damage from an EMP. Ensuring that human/machine interfaces are hardened against EMPs is of paramount importance.

Fission – Fission is a nuclear reaction where an atom is split apart. Fission reactions are simple to achieve with heavier, unstable elements such as Uranium or Plutonium. In closed systems with extreme heat and pressure it is possible to split atoms of much more stable elements, such as Helium. Fission of heavier elements typically produces less power and far more waste matter and radiation than Fusion.

FTL (Faster Than Light) – Refers to any mode of travel where a ship or object is able to travel faster than the speed of light (c). According to Einstein's theory of Special Relativity nothing can travel faster than the speed of light.

Fusion – Fusion is a nuclear reaction where atoms of one type (Hydrogen for example) are fused into atoms of another type (Helium in the case of Hydrogen fusion). Fusion was first discovered and tested in the H-Bombs (Hydrogen bombs) of the twentieth century. Fusion reactors are also used as the most common source of ship power from roughly the twenty fourth century on.

***g* (gee, gees, g-force)** – Represented as a lower-case g in italics, this symbol stands for gravity. On earth, at sea-level, the human body experiences 1*g*. A human sitting in a wheeled dragster race-car will achieve 4.2*gs* of horizontal g-force. Arial fighter jets will impose g-forces of 7-12*gs* on their pilots. Humans will often lose consciousness around 10*gs*. Unmodified humans will suffer serious injury or death at over 50*gs*. Starships will often impose burns as high as 20*gs* and provide special couches or beds for their passengers during such maneuvers. Modified starfighter pilots can withstand g-forces as high as 70*gs*.

Graviton – These are small massless particles that are emitted from objects with large mass, or by special generators capable of creating them without large masses. There are also negatively charged gravitons which push instead of pull. These are used in shielding systems in the form of Gravitational Waves. The *GSS Intrepid* uses a new system of channeled gravitons to create the artificial gravity in the crew areas of the ship.

Heliopause – The point where a star's solar wind stops relative to the interstellar medium. Though gravitational influences may stretch beyond this point, and some stellar objects, including the Oort cloud, typically lie beyond this point as well.

Heliosphere – The region of space contained within a star's heliopause. Despite the name, these are rarely spheres as most star's heliospheres are shaped like elongated water droplets as they race through the interstellar medium.

Helium-3 – This is a stable, non-radioactive isotope of Helium, produced by T3 Hydrogen decay, and is used in nuclear fusion reactors. The nucleus of the Helium-3 atom contains two protons, but only one neutron as opposed to the two neutrons in regular Helium. Helium-3 Can also be created by nuclear reactions that create Lithium-4 which decays into Helium-3.

HUD – Stands for Heads Up Display. It refers to any type of display where information about surroundings and other data is directly overlaid on a person's vision.

Link – Refers to an internal connection to computer networks. This connection is inside of a person and directly connects their brain to what is essentially the Internet in the fourth millennia. Methods of accessing the Link vary between retinal overlays to direct mental insertion of data.

Maglev – A shorthand term for magnetic levitation. First used commercially in 1984, most modern public transportation uses maglev to move vehicles without the friction caused by axles, rails, and wheels. The magnetic field is used to both support the vehicle and accelerate it. The acceleration and braking is provided by linear induction motors which act on the magnetic field provided by the maglev 'rail'. Maglev trains can achieve speeds of over one thousand kilometers per hour with very smooth and even acceleration.

Nano (nanoprobes, nanobots, etc...) – Refers to very small technology or robots. Something that is nanoscopic in size is one thousand times smaller than something that is microscopic in size.

Railgun – Railguns fire physical rounds, usually small pellets at speeds up to 10 kilometers per second by pushing the round through the barrel via a magnetic field. The concept is similar to that of a maglev train, but to move a smaller object much faster. Railguns were first conceived of in 1918 and the first actual magnetic particle accelerator was built in 1950. Originally railguns were massive, sometimes kilometers in size. By the twenty-second century reliable versions as small as a conventional rifle had been created.

Larger versions take the form of orbital railgun platforms which can fire sabot rounds or grapeshot at speeds over a hundred-thousand-kilometers per second.

Scattered Disk – Beyond a star system's EK Belt lies a region filled with comets, asteroids, and dwarf worlds. In the Sol System, this region begins roughly 50 AU from Sol and extends to the edge of the Oort cloud. While it contains the least mass of a system, a system's scattered disc typically contains hundreds of dwarf planets and fills an area nearly half a cubic light year.

Stasis – Early stasis systems were invented in the year 2541 as a method of 'cryogenically' freezing organic matter without using extreme cold (or lack of energy) to do so. The effect is similar in that all atomic motion is ceased, but not by the removal of energy by gradual cooling, but by removing the ability of the surrounding space to accept that energy and motion. There are varying degrees of effectiveness of stasis systems. The FGT and other groups possess the ability to put entire planets in stasis, while other groups only have the technology to put small items, such as people, into stasis. Personal stasis is often still referred to as cryostasis, though there is no cryogenic process involved.

Tritium – T3 (3H) is an isotope of hydrogen where the nucleus of the atom is made up of one proton and two neutrons as opposed to just a single proton and no neutrons in regular hydrogen (protium). T3 is radioactive and has a half-life of 12.32 years. It decays into Helium-3 through this process.

v – Represented as a lower case v in italics, this symbol stands for velocity. If a ship is increasing its speed it will be said that it is increasing *v*.

Van Allen belts – A radiation belt of energetic charged particles that is held in place around a magnetized planet, such as the Earth, by the planet's magnetic field. The Earth has two such belts and sometimes others may be temporarily created. The discovery of the belts is credited to James Van Allen, and as a result the Earth's belts are known as the Van Allen belts.

Vector – Vectors used are spatial vectors. Vector refers to both direction and rate of travel (speed or magnitude). Vector can be changed (direction) and increased (speed or magnitude).

GROUPS AND ORGANIZATIONS

FGT – The Future Generation Terraformers is a program started in 2352 with the purpose of terraforming worlds in advance of colony ships being sent to the worlds. Because terraforming of a world could take hundreds of years the FGT ships arrive and begin the process.

Once the world(s) being terraformed reached stage 3, a message was sent back to the Sol system with an 'open' date for the world(s) being terraformed. The GSS then handles the colony assignment.

A decade after the *Destiny Ascendant* left the Sol system in 3728 the FGT program was discontinued by the SolGov, making it the last FGT ship to leave. Because the FGT ships are all self-sustaining none of them came home after the program was discontinued—most of the ship's crews had spent generations in space and had no reason to return to Sol.

After the discontinuation FGT ships continued on their primary mission of terraforming worlds, but only communicated with the GSS and only when they had worlds completed.

Hand, The – The Hand is the common name of the Inner Stars Clandestine Uplift Operations. This bureau is responsible for managing and controlling the stability, and spread of technology within the Inner Stars. It operates exclusively under the direction of President Tomlinson.

GFF (Gedri Freedom Federation) – The GFF began as the political front for the ruling families and crime syndicates of Jericho. Over time they managed to gain seats in the system parliament, and eventually became the dominant party. The GFF also sends representatives to the Silstrand Alliance Senate.

Though they claim to be a legitimate political organization, everyone knows (though none can successfully prove) that all their funding and power still comes from the crime syndicates on Jericho.

Orion Guard – The Orion Guard is the name of the Orion Freedom Alliance's military. Within the Transcend, the term is often used to refer to the entire OFA, not just its military.

Scipio Federation/Empire – Externally, Scipio is known as a Federation, though it has, in recent decades, reformed itself as an empire, with Diana proclaiming herself Empress Supreme.

Located on the coreward side of the Silstrand Alliance, Scipio is vast and powerful, claiming over a thousand member stars, and exerting diplomatic influence far beyond its borders.

Though Scipio has always billed itself as an heir to Rome, Under Diana, the empire has further embraced those cultural artifacts.

Silstrand Alliance – The Silstrand Alliance (commonly referred to as the SA) is an alliance of 10 star systems, which lie 90 light years coreward of Sol.

The capital system is Silstrand, and the capital world also bears the same name. The Alliance was named by Peter Silva, who referred to the main G-class stars as a silver strand of light, running through a region filled with dimmer stars.

Many companies, worlds, and regions in the SA use Peter Silva's name.

The government of the SA is a quasi-parliamentary body.to which the member systems send representatives, which are called senators. The president of the SA is the senator with the largest party in the SA parliament.

Systems on the rimward side of the SA tend to democratically elect their senators separate from their local elections, while systems on the coreward side of the alliance nominate their representatives.

The population of the Silstrand Alliance is in excess of twenty-trillion humans, and over one trillion SAI.

Though the SA is an independent alliance, it is directly adjacent to the Scipio Federation, and not far from the ever expanding borders of the Hegemony of Worlds (AST).

SSF – Silstrand Space Force.

TSF – The Transcend Space Force is the overarching military of the Transcend Interstellar Alliance. It also shares an acronym with the ancient Terran Space Force.

PLACES

Coburn Station – Located above Trio in the Trio System of the Silstrand Alliance, this system is connected to its host world by the system's only space elevator.

Dauntless – A PetSil Scrapper, model 541A. Originally owned by a salvage company operating out of Trio, one of Maverick's shell corporations purchased it, and the crime lord eventually gifted the ship to Kylie Rhoads.

Freemont – The capital world of the Gedri system, Freemont is a cold, icy planet. Though there are some surface (mostly subterranean) settlements on Freemont, most of the populace lives in several massive orbital habitats.

Gedri (system) – A system on the core-ward fringe of the Silstrand Alliance. The Gedri System is the most corrupt and lawless of the worlds in the alliance and is rife with pirates and smugglers.

System Bodies:

Nepal – small terrestrial world orbiting at 96 million km.
Inner A-Belt – Asteroid belt orbiting at at 124 million km
Inner B-Belt – Asteroid belt orbiting at 211 million km
Freemont – Icy terrestrial world orbiting at 603 million km
Tapeka – Icy terrestrial world orbiting at 784 million km
Chiras – 0.64M*j* gas giant planet with 17 major moons orbiting at 3.3 billion km
Townsend – Red dwarf star orbiting at 4.48 billion km
Outer Asteroid belt – Thick asteroid belt orbiting at 6.8 billion km
Einendart – 1.7M*j* gas giant orbiting at 104 billion km with 23 major moons
Scattered Disk – the Gedri scattered disk contains hundreds of dwarf worlds and cold, icy objects.

Gedri (star) – The primary star in the Gedri system, this large, orange star is in the final stages of its life, with perhaps only a million years to go before it puffs off its outer layers and leaves behind a white dwarf stellar remnant.

Gedri masses 1.8 sols, has a radius of 25 sols, and a luminosity of 7.8 sols.

It is suspected that Gedri once had more rocky inner planets, but that when it turned into an orange giant, it consumed them, and now only one remains, though several asteroid belts lie in the inner system. It is debated as to whether or not they were created in the star's expansion, or by collisions from when Gedri captured the red dwarf star, Townsend.

Jericho – This planet, second in orbit of the red dwarf star, Townsend, was once terraformed and habitable, though its lack of a strong magnetic shield has caused it to lose much of its atmosphere as Townsend's solar wind wore it away.

Jericho is near Earth-sized with a circumference of 32,524km, 0.93*g*, and a rotation of 26 hours. The mean temperature on Jericho is 26C, though its possesses is only 0.49atm.

Deep valleys on Jericho still possess a dense enough atmosphere for humans to survive without breathing assistance, and several large liquid water seas and lakes exist on its surface.

Large cities once existed on Jericho's surface, and many are still occupied today, though they are under domes. The capital city of Montral also has a space elevator which reaches up to Laerdo Station.

Jericho is where the GFF holds the most power, even though the capital world of the Gedri system is the planet of Freemont.

Perseverance – This large, but cold, dwarf planet out in the fringes of the Gedri system is under heavy mining by GFF owned firms. Nearly all of the supply companies, and other service businesses are owned by fronts belonging to Maverick's syndicate.

Silstrand (HR-5279 / HD 122862) – The seat of the Silstrand Alliance government and the center of the Alliance's trade and commerce, the Silstrand System boasts three terraformed worlds, one with a ring and space elevators.

Silstrand Alliance – The Silstrand Alliance is a collection of worlds located roughly 90 light-years from Sol, which have banded together under an elected representative parliamentary government. The alliance consists of 10 major star systems.

Townsend – A red dwarf star (spectral class MV) in the Gedri system, Townsend orbits the system's primary star (Gedri) at a distance just over 30AU.

Townsend masses 0.338 sols, has a radius of 0.42 sols, and a luminosity of 0.0225 sols.

Thought the star exists within the Gedri system, it does not share the same elemental makeup as Gedri and is believed to have been captured by the primary star at some point in roughly three billion years ago.

Townsend has three planets in orbit of it, all captured from Gedri.

Nestra – A small, rocky planet only 8.9 million km from Townsend.
Jericho – A terrestrial world, 37 million km from Townsend.
Estace – A gas giant which orbits at a mean distance of 299 million km from townsend.

Trio – The fourth world from Trio Prime, the world is a terrestrial planet with a single space elevator which reaches Coburn Station. Though the world has a space elevator, the system is not well populated due to prior wars with the Scipio Federation.

Trio Prime (CP-67 2079 / HD 111232) – Trio lies on the core-ward edge of the Silstrand Alliance. It has one terraformed world known as Trio.

PEOPLE

Betty – Waitress at Nancy's Place, and commander of a mercenary company.

Finn – Owner of a mod/weapons/illegal AI shop on Heaven.

Gertrude – Heavily modified mod-tech working for Finn on Heaven.

Grayson – SSF Colonel working under General Samuel and assigned to the *Dauntless*.

Harken – Maverick's second in command, responsible for drugs, slavery and sex trade side businesses.

Jim Rogers – Pilot aboard the *Dauntless*.

Kylie Rhoads – Former SSF commander and captain/owner of the *Dauntless*.

Lana – Daughter of General Samuel, and unfortunate possessor of a weaponized version of Tanis's advanced nanotech.

Marge – Kylie's AI, purchased and installed on Heaven by Gertrude. Little of Marge's provenance is known.

Maverick – Leader of the most powerful crime syndicate in the GFF, and nominal ruler of Jerhicho.

Nadine – Crewmember of the *Dauntless* responsible for scan, comm, and weapons.

Samuel – General in the SFF, responsible for special weapons development, his daughter was kidnapped by Harken.

Winter – First mate, engineer, and muscle aboard the *Dauntless*.

ABOUT THE AUTHORS

Michael Cooper likes to think of himself as a jack of all trades (and hopes to become master of a few). When not writing, he can be found writing software, working in his shop at his latest carpentry project, or likely reading a book.

He shares his home with a precocious young girl, his wonderful wife (who also writes), two cats, a never-ending list of things he would like to build, and ideas...

Find out what's coming next at www.aeon14.com

* * * * *

Starship captains. Space battles. Dramatic relationships with big payoffs.

Chris J. Pike is an up and coming SF author, focused on writing in the Aeon14 universe. When not writing Science Fiction, he's watching the Expanse, the Killjoys, Firefly, and anything else that might go boom.

Follow along by liking his Facebook page at:
www.facebook.com/ChrisJPikeAuthor

Or sign up for his mailing list for news and updates.